A View from North Lochs

Aimsir Eachainn

Hector Macdonald

BIRLINN

This edition published in 2007 by
Birlinn Limited
West Newington House
10 Newington Road
Edinburgh EH9 1QS

www.birlinn.co.uk

ISBN 13: 978 1 84158 630 4
ISBN 10: 1 84158 630 7

British Library Cataloguing-In-Publication Data
A Catalogue record for this book is available from the British Library

Typeset in Minion Pro by Maria Streiter
Printed and bound by Cox and Wyman Ltd, Reading

CONTENTS

INTRODUCTION

There are very few people who can successfully translate humour into the written word. Take a look at what the professional humorists of the British media produce and you will find the confirmation. Some might raise an occasional smile, but the fingers of one hand would not be required to enumerate those who consistently achieve much more than that.

So, when a writer whose speciality is humour comes along and succeeds within his own potential readership in becoming the most widely-read, most-looked-forward-to, most-talked-about individual in print, then we know that a special and highly distinctive talent is involved. That was the achievement of Aimsir Eachainn – Hector Macdonald – who graced the pages of the *West Highland Free Press* for 14 charmed years.

Eachann's prodigious talent was all the more unusual for being largely confined to an audience of such modest size. Very often, on reading his column, I would be annoyed that it was being read by thousands rather than the millions that it deserved. Much of his writing was rooted in his own local environment and culture. But as a scatter of further-flung devotees came to appreciate, the humour, the pathos, the wisdom and insights contained in each View from North Lochs were truly universal.

Any regrets about Eachann not being accessible to a larger audience than the *Free Press* could offer were more than compensated for by the sense of pride and pleasure that his presence created for all who understood what the paper was meant to be. Eachann certainly empathised with its philosophy and purpose; indeed that was the factor which drew him to it in the first place.

Shortly after he had brought the family back to Leurbost, Eachann started contributing North Lochs notes to the Butt to Barra page of the *Stornoway Gazette*. This was the literary equivalent of placing a diamond in the middle of a cow-pat. Other districts of the Western Isles were represented by dutiful notes about weather, homecomings and – most frequently – bereavements. The life of North Lochs for this brief and halcyon period was reflected in the 'Greysheet' by flights of the surreal, tenuously based on local events and the rich cast of characters who were soon to become very familiar.

I was envious and wondered how these gems might be given a more hospitable home. What I did not then know was that Eachann's view of the *West Highland Free Press* as the natural outlet for his weekly writings was already well-formed. Fortunately, a mutual friend existed in the person of Neil MacPherson, who brought us together. It was the start not only of Aimsir Eachainn but also one of the most deeply-felt and rewarding friendships of my life.

I have never forgotten the sense of excitement when I read the first of Eachann's columns for the *Free Press* in June 1981. The image that it conjured up of Margaret Thatcher as the head "cutter" in the peat-bank demanding ever-great sacrifices of effort is as brilliant today as it was then, though the central character has long departed from the scene. Like everything else Eachann wrote, it stands the test of time. The humour transcends the context within which it was originally based.

Eachann's qualities as a writer reflected his personal characteristics. He had a fantastic sense of the ridiculous, a superb way with words and a tremendous humanity that informed all his attitudes and opinions. I have no doubt that if he had lived in Ireland, which was his other spiritual home, he would have been celebrated as a national as well as local treasure. He would have been published in the *Irish Times* and feted as a broadcaster who could always be relied on to bring linguistic artistry, in either language, to any debate. Scotland does not really have it in its cultural make-up to accord that sort of recognition to this kind of talent.

I remember one occasion. In 1983, when salmon "poaching" was a much bigger source of controversy than it is today, a public debate on the ethics of this activity was held in Portree. Eachann and I lined up on one side of the argument. The hall was packed, and I am sure many of his Skye readers had turned out to see what resemblance the North Lochs man bore to the illustration at the top of his column! It was a great occasion all round, but it was Eachann who stole the show with a hilarious account of the damage that would be caused to stocks if the "annual cull" did not take place. That was typical of his gentle humour; always coming at his subject from a direction that was just a little bit off the wall.

There was never malice in what Eachann wrote though he was perfectly capable of hitting his targets in a way that made it very difficult for them to complain. Well-measured irony or subtle ridicule can be more effective than any polemic in deflating the pompous or exposing the hypocritical. These were Eachann's chosen instruments and he wielded them beautifully. I only once heard him being taken to task when one pugnacious public figure in Lewis advised a startled Eachann that if he ever wrote about him again, he would be found at the bottom of his salmon cages!

When Eachann died, there was talk of a book but it took a long time before his beloved family could face up to that task. I am very glad that they have done so now. His work deserves to have an after-life and his devoted readers are due the opportunity to dip into this rich treasure trove of merriment and nostalgia. Eachann was a great talent, an original thinker, a wonderful human being. He was a Gael who could relate to all the peoples he encountered as a rounded citizen of the world. And all of that was reflected in what he wrote. Those who survive him have a lot to remember and be proud of.

Brian Wilson
August 2007

FOREWORD

This book is a tribute to my father, Hector Macdonald. It was a long-time dream of his to have a book published, but sadly, due to circumstances beyond his control, this ambition was unfulfilled. But in the twelve years since his death it has always been in our family's thoughts that his weekly writings in the *West Highland* deserved to be put into book form.

He wrote somewhere in the region of 800 columns over seventeen years, and to pick out the highlights was never going to be easy. The credit for doing so must go to my sister, Fiona, who, having raised her children to an age where they could now look after themselves, immersed herself in this project. Unlike me, Fiona did not inherit our father's patience, but unlike me, she did inherit his application, and the manner in which she went about this task is greatly to her credit.

I hope this book can be a tangible memorial for my mother, Maggie, who was the proofreader and inspiration for Aimsir Eachainn.

I hope also that this selection of columns rekindles fond memories for my father's friends, many of whom provided the characters for his stories, and I would like to thank them for the good grace with which they received their weekly dose of satire and slander.

Working on this book has evoked a lot of memories, all of them good, and I remember how I used to wonder where my father found the energy to write after working a twelve-hour shift in the real world. But writing was not like a job to him: he was just exploring a hobby and a talent that came easily.

Iain Macdonald
August 2007

Biography

Hector Macdonald was born in Ranish, on the Isle of Lewis, in the winter of 1945. He shared a black-house with his parents, a brother and some cattle. His early years in this most scenic of villages were a time for forming lifelong friendships with boys like Coinneach Iain, Roddy John, Wee Alex and Johnny Walker.

In 1956 the family upgraded to Leurbost, where he found new friends such as Roddy and Calum Iain Smith. And when Hector went to school in Stornoway he met Dodo and John D., who would later become the Garrabost Historian and the Barvas Navigator.

On leaving school he boarded the good ship Weather and studied meteorology, learning his trade on the high seas of the Atlantic, where he served under men who taught him the fine art of being a civil servant. Men such as Leslie and Archie Macdonald, who, despite the general consensus, were not brothers. Other lifelong friends he made in the Met Office were Norrie Munro and Alex Macdonald.

The seventies brought marriage to Maggie, two children and adventures in Africa with the Jacksons and the Macarthurs.

After enjoying the best parts the world had to offer, Hector returned to Leurbost and built a house on the croft with help of tradesmen such as Karachi, Kenny the Plumber, Roddy Danny and Angus Beattie. He was glad to be back home, where he enjoyed battling wits with the likes of Murdie Siareach and the West End Tory, John Allan. If Hector needed a mechanic, he had Aonghas Beag, and when he needed a strong back, he had Angie Hogg

He settled down and began to write for the *Stornoway Gazette* in 1979. This was the first outlet for his weekly columns before he was poached by the *West Highland Free Press*, and under the tutelage of Brian Wilson found a true home for a style of writing that could be described as thought-provoking, sometimes irreverent but nearly always funny.

A prolific reader, he enjoyed many styles of writing, from the poetry of Dylan Thomas to the adventures of Nevil Shute. But I would say he admired most the comic talents of mainstream authors such as James Thurber and Flann O'Brien and the less well known but brilliant Jaroslav Hasek and John Kennedy Toole.

He made the most of his time on earth. As well as working at the Met Office and writing, he started a business in the early eighties: Western Isles Salmon, which he founded with Calum Macdonald. They were the first small-time independent salmon farmers in the country, and although the business was fraught, they enjoyed the highs and suffered the lows without regret. This was also a time for learning new tricks from visionaries such as Donald Taylor and Neil MacPherson.

Hector lived life to the full and he always made time for his family. Trips abroad with his wife were always an experience to remember.

Stornoway Golf Club, the Criterion Bar and Donnie Campbell Bookies were some of the many local haunts that provided many hours of entertainment and inspiration. Mention must also be made of Comhairle nan Eilean Siar, who are an unfailing source for satire.

Hector died in 1995, which was of course sad for many reasons, one of which was because he had so much more to offer us as a writer.

Iain Macdonald
August 2007

1981

5 JUNE, 1981

MONDAY

Having found in their search for a diarist that Muggeridge would cost far too much, the *Free Press* finally had to settle for a puritan on free transfer from the *Stornoway Gazette*. There are probably a few Hearachs who will question the paper's wisdom, but that's the way the Hearachs are.

TUESDAY

I used to sleep well. Approaching middle age with nothing to worry about but the monthly letter from North Beach, the spread of sheep and rushes in Lochs, and the price of children's shoes in Bayhead, I used to sleep well. Even matters relating to the immortal soul and thoughts of an uncomfortable hereafter I had postponed until a bit nearer the end. Perhaps even contentment was not too strong a word to describe my condition, until last week. Suddenly all is changed. My beard has turned grey, my hair is falling out, I'm losing weight and I stumble through the day half-dead from lack of sleep.

The victim of a recurring nightmare, I wake up in the early hours screaming, sweating and fighting with the blankets and the other occupant of the bed. The dream is in glorious technicolour and the scene is so frightening I tremble even when mentioning it here. I am in the black depths of a three-deep peatbank that stretches into the mist with no end in sight. Throwing peat for all I'm worth, I am unable to keep up with the cutter, who is none other than Margaret Thatcher. Through parched throat I beg for a rest, but to no avail. The more I throw the faster she venomously cuts. My back is broken and I sob for mercy.

"Not until we reach our goal" is all I get from her. Our goal is Creag Sanntabhat forever receding on the distant horizon. Sometimes through the haze of exhaustion it is transformed into the Stock Exchange. To make matters worse, a row of gentlemen from the HIDB line the bank cheering, or jeering, I cannot make out which. Occasionally, on very bad nights, the spectators are from the head office of the Hydro Board chanting in unison: "More peat! More peat!" Not until I collapse face down in the peat do I escape the torment and then only to toss and turn restlessly, waiting for the dawn.

My friend and analyst the West End Tory can make nothing of the nightmare and shows little sympathy, callously suggesting it is something I must live with. His one stab at interpretation was way off the mark – something about deep lying guilt concerning my grandfather, a prewar Leurbost liberal who lived and ate well in the midst of poverty. I cannot even remember him. If this goes on for much longer I may be forced to seek refuge in strong drink.

WEDNESDAY

The main street in Stornoway, named Cromwell after an infamous 17th century hardman who made his money in the butchering business, has as pleasant a setting as you'll find in our hemisphere. Sadly, it is in the process of being defaced, not by young vandals, but by the managers of Lewis Crofters. On the glass door below the sign that tells us it is indeed the Crofters' Store they have pinned what looks, from the other side of the street, like a doormat with a picture of our future king and his bit of stuff. This sort of carry-on is downright disrespectful. I really don't know what the world is coming to.

THURSDAY

As if that wasn't enough, the sweet and normally soothing voice of Morag Stewart came over the air on Thursday morning with news of a disturbing nature. The Free Presbyterians of Lewis have let the world know they have no objection to the storing of bombs and warlike Americans in Melbost. It's all right for them when the big bang comes, with their passage assured, booked and paid for; but what about those of us who wasted our substance on riotous living? Have they no concern for their neighbours who are not ready to go yet? And if not, do they not realise they are inviting all kinds of heathens on to our island, including people who are not above the playing of polo and goodness knows what other games on the Sabbath?

DIHAOINE

Aig an aona bhanais feumaidh e bhith gun chuir seana ghille socharach sùil ann an tè a bhoireannaich taobh thall an Loch. Tha e coltach gun dh'fhaighnich e do dh'Ailean Dòmhnallach an iarradh e bean dha air an rèidio. Tha duine glè chunnartach muc ann am poc fhaighinn mar seo. Chan eil fhios cò às a dh'fhaodadh e freagairt fhaighinn. Fhuair fear à Crosabost fìor dhroch bhargan an Ceann Phàdraig. Chuir e sùil innte aig dannsa agus e làn stuth-cruaidh. Mar a bha e fhèin ag ràdh, 'Dhannsadh i air broga', ach tha e coltach gur e sin fhèin uireas a dhèanadh i. Co-dhiù, phòs e i air seota mòr sgadain agus 's ioma latha ghabh e aithreachas. 'S fheàrr dhut, 'ille, a dhol gha lorg thu fhèin, agus thoir an aire air feadhainn Ghlaschu, oir bidh tu beò, ma bhitheas tu beò, air fish-fingers agus chips.

Eachann Dòmhnallach

26 JUNE, 1981

MONDAY

Monday the 15th has always been a bad day for me and I expected the worst. I took the precaution of sleeping in a chair by the fire with a picture of Tony Benn by my side. He must have had some powers of protection because I got a good few hours' rest before the nightmare commenced.

She came walking across the Minch, golden mane flying in the wind, carrying the tairsgeir in one hand and a whip in the other. I thought I'd try a new strategy of attempting to outwork her but with no success. Her energy is unlimited. She has taken to singing while she cuts. Sometimes it's *Onward, Christian Soldiers*, and the voice is driving me mad. Occasionally she switches to *When The Saints Go Marching In*, then the cutting tempo increases. Voices of unseen gentlefolk cry 'Heah! Heah!' after every verse. All sense of time and place have long since gone but I think I see a great, unfamiliar river ahead. I fancied I saw a posse of men from the TUC coming to my rescue. I cried for help but they swept past us shouting: "You must go through the proper channels." Surely we must stop soon. The future looks dark.

TUESDAY

I had serious misgivings about disturbing my West End analyst on Ascot week but I found him in good humour, surrounded by tweeds. When I told him about the effect of Benn's picture he laughed loud and long, saying Mr Benn was an undercover agent for the establishment bent on the destruction of the Labour Party. Deep depression all day.

WEDNESDAY

All kinds of worrying changes are taking place in our island. The pubs are going downhill fast. They haven't really been the same since they started letting women in and I wouldn't be surprised if they (women) are responsible for the scenes that surround us in most Stornoway pubs in this sad day and age. If one should develop a thirst around the midday mark, as sometimes happens, it is almost impossible to quench it. You cannot get near the bar for young women wanting orange juice and hamburgers. If you finally succeed in getting your fist round a pint glass there's a good chance someone will drop a potato in it. Waitresses swish past you carrying trays laden with meat and gravy. All around you are the sounds of soup being slurped and lettuce being munched, and the rich smell of food threatening all the time to swamp the beautiful aroma of the hop. Something should be done about it. Why can't all these people eat at home and let the publican get on with his proper business? I blame it all on the working wife and the decline of the fish supper.

THURSDAY

The *Press & Journal* carried a story and photograph of Colin Maciver, a Laxay crofter who has succeeded in rearing a huge breed of Continental cow. No wonder the landlords want rid of him if he is going to clutter up valuable, dog-exercising land with these great hairy animals. Was reminded of a little snippet of information passed on to me recently by a Balallan crofter. A crofter with an MA who knows a thing or two. Did you know, he said, that if a tree on your croft grows to more than five foot six it becomes the property of the landlord? I wonder where they got the figure from. Is it the average height of a landlord, or could a tree of that height provide cover for a poacher? And, what is more worrying, will a cow of great stature come under the same law?

DIHAOINE

Thachair mi ri fear Àird Thung bho chionn ghoirid agus thug sinn còmhradh air na cunnartan a tha an cois a bhith toirt mhnathan dhachaigh às na bailtean mòra. Cha ghabh iad comhairle agus tha iad buileach cunnartach aig àm buain mhònach ma gheibh iad bhos do chionn anns a' pholl – feumaidh duine a bhith beò air a dhorgh ma tha e dol a ghleidheadh nan corragan. Bha mi ag innse dha mu na tubaistean a thachair air na Lochan timcheall air an tairsgeir. Tha e coltach, mas e an fhìrinn a th' ann, gun chaill fear bho taobh thall an Loch cluais. Bha fear Àird Thung ag ràdh gu bheil cùisean a cheart cho dona anns a' bhaile aca fhèin, ach tha dòigh ùr aca air na mnathan nach tuig Gàidhlig a cheannsachadh – 'yellow card' airson gearradh beag, agus 'red card' ma chailleas tu meur. Co-dhiù, feumaidh e bhith gu robh bruadar aige bho bha mi a' còmhradh ris agus fhuair mi litir bhuaithe: "Eachainn. Chaidh am beachd fhoillseachadh gur ann a' buain mòine air na Lochan a chaidh an fheadhainn a leanas a dhochann – Van Gogh, Dave Allen agus Moshe Dayan. A bheil susbainte sam bith anns a' bheachd seo? Ailig."

Tha mi cinnteach gu bheil, Ailig.

Eachann Dòmhnallach

31 JULY, 1981

FRIDAY

I was strolling through the narrows of Point Street in what I hoped would appear to be a purposeful manner but at the same time trying desperately to remember the reason for my trip to Stornoway. I bought some bread, fish fingers and milk anyway. You usually can't go far wrong with that sort of thing when you cannot remember what you were told to buy or borrow. (The reason for the milk is that Joe Black's is so full of preservative as to be absolutely undrinkable even with fried herring and new potatoes. I believe if they took a vote on it most of the customers would rather let it go sour in the natural way.) Then, to my astonishment, I found I had absentmindedly wandered into the Criterion. I had hardly taken my first sip of cold beer when Iain Crichton came breezing in and ordered a round. I had often wondered about the reason for his popularity. Now I know. To pay for the booze he pulled out a wad that would have choked an elephant. He peeled off, and this is as true as I'm standing here, a fifty pound note. A few of us gathered round to examine this rarity but no matter how much we pressed him he wouldn't tell where he keeps the machine. If I am wrong, and the notes are real, there is a moral here for all of us. If your sons and daughters have a notion to become brain surgeons or nuclear physicists, beat it out of them and get them to learn all about volts, amps and electric kettles. That is where the dough is.

THURSDAY

The advantages of having geriatric colleagues, or old mates depending on the net pay, is held by many to be easily outweighed by the disadvantages. I'm glad to say I'm not one of them. Those who are continually moaning about having to look after the aged and infirm perhaps haven't realised what we have gained in ancient folklore, shared wisdom and tall tales. Then, there are those who would grudge all the expensive retirement presents. This is surely an example of lack of imagination and short-sightedness. With inflation the way it is the few quid laid out on Bill

Maclean and Fingalstein should come back ten-fold in a few years' time. True, there was a lot of worry and nursing time involved as we moved into the computer age, but think of the lump sums. Although Fingalstein's has so far only yielded one can of Guinness, we all feel sure it is only a matter of time until his natural generosity manifests itself in a real hòro-gheallaidh.

MONDAY

You must have heard it asked a hundred times. Where do all these stories come from? Does someone sit at home behind partly drawn curtains fermenting malicious gossip or is there some truth in even the most unlikely yarn? No one should underestimate the power of gossip. Even if proved afterwards beyond shadow of doubt to be untrue, the damage done by rumour can never be undone. Some people believe we in the islands have a monopoly on gossip but this is nonsense. It is a worldwide plague, although it is probably true that it has more effect where everybody knows everyone else and reputations are easily shattered.

I blame it all on strong winds and defective hearing. When shouted from hilltop to hilltop against the prevailing westerly gale and through the bleating of sheep and the barking of dogs, messages easily get distorted. And even more so when passed on to the next hilltop, so that the final result bears little resemblance to the original text. For instance, an innocent crofter might shout to his partly-deaf neighbour: "Rug bò Chailein." Having digested this juicy titbit, the grateful but slightly deaf neighbour will rush to tell a friend: "Rug bean Chaluim." If the friend is a no-nonsense type he will put a stop to the whole silly business there and then with something like: "Ist, amadain. Boireannach a tha trì fichead bliadhna." However, if she (well, it is more likely than he) is a gossip, a wildly-exaggerated tale of a 60-year-old woman giving birth to triplets will spread like a heather fire.

Although I would hate to encourage this sort of thing, it probably does serve a useful purpose. The fear of gossip does even more than the fear of God to keep people on the straight and narrow path of righteousness.

TUESDAY

Last night a bald welder from Ranish disappeared over the Clisham towing a small caravan. He has not reported in and we fear the worst. If Van de Merwe is holding him I think I can safely say for the whole family that not one penny will be paid in the way of ransom. I told him he had been exposing his skin too much to the sun.

WEDNESDAY

I am seriously studying the pros and cons of the Social (or is it Socialist) Democratic Party. This could be the answer for the small property-owning progressive peasant who is frightened by Benn but who has given up hope of climbing into the Tory Party. It could take some time.

14 AUGUST, 1981

MONDAY

Amazing what one can pick up from the heavier Sunday papers. By scanning through the reviews and reading little snippets of biographies one could easily pass oneself off as being educated, or at least well read, without having to plough through the long boring books they used to write in the days before television. I was not at all surprised to learn Tolstoy was a Freemason. How else could he have got all that junk published? And his poor wife, having cleaned, cooked and generally danced attendance on him all day, was up half the night correcting his spelling. If fish fingers had been invented then she could have had all that done by nine o'clock and got a good night's sleep like any modern wife.

TUESDAY

It is now almost a year since the idea of a sponsored row from Loch Leurbost to the Star Inn was first mooted. After all that time it is still not easy to write or talk about it. It kindles painful memories not only in those who took part, but also in the relatives who gathered to wait anxiously on the pier. People tend to look away or change the subject when that terrible day is mentioned. Older citizens look at their shoes and mutter what sounds like a quick prayer – mysterious force that brought them back – can only be thankful they returned at all – unseen merciful hand on the tiller – tragedy miraculously avoided – men with family responsibilities reduced to the level of the lower animals, and much more of that sort of thing.

However, it seems the memory is slowly fading. Someone even had the nerve to suggest a similar outing this year but along a different route – Loch Leurbost to the Cleitear Hotel and back. Don't miss out. Book your place in a boat now. One consolation for a certain wife who will be nameless. If her husband should fall asleep by the fire with his wellies full of water, he is much lighter this year and easier to manhandle.

WEDNESDAY

I am now approaching the final stages in my preparation for a few days in South Uist and what better way to prepare than a quick visit to South Lochs to get the feel of the wilderness. I usually try to spend one day every year over in the land of my ancestors. Each year I give thanks that my great-great-grandfather had the good sense to move to the civilised north shore. There are certain rumour-mongers in Marvig who would have us believe he was chased across the Loch for sheep stealing, but I cannot accept that.

I have always entertained hope of going back to the South Side some day as a missionary, for, believe me, there is a great deal of scope for good work to be done "over there". Unfortunately my companion was a little uneasy and kept hurrying me on, so we didn't even have time to visit that famous tourist attraction, the 'Rob Fell Here' sign. I was surprised, though, at the progress they have made in the last year, what with salmon trout and even turbot farms.

Sometime I hope to spend a lengthy spell in Cromore before I write my half-novel. Murchadh Rodaidh could be the man-over-whom-the-rock-hangs and no one will recognise him. We could have all the characters wearing kilts and talking in stage-Scottish accents and of course they would have only a passing resemblance to any living person. Two-hundred-and-fifty pages of large print. There is a few bob to be made at that game.

THURSDAY
One of the most dangerous things around at the moment is the new potato. The problem is knowing when to stop, especially when they are taken along with salt herring. The effect is much the same as too much drink. If the new potatoes are taken in any quantity – say 12 or more – the consumer is likely to pass into a coma in the middle of the afternoon. Even when taken in moderation, about six or seven, they induce a drunk-like stupor and it is quite dangerous to drive. I wouldn't be surprised if those who detected a little unsteadiness in my gait today jumped to the wrong conclusion. Talking of food, you might be one of the lucky ones who caught a few of the fast disappearing mackerel. The cooking of mackerel is definitely something that should not be left to an imported wife. They generally have a mania for grilling, a cooking method not at all suited to that humble fish, because all that powerful oil is lost. I have it on the very best authority there is no cholesterol in the mackerel, so I've taken to pouring the oil on the new potatoes and washing the whole lot down with Guinness. Must have a snooze now.

FRIDAY
Now that Maggie Cunningham's picture has appeared on page two, I am under even more pressure to expose myself on page three. Beefcake, that's what the women want, said Fear Àird Thung when I met him the other day. So, I'm sending a photograph for next week's paper taken when I was in my prime.

SATURDAY
The cost of advertising is getting to the absolutely prohibitive stage. If I were to buy a few lines in the *Stornoway Gazette* to say I have a 12 cubic foot freezer for sale, God only knows what it would cost me, and if I were

to add that my phone number is 86–443 it would probably break me. [Note to accounts dept: deduct £1.20 from this man's fee – Ed.]

21 AUGUST, 1981

LAST WEEK

Little did I know when as a young man I stood looking over Lake Bangweulu, not far from where Stanley found Livingstone, that I too would, one day, have the opportunity to go forth among the less fortunate to do good work. When I waved goodbye to my neighbours on Monday 10th August and set off with my family to the Southern Isles, I was under no illusion about the magnitude of my task. The 60 treacherous miles between Leurbost and Leverburgh would in themselves have been enough to deter a weaker spirit. Roads climb almost vertically to over 2,000 feet, then plunge dizzily into ravines of terrifying sheerness and awe-inspiring beauty. Thank goodness I had my *Reader's Digest* with me. Our ageing vehicle, with 53,000 miles on the clock and a bald tyre, was a constant source of concern, but when duty calls it takes more than a bald tyre … (the reader should fill in two pages here describing the Harris hills). It was with immense relief and some surprise we found ourselves, at 10.00 am, in Leverburgh – a storm-lashed, picturesque little village with only 3,000 miles of rolling Atlantic Ocean between it and New York. At precisely 10.02, despite a force 8 south-easterly and only 20 yards' visibility, Captain Macaskill expertly manouevered his new 33 ft tupperware boat alongside the crumbling concrete jetty. Four-and-a-half minutes later we were off – our adventure had begun.

Time and again the Minch and the Atlantic backed away from each other and charged angrily to lock antlers like stags in October. Relentlessly those two proud seas tossed us high in the air and each time I looked across at my wife who had stood at my elbow (trying to keep it straight) all these years and wondered: "Is this it? Have we come so far together only to …" She caught my eye and whispered: "Don't worry, if the *Reader's Digest* won't buy it *The Scots Magazine* will."

Thanks to our Skipper, Donald (yes, we were all on first-name terms now: danger had drawn us together), we had miraculously pitched and tossed our way through 12½ miles of dangerous currents to arrive at our destination at 10.52 am. Our guide and driver, Gilleasbaig na Feusaige Ruaidhe, a native of the South Part, was faithfully waiting. "Ach, but it is good to see you," he cried in that delightful way they do. The 40 miles to Loch Eynort, my operational headquarters, were mercifully uneventful. (Slip in here four flowery paragraphs about gold-tinted sands – remote paradise – that sort of thing.)

The corrugations and innumerable potholes that strew the quaint, narrow roads all add to the unique character of the Dark Islands. We sincerely hope no well-meaning, Stornoway-based philistine has any plan to destroy this essential ingredient in Uist's appeal by building smooth wide highways.

That what I had set out to achieve would be difficult I did not doubt for one second. How could I succeed where so many had failed? What right had I to hope? The moment I set eyes on the majestic mountains that tower so triumphantly above the Loch, I knew somehow my mission would not be in vain. (Insert here two pages of fern-filled cliches that bring the slopes to life.) I will not pretend that everything went smoothly or that the scene is flawless – of course, it isn't. Here, I will quote another writer in *The Scots Magazine* who described so vividly "that concrete monstrosity at the end of the road." He was referring to our driver's new bungalow. Can nothing be done to hide this kind of ugliness from those of us who come to look for nature unblemished? Could not some architect design a simple, yet adequate, cave for the indigenous population? Then there was the pile of newly-delivered poles, belonging, we were informed, to the Hydro Electricity Board. What an abomination in the eyes of those who treasure the romance and cosy light of the tilley lamp.

Right from the outset I had decided to trust the natives completely and hope to win their confidence. This was a mistake. On the very first night they tried to poison me – or so I thought – a yellow liquid they acquired in a den of iniquity called Creagorry. I naturally took exception to this but later I discovered it was not intended as a poison. Apparently the indig can drink it with no ill effect and only incomers tend to be overcome. After that initial misunderstanding I made spectacular progress with my work. I do not intend to reveal my methods but I think the results speak for themselves. Naturally, I must leave it to others to judge and to praise my astonishing success, but perhaps I can mention three typical cases.

A well-known boatbuilder of Loch Eynort was looking pretty well reborn by the time I left and a hard-nosed sceptic, and reformed PhD, from Loch Carnan could very well skip the intermediate stages and go straight over to the Free Presbyterians. A holidaying English vet shook me warmly by the hand and thanked me, although he has not as yet committed himself. And that only brings us up to Tuesday.

* * *

Someone has started leaving the *Reader's Digest* and *The Scots Magazine* in our office lavatory. I'm sorry I'm so easily influenced.

28 AUGUST, 1981

MONDAY

The 10-year-olds of Leurbost have at last been brought to realise life can be tough. Up until now the path was smooth and free from nasty shocks. Over-protected at home, and mollycoddled in school by gentle women teachers, they were beginning to go soft. That is now ended. Today was the start of a new school year and they went back to a harsh new regime. A wild man has come over the mountains of Uig to show them what's what, and not before time.

He is obviously wealthy and already he is being held up to parents as an example. "Our teacher has five cars. He must be rich. Why aren't you?" I cannot explain that, but I'll tell you one thing: he steals pencils from children. Lifting biros in the Royal Bank is something we've all done, but pencils from children? I ask you. What next? Food from their mouths? Any more of this and I'll be along to sort him out.

TUESDAY

Talking of sorting people out, I'm expecting a visit from the Barvas Navigator any day now. He usually calls in on his way back from Venezuela. I'm doing some light training with a view to settling an old score. Nothing too strenuous – a little skipping and a few press-ups. It would be fatal to become musclebound so near the event. If I remember right, I had a sprained wrist and a damaged cartilage in my right knee that time he got the better of me behind the bicycle shed, but I feel I've taken better care of the corp in the intervening 20 years. I expect the decision to go my way this time.

Despite the lingering animosity I would not sink so low as to deny he sometimes has a good idea. He stopped in the Mediterranean on his way home last time – Malta, I think he said – where through sunburnt eyes he saw an astonishing number of English pensioners. Why not Hebridean pensioners, he thought. Why not indeed? Although our company is still in its infancy, I'm sure you can see the potential. Instead of cutting peat to warm all these old bones in the winter, we simply airlift everyone over 65 to a cheap spot in the sun. He has left the administration of the scheme in my hands, so please send your pension books to my secretary. You will get them back in April. There are a few minor snags but none that cannot be overcome. When I mentioned the project to the Bank Manager he said: "'S tric a thig fìrinn à beul deamhain."

WEDNESDAY

A short sermon now, if you can be serious for a minute. A new form of double-speak is emanating from the right. If repeated often enough, even the most transparently obvious lie will eventually be accepted as the truth. Although admittedly some take longer than others to be convinced that black is white. Our Prime Minister and Two-Gun Tex across the water are trying out a new one on us at the moment. They tell us that if you are going to talk peace you must go armed to the teeth. Your man has been watching too many of his own movies. If they admitted to keeping a dagger up the sleeve or tucked into the stocking when talking with forked tongue, we might understand, but to boast of going to talk peace with six-guns loaded and fully cocked is nonsensical. They may be right in thinking the only way to talk with the Rooshian is while holding him by the scruff of the neck (that's another argument altogether), but it is not peace. If that's what peace means, I'm an Englishman.

THURSDAY

Those who have been laughing at my goat would do well to read the following account of one of my ancestors and to remember we are not a clan to be trifled with.

Aon oidhche fhuar ann an dùbhlachd a' gheamhraidh bho chionn ceud gu leth bliadhna bha Coinneach an Tairbh a' tighinn bho bhoireannach à Grabhair. Bha e anns na cnuic os cionn Chalaboist agus gun guth aige gu robh duine air thalamh ach e fhèin. Ged a bha fradharc math aige (leughadh e am Bìoball ri solas Fir Chlis), bha Sàtan 's an gaol air a dhalladh cho mòr 's nach fhac' e an tarbh gus an robh e air a mhuin. Cha b' e shorthorns a bh' aca anns na làithean ud idir ach tairbh chaol ghlas nach biodh air an nàrachadh aig Aintree. Chan eil fios cia mheud mìle a ruith Coinneach sìos, suas agus timcheall chnuic agus an tarbh air a shàilean. 'S dòcha nan robh an talamh air bith rèidh gu robh e air a chasan a thoirt bhuaithe, ach cuimhnich gu robh dà chas a bharrachd air an tarbh. Mu dheireadh thàinig air Coinneach tionndadh agus aghaidh a chur air. Tha e coltach nach robh sabaiste air taobh thall an Loch a-riamh a leithid na tè ud. Fàgaidh sinn às dusan 'round' an-drasta, ach, 's e an deireadh a thàinig air an tarbh gun spìon Coinneach tè dha na casan-toisich às. 'S mise dubh-ogha Choinnich an Tairbh.

FRIDAY

Since the publication of my photograph in last week's paper the phone has not stopped ringing. I would remind the ladies I am a married man, much as I appreciate the offers. More than one old Leòdhasach has remarked on the resemblance between myself, my great-grandfather and John Knox. We are often taken for each other and I sometimes take advantage of the misunderstanding.

18 SEPTEMBER, 1981

MONDAY

As I was saying last week, fifty is not a moment too soon to get rid of them. To allow them to carry on in responsible jobs after that age is to invite disaster. On no account should anyone who took an active part in the last war be listened to on the subject of disarmament. They foolishly think they have seen the worst, so they don't try to imagine a catastrophe a million times greater. They also lived in a time when help for the wounded could be expected. When the holocaust comes, as it surely will, when you smell your own and your children's flesh burning, there will be no one to help because all around you there will be only the wailing of the half-dead. Perhaps you will be one of the lucky ones near the blast who will avoid the long drawn-out agony.

A great many people refuse to reflect on these horrors, and those who do, and then draw the obvious conclusion, are frequently suspected of being sympathetic towards Russian imperialism. (These suspicions are continually being nourished by official propaganda from those who profit most from the manufacture of weapons of destruction.) I don't understand what the desire to see the continuation of our civilisation has to do with political dogma.

Denis Healey said last week he thought the existence of nuclear bombs had kept the peace in Europe for the last 37 years. Or as my friend the Officer says: "THEY won't start a war nowadays because THEY also are part of the fodder." THEY might not start one deliberately but sooner or later it will come. Then we will fry. Our only chance is to start dismantling the bombs NOW! – all bombs. If the Russians move in, at least they will not have to bomb us first. Those who have always preached

"Better dead than Red" should retain some means of committing suicide. There is nothing like a good dwell on death to cheer one up.

TUESDAY

When your child comes home from school with a letter that starts "Dear Parent …", never make the mistake of thinking it's for you, the father. The father, as a letter from the local art teacher makes plain, can only consider himself the parent when the mother is not available. "Dear Parent," said the letter, "if you could spare one of daddy's old shirts …" Notice the female chauvinism here. Not "Dear Parent, can you spare one of your old shirts or one of the Ma's?" No fear of that. The writer cannot conceive of the notion the parent could be a man. Notice also the writer's lack of grasp of the economic priorities of our hard times. The father wears his old shirt. Why not ask for one of the mother's many discarded, almost-new shirts? I think this little example shows quite clearly the extent to which women are getting the upper hand in our society. Unless we men pull together we will soon be reduced to the level of the sgalag.

WEDNESDAY

Our football commentators are being a bit more cautious this time. About four years ago I remember a well-known, orange-haired TV personality saying to a visiting European manager: "I know we were great, but tell me how great, exactly, were we." The visitor knew just enough English to be embarrassed. Like everyone else who was largely to blame for Argentina, our friend with the hair is trying, on his way to Spain, not to repeat the folly of four years ago.

Sadly, Danny McGrain, our only world class player of recent years, is past his best. Dalglish, in the North Lochs view, has never looked more than merely competent. This team may have less talent than the infamous one of '78 but they are prepared to work harder and could very well make it to the quarter-finals. The blunderbuss Jordan scored a good goal tonight. It is a great pity he had to waste that one before the finals. He hasn't got that many in his store.

THURSDAY

Attracted by a familiar aroma, I followed my nose into a certain house in our own village where I found the occupier playing with his chemistry set. He had been given a recipe for strong ale by someone from Shader, Point, who will for the time being be nameless. One glance at the ingredients was enough to tell me it was a blatant attempt to bring the youth of our Parish to their knees. Enough is never enough for the Rubhach. We must now await the completion of the chemical action to see what percentage of poison the yeast can stand. Then we will retaliate.

FRIDAY

I met MacLennan of Kenneth St and found him to be in an unusually bad mood. He was full of bitterness about Stornoway ratepayers having to subsidise every Maw and Scorp between the Butt and Barra. Normally a good-natured sort of guy, he is only once-removed from the Maw himself. He even still retains a smattering of Gaelic. "We take you into our hostels and our school, teach you to read and write, and no sooner have we got the heather out of your ears than you turn round and attack us in print." It's a good job he doesn't drink. I'd like to find out what caused his bitterness.

SATURDAY

I see the *Free Press* has been attacked by the Press Barons and their lackeys. If anyone ever had any doubt about the paper's usefulness, it must surely now have been removed.

6 NOVEMBER, 1981

MONDAY

This warning may be too late for many of you but if it saves even one marriage my work will not have been in vain. As if there weren't enough causes of friction in the average household already, they had to give us the Rubik Cube. It is an even greater waste of time than television. Some people think Mr Rubik was – still is – an innocent Hungarian scientist bent on making a few bob for himself. There is much more to it than that. It is obviously a sinister Russian plot. Not since Stalin planned to flood the West with forged American dollars have they come up with a more devastating weapon than the Cube.

Apart from domestic squabbling over whose turn it is, work gets neglected. Peats don't get taken in, so fires go out, and the fish-fingers get burnt, but the puzzle remains unsolved. It doesn't help to be told every so often: "There's a little boy in school who can do it in two minutes." I am not ashamed to admit I gave up and bought the book, which makes it a little easier. Any day now I expect to get the colours in the right places, and then I'll start on the garage and mend the fence.

TUESDAY

I remember reading somewhere a long time ago some clever writer's idea of what the Gettysburg Address would have looked like if Eisenhower had been the man on the spot instead of Abraham Lincoln. The artist's impression of Eisenhower's efforts were thought at the time to be so far removed from the original masterpiece as it was possible to be. American political language had reached a new low and the writer probably thought the low would never get any lower. Then one day recently Reagan escaped from his speech writers and was left for a moment to broadcast his thoughts in his own words. I think they are worth reprinting here in case anyone missed them.

Asked about the likelihood of a "limited-theatre" nuclear exchange in Europe, Reagan replied: "Well, I would – if they realised that we, again – if we led them back to that stalemate only because that our retaliatory power, our seconds, or our strike at them after their first strike would be so destructive that they couldn't afford it. That would hold them off."

No one has claimed he was drunk, so we can assume that was the real Reagan speaking. And that is the man with his finger on the trigger! How do we know if his geography is any better? It is too easy to picture him briefing his pilots while pointing to Madrid, Toronto or Shawbost thinking these places are in Russia. Did it really come as a surprise to so many that he sees the whole of Europe as his aircraft carrier? Is there any hope at all, I ask you?

WEDNESDAY
Keeping depression at bay is never an easy task in these hard times. The causes are all too numerous: the weather, the pursers, the bombs or just the bleak future in general. Everyone has his own pet cause. For some it could be something as trivial as the overdraft or not having found all their sheep. For others it could be more serious. The death of a friend, perhaps. The confirmed Calvinist growing old with the mysterious sudden conversion eluding him has very little to smile about. The death of Gaelic. Too much booze. Loneliness. Unemployment. The list is too long.

Personally, I see nothing in the future more frightening than our children melting in the impending holocaust. As we rush towards our own extinction despair sometimes gives way to anger because it could be avoided. Someone, sometime, has to start dismantling the bombs. While we have no control over the Russians or the Americans, we do, in theory, have some control over our own lot. We can vote into power those who are prepared to take the first steps towards sanity. Paul Foot believes in banning the bomb. So does Michael Foot. Why not Donny Foot?

THURSDAY
Feeling a bit better today following a visit by not one but two West End Tories carrying good news about a son and heir to the estate and the customary plastic bag. It is unfashionable, almost unheard of in fact, to admit the other side have in their camp some honest men with sensible ideas. It is just that they are misguided and don't realise what their leaders really stand for.

Also, some good news in the *Stornoway Gazette*. According to a story on the front page, Lewis Offshore is not up for sale. I only wish I could believe it. Not that it would necessarily be a bad thing. Perhaps they could find new owners capable of securing some orders.

DIHAOINE

Cò a thachair rium an-dè ach Fear Àird Thung, Aristotle Jock Macnamarra. Chan eil càil air thalamh nach eil fios aig a' bhalach ud air. Thòisich e ag innse dhomh mar a fhuair na Sasannaich a' 'stiff upper lip'. Bha dùil agam fhìn a-riamh gur e an accent a ghlas an carbaird àrd aca, ach tha e coltach nach e. A rèir Aristotle 's e cuideam nam pith–helmets a bhiodh orra thall thairis a dh'fhàg iad mar a tha iad. Thàinig oirre a bhith còmhradh le dìreach gluasad beag air a' charbaird ìosal. 'S ann mar sin a rugadh an accent. Rud sam bith nach eil thu tuigse, faighnich do Mhacnamarra.

27 NOVEMBER, 1981

MONDAY

For the first time in 11 years my wife has taken to leaving the house every morning to go to work. I've been forbidden to mention the nature of the work and you wouldn't believe me anyway. Perhaps later in the year I'll be authorised to reveal more details.

In the meantime here I am on a Monday morning with the freedom of a silent empty house and I like it. There's a few jobs awaiting my attention but what's the hurry, haven't I got all day? I'll throw a peat on the fire, wander around and see what exactly is to be done. A slight leak on this dormer window, but what a view. A solitary boat chasing spent herring between Tavay and Cromore. The village of Crossbost still sleeping. Little children trudging their weary way to school. It's a cold morning but it doesn't make them hurry, although the girls seem to be making better progress. They try to avoid the puddles while the boys go out of their way to find them. I see a definite pattern developing now. The boys are falling way behind swinging their bags round their bodies and jumping in ditches. A little fighting and now and again an unprovoked attack on a sheep (good lad).

I see one tiny straggler at the tail end taking two steps forward and one back in dread. I wonder what's going on in his little head. Has he lost his dinner money? Or could he be heading for Neil's class?

Where do the girls get their sense of purpose from? Is it ambition at that early age? Anxiety about being late? Probably just more common sense. If only some of whatever it is could be transplanted in the young male, what couldn't he achieve.

I've moved to a downstairs window now. Calum Geal is up and about towing a reluctant ram in a yellow luminous oilskin (Calum, not the ram). Someone else peering from behind partly drawn curtains. What is it with these people? Have they nothing better to do? I like this fellow Jimmy Mack but I think I'll put on a record of the Chieftains. Turn it up full volume. Pity I stopped smoking. Never mind, at least I won't shave. I didn't think time would pass so quickly when there is so little to do. Maybe I'll wash the breakfast dishes a bit later on.

It's a nice relaxed life here on page three. No rushing about all over the country like the Leader. Aye, I could take more of this. I wonder if we could live on her pay and tell you-know-who where to stick … Steady on. Let's not be too hasty, it's only the first day.

TUESDAY

Once a month or so I go to the library to borrow a book. Occasionally I read, but more often than not I have a sneaky ulterior motive. Of course I make the usual pretence of browsing through the shelves, examining and rejecting, in scholarly fashion, obscure titles by even more obscure authors. After 10 minutes of this, or less if there is no one watching, I make for the new books. Very often in this pile you'll find the sort of thing I go for, and I pass this tip on to you in good faith.

Take a big one. Nothing less than 15 inches by 12 will do, and preferably weighing about 10 pounds. With this tome under your arm you march down town and into the Bank. On the way there you can score some valuable points if the book has a fancy name on the cover, like Chomsky, but it is in the Bank itself your labour is rewarded. If you've had one of these letters – please call at your convenience so that we can discuss your current account – the book is a must, but even if you have not, read on, because you never know the minute. I must stress again the book must look new and expensive. Words are unnecessary unless your interviewer is one of those who stares at the desk while lecturing, in which case you must draw his attention to your burden with something like "Sixteen pound fifty. I know I shouldn't have but I couldn't resist …" The man's eyes light up. Your name is cleared immediately. Here is a fellow, he says to himself, who spends his money not on foolishness but on the improvement of his mind. You walk out of there a freeman with your Declined to Report blessed and approved. If you should run into any snags, ring me; I have plenty of ploys in the same vein.

WEDNESDAY

Did you see those Irish boys in action tonight? What a team. It's a pity the English players couldn't have watched, perchance to pick up some of the basic skills. Yon K Keegan wouldn't have made the Lochs team before the war when we were all in our prime. Still, they got through, on sheer effort and Hungarian post-climactic lassitude, and that, they tell us, is what matters. It means trouble for the Scots. Not only will we see less of our own team on TV; there are all those English football hooligans. When they start to misbehave this time the Colemanators can call them British, as they did in Italy, and with a bit of luck the worldwide audience will assume they are Scottish. With brandy cheaper than Irn Bru, the real Scottish supporters will of course all be in jail or at the bullfighting challenging the bull.

THURSDAY

This sentimentality will be the death of us. Today, at the age of 88, Mairi Anna closes the door of the last black-house in N. Lochs and moves to a Stornoway council house. A sad day for Ranish because she will be very much missed. A sad day also for the traditionalists. You know the ones I mean. They would like to go back to the old days and the good ways. They usually live in centrally-heated luxury on at least 10 grand a year, and you can safely bet they never had to thatch a damp black-house or even go to the well. Give me a council house anytime, even in Plasterfield.

FRIDAY
I like to see so many people reading my column. It is almost as rewarding as getting paid.

18 DECEMBER, 1981

MONDAY
Less sheep and more cattle is a sermon I have often preached. It is easier said than done, though. I had expected to be treated lavishly tonight following a friend's trip to the market with two bullocks. No party, I'm afraid. He had to let them go at 34p per pound. I would give serious thought to the possibility of becoming a butcher but as I get older I have doubts about the wisdom of eating the flesh of other animals. Must seek advice on alternative diet.

TUESDAY
Listen. We have a lot to be thankful for. A big white house. Water coming through the tap. Electricity. A flush toilet inside the house. A barrel of salted flank for the winter. Every comfort, you would think, but what use is that if you cannot get a laugh. I mean to say, old chap, what is there to smile about in this age of affluence? Rolagan has retired and become a recluse. Ailean Sheonaidh and Thurber both gone. Some Stornoway taxi drivers rubbing their greedy paws in anticipation of the American Airforce. Mad men and women in control of our lives.

Someone who noticed the black cloud hanging over my head suggested I go along to the Beaver's shop to buy a book by that Australian Clive James. Worth every penny of £1.50, I was told, and full of laughs.

The author's not so critical friends on the back cover promised the same thing. "Enormously funny", "You can't put it down." And mine's a double whisky.

He seemed to know an awful lot of Greeks. (I didn't realise there were so many in Australia.) Quite interesting and all that, but damn the laugh did I get out of it.

WEDNESDAY

I see one ray of hope on the south-western horizon, however. This coming Friday a bunch of us intrepid pioneers intend to travel to the parish of Uig to celebrate the Leader's wedding. We are going unarmed right into the heart of Injun territory. But we are taking some precautions. We have a guide from Keose who spent a long time among these people. He speaks their language like a native and over the years he has won their trust. I feel his presence will afford us some protection. Bidh sinn beò ann an dòchas.

THURSDAY

If a man is determined to get married, there is little point in trying to talk him out of it. The more you remonstrate with him, the harder his attitude becomes. Confident in his own strength of character and ability to resist the debilitating influence of woman, he ignores your advice, and he goes ahead anyway.

You'll see little things at first, that seem trivial, like a missed editorial. But there are more important changes that become noticeable long before the wedding. A slight leaning to the right, then the typical lurch in the same direction. This is a phenomenon I've studied closely over many years. (It often comes with middle age even in those who avoid marriage.) A grudging respect for authority manifests itself. Property is acquired which must be protected from the masses. Sometimes they buy sheep. Finally they may go the whole hog and join the SDP. We must keep a wary eye on those who are foolhardy enough to tie the untieable knot.

FRIDAY

Talking of laughs, a teacher from the Castle invited me to submit my body to the College for experimental purposes. "The Haute Cuisine course has been underway for some time now, so it is probably safe to sample their work. Let's take a chance," he said. And we did.

I was sitting nervously weighing up the fourteen pieces of cutlery hoping I wouldn't let the East End down when who should come strolling in but a tableful of accountants from the Council's Department of Finance led by Ben the Director. Immediately I felt less apprehensive. Obviously, if nothing else, it had to be good value for money.

I thought the Poulet Saute Chausseur sauce a trifle on the sweet side; not quite how they used to make it in Ranish in the old days. The curry was definitely intended for the white man, and the pappadoms lacked the slightly singed taste preferred by the Ceylonese. There was no way I was going to try the Cat's Tongue. You have to draw the line somewhere. Still, all in all, I would not fall out with your man Mr Frost re presentation. He has a lot to put up with.

This sort of food is very enjoyable as a snack between meals, but when you are really hungry what you need is a well prepared cormorant, conger eel au gratin, or a well matured mackerel.

DISATHAIRN

Ma bhios sinn beò an t-seachdain sa tighinn feumaidh mi comhairle a thoirt oirbh mu thimcheall nan làithean gòrach a th' air thoiseach oirnn. Cha bhiodh e gu mòran feum an searmon a chur ann am Beurla, oir chan eil e mar fhasan aig muinntir na Beurla a bhith gam fosgladh fhèin a-mach mar a bhios luchd na Gàidhlig. Cuimhnich air an t-seanfhacal: D = (UG)2, far a bheil D = Staid mac an duine air Oidhche na Bliadhn' Ùir, U = Uisge-beatha, G = A h-uile facal Gaidhlig air a bheil fios aig an duine. Feuch, a chairdean, gum bi sibh ciallach.

1982

19 February, 1982

DILUAIN

Tha cuimhne agam aon oidhche geamhraidh, goirid mus do leum Mussolini air na h-Abyssinians, a dhol a chèilidh air Murchadh Saighdear, mar as minig a chaidh. Bha e ri sgrìobhadh 's a chùl ri Peigi. "Tha mi, bhalachaibh, air pìos bàrdachd a sgrìobhadh a-nochd – mi fhìn 's a' ghaoth a' còmhradh. Suidhibh sìos modhail agus leughaidh mi dhuibh rann no dhà. Seo mise a-nis a' bruidhinn ris a' ghaoith:

"Cò thuigeas neart nach fhaic an t-sùil 's nach bi gu bràth aig fois
ach fear bha tric a' càradh shiùil 's a chluicheadh bàla-cois.

"Seo a-nis a' ghaoth a' freagairt," arsa Murchadh.

"'S i," arsa Peigi, "agus gu leor dhith."

Anyone heard reciting the bard's verse in public bars or anywhere else will be hauled up in front of Colin Scott. On the other hand, serious students of his works will find me a reasonable man to deal with.

DIMAIRT

"Nach mòr ma-ta is feàrr an duine na caora?" (Mata, Caib. xii). Mothaichibh, a chàirdean, gur e ceist a bha am fear a sgrìobh na facail sin ri faighneachd. Tha e soilleir nach robh e cinnteach cò b' fheàrr. Carson eile tha comharradh-ceist an dèidh nam briathran? 'S dòcha air an làimh eile gur e bha e a' cur ceist air cò b' fheàrr DHETH duine na caora. Ann an 1982 san dùthaich bhochd 's eil sinn beò chan eil teagamh sam bith cò as fheàrr dheth. Tha £6.50 subsadaidh air a' chaora 's chan eil air a' chlann ach £5.25.

WEDNESDAY

Noticed you how speak the poor boys of Stornoway at whom there is neither one language nor the other complete. It was at one of them I heard this one:

"Nuair bha thu na do pheantair, bha thu math air
   whitewashaigeadh –
'S ioma balach brèagha mhill thu le do splashaigeadh."

If there is a reader out there somewhere who knows the rest of the "song", please send the complete version to the *Free Press* with a stamped addressed envelope. Payment on acceptance.

THURSDAY

I haven't seen Len Murray on TV for a long time and it worries me. I cannot tell if he is deliberately lying low or whether he has been silenced by THEM. He used to ring me on a Wednesday night for advice but he has not even been doing that recently. Have they got to him? It wouldn't surprise me, for they have certainly managed to silence many of his fellow trade unionists.

When unemployment reached two million, it caused a lot of ructions. Marches were planned and days of action. People seemed genuinely concerned and didn't hesitate to speak out against the hatchet men. Now the figure has reached three million, a disturbing change has become noticeable in workers' attitudes.

When news of a further 1,000 jobs lost is announced would-be protesters, the next potential batch, do not take to the streets. Instead they try to hide and keep quiet, hoping the Grim Reaperess will pass them by. Perhaps, they falsely hope, this latest sacrifice will satisfy her, and let us be thankful it's not us.

I don't know what our next move should be. I had hoped to gather a few of my own unemployed clan to go to Zimbabwe to help 'Ain Komo whose people came from Harris, but Mugabe foiled that plan.

FRIDAY

Murdie Siarach, well known for his far right political views, was last night elected secretary of the North Lochs Community Association, having no doubt planted his cronies in the darkest corners of the hall. It is only fair that you should know more about his character.

In his youth he roamed the oceans of the world as a ship's engineer. Then one day he said to himself: "Enough of this toil, I'll become a teacher." And he did. Now he seems content and, as he says himself, wouldn't dream of going back to working for a living. I only mentioned his politics because already I can sense his displeasure with our way of doing things. Let there be order and formality, you can almost hear him thinking. Over the years Dr Annie and I had built up a ceilidh atmosphere at N. Lochs meetings – everybody talking at the same time and no one listening, like an Irish parliament. Friendly chaos, you could say.

This approach is anathema to the narrow corridors of the rightist mind and already he has come out with foreign terms like agenda and matters arising. Of all the men I've known over the years with a mathematical bent, only Big Roddy himself had a touch of the anarchist. I think it comes from working daily with only three or four variables. They think somehow they can reproduce real life on the blackboard, which naturally leads them to suppose the big stick and mean monetary tactics can work. Only men of imagination in the middle ground understand that the variables are infinite and cannot be reduced to simple formulae. Yet I am not without hope for Murdie, because he came of solid stock on his grandfather's side.

19 MARCH, 1982

MONDAY

Eavesdropping is not a practice I admire, and I try to discourage it among those with whom I have any influence. However, there are times when you cannot help hearing whispered conversations that were not meant to be heard. When you are standing at the bar waiting for a friend, for instance. With your nose in your glass and your eyes focused on the froth, you make it plain to all present you couldn't give twopence for their idle chat. Even the most suspicious onlooker can see you are totally taken up with thoughts of great depth and importance. This puts them at their ease. Even the four furtive characters at the nearest table carelessly raise their voices. Pretty soon your ear cocks to a name, or names. Names that you and I know well but which cannot, of course, be mentioned here.

Twice recently snatches of low gossip have reached my innocent ears. There exists, if certain discerning Stornowegian observers can be believed, a "Gaelic Mafia" – a secret society more sinister even than the Freemasons. It is thought to hold total power and, we must assume, riches. The brothers have, it is whispered, the island of Lewis in their hands to do with as they see fit.

Their aim is subversion. They will not rest until the English language is spoken only at the speaker's peril. Their agents have wormed their way into the most important offices on our island, even into Comhairle Castle itself, where they openly and loudly speak their own language without hint of concern for Stornowegians and other who are without. We who "spoke the language when it was neither popular nor profitable" should keep our distance from them unless the Godfather makes us an offer we cannot refuse.

TUESDAY
I heard a new phrase today of which I can make nothing. Not that I was accused personally, although for all I know I could be one of the guilty ones. A certain lady I know well was told "to her face" she had a Council House Mentality. Is this a desirable state of mind? Is it contagious? Could it spread to private ghettos like Branahuie? Should we try to cultivate it or avoid it like the plague? If there is anyone out there who can shed a little light, please do. The Editor will pay handsomely.

WEDNESDAY

I ran into a certain Mr Campbell this morning. I hadn't seen him for a long time and I must say he looked very fit. But not, I'm afraid, very proper. No tie. Two buttons opened at the neck. General dishevelled appearance. Definitely not officer material. I offered him 2 to 1 against the betting shop but he wouldn't take me on. But wait you.

Talking of ties, I see young Mark Thatcher on the front page of *The Scotsman* today. He says he wouldn't dream of appearing at his mother's dinner table without a tie. I am pleased to see standards are not falling everywhere. There are certain boys in our Parish who wouldn't think twice of sitting to their herring in their wellies.

THURSDAY

What is the use of a poor crofter planting crocuses or anything else if he has a neighbour who trains his sheep to jump fences. (No names again, I'm afraid. The Editor is getting very strict on these matters.) I was restrained from action of a very violent nature only by visions of a future headline in the *Gazette*: "Mad Axeman Slaughters Neighbour's Sheep". There are other ways and means, however. An old gentleman in the village of Tong hit upon the ultimate deterrent when his neighbour's hens destroyed his crops. He set a baited longline along the perimeter of his property. I think whole barley is the bait I need.

A wealthy friend who is beginning to realise he cannot take it with him treated me to a dinner in the County Hotel. Now there's a steak for the working man. It was carried in on a large silver tray by two sturdy waitresses. The steak itself overlapped the plate by a good two inches and it was as thick and tender as a freshly-cut black peat. I have but one small criticism, for George the Chef was in good form: the bullock had obviously grazed excessively on reseeded pasture, in which case, as you all know, a slightly too tender cheesy texture can manifest itself. In these instances it is sufficient to wave the meat above the fire so the blood is retained. I'm afraid, Bill, that is all I can say for one pint of Guinness.

CHILDREN'S CORNER (or indoctrination of minors) Once upon

a lean time in the parish of Lochs there lived a big man who had some cows. He liked his cows very much but he liked his cars even more. He had more cars than cows. His wife didn't mind the cows but she hated the cars. Every time the man said he was going to get another car his wife roared furiously through her exhaust, "What about the groceries and the children's shoes." But the man didn't care because he was the boss. One day he went out and called the cows and the cars together to tell them some good news. He told them they were going to get an addition to the family – a lorry. The wee Fiesta flapped her wings in great joy and set about organising a welcoming party. The Landrover was also very happy because he would have a lot of fun pulling the lorry on a rope because the lorry was very old and stiff. The big shiny Rover, who never got excited about anything, just looked down his nose and said nothing. But the tractor, the poor tractor, was very unhappy. He cried and cried until his radiator was empty. "We don't need a lorry," he bawled, "I'll be made redundant." The cows were delighted. They held horns and danced round the cars. From now on they would never be hungry because the lorry would bring them hundreds and hundreds of bales of straw. The man's wife said maybe for her it would be the last straw. This made the big man very angry, for he liked to have his own way. He stamped his huge feet in rage, he beat the walls with his great fists, he backed the tractor into a deep ditch and he refused to play his accordion. Then he went and bought the lorry anyway. There was nothing the poor tractor or his wife could do because they were not in the farmworkers' union. So you see, children, better a weak union than no union at all.

4 JUNE, 1982

MONDAY

There are few nastier shocks than to learn after 12 years of marriage that your wife is keeping another man. I like to think I'm fairly broadminded about this sort of thing but it's the size of the cheques that hurt. Twenty quid here, 30 there and goodness knows how much in hard cash. I wouldn't mind so much if he helped around the croft, making hay, cutting peat and tasting the curries. But no. Your man does not appear to have a single scruple. His name, by the way, is Marshall Ward. It's his wife I feel sorry for.

TUESDAY

It may seem a bit late in the day to take an interest in the family purse and so it is. Had I been aware of what was going on I might have had my new boat by now. I would advise any young man foolish enough to be considering matrimony to take the financial reins from the start. Fair enough, let her buy the groceries; but beware of furniture salesmen. Look out also for obsessions like sweater-buying. I have unwittingly accumulated enough geansaidhs to last three lifetimes and she shows no signs of being cured of this expensive compulsion. I put it down to the deprivation of a Partick childhood.

WEDNESDAY

I must admit, though, that my only pair of shoes were a disgrace to the family. They were coming adrift at the stem and the left heel had been double declutched out of existence, so I reluctantly allowed myself to be dragged into Smith's shoe shop (Put's) – a shop I usually only go to before our annual sale of work to collect unwanted size twelve-and-a-halfs and jackets with three sleeves.

I came straight to the point and asked for the cheapest pair of shoes in the house. To my astonishment the Maitre de Maison produced a pair of sturdy brown leather shoes with a generous beam at 11 quid. As his cheapest pair last year cost 20, I thought I'd better make myself scarce with the goods before he discovered his mistake.

Later on in the Caberfeidh, having had two bottles of Guinness on an empty stomach. I noticed, or appeared to notice, that I had somehow managed to cross my right leg over my right thigh. Not wishing to draw attention to my slightly inebriated state, I said nothing at the time although I was fairly certain I'd been sold two shoes for the right foot.

(They are terribly bigoted in that shop and I thought it might be their way of celebrating the Pope's visit.) It is not quite that simple; the shoes fit too well. What seems to have happened is the soles of the shoes are as they should be but the uppers are both designed for the starboard side. It is most disconcerting, if you catch a glimpse of your own hind legs while walking along the road, to discover you are apparently hen-toed on one side and splay-footed on the other. I would take the shoes back, but what's the use? For I have never heard of anyone who got his money back from a Stornoway shopkeeper.

THURSDAY

Our man in Toxteth is back in Leurbost for a short break. He has not, as has been suggested by right-wing rumour-mongers, had his grant to study the workings of the inner Liverpudlian mind stopped following certain disrespectful remarks made about Charlie's wife. He is here to recover from city stress, to breathe some lead-free air and maybe write a bit. If anyone would like a long letter from him please get in touch with me, his agent, so that we can discuss that contemptible element "terms".

FRIDAY

I caught a glimpse of another minor writer in Stornoway today, Finlay J Macdonald. I have not, of course, read his *Crowdie and Cream* – I never read anything written by a woman or a man over 50 – but I did do him the great favour of delaying publication of my own novel until he's had a chance to make a bob or two on his. All I want in return is that he gets me an interview with Donny B on 'Pebble Mill' when my first "major work" appears.

SATURDAY

Those who paid money to watch the Scotland-England game were the victims of a blatant fraud. Whether the two managers conspired to defraud or whether they arrived separately at their decision to take things easy matters not. We, the punters, were seen off. We were denied the chance to evaluate our teams' chances in Spain.

For some reason known only to Jock Stein, Joe Jordan appeared in the first half, only to spend his time, as always, on all fours in the English penalty area. Dalglish continues to fool so many into thinking he is worth a place, and our old friend McGrain is sadly past it.

I have no hope at all for Scotland. The English team are looking better than they've done for years. I expect them to do very well.

To cheer us up after the match we had two musicians round for tea. Humperdink arrived early but George Melly was late as usual. Melly, obviously trying to establish a new image, was immaculately dressed in white silk scarf, rather conservative hat, camel-hair coat and sporting an exquisitely carved ivory-handled platinum-tipped walking stick. They fell immediately to heated discussion of the validity of grace notes in traditional Gaelic singing. So much more interesting than the usual talk one hears from one's medical colleagues of slipped discs and hernias.

11 JUNE, 1982

SUNDAY

Now that your man the Pope has gone home, will the good weather last? You probably remember the last time we had a decent spell of sunshine was when he came to Ireland. But that is not what I wanted to write about. What I really find fascinating is this continuing catholic/protestant squabbling. I've been studying the subject now for 20 years and I have reached a few conclusions which I will pass on to you here free of charge.

Not only is there no end in sight to this problem – it actually seems to be getting worse, which can be partly explained by the increasing numbers on the dole who have nothing better to do. Perhaps I should first of all explain my own position, which is out in no man's land as a sort of lapsed atheist. By that I mean I only acknowledge His existence in moments of grave emergency.

In these times of trouble, and there have not really been that many of them, I have been known to transmit a short prayer. Not much of a prayer. Something like: "In the absence of a plausible alternative explanation for The Mysteries it seems likely you exist, so please get me out of this scrape."

One such incident I remember from 1975. It happened in the middle of the Atlantic during a particularly violent storm. The deck for'ard of the bridge was buckled, but we pulled through. Now, seven years older and wiser, I realise the futility of my prayer because there was an engine-room-full of catholics down below offering their prayers in Latin, which would no doubt have jammed my broadcast. Or, if all the bigots I've listened to in the last week are correct, perhaps it was my prayer that saved the day.

I don't mean the mindless bigots who think the Pope is the power behind Celtic Football Club. No, it is the allegedly educated men with MAs and the like who puzzle and worry me most. Some of them were sick of the sight of the Pope on their TV screens, but like Mary Whitehouse and porn, they couldn't avert their gaze. Others astonished me with the bitterness of their remarks about John Paul (who seems a decent chap) and catholics in general. Pity I could understand, if they genuinely believe all catholics are doomed to everlasting fire; but why the hatred? Shouldn't these professing Christians seek out and befriend as many catholics as possible, perchance to convert them by stealth to what they believe to be the true faith?

One or two pointed to bigotry in the opposing camp as an excuse for their own stupid attitude. I wouldn't be surprised if our old friend, 'Fear of the Unknown', comes into it. Anyway, it seems education as generally understood is not the answer. Perhaps travel and the associated enforced mixing helps to combat prejudice. On the other hand, early training, if the brainwashing is efficient, is difficult to undo, and the narrow mind tends to get narrower as it ages.

If I am as free from prejudice as I think, I'm almost certain that happy condition is due, at least in part, to my father's corn. It troubled him throughout my early childhood, and every Sunday morning it flared up to its angry worst, which naturally meant he could not walk to church.

So, through the corn, I too escaped.

Not until much later did I learn, from older boys returning from Glasgow shipyards, the world was neatly divided into two distinct camps: us, the good guys, and them, the catholics. (These boys were not generally religious. In fact, for most of them the idea of man's chief end had no conformity unto the local norm.) Yet they sang the praises of King Billy, who was not renowned for his love of the Teuchter.

When my turn came to go out into the big bad world, it so happened a high proportion of my friends were N. Irish Fenians, with whom I found I had more in common than with other groups – they even spoke a sort of Gaelic. At that age I not only thought we were different to the non-Gaels – I thought we were a better tribe altogether. You will probably find such innocence hard to understand, but it actually took quite a while to dawn on me that catholic and fenian meant more or less the same. (We had strange history books in our school.) But these guys were all right! It didn't figure. OK, so they laughed at me not being allowed to whistle on a Sunday, but then I got my own back when they got the works at confession.

Mind you, I'm not all that keen on Popery and I like the name Free Church. I like free press. I like free anything, but how free is the Free Church? How many good footballers have you seen ruined by the cùram? And they are the sworn enemies of the Dance. Why? Does it really have to be the Grim Reaper? Sure, for the catholics he has to be the Grim Reaper, but for the favoured few should he not be the Jolly Reaper?

If I understand the matter correctly, and I have no reason to suspect I don't, the most unsurmountable obstacles to your average Calvinist's acceptance of John Paul are his claims to infallibility and to being a sort of clone of St Peter's. Personally, I have no problem here, being infallible myself, and I also have a similar relationship with St Paul.

Over a year now since I started laying my diaries open to the public, so perhaps it is time to stop and try something else before I start to reveal innermost feelings which are usually better kept hidden. You see, inside every extrovert there is an introvert trying to stay in.

30 JULY, 1982

MONDAY

Some of you will remember how I offered my "services" to the two local churches. Well, for two long months now I've been waiting anxiously every morning for that very important letter confirming my appointment – but, alas, in vain.

I realised there was a lot of opposition to my "call" in the ranks of the Free Church elders (I understand some of them would prefer Prof. Macleod) but the stand-in minister himself is obviously on my side. He went as far as to mention the subject from the pulpit last Sunday. He couldn't very well address me directly but he did urge those of us who felt we had a higher calling not to resist it. It seems the elders have more power than the minister.

I'm sorry, but I cannot wait any longer. There is nothing for it but to go over to the other side. With this very big step in mind I've started hearing confessions on Monday evenings. But don't, mind you, expect to find me a soft touch. If you've been a bad boy you could find yourself saying Hail Marys day and night right through till next weekend. You wouldn't believe the stories I could tell you. Not having taken any vows yet, I'm not obliged to keep any secrets, so watch this space for good gossip.

TUESDAY

Of all the good works I undertake in my spare time I can think of none more worthwhile than this confession business. Although I haven't had a lot of psychiatric training, I find it is one of these jobs you can pick up fairly easily as you go along.

After all, old chap, most people want only someone to listen to them. The mere act of getting it off the chest is often a cure in itself – in exceptionally difficult cases I encourage them to write abusive letters to the newspapers. This unfortunately tends to clutter the letters page with meaningless rubbish, but what does that matter if it brings relief to a troubled mind. With the Editor's permission I hope soon to introduce a regular agony column.

WEDNESDAY

It isn't often my duties take me to Carloway, which is a pity, because it's a quaint, picturesque little village full of quaint, picturesque people. Although picturesque is certainly not the way to describe Alex Mòr, the man I went to see in Carloway tonight.

The object of my mission was a last desperate attempt to prepare him for Saturday's Highland Games in Tong. To be more specific, our task was to reduce your man in two days from 17½ stone to a respectable, fighting 15. It took us less than five minutes to decide this was impossible, so we repaired to the Doune Braes instead. Now there's a pub for you. The only hostelry I could compare it with was the old multi-racial bar in Mogu on the Upper Zambesi when the mercenaries were in town. I would like to make it quite clear that we were not molested in any way, but this was no doubt due in part to Alex's presence. I was indeed glad that I had followed my old custom of befriending a large native when venturing into the bush, and perhaps it was just as well we hadn't reduced him to his fighting weight, for he looks more fearsome at 17½.

So we were respectfully treated by the indig, but I must say a few words about the new management. The Doune Braes has the very tidy annual turnover of £280,000 per year, so why do they have to charge 67p for a pint of beer? Even in the plush surroundings of pubs in the large town of Stornoway you can get your paw round a pint glass for 62p. And do they really have to add 3p to the nip because the natives take a few empty glasses home with their carry-outs? I wouldn't be surprised if the practice is illegal, and I've left the matter in the hands of consumer protection.

THURSDAY

Arnish is dead or dying, and already I am beginning to feel the pinch. Boys who used to buy out of turn now look at you accusingly as much as to say: Who's on the dole, me or you? I ran into a bunch of freshly-redundant in the Caberfeidh today and their spirits were low indeed – gone were the creaking tables of yesterday. Faced with the prospect of having to live on £38 a week, they become dull and poor company. I guess I'll have to look elsewhere for a laugh.

Some of them, however, admitted to having been cheered up enormously by the weasel Tebbit's speech on TV last night. According to Tebbit the man on the dole is now better off than he's ever been. Not that anyone needs to be on the dole anyway, for didn't the same Tebbit tell us not so long ago all we had to do was climb on a bicycle.

The bicycle line seems to be official now, at least as far as Jobcentre civil servants are concerned. The first question asked of all those who signed on today was: Are you prepared to travel? Where exactly they were expected to travel no one seemed to know. And has anyone paused to consider the chaos that will inevitably be caused by three million (soon to be four) cyclists tearing up and down the country drinking their redundancy money? The roads will not be safe, and what about when they start to maraud and to help themselves to the contents of the freezers of those of us who are better off? My all-too-frequent glimpses of the future become more terrifying every day.

SATURDAY

As I suspected earlier in the week, 17½ stone was far too much to carry. At the Tong Games today some of my elderly friends finally had to accept the inevitability of the ageing process. Alex Mòr, aged 46, and Neillie Chailein, 54, who reigned in the heavy events for so long, finally had to give way to youth. A young man from Shader an Taobh Siar aptly named Fury proved more than a match for the old hands. I am now looking for a strong local man whom we can train to take on the Siarachs at the Carloway Games next week. Atch's name has been mentioned, but I wonder if 36 is not too old to start.

13 AUGUST, 1982

MONDAY

One of the most pathetic sights I've seen in a long time was Joe Gormless in his Lordship's robes. Of all the union leaders bought and set up in this way by the Establishment, Joe seems the most ridiculous. He was very likely selected because of his accent – they cannot understand him even in the North of England.

This is not a new game. It was a well-established practice in the posh clubs of London one hundred years ago. Young men about town and their ladies could think of nothing better to liven up a party than to haul in a working man who would amuse them with his aaccent. Poor Joe. I'll say no more. It would be funny were it not so tragic.

TUESDAY

An old African neighbour with his wife and three children arrived to spend a few days with us. They were all born within a few miles of Victoria Falls, so they could take the heat of our Indian Summer. And of course they have been at war all their lives with toxic bugs and reptiles: puff adders, black mambas, spitting cobras, leopards, crocodiles, soldier ants, tsetse flies, mosquitoes – to name a small selection. "All these things I could take, but your midges, man: they're something else." I have to agree with him although it's about the only subject on which I do. When we become a Third World mini-power, which shouldn't be very long now, the World Health Organisation will make the eradication of midges a priority.

WEDNESDAY

I cannot remember a warmer day on the island of Lewis since World War Two. The temperature in Loch Leurbost got so high I had to sink my oysters to prevent premature spawning and consequent loss of weight before the sale. Old men of 70 were seen out of doors at our end of Leurbost stripped to the sleeveless pullover. Some old-timers in Sleepy

Hollow were seen out of doors. Even the sheep seemed to take a rest from their incessant destruction of the soil.

Over in Carloway where I had taken my overseas visitors to see their first Highland Games, it was over 80 in the shade if you could find any. It appeared that the entire Fraser Clan were competing in the heavy events and every man jack of them as near as dammit eight feet tall. But I have a plan to foil them next year at the first games on the new Creagan Dubh Park.

It is more or less a simple handicapping system. Anyone by the name of Fraser, whether tossing the caber or the sheaf, will be obliged to stand in a hole three feet deep. When throwing the hammer they will be expected to do so from a kneeling position. I am told these Frasers eat a whole bullock every day. I will say no more now, for Simon the eldest is a lawyer who could slap a writ on you before you could say Douglas Kesting.

But let us face up to the unpalatable truth. These games are getting repetitive and boring. That is why we plan to reintroduce the ancient art of bull-wrestling in Leurbost next year. Stop me if I've told you this one before, but the bloodsport known as bullwrassling had no finer exponent than my great-great-grandfather Coinneach – Coinneach an Tairbh, as they naturally named him after he tore one of the front legs off a lean Ayrshire bull in 1837. The men and the boys will almost certainly go their separate ways with this event. Book your seats now.

THURSDAY

I was not sorry to see the weather back to normal this afternoon. If you intend to spend your life on these islands, you must learn to like the rain. There is certainly no point in delaying a job, any job, because it is raining. The chances are you will eventually have to get wet doing whatever it is anyway.

I had a little job to do today from the boat with Calum Còigeach. Now there's a man who is at one with our climate. When it started spitting from a cold north-westerly direction I swear I saw him turning his face into the wind as if standing under a hot shower. I slowly changed course by way of experiment and, sure enough, again he faced into the rain to savour every exquisite drop. The only other time I witnessed this sort of truly Hebridean behaviour was last year down in Loch Eynort when I put to sea with two local sailors. One of them goes even further: he occasionally slips over the side, shouting "Man overboard!"

FRIDAY

Fell foul of some Englishmen and all the other women I know, except my wife who understands, and she thought calling a baby ugly – even a German one – was not in the best possible taste. Even Brian Wilson gave me a tongue-lashing when I met him in Radio nan Eilean. Is there no one left?

I was not surprised to receive a distress call from the local broadcasting station. Can you try to think of something to keep the last three listeners to "Feasgar Dihaoine" awake? Say, one of the old long-forgotten recipes? Or could you impersonate Coinneach MacIomhair? I thought it would be easier to give them the long-lost recipe for sweet and sour skate.

At great personal cost and inconvenience I rushed to Radio nan Eilean to record and then quickly to the Caberfeidh, where I persuaded Catriona to give us radio for 10 minutes instead of TV. The hungry working men who fill the public bar on a Friday evening – Tawse men, retired oil-men and the like – are still waiting for their sweet and sour skate. I cannot imagine why the skate fell foul of the local censor, Mr Macdonald, unless it was the passing mention of the skate's locally-renowned power as a fertility aid.

10 SEPTEMBER, 1982

LEWIS OFFSHORE – A GUIDE TO SURVIVAL

A long time ago an experienced Niseach naval man advised a young recruit, a fellow Leòdhasach: "Always have something in your hand and try to look intulligunt." This sound piece of advice is well worth remembering and there is no reason to suppose management, whether on- or off-shore, are any more difficult to fool now than they were in the Niseach's day.

Always to have something in your hand should not prove too difficult – a brush, a welding rod, a piece of paper or, if your rank merits it, a huge roll of linen with one corner unfurled to expose an extremely complicated drawing surrounded by powerful equations full of xs and ys squared and cubed. I once knew a man who spent three years, on "several thousand pounds a year", wandering round a certain head office with a sheet of graph-paper in his hand. No one knew what he did and for all I know he could still be getting away with it. I don't know what this has to do with the story, but he was married to a Rubhach.

So you can see, dear innocent children, the importance of having something in the hand. Although looks often lie, trying to look intelligent is equally desirable, but for some people, through no fault of their own, not so easy. The expression "intelligent-looking" is more often used to describe horses or dogs; if equine or canine impressions come easily to you, then you have nothing to worry about. (Oh, for a drop of Royal blood.) If, on the other hand, after long and diligent practice, you cannot imitate a collie or a thoroughbred stallion, you must do the best with what you've got. Try to keep your mouth closed: nothing could get you marked almost absent quicker than a gaping gob or, as it is sometimes called, a slack jaw. It is no use protesting as you're marched through the gates that your condition was caused by a gumboil. Take no chances.

In the struggle to look intelligent never forget the eyes. Industry has no time for poets and dreamers, so do not, upon pain of instant dismissal, let your unfocused gaze rest on a distant horizon. Let your eyes dance in your head like James Galway's, or at least move them quickly like a Lowlander. Better to be thought mad or shifty than dopey. So smarten up and look sharp. No one is going to pay you "several thousand pounds a year" if you go around in a trance.

Yes, the Niseach knew what he was talking about; but there are other factors to consider if you are to stay the course at Arnish. You must do a little crawling. Everyone does. And for every gaffer you must have a different style of fawning. They say imitation is a form of flattery, and they are all susceptible, even the Geordies.

Geordies have been very much on the move in recent years since they closed their shipyards, so there is a fair chance you'll have one for a gaffer. Blunt, outspoken – correction, very blunt – they pride themselves on their honesty, so no bribes. Essentially simple and easy to please. Talk to them about football and brown ale. It is worth going to the trouble of learning their language – a monosyllabic grunting loosely based on English.

The southern gentleman is not often found on sites such as Arnish where there is a chance they might get dirty. But you never know, so be prepared. Find a quiet spot on the Arnish Moor and practise a loud mirthless guffaw. What you say to this type (given the rare opportunity, for he likes to do the talking) does not matter; it's the way you say it. Mention your wealth, while at the same time taking great care not to spend any of it.

Shawbostians. Never been known to rise above the rank of private. Notoriously bad for the drink. Should a stray get a few stripes he is easily bribed with more drink.

South Africans. It seems unlikely that a yappie should have moved so far north of the Equator, but the danger cannot be ruled out. Very sensitive to Van De Merwe jokes, the rare, soon-to-be extinct great white bore of Africa is one of the toughest bosses you'll ever come across. So what can you do? If you're Hearach or Pakistani you have no chance: the rest of you stay out of the sun.

Uibhisteachs, Hearachs and Rubhachs. Unlikely to find these breeds in a position of authority due to their inbred bent for fighting and rioting.

Barrachs, Scousers, Irish and Stornowegians. Created to labour at the lower levels, but watch out for the odd one who makes boss. Unpredictable, generous, multifaceted chameleons. Great capacity for strong drink, so don't waste your money. Keep both eyes open all the time.

Flyemen. With the Portree Mod just round the corner this is no time to be frank.

Lochies. Natural, godfearing leaders of men. Fair yet strict. If you are fortunate enough to serve under this type, you have only to do your duty to the best of your ability. If your best falls short of our high standards, we understand and make allowances. Sure, we like a little respect. Call us by our first names in private but not, please, in front of the lads. The occasional "sir" does your prospects no harm. It does not seem much to ask for "several thousand pounds a year".

8 OCTOBER, 1982

MONDAY

I was pleasantly surprised to bump into an old buddy, one Johnnie Walker, the other day. After 21 years in London I must say he was looking remarkably well. I put this down to the relatively easy life lived by city men compared to our own hard struggle on the croft.

I couldn't help noticing my friend's still ultra-slim design and the wrinkle-free face. I suppose the fat-free English diet helps. What must it be like to be free of worry? No hay to dry nor livestock to feed, and no potatoes to lift. Still, I think I managed to hide my envy, choosing instead to make light of my troubles and generally putting a brave face on things.

John was my sidekick in the Grimshader days. I don't remember if I told you about Grimshader? The girls? No other village of comparable size in the whole world produced girls like Grimshader. Not only were they extremely beautiful, they were also incredibly plentiful (if that's the right word). For every fortunate boy born in that thrice-blessed village there were six girls. This naturally led to much restlessness in the neighbouring villages where we only had Alice (and she preferred the sophisticated Stornoway types). Not that we didn't meet some opposition from these "coves" in Grimshader, but they were no match. And we had Walker with the Golden Voice.

He would sidle up to Dòmhnall Iain Sheòrais's windows or Calum Iomhair's and serenade them in the Italian fashion. This occasionally led to unintended ructions but more often than not the ploy was successful. It meant, of course, Walker always had the pick of the paddock, but that didn't matter, for there were so many to spare. I wonder if Grimshader has changed. I don't think Walker has. For two pins I'd tell you about the night he got stuck in Dòmhnall Màiri Anna's window.

DIMAIRT

Here's a good tip for you in these inflationary times. Mar a dh'innis mi dhuibh ceud uair, 's e fìor dhroch phòsadh a rinn Calum Ruairidh Chaluim. Theab i mu dheireadh a chur a Thaigh nam Bochd. Cha do dh'fhag i fhèin 's a' chlann-nighean fiù cathair am broinn an taigh gun a losgadh le leisg fàd mònach a bhuain. Bha Calum aon latha a' còmhradh ri 'Ghuru', Seonaidh Choinnich.

" 'S e latha duilich sa bheil sinn beò, a Sheonaidh, ach cha bhi a bheul aig duine ri fhosgladh fhad 's a bhios aige na chuireas ceann-crìoch air fhèin."

"Nach fhearr dhut a' chiste a cheannach an-dràsta mus fhàs iad ro dhaor?" arsa Seonaidh.

"Nach eil fhios agad ged a dhèanainn-sa sin gu loisg na turraisgean i."

WEDNESDAY

Things have come to a pretty pass when honest men of the soil cannot show their faces in Stornoway without being harangued by the gentry of that town. I was accosted by MacLennan of Kenneth Street yesterday. "Look at them," he says. "Maws. Every second driver a Maw. Going down one way streets the wrong way. Generally making asses of themselves, holding up the traffic and shaking hands with passing traffic wardens. It reminds me," he says, "of rural sports day. Youse would come pouring off the bus and into Woollies for the brown paper carrier-bags." He then collapsed into a fit of laughter. "Youse would – 800 of youse – queue up for your threepenny icecream cones, then wander through the town like lost sheep." He left me, muttering about Scorps and laughing at his memories. Of course he was taught in Smith's Shoeshop. I'm told a lot of the town's youngsters still go there for their education. But I hope our councillors intend to do something about this subversive school of bad teaching.

THURSDAY

We had a rare treat tonight in the company of Seosaimhín Ní Bheaglaoich, Cathal Ó Searcaigh, Déaglán Mac a' Mháistir, Mícheál Ó Murchú and Colonel Ó Néill. How about that for a forward line? They came all the way from different parts of Ireland to entertain us in the Cross Inn, and I'll guarantee you those who took the trouble to travel to Ness would go ten times that distance to hear them again. Your man Déaglán Mac a' Mháistir on the uilleann pipes can only be described as a genius. I can think of no greater tribute to our visitors' talent than that even the Niseach latecomers were on their best behaviour, going for long spells without replenishing their empty glasses. Mac Thormoid Bhig kept order. Let's hope the Irish come back soon.

FRIDAY

I was given a present today of a tape by that powerful girl from Point called Ishbel MacAskill. How did the Rubhachs manage to keep this lady to themselves for so long? If you are not fortunate enough to be given this tape as a present, do not hesitate to go out and buy it for yourself.

SATURDAY

I must now go polish my shoes, have a haircut and see if I can borrow a suit from the West End Tory for the Mod. Sadly, this year, through lack of babysitters, I must take the goat in the boot.

15 October, 1982

I thought it best to keep the forecast from my family and fellow travellers, but I knew when the glass started to fall at midnight it was going to be a bad crossing. With the centre of the depression passing south of Tiree and pressure high at the Faroes, the isobars were drawn tighter than fiddle strings between the Butt and Cape Wrath.

The moment I climbed the gangway my worst fears were confirmed. A freshening Nor'easter was playing a high-pitched tune on the rigging and the Castle Grounds sycamores were howling ominously in the background.

A quick glance round the *Suilven*'s spartan saloon did little to ease my apprehension – a motley crew of denim-clad tourists and women carrying young children. With the exception of one young man from Cromore who was sipping Guinness at the bar at six in the morning, I knew there wasn't a soul on board I could count on when the going got rough. To make matters worse, I had packed no medicines – I make it a rule to carry not even so much as a stethoscope when on holiday. Yet the Hippocratic Oath is not taken lightly, so I made a mental note of those who would obviously be first to need comforting. A young Englishman talking at his girlfriend with the full power of his powerful voice, a member of the teaching profession and part-time writer, my own imported wife and peelly-wally offspring, and a man who looked as if he might belong to Achmore. Also, and this worried me, the skipper looked less mature than I like them – well under 70 and insufficiently weatherbeaten, as if he had spent too long on MV *Hebrides*.

We had barely passed the lighthouse when she started to roll unpredictably like a badly-ballasted drunk. I immediately instructed my family to proceed to the lower deck where motion is at a minimum. "I'll probably be needed up here," I said. "Yes, Walter," she said. "You must do what is best." "But first," I said, "I must check the security of the heavy vehicles."

As I had suspected, elementary precautions had been neglected.

An antiquated red lorry which I identified as belonging to a Keose accordionist was lurching dangerously fore and aft due to the absence of that useful modern device – the handbrake. I quickly chocked the wheels and sped to the upper deck, where already my services were desperately needed.

She was being badly buffeted on the port shoulder, inducing that corkscrew motion so unsettling to what Bobby Neillie calls "The Paper Stomach". Scenes of despair everywhere, but I couldn't stop to help them. It was all too clear to me that my navigational skills must this time take priority over the medical.

We now had Chicken Head off our port side, and a brief glimpse of the rising sun told me we were steering 075° against an 040° wave. The mad fool on the bridge was going to shake her to pieces. It was time to let him know I was on board. I took the steps four at a time, roughly brushing incompetent junior officers out of the way. I didn't have to tell the skipper who I was. He knew. "Of course you must take over," he said at once. "Thirty degrees to port," I yelled, "and reduce the revs to 750." Almost at once her action became a slow, steady ploughing. The skipper smiled. "Thank goodness you happened to be with us," he said.

But I wasn't happy. The stern was wallowing clumsily in the troughs much more than my experience would lead me to expect. In a matter of seconds I had deduced a poor distribution of ballast. "Too many MacBraynes' lorries towards the stern," I shouted. "What will we do, sir?" asked the skipper. "Move them for'ard?" "Nonsense, man," I barked. "Too late for that. Instruct that Sgiathanach chief steward to stand at the bow." He leapt to the tannoy to convey my orders. "The sharp end, man, the sharp end," I heard him scream at the steward. For the steward was indeed a Sgiathanach.

The message finally got through, and that simple manoeuvre saved the day. Before I made my way down below to soothe the sick I told them to steer that same course until 0700 hours precisely, then to head due south-east until we reached the shelter of the mainland. "That", I said, "will get her across in the space of six hours, and all very good."

As we meandered through the klondykers in the still waters of Loch Broom the crews gathered on the decks to cheer in Russian, Bulgarian and Polish. At Ullapool a large crowd had gathered on the pier to welcome us, and as usual reporters swarmed around in their hundreds. When we tied up I was besieged by grateful voyagers who pressed gifts on me which I naturally declined with dignity. "At least tell us your name," shouted one woman as I waved them farewell. "Walter," I said quietly, "Walter Murdy."

* * *

Cha d' fhuair mi leis an amadan ud Walter air innse dhuibh mu thuras Eachainn a Ghlaschu, ach ma bhitheas sinn beò an t-seachdain sa tighinn, mar tha fios math gum bi.

22 OCTOBER, 1982

INVERNESS

I notice all the children I know in Inverness are turning out bad. They talk about putting warums on hooks and things like that, despite the fact their parents come from places like Stornoway, Aberdeen, Garrabost and Newcastle. You might have thought these poor children were sufficiently handicapped without the additional burden of an Invernessian accent. Yet what can these parents do, short of sending them to expensive public schools, and whoever heard of anyone in the Highlands being so cruel except farmers and Lewis businessmen.

Not, mind you, that some of the aforementioned daddies couldn't afford Gordonstoun. I never saw the likes of it in my life – bidets, saunas and jacuzzis (that's a sort of giant bath that squirts water at you from all angles). There are other unmistakable signs that old crofting stock is being assimilated into middle-class Inverness.

But to get back to the children. Please don't waste your sympathy on them. They will go through life thinking their accent is not only good enough but the "best English in the whole warld".

GLASGOW

I consider myself very lucky to have found digs here on Byres Road with a woman from Mangersta, Uig. You must always think first of the stomach and how to keep it full: that is why I have always made sure I have the address of a Lewis woman when in a strange town. With a decent black pudding under the belt the black, unfriendly rushing city doesn't seem too bad. Even Blackpool, wherein I had always been led to believe every youth on achieving puberty acquired a brace of razors with which to slash innocent passers-by, is less intimidating when the crofter is well fed.

Anyway, here I am taking the young fellow to Celtic Park for the first time and I don't mind telling you I'm a little bit nervous. I drew some comfort from the green-and-white scarf round the boy's neck, but now I'm not so sure. The red-and-white Aberdonians, although relatively few in number, seemed drunker and noisier than our lot. Like all animals in the wild, I guess they make so much noise because they are afraid.

The concrete jungle of Barrowfield fascinates me. The sheer size of the words of the ground-to-tile graffiti must have used up considerable energy, not to mention paint. But this strange scene of devastation does not attract a second glance from our young fellow. I suppose TV has brought etc ... He would no doubt be more horrified if he could see where I spent my first nine years.

Now we are on the terracing he's taking a keen interest in the quick-silver horde of other nine-year-olds disgorged from the bowels of Barrowfield. Would he survive for long in their midst? I don't know. The first few days would be crucial. Kids learn quickly. I see he has already picked up some of their tricks, and has had his rump kicked gently by a policeman for leaning on the railings. Will this colour his view of authority later in life? I wouldn't be surprised.

Sadly, the game didn't go according to plan, with Aberdeen scoring three times and the Celts hardly at all. The referee was a member of the Clan Waddell, and that is all I am going to say about it.

Better luck at the Barras, though. I made a couple of good purchases –

presents for those left at home. Where the price says £7 I'll simply insert a three in front of the seven, they'll assume I bought the goods in Stornoway and so think me a generous fellow. Smart move, daddy.

SKYE

What a picturesque little island, but where are the people, especially the natives? Even the little village of Portree didn't seem all that crowded despite the visitors.

Of the first seven people I met on the so-called Isle of Smoke six were English and the seventh a Scot. There is no smoke without fire, but please don't think I disapprove of the situation. For if ever an island needed fresh blood, Skye is it.

According to those who are at the heart of the struggle to keep the language alive, or in Skye's case to resurrect it, emigrants from the south are the cause of all their problems. Abair nonsense. The death blow was struck long ago by Gaelic-speaking headmasters who taught us to be ashamed of the language. Many of them, to be fair, probably were too dim-witted to realise what they were doing. Anyway, it's almost all over now.

Although you can still hear a little Gaelic being spoken at the Mod, which happened to be taking place as I passed through last week, it is basically for the vast majority an occasion to meet old friends and perhaps to make new ones. The Mod is still worthwhile because occasionally people like Iain MacKay and Seonaidh Beag spontaneously burst into song. (I nearly said burst into flames there.) You will find this difficult to believe, but while Iain MacKay was letting it rip in the Royal Hotel on Friday night two old crows from a distant southern choir were trying to drown him out. This is, of course, the result of too much drink.

Up in a little hotel in Flodigarry I was threatened with physical violence by Black Angus. I think he heard me speaking English. In the same place I met and fell in love with a beautiful and mature lady from Barra – Flora Mac-something. I cannot remember now. Of course she had to pretend to reject my advances because her husband was there, but isn't that the way of it.

The accommodation shortage was desperate, but the Carloway boys got the better of the Skye jews – 12 of them paid for a single room and slept in two-hour shifts. It is good to get the last laugh.

1983

18 FEBRUARY, 1983

MONDAY

Another television programme for those who are still not sure whether or not they are full-blooded alcoholics. As soon as these horror movies start I go through to the kitchen and polish the silver or darn some socks. The amateurish approach of the presenters and the slipshod methods of the researchers turn me off. Dreadfully boring, you understand, for those of us scientists who have made a lifetime study of the subject. And where on earth do they find the doctors? Can they possibly be qualified?

Yet there was something about tonight's programme that held my attention for a while. One white-coated quack concluded, after many years' dedicated squandering of T. P. M., that some men could drink nine or ten pints of beer a day without becoming alcoholic. Was this supposed to be news to us? A fresh scientific statement? Why, I remember saying these very words to my wife as long ago as 1970.

To end this comical attempt at educational entertainment they produced a naive young doctor (obviously Punjab-failed) who announced with some excitement that a few stiff ones aid circulation. "Makes the blood less sticky," he cried as if he had made a genuine discovery. Had he been in the habit of studying my works he would have grasped this elementary fact some years ago. He would have read of how Kenny the Plumber, Rolagan and I managed, in extreme climatic conditions when all about us were falling, to last all day at the peats by making the blood less sticky with Trawler Rum. Mark my words, there is nothing on this earth worse than sticky blood.

The only worthwhile message in tonight's alcohol programme was the danger of not starting to drink early enough in life. This was shown quite clearly through the example of one middle-aged matron who couldn't cope with 12 nips a day just because she was too old when she started dramming. It is becoming increasingly obvious to me that nothing hastens the end more than total abstinence.

TUESDAY

I had intended to watch television every night this week (a depressing self-inflicted ordeal, but I have a good reason: I hear *The Sunday Times* are looking for a TV critic to compete with the smart young man at *The Observer*); but along comes a wealthy friend and treats me to a night out at the County Hotel. He couldn't have picked a better time because I felt my blood was turning a trifle sticky. House wine at five sheets a litre is good value – an excellent thinner.

WEDNESDAY

Back on duty again. Astonishing what one learns from television. For instance, some sourfaced newsreader tells me inflation is down to five per cent. This figure could very well be true if you have a £30,000 a year mortgage, but how do we calculate the rate for the average man on the croft? How about the bag of dross? At this time last year it cost £1.50: now it costs £2.50 – a mere 66 per cent. And the humble bag of chips – up from 20p last month to 25p this month, an annual rate of 300 per cent. It is difficult to know who to believe these days.

I wonder if the fellow who says the Queen's private fortune is only £200 million is telling the truth. If that is the sum total of her savings surely we should give her some more T. P. M. Hullo, hullo; I see the lovely Princess Margaret is off to the West Indies again with 17 bodyguards and a fancy man. Why not? What else could we do with the money? Give it to the poor and they would only eat and drink themselves to death.

THURSDAY

Thirteen years ago tonight I was a bachelor for the last time. My blood was extremely thin.

FRIDAY

It is not often I laugh or even smile in these troubled times. The few people who could make me laugh have all been dead for some years now. (Although I still meet them occasionally in bed at night, which annoys my wife. She objects strongly when I roar with laughter at 2am.) Yet tonight I laughed, while I was wide awake, at a comic genius called Freddie Starr. I hope we see more of this man and less of Michael Parkinson, the Tory Party Chairman.

SATURDAY

I pray the so-called art of American TV does not in any way mirror real life in that nation. If it does I'm glad I don't live there. Superfat corrupt politicians and violent law-enforcers.

Talking of corruption and nepotism, I will have an extremely juicy scoop for sensation-seekers just as soon as my investigations are complete and our lawyers have examined possible libel angles. Questions will be asked – if not in the House, at least in Comhairle Castle. I wouldn't be surprised to see some heads roll.

SUNDAY

Tonight I witnessed the most disgusting spectacle of the viewing year – the Crufts Dog Show. I watched it with the sound turned off, which made it all the more ridiculous. Ugly little canine sausages and long-legged monstrosities, all bred to obscene perfection, were paraded for judgement. Any true animal lover (not the type who hates humans) would have shot them all on compassionate grounds. He might have done the same for the owners who pranced around with their grotesque exhibits.

Confronted with this nauseating ultra-English phenomenon, I was making mental excuses for young nationalists when, lo and behold, the stage is commandeered by a kilted ponce – a professional Scotsman with a poodle. I was scared to turn the sound up in case he turned out to be a Sgiathanach transvestite.

On second thoughts, Rupert, I don't want the job.

11 MARCH, 1983

MONDAY

It gives me no pleasure whatsoever to quarrel publicly, once again, with my eminent colleagues Doctors Smith and MacAulay but it must be done. Normally we would conduct our disputation in Latin but the indigenous inhabitants of Portnaguran have no time for fancy affectation. All these poor people want is a pub. And of course they should have a pub. Every village on the island should have a pub. Maybe two or three pubs.

Why should the men of Portnaguran, every time they want to quench a thirst – or for that matter the men of Marvig – be crippled with the cost of a taxi to Stornoway? (One assumes they wouldn't risk the breathalyser.) Are they not all the more likely, having travelled so far, to try to quench a few thirsts at once? Yes, and perhaps carry out a plastic bagful to ward off future thirsts.

Availability leads to abuse, says Dr Smith. Even supposing he is right, which I don't believe for a moment, is it not better that drink should be available (because it always will be one way or another) in civilised surroundings rather than the half-bottle behind a peatstack? Is that not the attitude – keep it hidden – that led to our suicidal drinking habits in the first place?

Talking of availability, I remember staying for a short time in a sleepy little English village about the same size as Portnaguran. Although it was only 10 miles from the nearest large town it managed to support two pubs – I didn't notice much abuse apart from the occasional visiting Scotsman. I don't think the Englishman's sensible approach can be satisfactorily explained by his compulsion to save money.

At the other extreme of availability, or the lack of it, we have Norway. A regular visitor to that depressing country tells me you practically need a doctor's prescription to wet your whistle and yet the ever-increasing number of alcoholics would fill a fjord.

As for the peace and tranquility of Portnaguran, don't make me laugh. Compared with my East Anglian village – with two pubs, remember – Portnaguran is like Dodge City in the old days. And if they do have rare moments of peace it is only when most of the residents are up in Stornoway disturbing other people's peace. I feel there is little point in saying any more because I know I am right.

TUESDAY

A distressed woman in Portnaguran has just phoned me to complain about her peace being disturbed by two sheriff's officers. I understand they were cold sober and mean. A fine example of what can happen when men are deprived of their daily fix.

WEDNESDAY

In view of some of the decisions taken recently by our councillors perhaps there is something to be said after all for prohibition. Could they possibly have been sober when they invited these latter-day Patrick Sellars to loot our homes? From now on I think it only reasonable they should be asked to take a breathalyser test before important meetings.

THURSDAY

Having heard the Harris Tweed industry is doing that strange thing industries are prone to from time to time – booming – I called on my friend the West End Tory to discuss the national economic situation and the matter of a small loan for myself. I found him at the loom weaving a most unusual tweed a bit like an enormous hairnet. Never have I seen anything quite like it.

"Looks more like a net," I said.

"Exactly," says he, "a net for the Leaderene." His task, he told me with pride, was to weave a thousand miles of safety-net for the Government. A safety-net to catch those weaklings who fall off the slippery ladder to fame and fortune. I couldn't help noticing the mesh was extremely large, obviously designed to let the lean and hungry slip through.

He showed me his crock of gold, or crocks, to be precise. He hoards his savings, that is everything he earns, in old National Dried Milk tins like Maggie Thatcher's grandfather. There is no way I can get through to him that he and his type, Boadicea's disciples, are the prime cause of the recession. If the West End Tory and one other person of equal wealth went out tomorrow and spent a third of their pile, the extra trade generated would create 50 new jobs. But spending causes them so much pain.

FRIDAY

I would like to thank all those who wrote to inquire about my progress with the novel. Another snag, I'm afraid. Our hero, having had to break with a young widow because of village gossip, has turned his attention to Carloway. There, in the damp Atlantic spray, our man has laid siege to a matron in her 40s who is reported to have inherited a fortune from a long-lost Alaskan pioneer. The lady had started to respond to expensive gifts when she was suddenly laid low by the cùram. In the typically glassy-eyed mood of the newly-converted the gifts are parcelled and returned with a note saying: "This is bigger than both of us. I regret we are no longer intellectually compatible. Please return the shaver." I cannot see how we are going to get past this chapter.

17 JUNE, 1983

MONDAY

Many worse things could befall a man than to lose to Donald and Chrissie. Now that it is all over for a few years, perhaps forever if She decides elections are a waste of money, it must be admitted that Dòmhnall is not a bad old fellow. At least we can be thankful the seat did not fall to that other man Wilson. If only half the stories I heard last week are true, we had a very narrow escape indeed. The only serious accusation not made against him, and I cannot understand how they missed it, was cannibalism. I guess we managed to keep that quiet. The Communist smear was probably the most damaging and some of the accusers surprised me – men who have made the redistribution of wealth their lives' work. And others who have never done any work at all.

I knew another candidate who never figured in local gossip during the whole course of the campaign – a young man with a rare gift, an old-fashioned puritanical streak and a masochistic appetite for hard work I have only seen surpassed in my late uncle Tormod. But we must persevere. We must remember the trouble Galileo had persuading the Pope of his time that the earth was round.

TUESDAY

Perhaps too many people are so well off these days they can afford to get into big debt. The success of the unions in dragging them from the ashes has ironically turned them into little Tories. Perhaps also future candidates should learn from that Siarach charmer Murdo Morrison – he understands his potential support and has the right approach.

He tells a good story of a visit to a Stornoway lady. After the tea and customary niceties he said to her: "Remember, now, to vote for me. I am Murdo Morrison, Conservative."

"Ma-thà, yes, a ghràidh," said she. "Anything to get that woman out."

WEDNESDAY

When the lights are low, when the "damp hand of melancholy" rests heavily on your brow, you need a strong woman by your side. A woman who will prod you out of bed, mix your Disprins quietly and force you to eat your porridge for your own good.

At times like this I am moved to praise where I would normally slander. Just recently the imported wife has been working hard to improve her Gaelic. She feels she can never properly be a true native or appreciate peat to the full without the true Gaelicness of the true Gael. I have, of course, done all I can to help her. I have encouraged her to listen to Radio nan Eilean and to make a note of any word she cannot understand. This leads, naturally, to many queries but very often it is only a matter of local variation in pronunciation. If I am stuck I put her on to Doctor Finlay and if he cannot enlighten her there is always the local Tory candidate.

The other day, though, we were all beat. "I have a good one for you here," she said. "I have just been listening to Coinneach Maclomhair interviewing the director of engineering – you know that fellow who married your cousin Mary."

"Fine men," arsa mise. "You wouldn't pick anything bad up from these boys."

"I am not so sure," says she. "It sounded decidedly risqué to me. The subject of their talk, unless I got it wrong, was concrete mammary glands."

"I don't believe it," I said. "What were the exact words?"

"Clochan concrete. I am almost sure of it."

I immediately rushed to consult my only friend in Carloway to find out what sort of underhand shenanigans were going on. "What is this nonsense about clochan concrete your man Dr George has sprung on us, and are they going to be confined to Carloway? Come to think of it, are they going to be confined at all?"

He hadn't heard the programme himself but it only took him a minute to solve and explain the misunderstanding.

"The director is a civil engineer. Builds piers. Work it out for yourself."

THURSDAY

I was pleased to see an old buddy of mine coming off the Glasgow aircraft the other day on his way to an interview for an important job with the council. I was pleased because I knew him to be well qualified for the job and he had served his apprenticeship in a hard school. The sort of man I wouldn't mind having in charge of my children. After we had exchanged greetings I advised him to be on his way immediately and not be seen talking to me. But, alas, he must have been spotted. He didn't get the job. Stranger still, no one got it.

FRIDAY
Whenever I am feeling really low I phone the Garrabost historian. I don't remember if I told you about him before, but if I give you a brief outline of his character perhaps you'll understand why he should be the man to call when you are down.

He has a great enthusiasm for life which he sometimes demonstrates in public to such a degree he gets arrested. Although he has toned these outbursts down since he became an office-bearer in the Church of Scotland, he is still prone to spontaneous and alarming relapses to his old ways.

He recently took me to a certain place in Inverness where he warned me we must not talk about religion or politics. At 10pm I had to caution him; at 11 he was in the middle of the floor with his fists clenched raving like a madman about "that woman" and how he detested all she stood for.

At other times in the past, in a different mood, he would start to sing psalms loudly and off-tune. I have known him come off the ferry late at night and present himself at my door within the hour looking for action on the rivers. In his university years he did all his studying in a telephone kiosk. Obviously, then, the man to confide in when depressed.

After two sleepless nights I rang him up. His advice this time, I must say, surprised me. "Take yourself off to Africa," he said, "where there is much good work to be done for the foreign mission. Twenty million still to be converted in Central Africa alone. Given your present rate of success with the preaching of socialism in the Western Isles, the poor Africans should be safe enough."

24 JUNE, 1983

MONDAY

"Can we have a look at your mussels?" the officer kept asking when I took him out in the boat to see my little ones. "Sure, sure, plenty time, but first let us feed the salmon."

Then a few minutes later, "Can we see the mussels now. I'd like to see your mussels."

This development officer is getting on my nerves, I thought. The guy is obsessed with shellfish. If you've seen one mussel you've seen them all. Send a classical scholar to Cambridge nowadays and what do you get? A mussel and fiddler-crab maniac. Finally when I couldn't put him off any longer – he showed no interest in my smolts – I let him lift a couple of mussel ropes.

He left the island in the huff, muttering about short term profit merchants and stuff like that.

I suppose, to be honest, my mussel ropes had been neglected for some time, but when you get a new expensive toy you cannot be expected to content yourself with old home-made amusements.

Not that I have given up my shellfish experiments despite last year's disaster. In two weeks time I intend to set out some scallop-spat collectors between Tabhaigh and Rubha Ràdhainis. If any trawler, or anything that looks like a trawler or anything that could be mistaken for a trawler, approaches within shooting distance, it will be sunk. There will be no more warnings. Remember the *Belgrano*.

DIDÒMHNAICH

Now this is the sort of summer's day I remember from my childhood. Warm, cloudless, windless, swimming in the corn with the girls. Intent on exposing some acreage of skin to the sun, I dug out some of the old tropical gear and came downstairs prepared for the beach. The shorts, I suppose, were a bit tight but I wasn't quite prepared for my children's cruel reaction. "If he is going like that I am not going," said my daughter.

"Me neither," said the son, loyal as ever.

Day and night you slave for the little brats and what do you get? A fortune you spend to get them to this stage and they turn out to be ashamed of you.

SATURDAY

Little did I know, or should I say little did they know, when my mother and his were gutting herring in Yarmouth, that he would do this to me. I am talking of course about Iain Sheòrdaidh. For some reason he seems to be the man in charge of the selection of old crocks for the annual football match in Goathill in aid of Cancer Research. Last year he ignored me, the coward; this year he was craftier. He made certain I was on duty before he invited me and he knows I put service to Queen and Country before all else. Never mind, let him have his moment, I'll get him yet (he was never in the same league as his cousin Iain a' Chas. I hear he fell over the ball trying some fancy footwork).

THURSDAY

What is the greatest pleasure known to man? Does that seem too difficult a question? Can it be answered at all? Can we generalise to such an extent? I believe we can if we are speaking only about Gaelic man. Gaelic man more than any other species likes to eat. He likes to eat often and in large quantities. He likes curries – a taste developed in his seagoing days – he likes marag, white and black, he likes duff and potatoes, he likes a tail of the unexpected, but most of all he likes herring. Having been brought up on herring twice a day seven days a week, Gaelic man didn't fully realise how much he liked herring until they were taken from him. We were halfway through the first year of the ban before the enormity of our loss sank in. That year two brothers from our own village accidentally caught two herring. They took them home and fried them, each watching the other carefully to make sure there was no sneaky nibbling going on. Halfway through this rare feast the sight of the fast disappearing fish proved too much for the younger brother; he broke down and started to cry.

Yes, herring is the boy. I remember once getting a parcel of salt herring sent out to darkest Africa. Mail was slow and they had gone off a bit but still we picked the bones clean. Later on a Hearach neighbour who we thought was on holiday came to visit. He stood in the doorway, nostrils twitching, and screamed, "Youse have had salt herring." In a second he was down on all fours at the gash bin sucking the bones like a wild animal. He never forgave us for not keeping one.

If you should be lucky enough to get your hands on some herring, as I did today, you must exercise great care: it is all too easy to keep eating until you slump over the table. Fry gently for ten minutes, taking care the oil is trapped between the skin and the flesh, for the dunking of potatoes. Two and a half to three is sufficient for one person. At twenty-five pence each it is worth every penny. In fact it is worth much more than that. It is worth more than anything.

FRIDAY

Sometimes on sunny afternoons my daughter takes me to the Castle Grounds for a walk and teaches me a little about trees and wild flowers. We walk along the river to the sea and marvel at what has been provided for us. Naturally we often talk about how wonderful it would be to own the whole park – how much more pleasure we would get out of it. To stand in the shadow of the tall trees and be able to say, all this is mine. How much more intense our pleasure would be. For a start we could fence it off – a high fence with barbed wire to keep other people out. We could put up all sorts of notices. No entry, no walking, no touching, no feeling and no fishing. We would train dogs to guard us from the common horde. Then and only then could we properly appreciate the Castle Grounds. Sadly, it is too late to realise this dream, unless we can persuade the government it should be privatised.

1 JULY, 1983

MONDAY

Suddenly the other day (when else) I caught a glimpse of my own face in a mirror. I hadn't seen it for a long time because for the first 12 years of married life we were very poor and we didn't have a mirror. But now that we are quite rich we have a few of them.

Wealth brings its own problems. The deep criss-cross furrows under my eyes were not there the last time I looked and I'm sure my nose was pale and narrow. The whites of my eyes were certainly whiter and my beard was red.

The only sure-fire test of ageing mentally and physically is one's knowledge of the present Top Twenty. It occurred to me yesterday, when Gerry Davis was playing some of our old favourites and the daughter started complaining about my taste, just how ignorant I was of what is in or out at the present time. Anything seems to go these days. There are no fixed fashions. My old Beatles records are being recycled by the youngsters and I caught Maggie playing Sinatra yesterday (the summer wind came blowing in across Cromore). I have always liked a bit of everything but punk is not for me. This is not punk's fault, whoever he is; it is probably just that I am getting old. Dash it all, there is no probably about it.

I like this Dòmhnall Iain MacSween. I didn't know he could sing so well. Or maybe it's another MacSween, and not the political agitator.

TUESDAY

Talking of ceòl, I seem to remember arguing with Jo of the airwaves the other night (when else) about Scottish dance music and its depressing effect on seven generations of Highland men. Why, I asked her, is Scottish dance music so boring when Irish dance music is full of surprises? She didn't like it, of course. There is something fiercely nationalistic about the girl; she is also a Niseach.

We cannot lay the blame entirely at the fingers of Niall Cheòis and

Jimmy Shand; it must go deeper than that (up to the elbows!). It is probably the military influence. Even our reels were meant to be marched to. I can remember an old teacher saying: "You couldn't write like that." But then he was an old square. Me, I like to be with it. Meat Loaf and all kinds of heavy metal.

WEDNESDAY

Strange as it may seem, the ageing process does tend to miss the odd fellow here and there. The other day (yes) when out feeding my livestock with our young fellow, we noticed a slim figure bounding along the north shore of Loch Leurbost. His pace, without actually breaking into a jog, was astonishing. We increased the boat's speed to about eight knots, yet he seemed to be gaining on us. He had a blond balding appearance. One minute he was down on the beach, the next up on the grassy banks, weightless as a grey heron.

"I think," said our young fellow, "it is Duncan Norman" (a 24-year-old keep fit maniac cousin of ours). When we reached the pier only seconds ahead of the man the blond / balding head turned out to be grey. He was none other than our medicine man, Dr Murray. Dr Murray is thought to be 82.

THURSDAY

Three years ago I wrote about the almost unbelievably high number of bachelors in the small village of Leurbost. Forty-eight, I think we counted, of varying eligibility, and Karachi. They are all now that little bit more eligible because they are three years older and nearer the end – a fact that will not have escaped the notice of many a crafty young woman with an eye on the insurance bonanza.

But how can they be so certain of outlasting the men, you may quite rightly ask. You don't have to take my word for it. The statistics are the proof.

It is a sad but undeniably true fact of life, or death, that the men of Leurbost do not last long. Almost without exception they cash in their chips while their women are still in their prime. I cannot at the moment think of one man in Leurbost who has outlived his wife. Yet, immediately, I can count 10 women in our end of the village alone. This phenomenon is worthy of long and careful scientific study. How have all these widows managed it? And how do they keep out of the clutches of the law?

The answer is, of course, they do it stealthily over a long period with a variety of weapons, the two main ones being sheep and Golden Virginia. All winter three times a day they stuff their men with fatty mutton. Then, come summer, they encourage them to chase next winter's mutton on the hoof. Of course, their cholesterol carcasses cannot take it. To shorten the odds even further these conniving females buy their husbands tobacco by the bale. So inevitably we have a village full of widows.

One fellow I confidently expect to beat the odds is Angie Barney. I have managed to lay some money on him with the Stornoway bookie to last to at least 110. Whether I will be around to collect is, of course, very doubtful.

The mystery that remains is why the aforementioned 48 bachelors don't make a move for the freshly-liberated widows. We must do more to encourage these relationships. If they would even try living together in the modern way, perhaps something permanent could develop. Or is it that our bachelors have too highly-developed a sense of self-preservation and don't want to be the second notch in our widows' gun?

FRIDAY

"You must go and see the Grimshader road. Something has to be done," said Coinneach. He wanted to know why he paid rates and taxes if he couldn't have a decent road to Stornoway. The least a man should expect in this day and age is a tarred road to his place of work.

I cannot really get steamed up about roads. I think there are more important things to be done with the money, but the Grimshader road is something else. They wouldn't have it in Botswana. There are potholes at the bottom of the potholes and more potholes in the ruts. I would personally be prepared to sacrifice the newly-erected lamp posts in our own village if it means they could have a new surface on the Grimshader road. After all, I would like to buy Coinneach's Peugeot in a few years' time.

15 JULY, 1983

WEEKEND

Overseas readers of this column will probably accuse me of exaggeration when I claim the heat of the sun is such that when we abandon our cars for a short while we have to cover the steering wheels with towels to make them bearable on return. I would like to take this opportunity to state my nose is the way it is because of the sun and not the dirty drink, as my enemies would say.

Talking of abandoning cars reminds me of our Sgalpach traffic warden (TW3). The man is getting tough. Some say he is power-crazy and bent on rapid promotion through the ranks no matter what misery he leaves in his wake. (Agus cha bhi sin fada mura fàg e mise aig fois.)

My young daughter reckons he had a very unhappy childhood, that he was probably bullied in school, and now he is getting his own back. But I keep telling her the man is only doing his job. I believe in instilling respect for authority, with the exception of gamekeepers.

TUESDAY

A few years ago I remember writing that when unemployment reached four million our newspapers would contain nothing but stories and photographs of the Queen of England. To be honest, I didn't really believe it at the time. But look at the tabloids now. The great socialist paper the *Daily Record* leads the field. Lady Di on every page. Aye, and some of the posh ones, too. The Queen herself is now too old and ugly, so the fairy-tale princess has taken over.

I see the Queen found a broken bottle in Holyrood Park and was not amused. I should think not, too: the perpetrator of this outrage should be hanged.

WEDNESDAY

Which brings me to the week's great debate – to stretch their necks or not to stretch their necks. Bring back the rope, some say. Others say it is a barbarous, uncivilised act that belongs in the past.

Among those who go their separate paths are two of the Free Kirk's leading theologians, Rev Alec MacLeod and Prof Macleod. My cousin Alec is all for stringing them up, while Prof Macleod is not. The Prof is of the opinion the Bible is ambiguous on the issue and so one cannot with a clear conscience pull the lever. The Rev Alec like Khomeni says the Word is quite clear, and that he who takes life should pay with his life.

I am surprised these two gentlemen should differ on this matter. They are both analysers of great repute who are seldom troubled with doubt. When they are, they usually consult me and I hear their confession. But on this occasion they didn't, and went ahead and made opposing public statements. This is bad form, chaps. Gives the impression of a split in the ranks, encouraging heathens to attack us while we are divided.

Very often conclusions on these important issues, although arrived at through long and careful study, can all too easily be influenced by personal experience. Supposing, for instance, one came from a long line of sheepstealers who met their ends on the scaffold: is it not likely one would have inherited an aversion to hanging? Mind you, I am not for a moment casting any aspersions in the Professor's direction. Nor am I suggesting that the Rev Alec's ancestors suffered unduly at the hands of rustlers. But it is possible.

My own thoughts on the subject, although mysteriously I was not invited to express them on radio, are not fudged by any ambiguous instruction passed down by ancient Israelite goatherds: they are quite clear. In the first instance you cannot approve of hanging unless you are personally prepared to pull the rope with your own two hands; and secondly you must have caught the murderer in the act. Promotion-hungry law-enforcers cannot be trusted. Also, it depends on who was murdered. In some cases the murderer may have committed an act of great public service. I have a list here which for obvious reasons I cannot publish.

THURSDAY

Biadh agus beagan deoch. The next best thing to being wealthy is to have very wealthy, generous friends. This time it was a converted barn in Shawbost called Raebhat House. You bring your own plonk, which means your wealthy friend stays wealthy because he pays only a third of the normal hotel price and so he can take you out again and again. The great thing about Raebhat House is that at seven pounds a skull you can almost afford to treat yourself.

I have only one complaint. Although the portions are generous I suspect the cook is a health fiend. The onions and mushrooms were cooked in some strange fatless manner (steamed, perhaps) which may be all right for Englishmen but not good enough for men with properly-developed palates and appetites. The sirloin steak was extended slightly past the part of the animal usually referred to as sirloin and slightly overcooked if you like the blood running down your chin. But all in all I'm glad I skipped my customary afternoon fried herring.

DIHAOINE

Chuala mi tè mhath a-raoir ann an Raebhat House. Mar a tha fios agaib' fhèin, bha na Siaraich uabhasach fad' air ais. Cha robh iad a' dèanamh mòran am measg dhaoine eile agus mar sin cha robh iad ag ionnsachadh. Tha e coltach nuair a thàinig a' chiad chroman a Bharbhas, agus chan eil cho fada bhon àm sin, gu robh toileachas mòr anns a' bhaile. Thàinig iad a-mach às na taighean-dubha, òg is aosd, gus am faiceadh iad an t-inneal iongantach a bha seo. An sin 's ann a ghabh bodach 'fancy' garbh dheth agus dh'fhaighnich e am faigheadh e greis dheth. 'S ann a chòrd a' chùis cho math ris 's gun thobhaig e buntàta a' bhaile gu lèir. Chaidh am fear leis an robh an croman fiadhaich. "Thusa an sin," ars esan, "a' falbh a' bhaile a' dèanamh duine mòr dhìot fhèin le croman duin' eile."

22 JULY, 1983

MONDAY

At two o'clock this morning I was awakened by an intense pang of guilt. For ten minutes I paced the floor desperately trying to pinpoint the cause. What matter of great import had I forgotten? Or did I absentmindedly do something terrible to a friend or even to an enemy? Then I got it. I remembered I owed Malky some money. But where is he? I haven't seen him for ages. That should make me feel less guilty, but what if he is in jail somewhere and cannot raise the bail. I must try to settle my debts without delay so I can sleep nights.

Isn't access to a news sheet a wonderful thing. The mere mention of an outstanding few quid lets your creditor know you haven't forgotten. And after your having mentioned the matter publicly he will assume you intend to pay. This is the best idea I have had for some time. I could continue to write about this small debt indefinitely. It eases my conscience and at the same time gives the other fellow some hope. But the other fellow in this case is a smart cookie and will probably think of some way of getting back at me. Any intelligence on his movements will be gratefully received.

TUESDAY

I stopped at Parkend today and gave a lift to a young man with a beard who was trying to hitch a ride to town by waving one of his crutches in the air. I bet it always works. It transpired he had broken his leg in a motorbike accident. Had he known then what he knows now and what you and I knew long ago, he would have gathered himself together and crawled on to the Inverness plane. Instead, like so many before him, he allowed himself to be taken to Lewis Hospital where, sadly, they haven't got a bone man. Why have we not got a bone setter? Surely it is not too much to ask of a man who can whip out a gallbladder or diagnose a leaking heartvalve that he should be able to stick a few simple bones back together.

What would they think of a motor mechanic who only did carburettors? I don't think some of my eminent colleagues are worth the £40,000 a year we pay them. Speaking as a pulmonary man, I maintain it would be unreasonable to ask us or top neurosurgeons to waste time on bones and simple plumbing, but as for the rest of the ordinary quackery, I don't see why they shouldn't be jacks of all trades.

Another thing I would like to know, and I'm certainly not the only one, is why the aforementioned witch doctors insist on having a few goes at those unfortunate victims who come their way before finally packing them off to Raigmore. I am told they have carted some human beings off that Inverness plane with their feet pointing backwards.

WEDNESDAY

A visit from the Garrabost historian, who is on two weeks' parole, and I can hardly tell you how he disappoints me. Sooner or later the friends you liked the most will let you down. As they grow older the qualities you admired will wither and give way to the corrupting influenees of 20th century life.

He would deny it, of course, but the false god of material possession has him in its evil grasp. A man who was once indifferent to all that glitters has found comfort and joy in the shiny worldly body of a Vauxhall Cavalier. So proud is he of his new car that he will not bring it up my rough gravel path in case a small stone should dent the paintwork. Every few minutes he jumps up anxiously and looks out the window as if to divert any seagull that threatened to fly overhead. His is a sad case. It grieves me to see a man given over to the worship of property at a time in his life when he should be seeking a higher purpose.

THURSDAY

Among a crowd of Niseachs who came to celebrate a wedding in the Caberfeidh was Tormod a' Bhoxair (from this day forth it will be in order to use the letter 'x' in the Gaelic language. If challenged by some pedant don't hesitate to quote me as an authority). Anyway, as I was saying, I found Tormod a' Bhoxair at the bar. (A' brùchdail 's a' bromail.) "I think," he said, "you must be related to Calum Kennedy, the well known singer from Lochs."

This didn't please me at first, remembering the Kennedy's heavy jowls and numerous chins, so I was about to deny any connection with the south side of the Loch when I realised Tormod must have heard me singing in the toilet. He obviously spotted the similarity in tone and concluded we had to be blood relations. With this flattering thought in mind I am content to let anyone who likes think the Kennedy and I are cousins.

Later on it struck me it wasn't such a bright idea after all. What if people were to think I wrote "Make your way to Stornoway", or worse, "Rolling in the heather", or even, worse still, something about "Staying home in Kirkcaldy." If there are any three better reasons for the restoration of the rope I cannot think of them. For the time being I think I'll continue to deny any relationship with your man.

FRIDAY

I am almost sorry now I went along to Goathill tonight to watch the Hibs–Lewis Select game. Perhaps I should have been content with the memory of Smith, Johnstone, Reilly, Turnbull and Ormond. Not that we can compare the present forward line – if we can still use the expression – with the Famous Five, but I had hoped for something better: an exhibition of the skills we would expect from a team in Scotland's Premier Division. Of course it is partly our own fault. We have become highlight people.

The whole game has become so boring these days that we extract the rare exciting bits, like goals. Pretty soon it will be highlights of the highlights. It is partly our fault, but mainly the fault of managers who have allowed the game to become so boring.

This game tonight was one of the least entertaining I have ever seen. There was little to choose between the teams. With the exception of Nero, our boys seemed overawed. God knows why. One side scored a few goals. It doesn't matter which side or how many. It was that sort of game.

There was some evidence of lack of direction from management in both teams. The long hopeful ball is still a great favourite in Lewis and Scottish football, and it seems nothing will ever cure our players of this futile strategy. There is also a dearth of men who can beat two defenders and draw a third. Our running off the ball, a rare event, was too obvious. I must have a word with Murdie an Oighre because, somewhere along the way, he has taken the wrong turning. Sybil agrees with me.

5 AUGUST, 1983

MONDAY

The Glasgow lot are gone except for a few Paisley Fairies but any day now I expect the Anglos to arrive, led by Munro of Melbost. I am not sure what to do with these fellows this year. In times past there was nothing a starved exile liked better than a feed of herring and a game of golf. The herring we can still manage but the golf, I'm afraid, is nowadays beyond the shabby crofter's purse. There are still one or two country boys who can afford to play, like wealthy post officers, but for the average crofter on his humble croft the annual subscription is prohibitive.

I understand from intelligence reports a round of golf will set me back as a non-member four pounds sterling. I am sure you'll agree this is far too much – an increase way ahead of the pace of inflation. Obviously a deliberate ploy by that small clique of Stornoway businessmen to keep the club to themselves. Unable to blackball us like that other club, these capitalist hyenas, exploiters of cheap labour and racketeers of every description – in whose eyes the simple crofting man is no higher than a worm – raised the ante to the point where we had to choose between our small pleasures and our children's shoes. I don't know how I am going to break the news to Munro.

Still, there is always the fishing. They cannot keep that away from us, try as they might.

TUESDAY

As if that is not enough, Munro will also be sorry to hear our old friend Macdonald of Carloway is letting in himself big. At land and sea he has no luck. He has become, and it gives me no pleasure to say it, a burden to himself and others. I tried to make him train a little this year but he will not listen. He costs his wife £65 a week in fresh meat alone, yet these little Fraser boys are getting the better of him at the Highland Games. He just will not accept that at 47 you cannot sleep only three hours a night, drink like a fish and still expect to throw heavy weights around.

WEDNESDAY

Talking of heavyweights, who should visit me tonight but my favourite broadcaster, Maggie Cunningham. Her mission was to record my little ones at play, and that we did. My charges took an immediate liking to the microphone. They put on a fine display, jumping in tens and twelves and generally raising a loud hullabaloo.

Intent on feeding and recording, I was only vaguely aware of my interviewer's line of questioning. Only later on did I realise she had been getting at me – insinuating throughout my approach was that of the dilettante, comparing my attitude to the present project and to crofting in general to that of the Stornoway Gaelic Choir to the Gaelic language. But I forgive her.

Without warning the mist turned to thick fog. There I was adrift with Maggie in Loch Erisort, the visibility down to 10 yards and no compass. Can you imagine what our enemies, especially the reptiles of the gutter press, would have made of the situation. "Television star spends night on tidal reef with native medicine man." What opportunities for the punny new *Gazette*. Fortunately, the Sgalpach's inborn navigational sense saw us home safely.

THURSDAY

What has happened to the *Stornoway Gazette*? In old JSG's and Lord Longbottom's day it had a certain grey dignity you could almost respect.

Stories and headlines were composed with care and attention to detail. Little stories from the police courts were reported with cold indifference: now they are presented flippantly, with undisguised glee at the victim's misfortune. Is this what happens when a money-grubbing Tory with no interest in the community takes charge?

The paper goes to the expense of hiring a professional photographer (surely ten grand if they pay the proper rate) and then what happens? Wee Sammy produces photographs of quality, then they let loose some *Beano* fan to write the captions. Is it any wonder so many have stopped buying it? And the few who still read it do so only for the death notices. I only mention this because I care: no one wants to see a newspaper collapse.

For some time now I have been trying to persuade our own paper to go in for death and marriage notices. I have prepared a few in advance for my own friends. The style will shock those who were brought up on the *Gazette*, but I feel we should try to cheer up the bereaved and newly wed.

For example: Suddenly at his home last night Fiollaigean nam Fiadh, aged 86, passed away. And not before time. He was unique in being without a single redeeming feature. We are well rid of him. Or: Married at Crossbost Free Church yesterday, such-and-such to that flighty creature from Cromore. The fool! If only he knew what I know. And so on. I am sure it would work.

FRIDAY

Sandy Boots from Tanera with bottle of Morangie desperate to see my little ones. He takes one look at my two cages and promptly makes me an offer he thinks I cannot refuse. His 22 cages, Tanera, house and boat against my croft and site in Loch Leurbost. But naturally I turn him down. What is money to me? My daughter thought he reminded her of James Galway. The same accent and dancing eyes, she said. I think maybe she confused Galway with Danny McGrain.

SATURDAY

A call from Angus Peter Campbell to tell me he is coming to North Lochs next week to do some filming for Grampian. I hear he has taken a heavy Catholic cùram. I'm not sure how severe that is but I suppose I'd better watch my language.

23 SEPTEMBER, 1983

MONDAY

Now and again some of the men with whom I unfortunately have to consort succumb to the urge to tell me a joke. Usually along the lines of: "There was an Englishman, a Scotsman and an Irishman …" in the most unlikely situation. Sometimes the so-called jokes are crude and the teller is often a coarse sort of fellow who finds certain parts of the human anatomy amusing in themselves. This prince among bores often collars you at the bar and grabs you by the elbow as if he senses you would like to escape. Of course you should tell him to "go away" or plant one on his jaw, but instead you smile sympathetically, which of course he takes to mean you find him amusing. No wonder I drink so much.

My 10-year-old son woke me up at 12.30 yesterday afternoon to tell me a joke he'd heard on Andy Cameron. "How do you know when you're reading the paper upside down? Rangers are on the top of the league." I must say I found this very amusing, but only because it was told by a child.

Such a disrespectful reference to the mighty Rangers Football Club would not be tolerated from an adult. How can the downfall of this proud team be allowed to happen? Do opposing teams not realise they have a duty to lose so Rangers can appear above Celtic in the league table? I think it is a curse, myself, and it serves them right for offending their dedicated supporters by trying to sign a Catholic. Or are they being punished for their massive contribution to Tory Party funds?

Ha, ha. I bet you didn't know that one.

TUESDAY

Between you and me, I'm worried about my wife. At the tender age of 46 she has started to get small. We are not sure when exactly it began to happen. This reduction in physical stature is a slow process and obviously not the sort of thing you notice when you see the victim every day.

One of her occasional companions remarked innocently: "I thought we were about the same size." This didn't worry her at all, but next day another "friend" said: "I always thought you were taller than I am." Then I began to notice things at home. Like when she's painting the downstairs windows, she has to stand on two boxes. I am sure she used to manage on one, but thank goodness I am too much of a gentleman to say anything. If it's not one thing it's another: my first wife got too big.

WEDNESDAY

Much as I worry about Maggie's health, I worry a great deal more about my own. When we were poor we used to sit around and talk about our poverty. Now that we have everything we worry about our health.

Yesterday I had to go and consult my doctor about a slight chest infection. A new man, a member of the Beresford clan. And I must say I was impressed with his efficiency and general attitude to his job. I'm also pleased to say, being the younger man, he fully accepted my own diagnosis. Why, I hear you ask, should I have to consult another medical man when I have my own remedies at home? It is merely a case of job creation. Every day you read of doctors on the dole, and if we are, more and more of us, going to go in for homers, the situation can only get worse. Not that I normally approve of antibiotics, but if you are a man in a hurry who needs to get out and about, there is no great harm in resorting to modern drugs on rare occasions.

THURSDAY

Once or twice in a man's lifetime he will experience a moment to treasure. Some men prefer to savour those rare delights privately. Myself, I have to share them to extract the maximum pleasure.

Today I overheard an Englishman and a Fifer talking about money. No, they weren't planning to spend any, they were arguing heatedly about whether the Royal Bank stayed open until six or was it half-past on a Thursday.

"One thing is certain," I interjected to quieten them. "If you go to Stornoway now at half-past two it is certainly open at the moment."

They looked at me with that well-known mixture of pity and contempt and walked away. "What was all that about?" I asked a friend who understands these people better than I do. "Don't you realise the significance of the half-hour after six?" he said. "The shops are closed. There is no danger of being tempted to buy something."

FRIDAY

You may have noticed recently in this column that hardly a week goes by without some nasty remark about Skyemen. I would like to apologise for this immature behaviour. As I'm sure the more discerning among you will already have understood, it was nothing more than childish jealousy aroused by the visit of Princess Margaret to your beautiful island. Why this wonderful honour should have been bestowed on Skye rather than Lewis is not for us to question. We will now stop these envious digs at our neighbours and hope that some day we too will be blessed with a visitation.

21 OCTOBER, 1983

SUNDAY

We must not be afraid to break with tradition if we hope to hold the interest of a modern congregation. When the call comes, as it surely must now, I intend to preach in a style that may shock the elders but which I think, given strength, will attract the young and needy. Gone are the days of the wild man in the pulpit.

Do you remember that fellow they had in Back? He very nearly wrecked the box every Sunday. One morning he was in a particularly violent mood, jumping from wall to wall in the pulpit, bellowing and hammering the mahogany. Down below a frightened little boy was heard above the gnashing of teeth to ask his mother: "What will he do if he escapes?" We wouldn't like to revert to these methods.

What I would like to do is encourage debate. Each Sunday I will suggest a topic and we will get together in the County Hotel every Friday to argue. My word will, of course, be the final one.

It so happens that among the many paranormal gifts with which I have been blessed I can number the ability to communicate with the departed. Last night I had a long chat with two ancestors who had been dead for a long time – cousin Jacob and cousin John.

Cousin Jacob looked extremely well for someone who had been dead for 300 years. Not only was he in good shape physically, he was in high spirits and he played some lively tunes on his harp while we talked.

"You seem to have done all right for yourself on this side," I said.

"That I have," said Jacob. "I lack for nothing. A hundred nubile angels at my beck and call, the best cigars and fine malt whisky."

"You must have been a good man while you were alive. What did you do to deserve all this?"

"War, rape and pillage were my speciality. I also dabbled in fraud. I drank like a fish and beat my wife and children every Saturday night. As if that wasn't enough, I also strangled my social worker."

"How come you were not punished?"

"Ah, well, you see. I went on a big bender the week before I died and saw the light. One instant I was a drunken fiend, the next a reformed reborn character and my slate was swept clean. Sixty-nine years and fifty-one weeks of atrocities were atoned for in one frantic week of prayer. Here, have a cigar."

The ways are indeed mysterious and wonderful.

Cousin John had had a bad time. His cindered remains were pitiful to behold.

"They've given you the works," I said.

"Eighty years of fire and brimstone and an eternity of the same in store."

"What on earth did you do?" I said, trying to be punny to cheer him up.

"I did my utmost to help my fellow man. I went out among the poor of India and tried to heal the sick. I shared what I had with the less fortunate and encouraged them to believe their fate lay in their own hands. I suppose I was a sort of a humanist."

"Did you go to church at all?"

"Not much. Although I did treasurer for the Church of Scotland for a while and never once dipped my fingers in the till. I even gave half my salary to the Liberal Party. But that counted for nothing when the big day came. The board was made up of Free Presbyterians."

"It seems to me you've had a rough deal, cousin John, but I must leave you now and get back to sleep."

HANDS UP, those who think cousin Jacob and cousin John got what they deserved. I see. I'll have to spend more time with the Crossbost section of the flock.

MONDAY

It is firmly believed by the faceless men who control Gaelic broadcasting in the BBC that audiences are made up of Free Presbyterian ministers and children under 10. The unwritten rule, or perhaps it is written, is: Gaelic listeners must be protected, so stick to something simple; whatever you do, don't offend.

This voluntary censorship means we can only have news or music programmes. Humour is ruled out. Even Norman Maclean takes a tight grip of the reins when confronted with a BBC camera. Perhaps chat shows like *Fealla-Dhà 's a Trì* should have a studio audience mellowed with a pre-show dram.

There is another generally-accepted rule that Gaelic TV programmes should not be criticised. This is partly because they are a great rarity, but I suspect the main reason would-be critics do not criticise is that they don't want to spoil their own chances of a five-minute spot. For that reason I will say as little as possible about Rhino's sketch of last week. It came across as a mixture of "Playschool" and sterilised Kenny Everett. If five minutes of precious Gaelic TV time can be squandered like that, perhaps we don't deserve more than half an hour a week.

I thought John Carmichael and Joni looked very pretty in their new jumpers.

TUESDAY

I am often asked why I haven't joined the Lewis Film Society. The short answer is Leslie. For a long time I was locked up with Leslie on a ship where film-going was more or less compulsory. Your man was the organiser. Not only did he order obscure unheard-of movies full of hidden meaning and fancy directors' tricks, he always sat through every show facing us, studying audience reaction. I couldn't go through that again.

WEDNESDAY

My attention has been drawn to the strange migration pattern developing in north-west Scotland. The general trend for hundreds of years has been eastwards; now the shabby crofters of Achiltibute are moving in significant numbers across the Minch.

First to arrive were Sandy and Sheila Boots. Before I extend a hearty welcome I must first of all investigate their reasons for moving – make sure they aren't on the run. Any information will be gratefully received. In the meantime. Sandy will be setting up a fish farm consultancy. We will operate from Leurbost with, of course, 10 per cent for the Da.

Hot on Sandy's heels we expect Dòmhnall Chaluim. He is politically suspect. He once knew and admired the rich, but I think I may have caught him in time. His rehabilitation will probably be slow and painful.

4 NOVEMBER, 1983

MONDAY

There appears to be no cure for the Friday night wanderers. They no longer restrict their disruptive practices to Friday and Saturday. You are not safe in your own home on a Wednesday night. These boys cannot be beat. That you might have gone to bed when they call, far from being a deterrent, only adds to their satisfaction and lends some purpose to their mission. It is not that I don't sympathise with these poor unfortunates. I was myself once a not infrequent disturber of the peace.

At midnight or, even better, 2 am, you are for some unknown reason elated and filled with a sense of love for your friends. The only vital ingredient missing in their lives at that moment is your company. Once a target is selected there is no effective deterrent. If you already have one or two fellow-revellers in tow, so much the better. You can make more noise, disturb dogs, wives and children.

After a reluctant host – someone you know to have been teetotal for some time – has opened the door, he has had it. A cold northerly blowing into his house prevents too much protest. You're in. You lead with the white plastic bag as if it were a search warrant. He may pace the floor shivering in his night attire making impatient gestures and muttering about work in the morning, but eventually the sucker will have a wee one – just one, he says. Calling for glasses, you settle by the dying fire and proceed to air your views on politics and religion, which your host has almost certainly heard a thousand times before. If he sits down and accepts a second one you have him. Your mission has been accomplished. Another man has fallen.

TUESDAY

I thought I had the answer the other night. It could very well work for some, but I wouldn't advise the weak-livered to try it. Anyway, there are certain hard cases who cannot be reasoned with. A drastic measure, but you may want to try it.

When the intruder produces a bottle and calls for glasses, instead of whisky glasses you fetch two pint mugs. The contents are dispensed in one mad round, the reasoning being that in his condition he won't last long. Slàinte ... gulp, gulp. That's it. Sorry, I haven't a drop in the house. Certain characters will accept defeat at this stage. But not your man.

No matter, says he. Rummaging in the many folds and hidden crevices about his person, he produces another bottle. In desperation you try the same suicidal trick a second time. After which your companion – to whom you are now beginning to warm – instead of being dead as he should be, has become extremely lucid, like the elderly comotose when the end is nigh. You begin to marvel at his wisdom and are only too pleased when he finds another quartie in his wellingtons. Is there any answer apart from the monastery? Has everyone gone mad?

WEDNESDAY

I see before me a kind invitation from the Royal Bank. Not content with long-established means of getting me into debt, such as Access and overdrafts, they have thought of some new methods of enslavement. "Ask about our other services," they plead – "Rainbow Savings accounts," and here's a beauty: "Revolving Credit Accounts". They are being surprisingly honest in their choice of title for the Rainbow Savings Account – the tantalising pot of gold forever just out of reach. I think we'll forget about that one. The Revolving Credit Account sounds like the boy for me.

Presumably it goes round in ever-decreasing circles until eventually, like the bird in the song, it disappears. I haven't yet been in to ask how it works, but it sounds a bit like an idea my old shipmate Jackson had (in the lean old days, of course). Having got in deeply with his English bank, he had the good sense to open an account in Scotland. After a cautious start, to impress the new manager, he arranged a moderate overdraft. Off goes a small cheque to the English bank to keep the man down there happy for a while. For a short time we enjoyed a period of some prosperity, playing one off against the other until, eventually, one docking day, we were met on the pier by the debt collectors. At that time we were both in a position to skip the country for a year or two until the tide came in again. It's not easy nowadays. But perhaps this new Revolving Account is the answer.

THURSDAY

Tomorrow I had hoped to be in Inverness to officiate at the betrothal of my friend Kate Mhòr nan Airwaves. Sadly, I cannot make it and I cannot even send a telegram. I can only offer these two adventurous young people my warm congratulations as they start on this hazardous journey through life. May they prosper and seek guidance in the Good Book that their voyage be a calm one. And that their ways will be good ways. Let us hope their union is blessed with issue.

25 NOVEMBER, 1983

MONDAY

I have a very important message this week, so will all readers please pass the word around among the benighted minority who cannot spare the 20 pence or who cannot read. I would like to invite anyone and everyone who happens to have a dead animal on his hands to come and dump the carcase at Crossbost pier.

This fine monument to the first Job Creation scheme is tremendously convenient. Being able to drive down to the high water mark, you have no need to carry a dirty corpse for any distance – simply roll it out of the boot and leave it where it falls. But hurry while there is still room left. The shore on both sides of the pier is filling up fast with dead dogs, sheep, hens, rams' heads and all manner of refuse.

The pier is of course a favourite playground for North Lochs children and their pets, but do not let that worry you: hydatid doesn't always kill.

I have noticed from time to time people making use of the refuse cart which comes round once a week. Are these people aware of the cost of this service to the ratepayer? Why can they not bring their rubbish, like the public-spirited minority, to the shore? Old fences are particularly welcome: they enhance the natural beauty of the coastline and teach unwary navigators to keep their eyes open.

TUESDAY

Having started the week on a serious note, we may as well continue. I am pleased to see my important treatise, published last week, on the "Nine Fuses of Woman", has drawn a quick response, although not an uncritical one from my esteemed colleagues in the trade. One doctor, Iain Lom Smith of Stornoway, has written to thank me for explaining in simple terms (how could it be otherwise?) the workings of a typical female mind: for succeeding, as he puts it, where Freud and Jung have failed.

I take no pleasure whatever in being compared to Freud, a gluttonous Liberal MP, and I am not flattered by being classed with the infamous ex-Stornoway-airport fireman, Chung. Still, we won't fall out over that. Although Chung often did.

None of us in the medical profession should ever be too proud to seek a second opinion. Sometimes even the smartest GP can be steered off course by spurious symptoms that serve only to distract and divert attention from the main "fault". Dr Lom goes on to explain the "Peat in the Washing Machine Symdrome". Maggie, he diagnoses brilliantly, has fallen victim to my generosity. (It seems so clear to me now.)

Her responses are conditioned by genes spawned on the shores of Loch Gravir in that cloudy meteorological phenomenon, the mists of time. I should, of course, have spotted it myself. But there you are. (I wouldn't be surprised if our old friend Pavlov comes into it.)

Generously and foolishly I had bought Maggie every mod con in the business including a washing machine. How could I possibly foresee a Gravir child couldn't tell a washing machine from a three-legged prais?

I am disappointed with my eminent colleague's insinuation that I should have to call in N D or any other Trappist monk for a simple electrical fault.

WEDNESDAY

Wherever I roam in the town of Stornoway this day, I meet Lewis Offshore workers holding their heads, vomiting in the gutters, and generally behaving as if it were the first of January. It took me a long time to get to the bottom of this sad story. Some faithful servants were ashamed to tell the tale, while other would-be trade unionists were so eager to spill the beans I couldn't be sure they were not exaggerating.

The truth, to which I have 60 amused witnesses, is very nearly true. The obscenely-wealthy multinational company Brown & Root were so pleased with the recently-completed job at Arnish they decided to hold an end-of-contract soiree – at the scene of the crime.

When the staff had supped, giggled and cavorted in the inner sanctum, one lordly overseer, mellowed with ancient brandy, was heard to suggest the minions who had done the work should join in the merriment.

"What a jolly good idea," cried the chaps. "For he's a jolly good fellow, is good old Browned Root."

"We have a forty-ouncer left here," said a minor union-basher. "Let's call the boys in."

Some came. Most didn't. "There isn't much," said a plater, "J C Himself could do with one forty-ouncer and fifty welders." The staff are believed to have enjoyed the party.

THURSDAY

"Where have they gone?" I am often asked. Your unsavoury friends, the West End Tory, Karachi and all the other North Lochs characters. Nowhere, I'm afraid. They are still here and getting no better. I met the W E T the other night, had a few mugs, and still we parted the best of enemies. He still has the time-worn solution to the starving Third World – he would distribute the surplus when we have enough. When is that? I remember promising the Cnagan a haystack of tobacco when I started earning. But somehow I never seem to have enough.

Karachi is different. I am told he got married recently – three weeks ago. And this may very well be true. Someone moved into a caravan in our "desirable residential area" around that time, but as yet they haven't surfaced. There is a car parked outside, curtains are drawn, smoke occasionally rises, but there is no movement. If they do not bestir themselves this week some of the neighbours want to break the door down in the interests of decency. And no wonder. Beside the church.

Well do I remember the day Karachi was born. He entered the world with shoulder-length hair, weighing 17 lbs. He immediately started to walk and to graphite the Rayburn. We all agreed he was very advanced. God only knows what has happened since. I understand he has married a woman from Point.

FRIDAY

Bejay, but I seem to be rabbiting on this week. I don't know why, unless it's the big cheque I got from the *Free Press* last week. I don't know what happened to Saturday last week, dear editor. It was probably a bad line. Like being back with the *Stornoway G*. Don't worry. I wouldn't go back there for anything. I am probably the only man alive who ever got a 250,000 per cent pay rise.

9 December, 1983

SATURDAY

I hope readers who had anticipated my translation of Seumas's little work in this issue won't be too disappointed. It may take a little longer than I thought. Please be patient.

I'm suffering from delayed shock, having been driven from Aberdeen to Inverness by Maggie Cunningham in her new car, which for some reason she thinks is a VC-10. When she says "Fasten your seat belt – we're ready to go," she obviously means she is spiritually prepared for the other side. Hers is an extreme example of the personality change that affects otherwise normal people when they sit behind a wheel. Every other road-user becomes the enemy, to be humiliated and overtaken – preferably on hairpin bends. For one hundred hair-raising miles she snarled and blew her horn at other drivers and pedestrians alike. Bha pòlaichean an teileafòn a' dol seachad mar fiaclan cìr-mhìn. It's a miracle we're here today.

My medical advisers warned me to stay out of Stornoway this weekend and rest in the bosom of my family. Relax, they said, and watch some sport.

SUNDAY

While convalescing I've been catching up with the last few weeks' newspapers and magazines. Not much to amuse on the national scene these days – hardly worthwhile subscribing to *Punch* and *Private Eye*. Only the *Gazette* left. I see a woman of Bru has won herself a PhD for "sociological analysis of the relationship between culture and pattern of production, distribution and consumption of food in a Lewis village between the late 18th century and the present day".

I would be very grateful if anyone could steal this thesis for me so that my solicitors could peruse for plagiarism. I fear the entire fraudulent concoction could be based on a short book I wrote in the Forties entitled *Potato Blight and Psalms*. I am not making any definite accusations, but one must remember there are unscrupulous students around in these hard times who wouldn't hesitate to rewrite the Gospel according to Mark in sociological jargon and pass it off as their own.

I have just had delivered into my shaking hands a publication for the youth of the Free Church, *The Instructor*, in which someone has written a funny short story called "Sandy and Ann". We'll say nothing about the title. Here is the opening paragraph:– "The children were helping to clear the table when the doorbell rang. Father went to answer it and they were all delighted when he brought back a visitor, the minister."

The author is trying to amuse our little Free Church children – or is he being serious? If he or she is being serious, he/she is not of Free Church stock, otherwise he/she would know his credibility is lost with the word "delighted". Sandy and Ann, if they are like Alasdair and Mairi Ann before them, might be alarmed, despondent, frightened, worried or bored but never "delighted". Or they might have been trying to escape, in which case the author could have had the basis of a good yarn when the children were captured or lured back only to discover the minister wasn't such a bad fellow after all. Let's have a bit of realism, old chap. Remember the children were probably watching Hurricane Higgins when the bell rang. Furthermore, father would not have gone to answer the door. Perhaps the old man or the Da, but more likely the old lady.

A CHRISTMAS TALE FOR CHILDREN OF ALL AGES

Long ago, before double time was invented, almost everyone in Lewis was very poor and unhappy. Although they were often told poverty was next to Godliness and nothing to be ashamed of, they were still very unhappy. Unhappiest of all was wee Murdo from Garrynambreac. Murdo was a clever boy as boys from Garrynambreac went, although no doubt he would have been considered average in Marvig or Stornoway.

Murdo had no daddy because the daddy had been shot by game-keepers. His grandfather and all his uncles had also been shot by gamekeepers. Murdo didn't like gamekeepers. Neither did anyone in Garrynambreac except the minister and the headmaster.

Murdo's mother had been in service in a big house in Benbecula but when she got the sack she wasn't given £25,000 or anything like it. In fact she wasn't given anything at all.

So Murdo was always hungry. For breakfast he sometimes got a little oatmeal but usually there was only enough for the hens. And the hens had to get their share first, otherwise they wouldn't lay any eggs. Often, though the hens got all the oatmeal, they still didn't lay any eggs, which seemed unfair to Murdo. In the evening he usually had a cold potato. Occasionally when times were not quite so bad he would get a hot potato and for a rare treat and variety he might be given a hot potato with a cold potato.

He hardly ever got any milk because most of the milk had to be given to the calf and the remainder Murdo had to take to the Big House for rent. Once when he was carrying the milk to the landlord he was so thirsty he took a big drink from the pail. For this he was severely beaten, and next day he had to take the calf's share as well. Murdo often wondered if anyone ever had such a hard life.

When the minister came to see them – which he often did, because his mother was renowned for her piety – he was invariably offered a boiled egg and he even got butter on his oatcake. Murdo complained that his own oatcake was dry and difficult to swallow but the minister and his mother said he should be thankful and count his blessings. At this point, Murdo, who was getting smart and outspoken, voiced the opinion he wouldn't need to be much of a mathematician for that. Again Murdo was given a sound thrashing and sent to the lower end of the house to spend the night with the animals.

Things didn't get any better as he got older and thinner. When all the other boys got boots for the winter Murdo had to go to school in his bare feet. He couldn't afford to take a peat like the other boys, so the headmaster made him sit in the coldest corner of the room. He also got beaten more than the other boys who had daddies. Although he didn't understand what effectual calling and justification meant he could recite most of the psalms and the entire Catechism and he knew the multiplication tables. Also he often got beaten in the mornings before he had done anything because the headmaster had seen him after school. In those days if you saw the headmaster coming along the road you were expected to dive over a stone dyke before he clapped eyes on you because nothing caused greater offence than the sight of a Gaelic-speaking brat when the headmaster was off duty.

When Murdo was 14 his luck changed. He escaped from school and was made apprentice to a carter at two shillings a week. Around this time he also fell in love.

A rich man from the South who came to the village to set up a fish farm had a 16-year-old daughter of great charm and beauty. Murdo had never seen anyone like her, for the girls of the village all had coarse Gaelic faces. Her golden hair and lily-white features were seldom out of his mind. He also noticed her diamond rings and gold earrings and he had come to the conclusion if you had to count blessings it was better to do so in hard cash or negotiable precious metals. Even more important, he had cause to suspect his love was reciprocated. She had sometimes smiled and waved as he passed with his horse and cart. Yes, there was no doubt in his mind. She fancied him.

He was totally besotted. One day he nearly drove into the doctor's rose garden as he dreamed of his maiden. Murdo was still poor but no longer unhappy.

True, he had heard the rumour his fair-headed one was friendly with the Laird's son, but he didn't worry too much. The Laird's son had plenty money but he was stupid and ugly, and not a serious contender for his girl's affections.

Lo and behold, at that time there was a big man in the parish by the name of D H M Soval – a rich man with tractors and modern machinery. In a single morning he could spread more manure than Murdo could spread in a week with horse and cart. In a short time horses were out of business. Once again Murdo found himself in reduced circumstances, but he still had his love.

A big party was planned for Christmas at the Big House, and the beautiful princess, for that was how Murdo had come to think of her, had declared her intention to announce her choice of life partner. Murdo's mother being a Free Presbyterian didn't approve of Christmas or earrings and up until then he had missed out on the frankincense and myrrh. But this time she was prepared to make an exception, for she loved her son.

On the night everyone came to admire the radiant heiress and to listen to her speech. The Laird's son looked magnificent in his priceless tartan finery. Murdo stood in a dark corner in his borrowed shoes trying to hide his bare ankles. After they had all eaten of the best fallow hind and smoked salmon washed down with champagne and malt whisky, the princess came on stage to announce her engagement in the manner of the times.

"The Laird's son," she said, "is heir to a fortune. He has the means to keep me in the style to which I am accustomed, but I am afraid he is a bit of a creep. Murdo, on the other hand, is a penniless crofter and if I marry him I shall have to support him for the next 40 years until Santa Lawson comes along with the 40 million. Under the circumstances, much as I love Murdo, I have no choice but to marry the Laird's son."

Everyone except Murdo cheered like mad. The blonde may have looked dumb, but she was no mug. Boo, boo.

MORAL: The stupid and ugly can be made extremely attractive by money.

1984

24 FEBRUARY, 1984

MONDAY

Comhairle Castle, the White House, the Lubyanka ... all these names
are now out of date. Henceforth the edifice will be known as Taigh-
na-Cuts. Not to be confused with Taigh-na-Guts on the other side of
Sandwick Road, because Taigh-na-Guts, after much campaigning by the
inhabitants of Taigh-na-Cuts, is now a clean and sweet-smelling taigh.
Ironically, now that Taigh-na-Guts is being cleaned up, Taigh-na-Cuts
has started to give off a bad smell. There is thought to be something
rotten in the guts of Taigh-na-Cuts. We are optimistic, though, that a
thorough airing will soon clear the bad odour that, at present, lingers
over Sandwick Road.

TUESDAY

Education, it seems, is still held in great store by the majority of voters
in the Western Isles. Even in gentle North Lochs voices have been raised
in anger over the proposed closure of schools in our parish (if I dare use
the word "our" at the risk of having the chief paranoiac believing I mean
"my" parish).

So strong have feelings been running in Achmore that "our" councillor
felt the people of that village protested to the point of impertinence. It is
reassuring to hear a few adults are prepared to speak up in their children's
interests, but I find it difficult to believe the people of Achmore could
bring themselves to be impertinent.

Strangely enough, I notice most people have done little protesting
against cuts in art and music – the fields in which most of us as philistine
parents are least able to help our children. If pushed, many of us could
assist with multiplication tables, perhaps even with long division, but

how many parents know how to hold a chanter or draw a sheep? We are slipping back to the bad old ways. A few pennies can always be found for the basic elements that might make a child employable at 16, but money must not be spent on "luxuries" that could make the same child's journey through life more tolerable. These extras will again become the preserve of the few who can afford to buy them privately. Fortunately we still have one teacher in Leurbost school who will ensure the name of Jimmy Shand will live forever.

WEDNESDAY

Tonight I came back from a local Community Council meeting feeling more than a little depressed. It would appear there are a few in our midst still lacking in the smallest drop of that quality they would most like to project – Christian charity. Hypocrisy of an unusually high degree was in evidence.

A certain gentleman who shall be nameless finds it offensive that I feed my livestock on Sundays. Having been able to retire himself at an early age on a fat pension enhanced by the working of long Sunday hours, it takes a bit of nerve to complain about someone else putting to sea on a Sunday. I wouldn't be surprised if he feeds his own sheep on the Sabbath and takes a three-course dinner. Or are we up against that other old disease called "The-pleasure-of-having-enough-is-diminished-if-your-neighbour-has-anything".

Fortunately, the elders of the Free Church are not so narrow or blinkered as some would like to believe. Those of them I have encountered on stormy Sunday mornings realise I am not out for the fun of it. They have been understanding and helpful. Perhaps those who aspire to these positions, but haven't made it, have to be seen to be holier than thou.

THURSDAY

During the course of the next two weeks I intend to interview suitable candidates for the post of harbourmaster at "our" pier. I haven't advertised because I already have two or three men earmarked for the job. (Sure, isn't that the way it's done.)

There will be no salary, never mind double time for Sundays, but think of the prestige. We hope to supply a peaked gold-rimmed cap and a fine navy blue (what else?) uniform with as many rings on both sleeves as the lucky man can hold. The number will naturally depend on the length of arm, and it follows that a short-armed man with four rings will look and feel more important than a tall man with five. For this reason, although I don't want to discourage the likes of Seonaidh Fada, we will probably opt for the short variety. We all know the shorter the man the louder the voice, and a good harbourmaster has to be heard. Or, as a big friend of mine says, if the big fellows were as bad-tempered as the little fellows, there would be no little fellows left.

Prospective applicants, earmarked or otherwise, need not worry about having nothing to do – the moment a post is created work can be invented. (If Comhairle nan Eilean can have a museum curator surely we can have a harbourmaster.) And when the tide is out and the pier is high and dry, the lucky man can act as traffic warden.

Remember, time's running out. Apply now.

FRIDAY

Fourteen years of marriage behind us now, and I feel it incumbent upon me to pass a few tips to my younger friends about to embark on the hazardous journey.

The basis of a lasting relationship is respect. I'll give you a wee example. The other day, after a gruelling 12-hour shift, I phoned home and said: "I hope there is plenty of hot water. I want to have a bath." "My God," she said, "have you had an anonymous letter?"

On such a solid foundation of wifely respect so much can be built.

SATURDAY

That new watering-hole in Stornoway, the Rangers Supporters Club, is to be congratulated on the welcome given to thirsty strangers of whatever religious persuasion. Towards the weekend, when every other hostelry

in Stornoway was bolted and barred, three of us knocked on their door –
two Taoists and a Catholic. We were not only admitted, but treated
royally. I will never again listen to a bad word about this fine body of
men and women.

9 MARCH, 1984

A BALLAD OF MODERN TIMES

A Gang of Five, or was it Four,
Behind a secret Council door
Acting in suspicious manner
Said let us go and take a hammer
And together seal the fate
Of every little primary gate
To early education

A ha'penny less on the water rate
Will please the Secretary of State
Then he'll know we played the game
And we'll hide our burning shame
'Neath the innocent-sounding name
Of rationalisation

The Council knife was poised to drain
The lifesblood of the infant brain
In order for some time to gain
For pettyfoggers fat and vain
To scheme a way devoid of pain
To stay aboard the gravy train
Of rationalisation

Secure in the powerful voice of support
Of wealthy Stornoway business vote
And devious black theological backing
As ever in temporal charity lacking
They drew up the names of those for sacking
Through rationalisation

But they reckoned without the Carloway brick
Who goes by the name of old Calum Nick
Although he's taken his share of stick
He swayed to his feet and swore he would kick
Out rationalisation

And the bearded man from Ceose
Spared no effort for the cause
He parried the Convener's sword
With a cunning choice of word
And now we have a promise stored
For future generations

(Steady, baby, we're getting the rhythm now)

Now in these troubled times of strife
The common man was stirred to life—
Aye, and the common woman too,
Bremner, Pat, to name but two—
They formed a circle spread out in a bunch
And prepared the Matheson man to punch
Outweighed and outgunned by loudbeating gums
Expert at camouflaging badly-worked sums
With generalisations

But the crofting militia stood their ground
They traded punches pound for pound
Their arithmetic was found to be sound
And they easily carried the opening round
And won de-rationalisation

It is not my way to take personal credit
And our Leader may very well choose to edit
But my timely compassionate intervention
In the cause of relieving female tension
Must surely rate a risqué mention
Against rationalisation

While all this was taking place
Another Gang had lost much face
Intent on fighting Bannockburn
Hoping still the tide will turn
Against the stubborn mules who spurn
Nation-alisation

No shade of sadness no blush of shame
Over the face of their Leader came
But he thought it better before be spoke
At the risk of having his neighbours choke
To raise a cloud of Condor smoke
On rationalisation

His supporters ranted and vented their rage
With angry betters to the edition's page.
No one told him, he didnae ken —
If only someone had lifted a pen
Oor Donald would then have had the gen

On rationalisation
But we musn't forget the teachers who
When faced with the order of the shoe
Rallied around ungrateful brats
And railed against the dirty rats
And spat their venom in the oily vat
Of rationalisation

Here is a more charitable verse from our ten-year-old, who entered the spirit of the rhyming game. He lacks cynicism. Bad schooling, obviously.

Now Mr Matheson, Boss of the Isles,
Looked and rummaged in all his files
But not even he could find the key
That would open the schools for you and me.

Veritas XVI

20 APRIL, 1984

DILUAIN

'S fhada bho bha dùil agam barrachd feum a dhèanamh dhe na h-ochd àicearan fearainn tha eadar mi 's an cladach ris an can sinn a' chroit no "an lot". Aig aon àm bha leth-dhùil agam gur dòch' gum faighinn dà mhìle cearc, ach bha feagal orm gu leumadh Dòmhnall Beag Cheann Ùrnabhaigh. Ach nuair a thàinig IDP thuirt mi rium fhìn, Seo mo sheans. Cuiridh mi, arsa mise, a' chroit gu lèir fo asparagus. Agus mur b' e gun tàinig Eachainn Ruadh a chèilidh orm o chionn chealla-deug 's dòcha gu robh mi air tòiseachadh gu seo. A bhroinein bhochd, ars esan, 's e bualadh a bhios air cùl a' chinn, na dh'innis do mhàthair càil idir dhut? An cuala tu riamh mu dheidhinn a' chiad duine a thàinig dhachaigh an seo le speal le dà chas oirre? Thionail iad às a h-uile còrnair a dh'fhanaid air. An t-amadan, dh'èigh iad, bristidh e dhruim, agus dh'fhalbh iad dhachaigh

113

chun nan seann spealan aona-chasach a bha aca bho linn Nòah.

Cò aig tha fios nach robh iad ceart. 'S dòcha nach fhàsadh asparagus co-dhiù.

TUESDAY

These few words of the old Celtic warriors must add up to about 150. Not a lot, you might think: not a lot to be proud of. But do you realise these 150 words bring my lifetime's total to approximately 6,000? This grand total of 6,000 words doesn't seem much when set against Dòmhnall Donn's billion words for the *Stornoway Gazette*. I'm afraid it is a pretty thin folder compared with any other journalist's, alive or dead, you care to mention. Certain people I know write more than 6,000 words to the Inland Revenue each year and probably some women leave longer notes for their milkmen. Yet my 6,000 native words represent an achievement unequalled by anyone anywhere. Apart from their scholarly appeal and their unusual form, my collected Gaelic works are unique in a way that says a great deal about the perilous state of the language. The usual small prize can be won on Thursday by those who know what I'm talking about.

WEDNESDAY

Last week, you will recall, I asked what a certain group of British Airways passengers had in common. The all-too-obvious answer was that none of us had paid for our own tickets. Of course I don't travel much, so I thought that was something unusual. Since then I've been to the airport a few times and now I realise no one can afford to travel these days unless someone else is paying for his ticket. It is rare indeed to spot a passenger who isn't on expenses.

If the £36 it costs to fly to Inverness were reduced to £18, you would attract three times as many passengers. As I've been telling BA's management for years, even allowing for a slight increase in fuel consumption, they would immediately show a 30% increase in revenue. But what do the cretins do? Every time someone shouts "loss" they slap a fiver on the fare and lose five passengers. I guess they must be economists.

Ken Livingstone slashed fares on London Transport, persuaded people to use public transport and saved the GLC a fortune. Sadly, the ermine-clad lady ratepayers of Belgravia cannot stand the thought of proles travelling cheaply: they've told Herself to get rid of the GLC. Do you sometimes feel you're going mad?

THURSDAY

Following publication of the last *Free Press*, I am besieged by angry, mainly female, telephone callers. How dare I make disrespectful references to ministers of religion and members of the Labour Party? Listen, mate, it's a free country. Isn't it? We can say what we like about who we like. OK?

Anyway, in a couple of years' time I expect to be quite rich. Perhaps £20,000 a year. How could I stay in the Labour Party? When you are earning twenty grand it is time to support the Party that is going to protect you from the Russians and Social Security scroungers. Naturally you must prepare the ground in advance. Start moving to the right long before you have arrived. That way, when you do strike oil you can say: Honest, it's not my money; I'm here through conviction. And if the SNP don't deliver the goods there is always the Tory Party.

The choice of Church when you've made your pile can be very important. Remember you are a busy man: you don't want to waste your time on theological disputation. Martins Memorial sounds like the very place. I'm told the greatest problem faced by the elders of that kirk on a Sunday morning is which movie to show.

FRIDAY

Talking of God and godlessness, I find it reassuring that a minister of religion should spare the time to come and visit me personally, knowing as he does I don't "go out". I thought at first he Mafia had set the priests on me but now I realise your man was motivated purely by concern for my soul.

I appreciate this concern but I find it difficult to get across that my lack of faith is not a deliberate act of defiance, not a childish desire to shock or to be different. I can no more help my state of mind than my visitor can dilute his holiness. That we might one day in eternity meet again our friends seems to me, with the exception of some relations, an attractive prospect – an idea most people who have ever loved anyone would embrace if they could. But as someone said recently: "Emotionally I am with you but I cannot get my mind to follow."

13 JULY, 1984

MONDAY

Can there possibly be any other corner of the civilised world where the toiling masses spend their summer holiday hauling peat and shearing sheep? I doubt it. The heathen savages of the Third World have the sense to sit in the shade of the jacaranda sipping beer when the sun is at its zenith. The few remaining workers of industrial nations head for the Costa Del Sol to recharge their batteries on cheap wine. These people are not burdened with guilt and they will be found innocent on Judgement Day because they know nothing of sheep. Only here in the Fourth World do the inhabitants seek salvation through self-mortification and the profound misery that can only be attained in "the fank" on a hot day.

An acquaintance of mine tells me he sheared 340 sheep last week (I would call him a friend but for that same perversion). He couldn't straighten his back and he could walk only with great difficulty, but he wore the unmistakable smile of deep satisfaction. He had piled a few more inches on a worthless wool mountain and reduced his life-expectancy by several years. Consider how much better his time would have been spent fishing or setting ropes for mussel spat, helping to feed the nation.

I have not yet had time to contact my eminent colleagues to check the number of shearing heart attacks this year but I fear the usual savage toll has been taken. This Bo-Peepearachd will be the death of us all. Maybe then the land will get a chance to recover.

TUESDAY

In addition to having had to handle sheep, my so-called holiday was marred by several disturbing occurrences reported in the national news. The Royal Family seem determined to destroy forever the peace of the Sabbath. Our future King's polo pony runs amok on a Sunday morning, and I'm not surprised. While, at the same time, his father attends a shooting match in Wales. A shooting match, no less. With guns. And bullets: is it any wonder the Free Presbyterians feel compelled to transmit special prayers for Royalty. I only hope they are not too late.

As if that were not enough, an English archbishop – i.e. "an ecclesiastical dignitary one point holier than a bishop" – casts doubt on the Immaculate Conception. Poor fool. He need have no doubt on that score. There are innumerable recorded instances of this phenomenon in Ireland and the North-west of Scotland alone. Sure, I don't know how it happened: I never done nothing.

Remember Jodo Rem: "If I were a jolly archbishop / On Friday I'd eat all the fish up: / Salmon and flounders and smelts, / On other days everything else."

WEDNESDAY

My attention has been drawn to reports in the newspapers concerning a certain gentleman of our own medical profession who intends to produce a new "cure-all" at his base in Harris. He couldn't have picked a better spot to start his experiment. If he can come up with a medicine to keep blood flowing through the mutton-clogged arteries of the average Hearach, his success is assured.

Much as I admire this blatant piece of paddyquackery, I have to issue yet another writ. What is more, this time I can count on the support of NCC. Your man hopes to manufacture his drug from the oil of protected species such as seal and herring. And he has the gall to set up on my doorstep. Older readers of this page know very well I've been treating my patients for years with fish oil. I detest these interminable wranglings in the law courts, but I have no choice.

THURSDAY

Can anyone help Blodwen? Buried in an unusually heavy sack of fan mail this morning I find a letter from a lonely Stornoway spinster called Blodwen. She says she is driven to distraction by talk of all these North Lochs bachelors. She regrets Karachi passed her by and some grey-haired jogger I cannot identify.

I don't think the jogger is Alochie, and if, as you say, Blodwen, the New York ladies couldnae catch him, I don't give much for your chances despite your "fine legs and strong back". As far as Karachi is concerned, you probably had a narrow escape. He is today the proud father of an 18lb baby boy, and there are probably many more on the way, for he came from a tribe renowned for their fecundity.

You mention a preference for the athletic type, which narrows the field. I would recommend the Bosun, Murdie Siarach or the West End Tory – all extremely wealthy men and teetotallers of varying degree. As physical specimens they are past their best, but they waste no energy on unproductive pursuits such as jogging. If carefully nursed they probably have a good few years left in them yet.

You don't specifically mention marriage, but I am sure in these liberated times an arrangement could be concluded to suit all parties. Let me know how you get on.

FRIDAY

To Goathill Park for the Jock Stein Cup Final, and from there quickly to the Caberfeidh to celebrate a well-earned draw. (I presume the ref didn't record the two offside goals scored by Point in the last 10 minutes.)

It says much for the sporting nature of the Lochs team that they didn't complain when Point brought on a twelfth man after 15 minutes, but that is the way we are in Lochs. We play for the fun of it, although, if in 90 minutes you don't string three passes together, it is not much fun for the spectators.

SATURDAY

I must mention in passing, and I probably will very soon, today's fish supper in the fishing port of Stornoway, a sliver of frozen cod at £1.04 plus fat. Not many minutes earlier young Dr MacPherson had been telling me the Sgalpachs have to stop fishing for herring through lack of demand. If anyone can explain this madness to me he will receive a substantial reward.

I must as always give credit where credit is due. In this instance the County Hotel. Their fried herring bar lunch is fine and well-cooked, but I must point out that the normal quantity for a working man is four, not two.

29 JULY, 1984

MONDAY

When the air temperature reaches 20 Deg., as it has done on several days recently, the majority of white-skinned men, women and children are overcome by a peculiar madness. Instead of looking for the shade of an oak tree or the cool comfort of a public bar, they succumb to this strange urge to find a sandy beach and to expose their tender skins to the harmful rays of the sun. My own family are sorely afflicted with this madness, which is why I came to find myself on a crowded Bosta beach the other day without cover or relief from the hot sun, and I hate it. Sand gets everywhere. The sun burns my sensitive skin, no doubt increasing the risk of catching prickly heat, skin cancer and a host of other deadly diseases. Only mad dogs and Englishmen used to go out in the midday sun; now all the white races do it.

If you take a walk through Africa you'll find the black man has the common sense to sit in the shade of a tree when the sun is at its zenith. In the Orient the natives avoid direct sunlight like the plague. And so they should. Another couple of summers like this one and our women will look like these Australians you sometimes meet with dried-up, wrinkled hides. As it is, if I took my wife to South Africa nowadays, we would have to use separate entrances. Of course there is a lot of Spanish blood there (great-grandmother from Harris).

TUESDAY

Maximum temperature 23.7 and do you know what I see all around me? Seventy-year-old men in heavy boilersuits shearing sheep. Now this is really asking for it. I would urge my medical colleagues to get together immediately and put a stop to this crazy behaviour. Better they should spend the day in the pub. And it is not just the old men. One contemporary of my own who suffers from hypertension sheared 200 sheep between two nightshifts. I'm saying no more.

WEDNESDAY

One class of gentleman you will never catch shearing sheep is the Glasgow Fairy – you know, these fellows who assume everyone is on holiday when they are. They do a lot of roaming and visiting with white plastic bags. They tarry all night and let their hearts be merry. You will probably have heard they were stuck in Ullapool for two days when the ferry broke down. This was of course no accident.

The variable pitch prop was deliberately "fixed" by a friend of mine who says he has never had a decent night's sleep during the last fortnight in July with the ructions raised by the Fairies. Unfortunately the people of Ullapool hired expert engineers at great expense to get the boat repaired and rid of them as soon as possible. And believe me, the people of Ullapool do not go to expense, great or small, without good reason. Still, two days' peace are better than none.

THURSDAY

For two weeks now I've been acutely aware of a lightening burden, almost as if I'd got rid of a raging toothache or prickly heat. Try as I might, I could not put my finger on the cause. Then someone told me Murdie Siarach is on holiday in New Zealand.

Certain people who are close to him suggested he had gone to buy

South Island but I know different. He is much too attached to his loot to lay out that kind of money. You see, I know what he is up to.

Many local pundits had him marked as a confirmed bachelor but my investigations reveal he has been engaged for years, to a big black Maori with a bone through her nose, and he hasn't got the nerve to take her home to Sleepy Hollow. And then his political party is notorious for its racial prejudice. What can the man do? Perhaps this time he'll pick up the courage.

FRIDAY

At enormous personal cost I took my wife out to the Caberfeidh. After a beautiful meal at home before we left, we were splendidly entertained by the Boys of the Lough. I am not sure if there isn't something blasphemous about the title of one of their tunes – "The Mason's Apron". Who are they to make fun of that most beautiful lambskin symbol of innocence?

Among the audience I found a lost tribe I'd been searching for since 1965. Do you remember them? Big, strong, Aran-sweatered, pint-drinking. Wild Rover-singing girls. They liked to stand at the bar in those days but now, approaching their 40th year, they realise they look better sitting down.

Wee Alex nearly married a few of them but they were a restless lot. I see many of them are still either unaccompanied or attached to timid-looking little men. There but for the grace of G. go so many of us.

10 AUGUST, 1984

ONE SUNDAY NIGHT IN THE LIFE OF A SALMON FARMER
Woke at 3am after two hours of fitful slumber. Bathed in sweat. Red spots in front of eyes. Red spots on belly of fish. Maggie snoring gently, blissfully unaware of crisis. Better not to tell her until certain. Certain things a man must face alone.

Red spots on 90 per cent of fish. Has to be (according to Jonathan Shepherd's book, page 151) vibriosis aquillarum. Sounds deadly.

Unable to concentrate. Trains in skull running in opposite directions threatening to crash and explode feeble brain. Better get up and walk floor for a bit. Red spots on sheepskin rug.

Downstairs for another browse in Dr Shepherd's bible. Might be better to open the other Bible occasionally. Pace around cold kitchen floor. Bare foot in cat's milk. Troubles never come singly.

Grey dawn throws enough light on book to make out gruesome print of furunculosis. Holy Moses. Surely not. Couldn't be that. Heavy mortalities. Debtors' prison till teeth rot. Wife and children begging on the street.

Dive to cupboard for slug of gin. Calm down, now. That's a bit better. Swallow pride and go for second opinion. Perhaps the local vet? No, they say Doctor MacIntosh is better. But, like me, good with trees but no experience with fish. May call the High Priest of Fish Pathology, Ted Needham. On third thoughts, go straight to the top: spare no expense. Call Sandy Boots. Have to wait for morning, though, Another swig. Doze through half-hour of further nightmare. Red spots on gin bottle.

Five am. Mind in turmoil. Another look in book, page 171 this time. Must settle for vibriosis after all. Common in eels, hence name. Aquillarum. Internal bleeding. Liquification of the kidneys. Dear Lord, is there any hope? Should have settled for poultry or a few bullocks. Sheep, even. To treat or not to treat? That is the question. Couldn't sell for 10 weeks afterwards. Perhaps should wait hopefully for polar front and drop in temperature. Wishful thinking – temp still rising for six weeks. Maybe too late then.

Fantastic images. Picture on wall beginning to resemble bacterial kidney disease. Could be horrors? Page 172 says vibriosis bacterium similar to cholera in hums. Holy Mary, Mother of God. Hope the old fellow didn't eat that one. No choice now; have to treat.

Consult tables. Two hundred kilos of oxytetracycline. Cost an arm and a leg, but cannot be helped. Enough to save the entire diseased population of Uganda. This is no time for moral qualms. Loans to be met.

Call partner to share misery. Refuses to be alarmed. Incurable optimist.

Totally irresponsible. Call Bosun. He's worse. Says probably a touch of measles. God love us all. Who will rid me of these troublesome spots?

In desperation dig out manuscript and do 50 minutes of panicky work on The Novel. Unlikely to solve financial problems, but perhaps sufficiently boring to win critical acclaim. Who knows, perhaps a small step towards immortality. Glad I planted all these trees now. Important to live in their memories if one has to end it all. Drastic selfish action, that. Lack of moral fibre. Also complicates insurance claims.

More gin. Fall into short coma. Nine am. Drag weary body to surgery to start the day's work. Humans can be difficult, too. They talk too much. Try to force you to diagnose their imagined illness. But at least they talk.

MONDAY

Financial and all other worries dissolve at the thought of seeing the gorgeous Princess Margaret tomorrow. Will stay up all night if necessary to ensure good view of this symbol of all that is best in British life. Instructed my staff to gather mussels, oysters, lobsters, salmon and prawns, with view to presenting same to Her Most Gracious Royal Highness. Am not without hope of invitation to dine on board the Royal Yacht. Have even painted kitchen table in case she decides to call on me.

TUESDAY

I didn't feel it was right to go and meet the Princess in so black a mood, so I went along to the Caberfeidh to be lifted by Norman Maclean. I thought for some reason that one manic depressive might be able to help another. And help me he certainly did, but – although I didn't have time for a thorough analysis – perhaps I was wrong to place Norman in the manic depressive category. (You know what I mean by manic depressive – one day Freddie Starr, the next a Free Church deacon.)

In fact Norman is in such robust health, mentally and physically, it sometimes becomes unbearable for him. He feels he must, from time to time, go in for drastic self-mutilation.

He has some good stories on this tour – and all true, of course. Especially the one about Donald Macdonald the Spy – the social structure of an island explained in one short, funny line. Not that I would repeat it here even if I could remember a joke: instead I recommend you go along, pay your three quid and listen to him. If you doubt my assessment of his physical fitness, go and see him play the bagpipes lying on his back.

I feel sufficiently cheerful now to entertain the Princess. I'm only sorry she missed Norman last night.

7 SEPTEMBER, 1984

TUESDAY

All last week a grim struggle for power raged across our planet's stratosphere. Somewhere between the heavens above and the earth beneath the disembodied spirits of two long dead Ranish peasants fought a desperate battle for control of the elements. But to begin at the beginning. It all started here on earth – a conflict of interests between Coinneach Iain and me. Coinneach is a sheep- and cattleman who needs dry weather to make winter fodder. I, on the other hand, wanted three days of continuous rain to cleanse my charges of lice. An insignificant dispute, you might think, and not something over which to end a lifelong friendship, but business is business. I knew Coinneach would not hesitate to invoke the powers of his dead ancestors, so naturally I had to do the same. In this way did Dòmhnall 'Ain Chaluim 'Ain and Prabag enter the fray.

Prabag, my maternal grandmother, knew where to find a certain well under a certain hill and she had the 'cnocan'. Of that there can be no doubt. The officer Coinneach's father and son of Dòmhnall 'Ain Chaluim 'Ain tells a story of when, as a young man, he studied the black arts under the guidance of Prabag.

One day when the larder was empty but when fishing conditions were far from favourable (a cold easterly), Prabag allowed the young 'officer' to accompany her on a rock fishing expedition. He was allocated a position on one side of Tughair and she perched on the other. But before she made her first cast, the officer reports, she performed what sounds not unlike a sword dance, stepping nimbly back and fore across the rod along its full length. One hour later Prabag had landed seven fine wrasse and a few codling. The officer hadn't had a single bite.

I could give you several examples as proof of her immense power but I think that is enough. Dòmhnall 'Ain Chaluim 'Ain was considered only average in this respect. Events in the last few days demonstrate quite clearly that Prabag has lost none of her supernatural influence since crossing over to the other side.

A depression with a vigorous occluded front was moving in from the Atlantic promising to bring us much rain. At the same time a developing ridge of high pressure to the north threatened, with some help from Dòmhnall 'Ain Chaluim 'Ain, to push the rain belt south of us across Central Scotland. For three days they fought each other with neither giving any ground. Finally the ridge collapsed and the front moved north across the Clisham. Prabag had won. To ask for the assistance of paranormal forces is not something I like to do, but I think you'll agree this was an emergency. People often say to me, "You are a lucky man," but I know it is not luck.

WEDNESDAY

We must act and act now if we are to preserve our freedom. According to the learned and far-seeing Col David Hickey, brother of the notorious *Daily Express* gossip columnist, our island fortress is open to infiltration by KGB agents, moles and subversive elements of every alien creed. Our immediate task is to identify them, expose them for what they are, and then shoot them. If peace is to be preserved, we who are charged with that responsibility must arm ourselves to the teeth. Dig out the old 303s and don't hesitate to use them. If you suspect your neighbour is in the pay of a foreign power, blast him. The time for talking is past; we may already be too late.

Identification is never easy, so I will set down a few simple guidelines. Do not waste your time looking for infiltrators in the ranks of CND.

Neither will you find them among the bearded supporters of socialist parties. They are too clever for that. Your genuine ten carat spy is a smart fellow. He is much more likely to be a pillar of the Establishment – a clean-shaven, well dressed member of the professional classes. Your accountant, your bank manager, or your friendly policeman. Yes, perhaps your church deacon or even your big brother. Beware at all times of anyone who is given to voicing loud support for the extreme right. If you stop to think about it, you will not find bank robbers going about their non-felonious business with nylon stockings pulled over their heads. They are not daft. Neither is the average Russian or American spy.

So what do we do first? We form a secret defence force, that's what we do. A modern Home Guard. Every man will be trained to kill with one blow. Look closely at your neighbour with the three-piece suit and the CB radio. Be especcially watchful of taxi drivers. Any suspicious transmission, let him have it on the back of the neck. Peace, brother. Remember you've done it for peace. Needless to say, you will not, for obvious reasons, hear any more of our new Home Guard.

THURSDAY
On the subject of national security, I am glad to see we can still rely on Sir Keith Joseph to come up with a good one. The Mad Monk, as his enemies call him, is clever enough to realise that the most dangerous enemies of the state are at large in the classroom. He wants to see more patriotic history taught in our schools. He has not specified exactly from which date he wants to start re-writing history. Perhaps we can assume 2,000 years ago, or so ...

"These things were done in Lancashire beyond Birmingham, where John was baptising ... Jesus turned and saw them following, and saith unto them, what seek ye? They said unto him, Rabbi, where dwellest thou? He said unto them, come and see. They came and saw where he dwelt, and abode with him that day in his home town of Canterbury in the county of Kent ... The day following Jesus would go forth into Yorkshire, and findeth Philip, and saith unto him, behold an Englishman indeed, in whom is no guile. Nathanael saith unto him, whence knowest thou me? Jesus answered and saith unto him, before that Philip called thee, when thou wast in Oxford, I saw thee …"

I cannot see the Welsh and Scottish Nats letting him away with that: there will have to be several versions. Dear me, there is so much re-writing to be done. Will we ever get to the beating back of the Roman Legions in the English Channel, never mind the defeat of the Russian Bolsheviks?

14 SEPTEMBER, 1984

MONDAY

I'm sorry. I know I'm late. The deadline was two hours ago but, you see, it's like this. I must, absolutely must, watch *Coronation Street*. First Leslie – who until recently only watched obscure BBC2 French movies – told me what an excellent production *Coronation Street* is, then some other highbrowed critic on Channel 4 digressed to mention this "wonderfully written long-running soap opera".

What could I do? Pride, vanity, call it what you like, but if there is a new cult on the go I want to be in on it. No one wants to be pointed out on the Aignish cocktail circuit as a crofting yokel who has not grasped the significance of this essentially popular, yet meaningful, expression of so much that is worthwhile in working-class relationships and aspirations.

Which is why I am at this moment almost totally engrossed in "it". I say "almost" because a part of my attention and energy is diverted towards my notebook, wherein, from time to time, I jot down what I judge will be interpreted as intelligent observation. Pity the *Street* fan who has the misfortune to encounter me tomorrow. His threadbare cloak of so-called analytical comment I will shred contemptuously with my scalpel-sharp rapier of rehearsed wit.

"A window on a hitherto hidden subculture … cosy portrayal of neighbourly provincial co-existence … A *Coronation Street* couldn't be done in Gaelic, y'know. It has, how shall I put it … no soul. Celtic consciousness does not sink … But that is beside the point. Yes, yes, I'll grant you that, it's all there – the council house mentality, semi-detached preoccupation with trivia: there is a certain charm in its simplicity, but, I say, old chap, is it art? I mean, is it really art?"

Enter noisy offspring: "Can I switch over, I want to see a sports quiz?"

"Do you mind. I am watching *Coronation Street*."

"That's *Crossroads* you've got, you old fool."

My God. The shame of it. What a narrow escape. Can you imagine the smart set sniggering as I expounded? What would Leslie have thought?

TUESDAY

I realise only too well what I have unleashed on the poor unsuspecting radio audience of this tiny but proud Scottish nation. And I apologise in advance. For the next six days until the next *Free Press* appears you will hear nothing on your receivers but this latest *Coronation Street* cult that has the Highlands and Islands in its grip. One hardly dares open one's mouth these days, knowing, as one does, one's words will be plagiarised by the BBC and broadcast as news five times every day for a week.

Take for example my little filler last week on the Uist–Harris mink traps. I only slipped it in to fill a gap left by an advert withdrawn by some monarchist, yet it became a major BBC news item. What the effect will be if they ever catch a mink does not bear contemplation. The guga–Greenpeace story, which I thought better to suppress at this time last year, is still rolling. Ten days later, after every broadcasting station in Scotland had milked it dry, old Tom Weir manages to hang a thousand words on it in the *Glasgow Herald*. I have written to the BBC (and I expect to be paid for it) suggesting it would be cheaper to broadcast directly from the Old School, Breakish.

Here is a good one for you. I was walking down the road the other day when I met a man leading a horse. The horse is 16 years old and the last in Lewis. Ring 86443 for interviews.

WEDNESDAY

If you think you detected a note of bitterness in yesterday's notes, you were quite right, and there is a good reason for it: I did not receive my two gugas this year. I thought I did but I didn't.

Let me explain. A parcel arrived with two guga-like objects which Maggie took to be the real thing. Despite several boilings they still refused to yield to the carver. Neither could they be torn apart nor chopped with an axe, never mind chewed. A painstaking investigation revealed that the two gugas were Bill Lawson's discarded trainers. There is a good wee story there but of course I cannot retail it, knowing your man will be pestered for years by the BBC.

THURSDAY

The *Free Press* has been on the streets for only three hours, yet already 75 crofters have phoned to claim their two million quid. Naturally I suspected some skullduggery. And sure enough, the Skyemen had been at it – cutting ears off stray sheep and forging their own marks. When our inspectors called to check several claims, homemade ears were still bleeding profusely. Regrettably I must withdraw last week's offer of two million until we can devise some method of making the game foolproof.

What hurt me even more was the number of Skyemen who laughed and jested unmercifully about last week's drawing of a sheep's head. For years, you see, Skyemen have made mock of the Lewis sheep with its sparse straggly wool and fleshless legs. "Where did you find last week's model? Ha, ha, ha. Imported from Skye, was it?" And much more of the same. The ignorant fools didn't realise that was a drawing of a post-IDP sheep (with fur right down to its ankles).

FRIDAY

My admiration for the strong men of Ness I have never tried to hide. Their achievement on the football field – at home and overseas – deserves praise and applause.

But, ask yourselves this: could they have done it on a diet of cormorant or corncrake? I doubt it. When the conservationists arrive in Ness, show them the cup. Fill it with guga-soup and pass it amongst them. They will then "waste not their time in windy argument", but let the matter drop.

21 SEPTEMBER, 1984

MONDAY

It was 12.30 BST on Sunday morning when they broke the news of little Hooray Henry to me. Several friends had gathered to join in the festivities, knowing I would be very excited and likely to break out the malt. Hooray, hooray, we all shouted. Everyone turned to his neighbour and shook hands, all crying with sheer happiness. It was almost like New Year's Eve, only much jollier, naturally, because we were all so thrilled at the thought of another gorgeous little royal bairn.

Among my visitors was Allan MacDonald. The Piper of Glenuig. A strange coincidence, you might think, that he should be present when we heard of the royal birth. Too strange? Yes, that's what I thought. Perhaps it was more good fortune. Perhaps it was divine guidance.

In any case, out came the pipes, and Allan was about to strike up when he noticed the time. Formerly it wouldn't have bothered him, but since he had arrived on Lewis on Friday he had developed a light-to-moderate cùram (if it gets heavier he'll probably burn his bagpipes). However, I reminded him we were on BST; reassured, Allan piped young Henry into his first Sabbath. He played a tune not often heard on bagpipes, *Rule Britannia*, and we all stood up and saluted. There was not a dry eye in the house. I feel I can safely claim that no one present will ever forget the intensity of emotion that threatened to overwhelm us on the night we heard of little Henry.

TUESDAY

Many of you will be saddened to hear that as you read this the editor is at the same time reading my letter of resignation. Although I have enjoyed keeping a diary for the last few years, the truth is the *Free Press* can no longer afford me. They must now, I'm sorry to say, look for an English-writing diarist because there's one guy here who will never again scribble as much as a note to the milk person in that cheap language.

Seall seo, fichead mìle not sa bhliadhna. What do you think of that, then? Amazing the number of people who can read that although they couldn't speak a word when it was neither popular nor profitable, and who still probably couldn't give you the Gaelic for sea urchin.

Because of its increasing rarity, every word written in Gaelic is now worth ten times its English equivalent. I think I did my little bit to bring this about when I stopped writing Gaelic several years ago. We had some evidence that too many people were trying to read the language. It was threatening to become popular, and that would never do; down would come the rates. But now I must start again. I have to prove I can do it if I am to hold any hope of getting interviewed for the 20-grand CNAG job.

WEDNESDAY

Yesterday my future looked good. Twenty thousand a year, and plenty of time to pursue hobbies. But, alas, I have bad news. I have it on high authority that a certain gentleman who didn't speak the language when it was neither popular nor profitable has been heavily tipped for the job. Dash it all, I wouldn't mind; but he's not even a Freemason nor a Hibernian. All is not yet lost, though. I know as many important and influential people as he does – perhaps more.

THURSDAY

Talking of Masons, you may have noticed we have had a lot of bad press in recent times. I have personally no doubt whatsoever that this carefully orchestrated attack on our charitable and worshipful lodge is a fiendish Roman plot. This present Tory Pope has been, in my opinion, much too outspoken in his criticism of our worshipful brotherhood. He should take care, and remember what happened to one of his predecessors. And the same goes for the Wee Free critics who write to the *Stornoway Gazette* trying to identify our worshipful lodge as the antichrist. My advice to both these aggressors is to keep their traps shut if they know what's good for them.

I feel I can honestly say, for myself and most of my brothers on The Square, that we would never use the Handshake to secure a job. Of course I cannot speak for every single Mason; there is no organisation without its black sheep. There may very well be one or two who have used the brotherhood for their own ends, but all I can say is that they are no more Masons than Maxwell is a socialist.

In any case, I think all you critics are driven by envy and nosiness, and if we want to ponce about with our left breasts exposed and trousers rolled up, that is our business.

FRIDAY

It has now been made very clear to me by the inner cabinet of the Gaelic Mafia that I have no chance of the big job. But I don't care any more. I've formed a splinter group, CNAP (short for CNAP Mòr Airgid). Our chief aim will be to rescue Gaelic from the middle-classes and give it back to those who spoke it when it was neither P nor P. There will be a branch in every village doing all sorts of devious work to destroy CNAG. Everyone, and not just the big man, will receive £21,000 a year. The only qualification we insist on is that applicants should have been born in a black-house.

SATURDAY

As you know, I've been praying for rain. A dangerous business, praying, when you're not familiar with the technicalities of transmission. If you're not careful when asking for rain, you could end up with a 40 days and 40 nights job. I think perhaps I used the wrong language – Gaelic and Hebrew. Clearly, you are more likely to get a little of what you need if you pray in English.

19 October, 1984

BLOODY FORELAND, DONEGAL — TUESDAY

Looking west to Tory Island isn't all that different to the view from North Lochs across to Cromore if you close an eye. The faces you pass on the road are very similar. As a matter of fact, I spoke to a small red-haired man yesterday whom I took to be one of bodaich bheag Leumrabhaigh, but he turned out to be a member of the Inishbofin clan.

Like the cousins in Lemreway, everyone has red hair. Their Gaelic is slightly different but the difference tends to evaporate after a few snorts of Bushmills. The people of Tory Island are a much darker race, almost as black as the men of Scalpay. I didn't meet anyone from Tory this time; like the Sgalpachs, they don't mix or come to the mainland much. Whether they are as suspicious of mainlanders as the Sgalpachs I cannot say yet. What we can be sure of, though, is that they are not half as rich as the Sgalpachs. And certainly, they are not as well off as the mainlanders of Donegal.

When I last visited Gortahork, Donegal, 18 years ago I would say the mass of the population were as poor if not poorer than their counterparts in the Western Isles (outside Stornoway, of course). Their standard of housing was, if you can imagine it, lower than our own in Ranish, and their services were on a par with Rhenigidale. When I drove into Donegal the other day my first conclusion was that they must all have won the football pools.

While we were building ordinary dwellings with a little help from the Government – and the boys who were lifting table houses on their own heads – the men of Donegal were building villas and mansions. The transformation is astonishing. You can now go for a long walk round the average house here without going outside. And they still have Gaelic and peat and cattle. I suspect the reason we no longer have cattle is that they cannot be toilet-trained. And of course there will soon be trouble with planning permission for manure heaps.

I find it difficult to understand the layout of the Gaeltacht areas. One minute you are in an all-English village, the next one doesn't use that language at all. It is as if you were suddenly transported from Matheson Road to Mangersta.

YESTERDAY

I drove some 200 miles round the country of Donegal, all the while uneasily aware of something missing. There were any number of sheep on the roads and tractors hauling peat to make me feel at home. Yet I was very conscious of a missing familiar ingredient. Maggie was first to think of it – no IDP fences. Hardly a new fence post to be seen between Fanad Head and Burtonport. There must surely be an opportunity for some deal here. Could we perhaps swop half our new EEC fencing for some of their livestock? We could throw in half a million sheep because it strikes me they are falling behind with bullrushes.

To get to a subject much more interesting than sheep, yesterday I visited a huge salmon farm in Mulroy Bay. The following is an urgent message in code for the boys in the loch: S2s – 800 gm. Second autumn mature fish 12 lbs. Where are we going wrong? Please take immediate steps to remedy. Will contact soon.

Sadly, the salmon farm is owned by a big Norwegian concern. I have also since learned that many of the mansions I noticed yesterday are owned by retired gentlemen from without. Chan ann an aon àite tha 'n t-olc.

Down in Burtonport at the fishermen's co-op I found your man Eugene Hannigan trying to out-MacPherson MacPherson – packing dogfish for a long journey to wherever they eat these things. He obviously picked up a few tips on his visit to the Stornoway co-op.

You may well wonder what I am doing in Donegal when most of my cronies are making merry at the Mod in Inverness. It is very simple. My wife, who has years of nursing experience, considered my liver would not stand one more Mod.

Mar sin leibh an dràsta, agus feuch gum bi sibh ciallach, Eachann.

26 OCTOBER, 1984

MONDAY

Did I ever complain about MacBraynes' catering? If I did I'm sorry. I realise now that as ferries go they are somewhere near the middle of the league table. At the bottom is the Sealink *Antrim Princess* that transports people from Stranraer to Larne on a Sunday in much the same fashion as slaves were ferried last century. Second class passengers might as well be shackled together. There is only enough deck space for two people to be sick at a time.

And after they've been to the canteen they need to be sick. Catering staff are all Prods and are trying to poison second-class passengers. Or they are all Catholic and are trying to do away with travelling soldiers. Mercifully, the voyage only lasts two and a half hours, and the Guinness is good.

TUESDAY

Talking of Guinness, you should bear in mind if you're ever going to the Republic that it costs £9.20 a gallon. Petrol is only £2.80.

There is a desperate imbalance there. Some cars will do 50 miles to the gallon, whereas few drivers can manage 30 miles on a gallon of Guinness. I have pointed this out to their Bord Fáilte and expect to see some rationalisation when I return next year.

I also complained about the roads in Donegal. Heavy swell everywhere. (I wonder if DHM ever had a contract there.) Your man said: "I know, they are wild altogether; if we had new roads we'd be flying."

WEDNESDAY

If you ask me, there are too many fast new roads nowadays. The trouble with this is you don't really go places anymore. You nearly go there.

You very nearly see Stirling, you pass over Glasgow, fly past Kilmarnock and Ayr at 70 miles an hour – which is a good thing for the man in a hurry, but bad for those of us who lapse into dwams. "What was that sign back there?" "I think it said 'Derry'," says she. "We're on the wrong road, then." "What, again?" says she again.

You don't really have to go into Derry on your way to the border if you take the right road. I didn't, and ended up in the Bogside. It would take too much time on the telephone to try to convey the gloom and hopelessness of the Bogside. I find city slums depressing at the best of times, but this was a deeper than normal depression. The huge murals of black-hooded IRA figures are very artistic but chilling. It didn't strike me as a place in which to loiter too long.

THURSDAY

And what is the war all about? When the first rumblings started in 1968 it was all very simple and easy to understand. Catholics in Belfast only wanted to be treated like Protestants, given the same chance of a job and the same voting rights. If the fat cats of the Royal Avenues had had any sense of self-preservation it could all have been avoided. They didn't seem to possess the old Tory cunning. They couldn't see that by giving a little they could maybe avoid some day having to give it all.

If the powers-that-be had exercised a little common sense and "fair play to your man", the average rebel singer would perhaps be happy to sing his rebel songs under the Union Jack. It is certainly likely he would not now be trying to bomb his way into a Republic with an inferior health service, £1,000 a year road insurance and a £1.15 pint. They're not all fools.

FRIDAY

Having more or less solved the Irish problem in six days, I returned to Scotland on the *Galloway Princess* – a clean, spacious, luxurious boat. Why a luxury liner one day and a cattle boat the next? I really cannot understand these people.

SATURDAY

Having taken the son and heir to Parkhead last Saturday, I thought to complete his education we should go to Ibrox today. At least there is no chance of him getting lost in the crowd at Ibrox. To make up for the lack of noisy support, Rangers tried to compensate with noisy music from very loud speakers. Rangers management seem to be under the impression that anti-Celtic songs will compensate for poor play – even when they are playing the likes of wee Dumbarton.

Part of the fun these days, and a great challenge, is to try and come back from a football match with your car in one piece. The little street urchins of Parkhead and Ibrox have a lucrative protection racket going. They offer to watch your car, and I would advise you to pay. For these little buggers have a great sense of humour.

One man I know said: "No, thanks, you don't need to watch my car. I have an Alsatian in the back." When he returned after the match he found all four tyres flat and a note on the windscreen saying: "Get your dug to blow your tyres up."

9 NOVEMBER, 1984

MONDAY

This diary of a modern crofter is brought to you this Monday morning with great difficulty. The words I search for to describe my lethargic and apathetic state of mind are difficult to find, even if I could be bothered. And if that was not enough, every few minutes Leslie looks over my shoulder and says: "Is that all you've done?" Ten years ago I would have strangled him but as I get older I become increasingly calm and tolerant. Anyway, it is all too much of an effort. And he would probably take too long to strangle.

Ist, 'ere 'e comes again. Plod, plod, flip, flop. "And another fing, 'Ec, you always promise us more next week but it never materialises. Lawsuits and the Queen Mum's gambling, that sort of fing …"

One of these days I will finish him off. But he does have a point there. I never do tell you the outcome of my court cases. To tell the truth, the few I've pursued to a conclusion have gone against me. One grows accustomed to sneering mock-concerned questions from the bench: "Do you wish time to pay? Is it too much to hope we won't see you here again for some time? I hope your tap-dancing will be none the worse for your fall from the Lewis Hotel bar on the night in question."

Never a genuine humane enquiry such as we often heard from the late lamented procurator fiscal, Colin Scott (Senior). Like when one travelling person attacked another travelling person with his bagpipe: "Were you not afraid you'd damage the drones, man?" No one cares nowadays. Thirty pounds and a year on your bike if you have the civility to accept any hospitality at all, and never mind if you're in poor health. As for the civil actions I have to raise from time to time, I always take pity on the enemy before the day of judgement and settle for peanuts. Possibly another excuse for not being bothered. But who cares.

TUESDAY

Talking of civil law, it is a very foolish man who does not take care of the formalities, who does not look to the future as it will inevitably be seen one day through the beady eyes of the legal profession. Look at my own predicament this last week. There was the old fellow in hospital awaiting a trip to the operating theatre and all the relations could think of bringing him were grapes, orange juice and tobacco. Not one of the so-called caring cousins had the presence of mind to enquire if he'd made a Will. I wouldn't like you to think me callous, but many's the poor innocent heir has had his inheritance swallowed by that ravenous beast the Revenue Inspector. Please believe me, the Last Will and Testament is not a subject I raise with any pleasure in a surgical ward, but the old fellow understood: "Bring me a Public Notary," he said. "Try to find one who doesn't look like an undertaker." I like a man who can joke on his way to the table.

WEDNESDAY

Due to the hospitalisation of the old fellow, I have now spent two consecutive Saturdays manhandling sheep. Hauling them off trailers and back onto trailers, lifting them into a bath and, worst of all, chasing them in wellingtons through high heather and dragging them vast distances by the horns. Those of you with any medical training will, of course, have realised that if I were the typical office slob I would by now be up there on the machine beside the old fellow. Which is why I have always tried to keep in shape. The body must be treated with respect.

Twenty sheep, like golf, is a good hobby, as long as they don't get in the way of real work. I've often said this to the brother, but what's the use? Better to send them to Ethiopia and buy a mussel raft. But 300 sheep! Now, that is a different matter altogether.

Tommy and Coinneach, the last two real crofters in North Lochs, tell me they expect to earn a small fortune from sheep and cattle in the coming year. I'm not sure, though, that their decision to pay £600 for two Suffolk tups was a sound idea. They look much too pretty, these rams, with their tightly-permed curls. They could very well turn out to be a bit peculiar. I suppose we won't know until next Spring. And the IDP appointment of a ram's hairdresser is going a bit too far.

THURSDAY

Two Gaelic programmes on the same date, one in the evening and one in the middle of the night. You have to hand it to your man Neil Fraser. He must be a powerful and influential man to get an early evening slot. But I must confess to being a bit disappointed he didn't offer me a job. I can only think this is because he knows I'm in love with his wife.

Not that I could have accepted in any case. I have now settled my long-lasting dispute with Grampian and accepted their latest offer of £200 per minute. I expect Maggie will also be back on 'Crann Tara' next week. Her little boy will be three weeks old and surely, if he is a true Sgalpach, ready to travel to Aberdeen for the money.

I worried a little when APC moved upstairs to his new £48,000-a-year post, but I needn't have done. Your man D J Macdonald has, you know, warmth. One of the advantages of being transmitted in the middle of the night is that the other channels have closed down. Another is that the critics are usually drunk by that time and easy to please. 'Prosbaig', on the other hand, has to compete with the silly English programmes that are so popular with the undiscerning masses. But it is good – a pretty fair imitation of *Crann Tara*. Kenny MacIver, now that he is not in so much of a hurry, has developed into a smart but sensitive interviewer. I had to promise I'd say that to get on his new Friday evening programme from Radio nan Eilean. That is the way things work in this business.

FRIDAY
Any minute now I expect to hear old Jungle-Brow has been re-elected to the White House. This doesn't worry me as much as it used to because anyone who is so obviously incompetent and senile will not be left to make decisions on his own. Which means the U S of A will be governed by committee.

Again, I have not allowed time to reveal the QM's betting scandal. Maybe next week.

23 NOVEMBER, 1984

Dear Jackson,
Words cannot describe my disappointment at your decision to buy a house in the Isle of White. I'm sure your ancestors in Arran are at this moment stirring restlessly in their graves.

Why, man? Why? They haven't even got IDP there. And isn't the place full of retired public school boys? It sounds to me very much like the sort of place you could catch AIDS in. Would you not have done better to have settled here and taken a chance on the cùram?

By my reckoning that is nine years you've been relieving the Arabs of their ill-gotten spondulies. It's a great pity you didn't come here: I could have shown you so many ways of investing your money. The Isle of White, for God's sake. I'm sorry to keep harping on about it but it just isn't you. You, the man who owned the only horse in Barotzeland. (By the way, the reason for this open letter is that I refuse to put pen to paper these days unless I get paid for it.) Is it not strange that men like yourself who might have been able to cope with our harsh unyielding habitat tend to go to places like the Isle of White while your man and others like him are attracted to our islands.

I have this theory – I cannot remember if I told you before – that we on these islands are the victims of a nasty conspiracy. The powers-that-be are gradually encouraging their least desirable mainland residents to migrate to the Hebrides, until one day the indigenous population will find their presence unbearable and leave. Then of, course, they can do what they like with the place. Clever, what?

I've learned quite a few tricks since I started this journalism, and I'll give you a good tip now. Remember the plans you made to sail down the Zambesi from Angola to the sea, then write a book and make a fortune from it, but never got round to it? Well, it doesn't matter. You can still write the book as if you had done it. That is what journalists do all the time. Smart boys!

Thanks for the photographs of your family. Kate seems to be wearing well and the boys look very much like yourself, but I always think that doesn't matter as long as they are healthy. My own family, I am pleased to say, are fine and Maggie is still the same wonderful economist. She must be, because I am able to maintain them all with only four jobs. Example: she goes to Inverness once a week for the shopping because the big stores there are a few pennies cheaper than Stornoway. Not many wives would think of that.

Fiona worries me. Only 13 and already her head is full of nonsense about women's rights. Comes home with phrases like 'male chauvinist' and stuff like that. I blame her acquaintances, but what can you do? You cannot isolate them. She pals around with the daughter of a mad bohemian artist from Keose, and I think she has been influenced by Brian Wilson's wife. Ha, ha. They hate that. Someone's wife, as if they were not a person in their own right.

Iain is a problem in other ways, but he is cheap to run. He seems to get sufficient nourishment from Celtic badges. That is a Glasgow football team, and wait till I tell you … they are Catholic. I tried to beat him out of it but he is getting too big for me.

I don't think I told you before about this fish-farming craze that's swept the Western Isles. Naturally, being fashion-conscious, I started to dabble (in the usual dilettante manner), but now the whole thing is beginning to take over my life. See that word dilettante: if you ever use it, be careful. Once when I was writing for a downmarket paper I used the plural 'i' (can one ever forget one's Classical training?) and some pillock changed it to an 'e'. Result: all residents of Matheson Road accusing each other, not realising I was talking about the whole street.

But to get back to this fish-farming business. I think it is more than a passing phase. In a mad impulsive moment I threw in with some Norwegian marketing shark. You know me, I'll go along with any bore who is bugging me to get rid of him. Now I may be forced to take a time-consuming interest in the whole sordid business world.

Remember MacPherson who went to Antarctica? A competent Classics scholar in his day, now his brain has turned to porridge – nothing there but skate and lemon sole. Try to have an intelligent discussion with him about the market economy and he says, Which one? Billingsgate or Boulogne? My whole way of life may soon depend on the vagaries of the French fish market.

Incidentally, next time you come to UK don't worry about the phrase 'market economy'. Everyone talks about it but no one knows what it means.

Strangely enough, Gaelic still survives, but only just. As you know, it had become almost exclusively the language of prayer, classroom and sheep's earmarks. But now even prayer is done in English. A few dedicated individuals still work hard for her survival and I should be in there helping but I'm too lazy. Was it you who said to me once we were a nation of drunken dreamers? Listen, mate, it's all right for me to say that, but you watch it.

More sheep than ever, I'm afraid. You may have read recently of these funny new hornless rams they've started importing here? Curly, pretty things. Well, it turns out they couldn't take the climate. They are all sick and they are giving them antibiotics, but if you ask me they are wasting their time. It is probably You Know What.

Remember, whatever you do, guard this letter with your life. It will be worth a small fortune when my novel comes out. I know these things are usually done in the reverse order but it is nice to be different. And I know you subscribe, so it kills several birds with the one stone. Lazy and frugal as ever.

Yours till the cows come home.

Eachann

30 NOVEMBER, 1984

PS … Remember that night on Gibbs Hill after O'Toole's wedding? Coming back with no teeth and being pulled from the James Watt Dock? Do you too sometimes take a nostalgic glance over your shoulder? And that terrible fight in the Govan Town Hall after which you bled all the way to Bath and they had to cut your shoe off? Great times, eh? Best of all, the night you fought Pete Sanchez, wrecked the house and stitches were required all round. I sometimes tell the story of the night you and that mad Latvian pilot were arrested for throwing stones through the window of the Russian embassy in Lusaka, and the time you and Carrots made the *News of the World*. I tell you, man, youngsters nowadays don't know how to enjoy themselves. I often wonder if it was my Christian upbringing that prevented me taking part in your worst excesses.

Y.T.T.C.C.H.,
E.

An extraordinary thing is happening in this little Scottish nation of ours in this Year of our Lord 1984.

This Government that preaches self-reliance has always had to draw much of its support from the seedy fly-by-nights and cheap crooks sometimes called middlemen – parasites in the main (but more often on land), jackals who fed off our starving carcases but who fed well because our carcases were many. Aided and abetted by High Tories, these Little Tories squeezed too hard until eventually the meek majority got together and said, Let us circumnavigate these middlemen. You have to laugh at the irony. Call me a sadist if you like, but there is no sweeter music to my ear than the sound of a whingeing middleman crying: "I've been robbed."

But if these Scottish middlemen lack brain, they make up for it with a superabundance of low cunning. They are capable of subversion if guided and manipulated by a higher intelligence. And it is never difficult to find someone to subvert – a greedy malcontent on the fringe of the pack who is easily picked off. If you get one you'll soon get two, and before long the power of the majority is broken. Only sometimes it doesn't work. The majority is getting smart. Of course there are reasonable middlemen – even in the fishing industry – but they are probably Labour supporters.

All the characters not mentioned in this story are entirely imaginary and bear no relation to anyone you and I know well.

Got into a spot of bother again last week with the Women's Liberation Army. I was accused of trying to do them down – me of all people, who has worked tirelessly in the cause of women's freedom for half a lifetime.

Do you realise every time a woman is liberated some poor man is released from the clutches of a dragon? Such is the power of the dragons' propaganda that a million men I know personally are brainwashed into thinking theirs is a normal existence. Of course, most of these married men are by now so demoralised they are terrified if you show them a glimpse of freedom. Which is why they resist women's liberation with all their might. Of course, they don't have to fight too hard, and it is not men's superior strength that will ensure victory but the fifth colomn of scheming vixens who know when they are onto a good thing. But please don't count me among them: I am with the liberators.

You have to hand it to Coinneach Mòr. Is there any other radio presenter in the whole kingdom who would invite his newspaper critics onto his programme so they could reiterate their criticisms on the air?

Once again I must try to get through to your man, because it seems he still confuses wit with humour. You cannot plan wit: you cannot say, "At five o'clock next Friday I am going to be witty." Maybe you can do it in English. Any old fool can amuse the English, but a Gaelic audience is more demanding. Humour, on the other hand, you can and should plan, but what is the use of talking.

Only the other day I was very nearly witty. Given another two seconds I could have made it. I happened to be talking to a smartass Cornishman and some others on the telephone, giving my usual sermon on the regrettable necessity of having to work on the Lord's Day. "I thought they were all the Lord's days," said the Cornishman. "You must," arsa mise, "be a very holy man." But too late as usual: he had hung up.

There was one other time. I think it was in Fingalstein's day. I shouted something funny after him but he had shut the door behind him.

That's the story of my life. Twice I've been witty and there's been no one there to vouch for me – certainly no one with a microphone.

Talking of holy persons, I couldn't help noticing the huge number of those who drove up to Crossbost Free Church the other Sunday in gleaming new Cavaliers. Neither could I help comparing their limousines with my own shabby second-hand Japanese thing and wondering how the system works.

How do these fellows get on so well when they go "that way?" I cannot remember any promises of instant reward for good behaviour on this side. Naturally, those of us who waste our substance on riotous living will be left with only wet change, but I am still puzzled as to why these other guys should do so well on this side. Should they not be made to suffer a little now when they have high hopes of better things to come later on?

I will not remind them again how narrow the eye of a needle can be, but I will warn them of a dream I had the other night. We have all passed on. I remember flying around in my golden winged chariot and waving to Alec George and Murdie Siarach as I overtook them on their rusty motorbikes.

7 December, 1984

At a time when most crofters are desperately trying to improve their stock by importing fancy rams, you have to admire Karachi's courage.

Somewhere – possibly the Middle East – he has acquired one of the meanest-looking beasts ever seen in the East End of Leurbost. And he hasn't the decency to keep it hidden but tethers the animal instead in his potato patch where it is clearly visible from the main road, and guaranteed to cause the maximum offence to passing sheepmen.

Never in the history of Bo Peepaireachd have we seen its like. Viewed from the front, only head and horns are visible, such is the narrowness of the corp. From the side it appears to have a camel-like hump above its forequarters, then further aft a deep hollow as if it had been ridden to hounds. Apparently the previous owner hadn't sheared the brute for years. Probably because he couldn't bear to look at it in its nakedness. The result is a tufted patchwork effect like a half-plucked chicken. There is talk of sending for the Cruelty.

But worse still, wait till I tell you this one, this scrawny apology for a tup has already acquired some notoriety as a rake. On its first night in the village it broke down a fence and got at some yearlings belonging to a fastidious neighbouring shepherd. Yearlings, I might add, that had been carefully segregated to be kept pure for some fancy class of English ram next year. The neighbour is still under sedation, and his family are worried. As if this were not enough, your man Karachi has the audacity to demand stud fees. One day he'll go too far.

On the subject of rams, I must mention an interesting chat I had with my butcher the other day. I asked him if he had stopped mincing rams' flesh for his beef sausages, but he didn't fall for that one. Too smart. We then proceeded to small-talk and gossip about his regular customers, and I am sure he won't mind if I pass some of it on to you here.

"Do you know," he told me, "if it wasn't for youse country customers I would have gone bust years ago. The average Maw cailleach comes in weekly and orders 5lbs of beef, a plastic bag full of chops, a basinful of sausages and a hod load of suet for the duff. Town ladies," he says, "they are different. They drive up in their BMWs and ask for two chops, four sausages and please cut the fat off."

This puzzled me because I had always assumed Stornowegians were more or less like ourselves apart from their terrible accent. I had thought that except for their use of the old Cockney word 'Cove' they had no English habits. Now I hear they are into buying two chops. What next? Unstewed tea?

The apparently simple act of getting drunk I believe to be an expression of faith in one's fellow humans almost up there on a par with the trust demonstrated at Masonic initiations. Which is why a certain type of fellow we both know will never be seen drunk. Not that I would like anyone to make a habit of getting drunk.

But now that we are approaching the silly season I must once again warn you of the dangers of extreme sobriety. Only last week I came across an instance of this common failing among men.

At a private soiree in the Lewis Hotel (to bid farewell to Ken Dunlop who wasn't the worst, and who left his house to the Free Church), most of those present, being away from their wives for the evening and so having to rely on their own willpower, were quite tired by the end of the night. At times like these Leslie always shows his true worth. Being the only one in a condition to navigate, he did the decent thing and ferried his dazed (but eminent) colleagues home. (Norman Tebbit would have been surprised to learn that a man with no money could have been a Samaritan.) Unfortunately some of one's colleagues were unable to locate and direct the Samaritan, which meant he arrived at his own home at a disgustingly late hour. They say he stood on the cat and raised a terrible commotion. The result was a severe mauling by a wife who refused to believe anyone could be out till three in the morning and still be sober. Sally comes from Glasgow.

At the aforementioned party all present ate sparingly from a cold table. Contrast this modest meal with the gargantuan feast on which members and guests of the Rotary Club gorged themselves in Lews

Castle College on the previous Friday. I am reliably informed (by an informer, what else) that the courses numbered fifteen, each surpassing its predecessor in excellence of Haute Cuisine, and all this served in quantities bordering on the obscene. An educated estimator who was present thought a small African country could have been fed for a week on the protein one of these Rotarians put away on the night.

To begin with there were oysters, scallops, smoked salmon and a large variety of crustaceans in dry white wine to sharpen the palate. What followed we cannot describe accurately because my informer, who is not much travelled, didn't recognise the different meats and subtle sauces under which the tables creaked. He just asked me to imagine a bullock and a stag swimming in a lake of brandy sauce.

It didn't surprise me that the businessmen of Stornoway should flaunt their wealth in such a hideous display of gluttony. But I was disappointed to hear several of my medical colleagues were present. One doesn't expect one's own profession to be associated with hedonistic gratification of base animal lust.

What else can I say except plead for an invitation next year.

1985

1 FEBRUARY, 1985

MONDAY

Several of my close associates in the Free Church are concerned about matters financial within the Church. I have always encouraged these people to unburden their troubled minds in my presence, and in most instances I am able to send them on their way with a lighter load. But, and I cannot stress the "but" too much, they can only look to me for guidance if their problem is of a spiritual nature. If they want to talk about this sort of thing, the town of Stornoway is teeming with bankers, accountants, solicitors and several other categories of shyster who will counsel them on money matters and finally relieve them of most of it, thereby solving their problem.

You'll be pleased to hear I soon sent this lot (two elders and an elderly daycon) packing, but not before I had taken the time to read them a stern lecture:

So the Church is short of money, is that it? What do you expect? If you elect to go for private medicine, be it for body or soul, then you must pay dearly for it. The moment you place your soul in the care of the Free Church – a Church that is independent of the State and the corrupting wealth of Rome – you must dig into your pocket, and dig deep. Remember, private medicine was your choice. Private sector palaces have to be maintained by those who build them. If you must surround yourselves by the vulgar trappings of wealth, to arouse envy in misguided adherents to inferior faith, then you are no better than they are. This is not your place. Go back whence you came. Seek an Anglican place of worship with all its gaudy attractions. Go on your bended knees before glittering false images. Join your Martins and your St Columbases where the wine is probably led in by a piper.

Seek fool's gold and ye shall surely find it, I yelled, but don't talk to me about money, I'm afraid I got quite carried away for a moment. Then I calmed down and suggested they try to raise money through a sale of work or ask the Free Presbyterians for a loan. But I fear my message was lost on them.

TUESDAY

The words stick in the throat of my biro but I'm afraid I must quote from young Wilson's piece in last week's paper. "Journalists only part with advice for money – we're a bit like doctors in this respect." It is not going too far to say I was exceeding wroth when I read this libel. As a matter of fact, my wife had to wet my lips with malt before I could speak. The paper had slipped to the floor and a full 10 minutes had elapsed before I found the strength to pick it up and make sure I had not misread his statement. I was, alas, not mistaken.

Like doctors, indeed. In a moment I was back on the shores of Lake Tanganyika. I could see it as plainly as though it were yesterday: handing out penicillin to sick children who had given up hope; stitching and restitching pathetic creatures who had been mauled by leopards; and, most rewarding of all memories, the wide-open grateful eyes of a waif cured of King's Evil. Is the lingering image of these worshipping eyes not sufficient reward for any medicine man? The insulting accusation that doctors only work for money makes me tremble with rage.

That journalists always demand payment I do not for a moment doubt. But, as for the laughable pretence that they usually get it … Pardon me if I permit myself a sardonic (wry) smile.

WEDNESDAY

I have a letter here from the HIDB that is no laughing matter – a communication designed and worded to cause the maximum offence. "Enclosed," says a man I thought was my friend, "is a 'paper' on mussels written by such and such and this other fellow. I hope you'll find it helpful."

Helpful! Mussels!! By these two? Me? Who practically invented the cultivated mussel as it is known today? Who took GMK and RMD under his wing and taught them all there is to know about mussels back in '78? Who else. Not that I want recognition or reward. I considered it my duty. Would they, one wonders, send a Grade One instruction manual on the art of boxing to Mohammed Ali. Send your kindergarten pamphlets to Willie Burns, Calum Dan and other first-year apprentices, but let's have a little respect for the pioneers.

Please do not think I have any disregard for the authors of this 'paper', for they have made excellent progress. But I see they are still up to their old tricks: "Have you any comments to add?" ends the letter. I certainly have not. The time for that sort of thing is long gone. We have now entered the commercial phase of the operation and it is every man for himself. Certainly, a great deal of scientific discovery has been made in the last six months but I can assure you and them it is safely locked up in the file marked "confidential". Anyone who wants comment at this stage pays through the nose.

THURSDAY

My annual search for two new shoes took me to the Millionaire Cobbler's warehouse on Kenneth Street. There was a very big crowd in her on the day and it was very hard to find anyone in the head of his earning. A banker and a baker came into the company and it was not long until an undertaker came among them also. There was not even a civil servant who was not there who is related to The Cobbler. A girl or two were walking about with shoes in their hands and if they were selling or buying you are asking me a question I cannot answer. There was a lot of talking and shouting and laughing and the confusion was as big as any fank you ever saw. At the end of 10 minutes I had made up my mind to go to another shop when a new one I hadn't seen till then came to where I was standing and gave me a box of new shoes nine-and-a-half. It was after hand I thought maybe he was one on the same business as myself but by that time I had taken my legs with me out of the shop and I hadn't parted with a brown penny.

FRIDAY

I have only one thing to say about the Point Labour Party's Burns Night, and I know the chairman, Donald Macdonald, would say it with me. I was dismayed to see several people lighting up their cigarettes before The Queen had been toasted.

15 FEBRUARY, 1985

SUNDAY

For those who cannot "get out" the Sunday afternoon BBC sermon is a tolerable consolation (and of course there is no collection). But I'm afraid all is not well with the BBC. Today I switched on as usual immediately after the pudding and settled down for some thunder and lightning, but thunder and lightning came there none.

The broadcasting preacher's soft-spoken transmission seemed familiar, yet I couldn't place it at first. The accent was unmistakably of Uibhist origin, although, I surmised, modified and refined by exposure to the tone of a more advanced society. The voice, I thought for a moment, of one of those wishy-washy liberal Church of Scotland ministers. But I was wrong. It was worse than that. Much worse. Yes, you've guessed: a Catholic, and none other than your man the water ski-ing priest, John Archie.

I suppose I should have closed my ears but I'm glad I didn't because now I am able to warn our youth – to prepare them for these unexpected onslaughts of expert propaganda and to strengthen their defences against the trained manipulator. Believe me, the cunning of these fellows must never be underestimated. Although some of us have the conviction and resource to come through such a broadcast unscathed, there are others who, although thinking themselves sufficiently cloaked against evil influence, would be better to switch the wireless off at the wall.

You would think to listen to some of these phoney ecclesiastics they were as holy as your own minister. The beguiling voice of sweet reason. But do not be fooled. That is all part of their game. This talk of one Christian is as good as another – ecumenism, I think they call it – is merely the fabric with which they weave their web. Lower your guard for one instant and, take it from me, you are ensnared. Once these boys get their gory talons into you, you're done for. Your mind is no longer your own. You might as well wrap your soul in a parcel and send it to the Vatican. Yes, you'll remember my words then. Too late, my friends, Too late.

MONDAY

I seen a good one the other day. According to the "other paper", a young gentleman from Laxdale was fined £250 for introducing a new crop to the crofting territories. This seems a harsh and unjust sentence with which to reward a youngster with the ingenuity and courage to attempt something new in horticulture.

For generations we have been criticised for not making full use of our native sod. (Remember Professor Lodge.) Yet here we have a boy who manages, without an IDP grant, to grow a plant that does not normally thrive in cold climates, and for his trouble he is hauled up before the beak. Had he managed to grow a really dangerous narcotic like tobacco he would probably have been given some award for industry.

Unlike some of my medical colleagues, I would not make the rash claim that cannabis is totally harmless. It is difficult for our generation to judge its short term effects: having been soaked in alcohol for half a lifetime, our judgement is clouded and our sensitivity numbed. Very likely it is all a Jesuit plot.

TUESDAY

Without question I live in a very strange household. I came down to breakfast this morning to find a man sitting at the table strumming a guitar and singing folk songs to a sizeable and appreciative audience – except for the man who was playing snooker with our neurotic cat and a fellow who was yelling into the telephone as if he didn't believe it really worked. A departed visitor, an early-rising journalist, had eaten my black puddings and left me only the empty plastic rings.

I couldn't get into the bathroom, because another regular caller with a bowel disorder spends every morning in there waiting for something to happen. The radio was on (is it ever off?) and the local station was either experiencing bad electrical interference or someone was doing an exciting interview. In the midst of all this a child was hurriedly doing last night's homework.

Nobody pays any attention to me, so there is nothing for it but to leave for the loch and the therapeutic company of my little ones. It is all right for her – she worked for years in Gartnavel mental hospital – but it would have driven my first wife mad.

WEDNESDAY

One tries, of course, to do the best for one's children. One encourages them to read the right books, to eat wholemeal bread, and to play chess. On MacLennan Kenneth Street's advice one beggars oneself buying a computer for their education. And what for, one asks? One comes home of an evening to find the eldest reading a book by Billy Connolly and Number Two asking if one would teach him five-card stud poker. Where did one go wrong?

THURSDAY

Regular readers of my daily recordings have detected something which I obviously couldn't see. Several have written kind letters suggesting I need a long rest. They point out passages to me that clearly reveal signs of overwork, and perhaps they are right.

But can I help myself? No. It's the Protestant work ethic, you see. Unless I work 16 hours a day I am burdened with a crushing weight of guilt. However, I am always open to advice and have been looking through the brochures for a suitable long holiday.

Let's have a look at this one in the *Glasgow Herald*: Greenland adventure cruise on the luxury liner *Astor*. Calling in Shetland, Faroes, Iceland and Greenland. £1,170. Friday night dancing. Exciting Flora (who she?) and the polar bears. Bubbling geysers in Iceland. Oh, dear. What's this? Two delightful Scottish lecturers, Tom Weir and the Rev James Currie (bubbling geezers again), will bore you round the North Atlantic. But wait a minute, maybe that's not such a bad idea. These two geezers should take the edge off any enjoyment and help to keep guilt at bay.

FRIDAY

Talking of Friday night dancing, I find myself in the Caberfeidh Hotel by kind invitation of the combined Hebridean dilettantes. My invitation is clearly a Gaelic choirs' PR exercise. They would like to see reported how they deport themselves in private relaxation – with restraint and dignity and as much decorum as is possible for any man dancing in women's clothing.

However, because I enjoyed myself and because I can only write the truth, I feel it would be unfair of me to say anything.

22 FEBRUARY, 1985

MONDAY

Two times today I narrowly escaped death at the hands of women. In both instances the guilty women were oldish – over forty – and in charge of motor vehicles. Under no circumstances could they be deemed to be drivers, not even in the dock where they will almost certainly find themselves soon. To qualify for the title "driver" a "person" must have the ability to fool an examiner, for half an hour or so, that she is in control of the car. We must assume the two women who nearly finished me off today passed their tests in the miniskirt era or else had the good fortune to meet an examiner who was easily bought with cash.

The first nearly had me at the Manor roundabout. She arrived from the east, down Coulegrein way, and stopped at the roundabout for a while to admire the scenery. She let two cars pass but decided two was plenty. Mine was the third. She shot across my bow several yards after I thought I had already passed her, no doubt muttering to herself some old Coulegrein warcry like: "Let two into town, mow the third down."

The second old bag ambushed me on Sandwick Road. I was making my nervous way towards the airport, possibly at 31.5 miles an hour as one sometimes does to keep up with the traffic, when, lo and behold, a westward-bounder suddenly remembered an appointment in Goathill. She made a violent suicidal swing to starboard, missing my nose by five millimetres. Her ashen-faced passenger, a middle-aged man who for all I know could be her husband, tried to make apologetic signs to me (or else he was crossing himself).

I need hardly remind you that all this took place on Communion Monday. What I want to know is: what protection does the law afford those of us who fall victim to female motorists who are temporarily unhinged or possessed by extra-terrestrial invaders? Is it not about time the law carried machines to record danger-levels?

Imagine for a moment what the outcome might have been if my brakes were anything other than perfect. Blood and guts all over the road, and some of us not ready to go. Suppose, further, I had accepted an uncharacteristic third sherry – curtains for your man, and the woman on a spiritual high walks or floats from the court Scott-free.

Even the best of women drivers should never be trusted with any vehicle more powerful than a pram. I would certainly never let my wife drive.

TUESDAY

On this day 15 years ago I got married to Maggie. I only wish I'd got married earlier to someone else for a while. It is the custom on occasions such as this for men and women to proclaim that they are happily married, but how do they know? Most of them have only been married to each other. On what do they base their assessment of happiness? Even if we accept that there is no such thing as happiness – only varying degrees of misery – we still need some yardstick against which to measure our misery. (Would I have been so miserable with Maria that sold the ferrets?) To make any sort of valid comparison a sample of two or three would seem the absolute minimum if you want to be certain your angel isn't a pig in a poke.

Of course, it doesn't naturally follow that No 2 is going to be any better than No 1. You could sack your first wife only to find the second is an even worse bargain. But at least you are in a position to know. It is quite possible, and this should drive my point home, that Denis Thatcher thinks he is happily married. A brief flirtation with Shirley Williams would open his eyes to the misery that had been his lot (varying degrees again).

WEDNESDAY

The normally peace-loving people of Carloway took to the streets today to protest against the inhuman decision to close their police station. Unprecedented scenes of public outrage greeted observers and journalists who had travelled from all over the country to witness at first hand the frustration and despair of a demoralised community.

"What we are faced with here," said one shocked citizen, "is a total breakdown in law and order. Do you realise," he went on, "that if a poacher is seen on the river it takes a patrol car one hour to come from Stornoway? Not good enough."

Interviewed at the Doune Braes Hotel, the customer known as One-Eyed Jack said: "Without a polis this place wud be open 24 hours a day. When would we get a chance to drink the carry-outs?"

So the marching and banner-waving continued. A save-the-polis deputation from Shawbost led by Seonaidh Leòid had to be arrested. There is talk of moving a UN force into the area until the matter is resolved.

In stark contrast to the present riotous scenes in Carloway, the last recorded crime in its history refers to the mysterious disappearance of a sheep from a certain barn in 1897. North Lochs is probably unique in never having needed a police station.

THURSDAY

St Valentine's Day. Up at the crack of dawn to prepare the breakfast and to warm the house up for her descent. I know I am in a minority in this Celtic warrior nation, but I think the least a man can do for his wife once a year is make the breakfast.

FRIDAY

To celebrate the Brass Wedding a fairly wealthy friend took us out to dinner. The County was fully booked, so we had to go to one of the bigger hotels which I will not name because, although I was desperately unlucky myself, my friends were happy with their food. But what do they know. "Aha," I said to Maggie when the 'steak' arrived. "Your auntie must have got a job in the kitchen here. You know the one with the flavour-extractor in her fingertips." Not only had the flavour been extracted, but every molecule of moisture had also been removed. Only afterwards did it occur to me that maybe what I had on my plate was a slab of reconstituted soya beans. I have kept a wad for analysis.

29 MARCH, 1985

COUNTRY DIARY

Soon I expect a young woman to start work with our boys in the loch as part of her training in fish farming. Having done some very basic learning with Atlantic Sea in Uig and a little theory in Inverness Technical College, she is now being sent to The Bosun to be, as it were, finished. Normally I wouldn't give my blessing to this piece of progressive lunacy but in Jan's case (for it is she) I feel I can make an exception because she handles a boat like a man. There, I hasten to add, the resemblance ends.

A strange turning of the tide here: Jan is engaged to the grandson of the late Iain Mhurchaidh, 8 Ranish, one of the best and last lobster fishermen of North Lochs. If Iain met a woman on his way to the boat, and he usually chose a tortuous route to narrow the odds, he would turn back and cancel the day's fishing. The notion of stepping into a boat with a woman would have seemed to him too ridiculous to contemplate. But, there you are, now we have a woman Prime Minister.

But this is not an aspect of sea-womanship that worries me: I am not superstitious. Although I believe there are certain jobs that are more suited to the male of the species — such as hauling anchors, turfing peat, throwing the hammer and leading parliamentary parties — I am in favour of giving them a chance to prove they can make a mess of these man jobs. Fish farming, you'll notice, was not listed among my masculine jobs because it has already been proven in Marvig and Loch Grimshader that young salmon feed better from a woman's hand (although it is rumoured the fish grow soft and colourless). No, what worries me is the effect of woman on the men in a crew.

About 20 years ago I was able to study for a whole year the behaviour of men and boys isolated from women on a small tropical island. When I say they were isolated I mean there were no women resident on the island and the island was only one and a half miles long. Yet for most of the time these 500 men of mixed nationality got on well. They worked, played football, drank and swam together with no squabbling over territory or fighting in the autumn. Rank was of no consequence, officers large and petty lived with one another in temporary truce and financial status was unimportant because there were no private cars or houses. (Fortunately there were natives to look down on, but that's another story.)

Yet every so often this Brave New World tranquillity was disrupted for a day or two when an air stewardess had to make a brief stopover. Your level-headed soft English neighbour who wrote to his wife twice a day started to behave like an idiot — posing and telling tall stories about how he just missed being selected for the Olympic sailing team. The scruffiest Scotsman you ever did see would appear in the bar with one of these ridiculous bandages round his waist. Frail non-swimmers would flex their imaginary museles and dive dangerously off the pier. Non-smoking near-teetotalers would light up huge cigars and order large Napoleon brandies — all in crazy hopeful expectation of being noticed and singled out from among another 500 fools. Those of us who feigned a calculated disinterest, hoping that might do the trick, were no better and no luckier.

A far cry from Loch Leurbost, I hear you mutter, but I am not so sure. I recollect and worry particularly about non-swimming high-divers trying to impress. Worse, I worry about Ranish boys who might have been influenced by Iain Mhurchaidh and who might go on strike when Jan makes her debut. We wish her all the best in her finishing school and we can assure her there will be none of the chauvinistic behaviour she experienced in Uig. During working hours in Leurbost she will be treated like a man.

TOWN DIARY

Although I am not myself a churchgoer, I try to befriend those who are, because when it comes to gossip churchgoers are streets ahead of pubgoers. I heard several good ones the other day — all from churchgoers. Careful investigation among pubgoers proved all the stories to be untrue, but that is poor reason for not repeating them here.

Quite recently in Stornoway a new pub, an extension to the Star Inn, was opened and named Zebo's in honour of an old dedicated customer. The name "Zebo" mounted on the west gable-end mysteriously disappeared early last week.

The first rumour had it that Zebo had died and that the sign was lowered as a show of respect. Then it was confirmed that the original "Zebo Company" had insisted on its removal. Several other "genuine" explanations for Zebo's comedown were broadcast, but best of all was the story that our man Zebo had seen the light and wanted this monument to his former way of life obliterated. This one was welcomed by both evangelists and enemies of the true gospel as a "cracker" — the former to demonstrate the power and the fact that it is never too late, and the latter to prove how shallow and showy is the nature of conversion in the only "true faith".

In fact, the sign was taken down to be repainted.

If I ever get the cùram I will not have these diaries burnt but will instead hold them aloft as an example of how meaningless was my existence before "she blew", and there is nothing more meaningless than meaningless. (Why should anything make sense? Answer me that one, cousin.)

From that other town, the capital of the Highlands, I have recently missed the voice of my favourite Radio Highland broadcaster. Rumour in Zebo's has it she has been domesticated and is raising turkeys in Suffolk. Please believe me, I have nothing against harsh East Coast accents but one grows accustomed to, even looks forward to, her soft West Coast tones and her belligerent style of interviewing. If it is anything I said, I'm sorry, I didn't mean it, please come back.

19 APRIL, 1985

SUNDAY

On this first Sunday back from holiday I get up out of bed at 1.30pm in response to an announcement that dinner is ready. Although I am very hungry, I get up reluctantly because sometimes I am so lazy that hunger pangs are easier to endure than the stress and anguish through which I must go every time I have to leave my bed. In the past when spiritually dehydrated I have often taken a lukewarm slug from the hot water bottle rather than force myself across the Arctic waste that lies between me and the bathroom.

This morning it is even harder than usual to get up because yesterday afternoon I stopped smoking, so I know I will be bad-tempered and will probably try to find fault with those who are nearest and dearest to me. It doesn't take long. She knows I like carrots and turnips to be well cooked. I don't mind raw carrots or raw turnips but I hate them half-cooked. If you are going to bother cooking vegetables you might as well persevere until the damn things are fully softened. For God's sake, I've told her often enough, if I wanted half-cooked carrots I would ask for half-cooked carrots. But this time I say nothing. I maintain a sullen silence throughout the meal and go straight back to bed as soon as I've finished.

Unfortunately I cannot get to sleep for brooding over the knowledge I could have slept for another 10 minutes if she'd cooked the veg properly. And other things.

MONDAY

Things are no better this morning. I am destined to be surrounded by incompetence at home and at work and have great difficulty sleeping in either place now. My physician says I drink too much and that maybe that last tour of seven towns in nine days through five opening-time-zones was too much for me. (If I said anything about the folks back home, I'm sure they deserved it.) The empty bags under my eyes are grey and wrinkled and the lids droop sometimes like Onassis's (lids). Instead of taking my physician on tour with me next time as suggested, I think I will do away with second opinions altogether and heal myself with vigorous exercise and spartan self-denial.

TUESDAY

The reasons for wallowing in self-pity this week go deeper than the usual chemical changes caused by holiday excess. I was dealt a dirty blow the other night when the ref was looking the other way. My armoury of faith is shattered and the most annoying part is I cannot say too much because of something called sub judice.

Happily there is nothing yet in the law books to prevent us discussing the fascinating subject(s) of crime and punishment. One of the buff envelopes lying behind the front door (after the holiday as usual) contained an alarming message from the Prudential informing me of their regretted decision to increase my household insurance because "your area is now included in the high-crime rate group". We had a good laugh. I showed it to everyone I know and they all laughed. Even the debt collector Duncan Geal himself found it amusing and we laughed together. High-crime area ... ha, ha. Maybe they've confused Liverpool and Leurbost, said someone, and we all guffawed. Two days later I was robbed of something that cannot be insured. Let me make it quite clear, there is no evidence whatsoever that in any way implicates the Prudential – it was merely a remarkable coincidence.

WEDNESDAY

Even in the hardened and embittered autumn of my days I was shocked to learn or relearn the casual conscienceless manner in which one man is prepared to condemn another (especially if the other is a friend). Give a dog a bad name and you might indeed as well shoot it: in fact you would do better to shoot it in the first place and it would immediately acquire a good name. None of this affects my views on hanging very much although I begin to see that an over-liberal approach to punishment can be a costly business. I also see how easy it would be to hang the wrong person and how little it matters to some people as long as someone is hanged. I still believe hanging serves no purpose as a deterrent but it does offer the grim satisfaction of revenge. As I said, we have this sub judice thing, but I think I am allowed to say that when we catch "them" they will be given a fair open trial before they are hanged.

DIARDAOIN

Tha mi 'n dùil nach fhalbh mi tuilleadh. Cha chreid mi nach e sin na facail a bh' aig Fionnlagh an t-seachdain a chaidh. Nach e Sàtan a th' air am balach bochd a dhalladh. Mo gheibh mise mo chasan às an t-sùil-chruthaich tha seo aon uair eile, cha till mi tuilleadh. Tha rudeigin mì-nàdarrach mu thimcheall an eilein tha seo – mar gum biodh daoine nan leth-ruith chun a' bhàis le dearg eagal am beatha.

FRIDAY

It seems easier to get on with "this life" in the cities: they seem to manage the running of it better, probably because they have nature pretty well under control and there is generally less preoccupation with the next round. Most of them feel they could only live as a cog in the engine-rooms of the nation. Of course many of them have never known anything better and would probably wither without daily contact with another half-million souls. But I must remind them:

"Great things are done when men meet mountain sheep; This is not done by jostling in the street."

To think that these words were written long before IDP and earth-moving equipment.

26 APRIL, 1985

MONDAY

Seldom, in the course of 10 days, has anyone suffered two devastating blows to the belly and survived. One, from an unknown burglar, is easily shaken off, but the second, from an alleged friend, has opened a wound that only time and whisky can heal. This co-called comrade, an Uibhisteach, made an offer behind my back for the *Serene* that couldn't be refused.

I have never made a secret of my 10-year love affair for the *Serene*. My wife knew and made allowances; my children understood my need and promised to save, when the time came, from their Job Creation money enough to lay a deposit. At one stage I entertained some hope of winning her through a bet but the crafty owner stopped playing golf when his handicap was reduced to a realistic figure. And talking of figures, that was what first got to me. It was not a weakness for wood or mere infatuation with her traditional clinker build; it was her shape – the swan-slim neck, the subtle swelling of her breast, her adequate yet somehow slender waist growing out of beamy load-bearing hips that tapered quickly but not too quickly to a streamlined stern. To think that at this moment she is being pawed by the horny unappreciative hands of one whose only advantage over me was money.

Forgive me. This is no place for tears or the revelation of futile fantasy. I should have known she would always remain elusively just beyond my reach. Yet you must bear with me through this painful time because it is three in the morning and there is no one else to share my burden.

TUESDAY

It is no use; save your breath. I cannot be consoled. When day breaks in one hour's time the *Serene* will leave Stornoway's inner harbour and I expect I will never see her again. Indeed, I will be surprised if anyone sees her again because I have just given "them" a weather forecast. (This is a hobby I haven't mentioned before because my methods are not officially recognised.)

The behaviour of the plovers and lapwings on the Church of Scotland glebe alerted me to sudden unseasonal change. Then the snipe stopped drumming – a sure sign of an impending cold northerly gale. By all means, I told the brute, a fine day, set sail immediately.

Callous? Cold-blooded? Violent vengeance, did you say? OK, perhaps I am cruel; but remember the *Serene* has fallen into the hands of philistines. I sent them out into a storm but consider what David did to them. These heathens are not ashamed to admit they intend to abuse her gathering mussels, and who knows what other obscene maltreatment might they conceive in their depravity.

But I'll tell you this one: by the time they hit the Shiants this morning, lapsed or no, they'll be muttering Hail Marys and making rosary beads from ballbearings. Yes, and probably offering anything they might have picked up in the way of strong, Presbyterian prayer as an each-way bet.

WEDNESDAY

I am desperately sorry for my deeds and despicable thoughts of the last two days. Not since Johnnie Walker attempted to come between me and Alice at the age of 15 have I lost control and lashed out with such malicious intent. (It took me another six years to learn that boats retain their beauty longer than women.) This latent violence that we all possess at varying depth can be partially excused when it erupts in the heat of the moment: when it is premeditated as it was with the "forecast" we should be shown little mercy. Another bad example of what can happen when the means of destruction are too readily available. Perhaps the fact that I am sorry means I am not a psychopath and am unlikely to do the same again. Yet I cannot be sure, so I am taking up golf.

THURSDAY

As a self-imposed penance golf has no equal. There is no other outlet for suppressed anger, frustration and excess energy (after 40) that can remotely compare with golf. When you make a spectacle of yourself you are on your own. There is no opponent standing directly in the line of fire (although that is often the safest position), so you punish the guilty one – yourself. I have seen grown men tearing their own hair out and stamping on their balls in rage and I have heard language the like of which you wouldn't hear on the Ullapool–Inverness bus.

If you must punish yourself, play golf. It is the ultimate self-flagellation and a fitting sentence for someone who would give a sailor a bum forecast. I am not surprised it is one of the few pastimes approved by the Deacons Court for members and ministers of the Free Church.

FRIDAY

In Stornoway Town Hall tonight I witnessed what can only be described as a vicious attack on the Free Presbyterian Church. A play, if we may dignify it with the title, twisted from a fine sensitive novel about the north-west. Twisted in a manner designed to cause the maximum offence and to savage all that we hold dear. And performed with relish by a gang composed, we may assume, of Communists, Catholics and probable Mormons – led by Simon, who should know better. I had to draw on my inner reserve of strength and willpower to force myself to stay to the end.

It distresses me to record that the full-house audience laughed frequently and applauded loudly at the finish. To tell the truth, I myself enjoyed the play and Ossian enormously but I have been taking lessons in criticism from NM of the *Stornoway Gazette*.

SATURDAY

The beef-burgers advertised on the *Suilven* blackboard are made from spam and gravel.

24 MAY, 1985

One day in May of Eighty-five
When IDP was still alive
A mystery man of noble breeding
Who doesn't often do much reading
Hearing I don't know who from
Of our Holy Aid Program
Remembered in the nick of time
That sometime early in his prime
Somewhere in the Scottish Highlands
He had acquired a distant island
À bon compte

Associates within the City
To whom the Comte was just a titty
Were summoned to the great man's table
Whereat your man was quickly able
To show them on a large-scale map
A glorious little magic tap
Through which flowed a golden stream
Too rich for native island dreams
And so was hatched the humble plan
Of our landlord de la Lanne
The Comte

Perhaps he wasn't such a dope
The City sharks began to hope
But they say the cupboard's bare
How can you a millionaire
Expect to get a decent share
Of what is no longer there
And tell us how an English wooftah

Can pass himself off as a croftah
Members of the Highland Board
Can tell a farmer from a toad
You Comte

The old Comte smiled the knowing smile
Of one who knows he has the style
The accent and the charm and wit
To coax the Board to part with it
OK so I'm a millionaire
Lacking some in savoir-faire
But God is good, His servant's better
We'll get him to write the letter
We're all dreamers here you know
And all we dream of is cash flow
Us Comtes

PR men and advisers swore
They'd never heard the like before
By gosh we think you are a winner
How fortunate you're not a sinner
Yet we must tread a careful path
We dare not risk the native wrath
When all this cash begins to flow
Past little Bernera's rocky shore
Prying peasant eyes will covet
We must pretend there's something in it
For non-Comtes

And with respect, sir, there remains
Before our losses become gains
The miraculous new process
That almost overnight transposes

A soft slick City ageing charmer
Bred in habitat much warmer
Cosseted by maid and gardener
Into a septuagenarian farmer
Of the reigning king of fish
Red enough to grace a dish
Fit for a Comte

Fear not said the jolly Comte
I know what fellow-croftahs want
What's more I know what most appeals
To those who are empowered to deal
From underneath their loaded sleeve
The missing card I think you feel
We must produce to get a grant
At a healthy some per cent
Unless the answer lies for certain
In the modern myth of tartan
I'm a Comte

Tartan collars for the clergy
Tartan boots for Murd and Erchie
Will make our little isle so rich
We'll have to build another bridge
Although the bridge must not be low
Enough to ever stop cash flow
For island girls I promise fame
Full employment without shame
For every little Miss Demeanour
Will answer to the vice-convener
And the Comte

I'll impress both CNAG and Comunn
On their Radio nan Eilean
Despite my lack of savoir-faire
When Rusty asks me on the air
The rustics listening to my act
Will never guess I'm short of tact
Their Garlic language has no bounds
Of hollow words and empty sounds
Like on ne sait a quoi s'en tenir sur son comte.*

* Because I didn't give my French teacher, the well-meaning Miss Ross, the attention she deserved, I had to look that last phrase picked up in a bad place in Zaire up in the dictionary. It said: "We do not know what to make of him (or it)."

We hope the BBC will release a tape of the Comte's interview soon. A snip at £10.50.

26 JULY, 1985

Dear Jackson,

These are very busy days for your man. They would be even busier were it not for the invaluable assistance I've received from young students fresh out of medical school. I still refer to them as students because, although they have passed their finals, they have everything to learn and they know it. That is why they come to me. If you looked in the records of Dundee University you would find that these newly-graduated youngsters are officially seconded for further training to my neighbouring practitioner Dr Bayliss, but that is merely to appease a rigid medical bureaucracy that does not recognise the old ways. By the way, were you one of the snobs who opted for the title "St Andrews" when given the choice at Dundee in the early days? I think young Wilson on page three was.

I mean no disrespect to my eminent neighbouring colleague but I am sure she knows that students use her to get, as it were, close to me (who studied under Duncan himself). Where else, pray tell me, could they find the mysteries of Central African doctoring, remedies originating in the mists of Celtic antiquity (passed down by port-à-beul), rough and ready weathership cures and modern medicine all rolled into the one small middle-aged man? Where else.

But that is enough of my humdrum existence. I see from your own letter you are now more or less Numero Uno in the Gulf. You seem to have the sheiks by the beard – open cheques dropping through your letterbox, and special dispensation for the grog. You always did have a smooth tongue. Still, it's a shame you didn't follow a career in the Civil Service as we originally planned. You will not have seen the papers yet but the headlines tell us that top Civil Servants and Rear-Admirals are to get a significant pay rise bringing their earnings before expenses from £51,000 to £75,000. That is even more than we make and damn near as much as dentists, who now rake in £100,000 a year – and every man jack of them as thick as an old sailor's gums, except of course when it comes to counting shekels. Perhaps she has her reasons for these rather large rises for top people but I cannot help thinking she was wrong to include Rear-Admirals. Is this what we might call putting a premium on aids?

To change the subject quite drastically, you probably cannot remember the day my son and heir was born in Lusaka. You were lost down the Zambezi on some fool crocodile hunt – you were going through your Hemingway phase then. Anyway, while the drama unfolded in the Medical Aid Hospital some of us were celebrating in the golf club with the touring professionals. Among them was a young fellow (then) with the famous name Christy O'Connor. He liked a dram and kept the party going. Played the box better than Niall Cheòis. He smacked the ball well too, and proved it this year when he broke the course record at Sandwich.

Naturally, I followed this year's Open closely. Not often anyone I know wins anything. Now listen, I am not saying British broadcasting is in any way biased or that there is any anti-Irish undercurrent in Britain as a whole, yet they leave themselves open to this sort of accusation with their coverage of this year's major sporting event – if we may pretend for a moment that golf is a sport. Christy was seldom more than two strokes off the pace, yet somehow he never seemed to be within camera range. That's television. In *The Guardian* and *Punch* Frank Keating, the only sports reporter with pretension to writer status, composed his week's work around a spoilt English brat called Faldo. Faldo failed as always but that didn't matter: copy had been filed before the game. In the meantime the big American names collapsed and confused the script but that didn't worry that bastion of the truth *The Observer*. Nicklaus and Watson were hiding in disgrace, so they featured on their sports page a large photograph of a Spaniard who had also forgotten his lines. In the accompanying three thousand words they "accidentally" managed to avoid any reference to O'Connor, who won £26,000. He speaks Gaelic but I'm not saying that has anything to do with it. Perhaps the reason he was so quickly forgotten was Lyle. A Wasp name appeared on the leader board and the broadcasters relaxed. It didn't matter that his name was followed by 'Scot' (in brackets), the English loved him and hailed a British victory. Neither did it matter to the Scots that he spoke with his natural Midlands accent: he was one of "ours".

I wonder if my children with their blonde hair (what a stroke of luck?) will ever be hailed in Zambia as "ours". As for yours, with their touch of England, Isle of Arran, Africa and Arabia ... well, who knows what sort of nationalism they might embrace. Persuade them if you can to become dentists.

Forgive me for lapsing from the usual chatty style but I am terribly frustrated by our box and papers. I have many things to tell you but I am in a desperate hurry. Maggie thinks a touch of the sun might rejuvenate me, so is dragging me off to Portugal today. It is surprisingly easy to arrange a journey between Glasgow and Portugal because MacBraynes' are not involved: the little bit journey in between could prove impossible for the opposite reason. Remember when you come on holiday to give me a whistle from Ullapool. I'll come for you in my new tupperware boat. Not only will it save time, you will not have to eat on the *Suilven*.

Talking of eating, since you ask how the farmed salmon are coming on I'll tell you a good one. I called on the old fellow the other day and found him eating a greyish-pink mess. What, arsa mise, is that? A wild salmon, says he. Well, do you know what, I tasted it and had to rush to the cages to pull one of my own out to get the taste of that wild stuff out of my mouth. Not only does it look and taste vile, you never know where it's been. Must go.

Yours aye,
Eachann

PS Please send me a photograph of your liver.

16 AUGUST, 1985

THE HOLIDAY
DAY ONE
Glasgow Airport's international departure lounge is not a comfortable place for the nervous flyer. They keep it hot, presumably so you'll get accustomed to your destination's climate; they imprison you one hour before your flight; and as if that were not enough, they fill the lounge with Glaswegians – a tolerable breed in their natural habitat, but in the upper troposphere a potentially lethal cargo.

Across the table from me a very fat man and his equally heavy wife are downing large vodkas at a furious pace. They are already sweating profusely. I wonder if they read in the morning papers that the temperature at Faro Airport is 90 degrees. Although I cannot hear what they are saying, a simmering matrimonial dispute is evident. They are sitting at a 45-degree angle to each other and have to whisper their disagreements over their shoulders. I would guess one or the other would have preferred to go to Dunoon or Blackpool. If they were my patients I would have advised Dunoon.

Behind me a group of young boys are already well bevvied and noisy. One of them has obviously been to the Algarve before: "Wait till you see the %@£??£ out there, boys." Loud laughter. Further information on the

Portuguese female anatomy is disseminated, heavily spiced with crude innuendo. I begin to have doubts about the whole holiday. I am thankful that my sheltered clerical friends back home were spared this dreadful embarrassment and I remember thinking: "Right now I could be the Rev Angus Smith sitting here and these louts wouldn't care. And my poor wife. How fortunate that she once nursed Norman Maclean."

It occurs to me, not for the first time, how stupid it is for airlines to permit smoking on flights out of Scottish airports. The slightest spark could ignite the cabin's atmosphere, composed as it is mainly of alcoholic gases. On the other hand, clouds of cigarette smoke keeps oxygen at a minimal level, reducing the risk of explosion. Nevertheless I fill two pages with invaluable suggestions for the Dan Air captain. I know him well, of course. John something or other; we did our training together.

Flying at 32,000 feet over the English Channel, I take, as always, a keen scientific interest in my surroundings (not least in the large gentleman who is by now into the duty free grog and who would probably explode in the event of pressurisation failure). I see a considerable amount of cirrus above us and I make a note to reprimand these fools in the Met Office who never report cirrus above 30,000 feet. Or can it be the Dan Air altimeter? Anyway, it doesn't matter because the Iberian Peninsula is cloudless and the highest mountain en route, if I remember right, is no higher than Ben Nevis. Twice I have to go up front to suggest minor alternations in course to avoid clear air turbulence and the captain is wise enough to obey instantly. These small diversions are usually frowned upon but in this instance they don't matter because Spanish air traffic controllers are on strike. How much more comfortable our flights would be if they all went on strike permanently.

In a long taxi queue at Faro Airport I have in front of me a southern English gentleman who is travelling alone. I would guess he is called Peregrine. Peregrine is never really alone because he wonders aloud. So loud that the whole taxi queue can hear him. "Extraordinary, all these empty taxis for Faro. Funny system. Surely some of them could be hired for western destinations. Damn strange foreigners. I'll bet money talks, though." I am pleased to say when we passed him in our taxi 20 minutes later he was gesticulating wildly among a group of local gestapo and taxi drivers who clearly found his money didn't talk as loud as he did.

Forty minutes of fast driving later, but only £10 lighter, we arrive at our little self-catering flat in a small village near Albifeira. The hypnotic aroma of the eucalyptus immediately brings on a biblical mood. So I spend half-an-hour in meditation while Maggie unpacks.

My period of peace is interrupted by the apartment's caretaker (the apartments are British-owned, of course). Like many entrepreneurs, he knows what goes on locally, and like all entrepreneurs, he knows most about money. "You have government elections coming up soon," I said because I couldn't think of anything else. "Yes," he said. "Another one" – dismissing politics and politicians with a snort. "Now about money. No need to go to the bank. I'll give you such and such," he said, mentioning a figure some 10 per cent better than the Scrooges in Stornoway's Royal Bank had given me. "You are quite right," I said. "There are more important things than politics." Sadly, he would have nothing to do with Maggie's fivers, saved out of her Family Allowance, because they were Scottish.

I was outraged. I threatened him with media exposure, physical violence, eternal damnation and finally with Donald Stewart. At the mention of the latter's name he affected a bland posture of ignorance which I must assume was feigned and well practised. He offers me tickets for a bullfight. I laugh at a Portuguese bullfight as Ernesto would have laughed. He smiles. He understands.

I send him on his way and proceed to inspect the flat with a view to bad-tempered grousing in the morning. I am disappointed. Not a cockroach in sight. Only two familiar splashes of blood on the wall above the bed. I never worried much about mosquitoes in the old days. On the whole they are much less of a nuisance than our midges. Yet in these terribly uncertain times one doesn't like to be at the mercy of a bloodsucking insect whose last port of call could well have been a gentleman suffering from what the French call "the English disease".

We go out in search of food, because that is what self-catering means if the housewife has been influenced by the MDFU (Movement for the Destruction of the Family Unit). Not long ago I read somewhere of Clement Freud's search for Portuguese cuisine. He couldn't find it, through no fault of his own, because unlike me he is not a peasant. Portuguese cuisine begins and ends with sardines, much the same as ours began with herring and ended in fishmeal.

I order some drinks while waiting for my sardines – two Cokes, a large brandy and a small lager. If my calculations are correct the round comes to £1.20 and I think I am going to enjoy it here. If I am wrong and it's £12.00 I am already in trouble, so I am going to enjoy it anyway.

On every corner you meet British girls desperately urging you to visit new timeshare apartments with swimming pools, games (??) and – wait for it – donkey rides. Nearly everyone declines these invitations. Even the English, I am told, cannot be attracted by the free lunch. I feel sorry for the girls on commission but my friends in Greenpeace will be pleased to hear the donkey seldom has to move from the shade.

DAY TWO

I'm a rover, seldom sober ... Sorry, ours is a nudist beach. We got it at half price. There are 12 days to go. This is my first attempt at a proper diary. I shall have to pace myself. It takes much more time and space than I anticipated. The rest of the holiday will be published in booklet form in time for Christmas. Title – *In Search of Portugal (or Looking SSW)*, £24.50 plus post and package.

PS Who is this MacVicar fellow who had tenancy of these sacred columns while I was on holiday? I hope he's not a Catholic.

13 SEPTEMBER, 1985

MONDAY

It is not often I get the better of Leslie, since he stopped playing poker. Sally put the five card stud shackles on him the first time we let him ashore on his own. But when it comes to bus timetables, be they in deepest Sussex or remote Caithness, he is in a class of his own – a class of one, to be exact, because he is the only person I've ever met who cares passionately about bus routes and timetables.

He is also an expert on movies and movie-making. Quite honestly, I think he should have went in for something.

If there is anything worth watching on TV he usually lets me know well in advance. Today he shambled into my office with a noticeable display of excitement about his considerable personage. "It is absolutely imperative you see tonight's documentary on the concentration camps, suppressed – I don't know why – for 40 years." My reply: "Leslie," arsa mise, "you have misread your *Radio Times*. I was up until 12.30 watching it and all night thinking about it." I am still thinking about it.

This film should have been shown not at midnight but instead of *Coronation Street*. It should be shown once a week for evermore as a constant reminder of what we are capable of. Orwell, honestly, thought it couldn't happen in Britain. I hae ma doots.

TUESDAY

Anyway, this is not the page to weep upon. If that is your taste, turn to page three. This page is where you expect to find fun, or ridiculous optimism.

I know now that I am an optimist, or at least not a perfect pessimist. Otherwise, as the Navigator's wife said the other night, I would have no option but to do away with myself at once. The trouble is that takes great courage. My lack of courage must make me an optimist. Did you ever read Kafka? His problem was he wouldn't let himself take the cùram. Although hardly yet on his level, I am trying desperately for the cùram, but it won't come on me.

I sometimes rest in the horizontal at my place of work with all the windows open, waiting for the cùram to float in. What do I get? Leslie flops down the corridor trying to sell me tickets for the Film Society at £14 a go. The Devil, I need hardly remind you, takes many gross and deceptive forms. He can also be a very persuasive salesman. I find myself forking out £14 to see *The Killing Game* on Saturday night because this smoothie tells me if I don't it could cost me £2. I am easily baffled by economics and sometimes wonder how I became a successful businessman.

WEDNESDAY

Before I became a businessman I had, as you know, done many things. What I am going to tell you now you must keep strictly to yourselves because the nation's security is at risk.

It was early in 1940. We were in the South Atlantic trying to dodge a German raider who was trying to dodge us. I had only just climbed onto the bridge to relieve my Number One. It was a calm and uneventful night until then. "No need," said the Mate. "You must keep a clear head for decision-making." "Nonsense," I snapped. I was never one to shirk a watch despite the burden of my administrative responsibility. I even insisted the look-out man get his head down. That is the way I was. That was also my first mistake in an otherwise blameless career. Not many minutes had passed when I took a burst of shrapnel in the lower abdomen. That was how the dirty dogs fought.

THURSDAY

Needless to say, I was invalided out and within a matter of months found myself in Stornoway's Castle Grounds in the Home Guard under Captain Scott Senior. An ignominious end to a promising career, I imagine you saying. How very, very wrong you can be. Had it not been for C S Senior and me, how very differently it all could have ended.

True enough, our resources were limited – a few hundred Siarachs with bad hearing and cromans for weapons. But, as history now allows me to tell, this pathetic-looking band of ill-equipped men met and blootered Hitler's main assault force at the Butt of Lewis while his diversionary force drew attention at Dunkirk. This has been one of the best-kept secrets of the war and, as I said, perhaps not yet ready for general release. So, cùm agad fhèin e.

FRIDAY

Is it any wonder, with the SAS all around us, that I am called in as adviser to the local Home Guard? I am certain Captain Scott Junior will graciously concede as one officer to another that at times like these experience is all-important. Yet I am reluctant to take absolute command and would rather see what the youngsters will make of it. I let C S Junior take over.

He has the brilliant idea of releasing all the monofilament nets confiscated from poachers to the local Dad's Army for the purpose of securing the perimeter of the airfield. I make a half-hearted attempt to tell him that most SAS men can see better than salmon even at sea, let alone on Sandwick common grazings, where even the Melbost cailleachs can spot the nets from a passing bus. He is a desperately headstrong character and insists on the mono. I didn't fear for the SAS men, but who's going to pay the damages if ex-councillor Willie John Macdonald is found enmeshed in a net tomorrow morning? As a last desperate ploy the local administration came up with a typical army solution for an unbreakable code – Gaelic.

As I said before, I cannot give too much away, but surely our intelligence officers should have checked the surnames of the SAS Regiment. I wonder if the name Donald Macdonald would have meant anything to them? I believe it is a pseudonym often used by Rooshian spies.

4 OCTOBER, 1985

MONDAY MORNING

After a day's unimaginable boredom at the office it is extremely difficult to force oneself to record details of the drudgery in diary form. But it must be done, if only so that generations yet unborn can read and marvel at the miseries that drove their ancestors to despair.

At nine o'clock I read several instruments and recorded the results in a ledger and passed them to the nation. As soon as I had done that I transferred the readings to another page to be stored for posterity. Then

I tore several yards of paper off the teleprinter and cut it into neat two-foot strips and hung them on a clip. At ten past nine I strolled along the corridor to the lavatory, only to find it engaged. This infuriated me because everyone knows I always go to the lavatory at this time. My physical equilibrium, not to mention my emotional stability, is totally dependent on getting to the lavatory at ten past nine. There is clearly a move afoot among my colleagues to rock these delicate balances.

Although no changes have taken place in atmospheric conditions, and despite my distressed condition, I once again read the same figures and enter in the good book, carefully. I always try to be careful, even when deprived of my toilet, because carelessness in field experiments will render the analyst's work void and the experiment futile. However, just for badness I cut the teleprinter strips into uneven lengths of two and two-and-a-half feet. That'll teach them. In a moment of uncharacteristic idleness I wonder if the man in the toilet is tearing the paper in single sheets or double.

In a matter of minutes it is time to record the same figures again. I wander outside to take stock of the celestial dome and I notice a cumulonimbus developing over Stornoway (probably generated by heat from the *Gazette* office). At the same time I catch a glimpse of my own reflection in a window. The tail of my shirt is hanging out, flapping in the wind, and my jerkin is ballooned up behind me, almost – I imagine for a second – like a cumulonimbus. I reprimand myself for being unscientifically fanciful but still I hop up and down and the resemblance grows. Disregarding a subconscious warning that I might be going mad, I wonder if it could be possible to shake off the depressing gravitational forces that are dragging me down. The freedom of the skies seems irresistible. I jump a little higher ... and higher ... I am away ...

Intoxicated with my release from bondage and my new-found unlimited powers, I immediately begin to take advantage. My first victim is a poor farmer attempting to gather hay in Moss End. He has only just laid the foundation of his first stack and is probably giving thanks for a few hours sunshine when I nonchalantly drift over him to let loose a torrential downpour. While still gloating I see a glorious opportunity for revenge – a British Airways 748 coming across the Minch. I'll teach them, I think, to raise fares and divert to Glasgow at the flimsiest excuse. I hope the aircraft is full of councillors and officials on expenses because I blow up my anvil and belch up a tremendous turbulence that threatens to blow her wings off. Still chortling, I retire to rest on the Harris hills and wonder if anyone ever had so much fun. But sitting on cold mountain tops can be desperately bad for the haemer … hem … – piles. So I push myself up into the south-westerly wind and allow myself to be carried over Loch Leurbost …

Even from 20,000 feet I can see that the figures on the rafts are strangely motionless. However, I let them off with a warning rumble of thunder. Above Point I detect that they are all tuned into the Labour Party Conference when they should be making hay. I content myself with a small electrical storm – just enough interference to blot out reception and drive them back to work.

But a cumulonimbus, although powerful, has a very short life. I am acutely aware of approaching old age. As I draw near the airport for my final ploy I can no longer raise a decent anvil and my intended violent hailstorm is a mere dribble. Worn out but intensely happy, I stumble back into the office. My sympathy knows no bounds for those who are chained to desks and meaningless tasks for a lifetime.

MONDAY AFTERNOON
On the way home two labouring types in the Caberfeidh comment on how tired I look. They ask amidst much sniggering how anyone can be exhausted sitting on his bum in an office all day. The poor ignorant fools cannot be expected to understand what you and I go through, but nevertheless I read them a stern lecture on the stress and strain attached to brain work.

One of them holds out a calloused hand and says: "That is what real work does to you." A newcomer, a stranger, proudly exhibits a broken thumb as proof of his honest toil. "What are you anyway?" he asks.

"A teacher?"

"Of a sort," I reply, "and sometimes I play God." Hostility and suspicion force me to leave after one instead of my customary two.

11 OCTOBER, 1985

MONDAY

I met the Barvas Navigator in the Caledonian Hotel the other day. He was on his way to Cairo and I was bound for North Lochs. I'll say this for him: if he felt envious that I should be heading for the lush pastures of God's green acre while he was destined for the barren wastes of Arabia, his expression didn't betray it. As a matter of fact he appeared unusually cheerful, smiling and occasionally laughing out loud as if he'd scored a goal against Point. Of course I couldn't ask him what was so funny because that was obviously what he wanted me to ask. I cannot grant him that satisfaction because we have known each other too long.

"You're not looking too good," I said. (He works for an American company. He is as fat as a pig, disgustingly healthy and the colour of freshly-cut black peat.)

"I know," he said, the smug blaigeard, "I need a holiday. I've booked a safari tour in East Africa."

"Fine, Captain Smith," arsa mise, "fine, if you like that sort of thing."

Funny thing is, or was, when he was young and a poor apprentice with Denholm's, a tour of East African ports would have seemed a hellish chore. Amazing how wealth alters perspective. The view seems always to improve the higher one steps. From the bridge it is at its best.

TUESDAY

The funny thing is that because of our poverty-stricken childhood we continue to make ridiculous economies even now. The Navigator will, as is the way with the rich (they are different from you and me), get from Cairo to Nairobi for nothing. His wife, Christine of the Million Tortures, will have to pay her own way. Now, as every schoolboy who reads the

Daily Telegraph knows, no one buys his own ticket for an international flight nowadays. How to get round this unnecessary expense was the Navigator's only concern. Was it possible, he wondered, to send her steerage? He is full of these quaint old expressions.

Of course he found a way. He always does. Apparently, while catching up with the last six months' newspapers, he learned of the Nigerian method. He has had our carpenter nail a large airy box together and is sending Christine to Nairobi air freight. I deplore this miserly approach to matrimony and will only forgive him if he sends the box back full of cigars.

WEDNESDAY

Please do not adjust your spectacles, for this is another true story. All the characters are alive and well and can be found in the Caley every Friday night. I retail the story only because so many of you are worried about your shares in British Telecom.

It all began last Spring when a friend of mine in Ranish became concerned about his old fellow. The old man's behaviour was becoming rather irrational – threatening to leave his money to a cat and dog home, that sort of thing. My friend thought he had better get the phone put in for the Da.

British Telecom responded to his request with the astonishing speed and eagerness to please that is only to be found in newly-stolen companies. A tunnel was dug, a coil of wire appeared in the lobby and then the tunnellers disappeared. Co-dhiù, after a decent interval – six months – Coinneach phoned BT HQ in Inverness where they speak the best English in the warld and asked what was keeping his phone. "Ah," said the man with the warums in this mouth, "you need a pole." There followed a lengthy argument during which my friend who is stunningly articulate in both languages tried to convey the message that the line was already "in" and all he needed was the plastic bit at the end. "I am sorry, you stupid coastwester," said the Invernessy man, "you need a pole."

So what the heck, though Coinneach; if he wants to send a pole I'll get three strainers out of it. But no. When the linesman arrived with a pole on his roof-rack he said: "I think I recognise the terrain. I have already run a line into this house." They didn't leave the pole, though.

WEDNESDAY

How local should a local radio station be? What is the crazy reasoning behind this latest move to colonise Inverness where 99.9 per cent of the population are ignorant of Gaelic (and English) and tuned into Moray Firth Radio? Radio nan Eilean was news-orientated from the beginning and very good at it. By news, I mean local news. Any other kind makes no sense because the audience has already heard it in English.

Alan Macdonald was as narrow-minded in some ways as the narrowest of the Wee Free. He had the audacity once to censor a piece I did on "the skate as an aphrodisiac", at a time. I might add, when the birth-rate was falling in the islands. But he was very good at news.

Coinneach Mòr and Ciorstag had probably the biggest audience ever of a Gaelic programme in *Feasgar Dihaoine*. It was of course very lowbrow. Those who direct operations do not like to think that Gaelic listeners have a *Coronation Street*-sized brow. Maybe they are right, but if you want the attention of the carefree masses you don't start with Sorley. Try the old-style *Feasgar Dihaoine* first and introduce the big words gradually.

Better, perhaps, to drop news altogether and save your money for the plays Angus Peter and I are going to write this winter.

THURSDAY

Talking of millionaires, which we weren't … It seems Allan Grant is determined to become a millionaire before I am. Rumour has it he has bought the Bruar Falls Hotel, near Blair Atholl. Allan intends to continue the tradition in Grant hotels of giving free drams to anyone who speaks Gaelic. He will, of course, continue to supply Western Isles salmon as he did in the Four Seasons in Ullapool. This product will not be free. On the contrary, it will be extremely expensive because it is the best.

25 October, 1985

Dear Maggie,

Thank you very much. Yes, I am as well as can be expected. As well, that is, as anyone can be who is left on his own to run a home, a croft, a fish farm, a cat, three hotels and a turf accountant's establishment while his family and business partners enjoy themselves on the mainland. Please don't think for a moment I begrudge you your spree in Inverness so soon after your fortnight on the Algarve because I don't. On the contrary, I approve wholeheartedly of your willingness to travel so far from home is search of bargains. Good housekeeping is something I have learned to appreciate.

I'm pleased to say that, yes, I am managing to feed myself fairly well. The bowl of cornbeef hash you froze did for three meals as you predicted. On Saturday I shared my salt herring with Karachi, but we didn't go to town afterwards although we were very thirsty. True, we went the night before, but only because your man needed milk and the local shop was closed. You say you heard I was seen in the vicinity of the pubs with Kenny the plumber on Friday but I can assure you that we had a very good reason. We desperately needed some drainage items and it is hardly our fault if every shop and service in town closes between one and two, which is when we happened to arrive. Only the pubs stay open at this time and I am sure you would rather we took shelter than chance catching our death of cold. Incidentally, don't you find it strange that pubs can manage staggered lunch breaks while shops cannot?

You mention having met people on their way to and from the Mod. I honestly thought this year's had been cancelled that time we stopped saving. But I get easily confused these days with so many folk festivals about. I asked several old fellows here in North Lochs what the word 'mod' means and no one seems to know. I am not sure it has much to do with us but as long as people enjoy it, and many seem to do so, they should be allowed to frolic to their heart's content. I might even have done some frolicking myself if I had remembered. But even if I had we cannot all leave the island at the same time, can we? By the way, did you see Calum? You say you met Donald John MacSween looking for a head transplant. Did he say if this was a result of the Mod or the dawning of common sense? Or has he taken religion?

I am pleased to hear you finally managed to get your father to do something about a Will. Not that we wanted a penny, of course, but it seemed a shame to leave it all to the church when there are so many other worthy causes in need of support. I'm sure he'll sleep easier now having made some provision for you, his own daughter. Did he, by the by, mention a figure?

Thanks for your cutting from the *Daily Express* of Nicholas Fairbairn's article. As you know, I have long been an admirer of his and I'm glad to learn he has gone to see for himself what conditions are like in the native 'locations' so he can inform his readers in this country of ignoramuses. Wasn't it brave of him to venture into Soweto in these troubled times to witness at first hand the perfectly "adequate" housing provided for three million idle blacks by our "wealth-creating" allies the Boers? We so seldom nowadays get to read the truth in our newspapers, which have largely been taken over by leftist subversives who would have us believe the Bantu are oppressed. The same distorters of truth have suggested that my learned friend Fairbairn didn't come closer to a shanty town than a five-star hotel in Jo'burg. I would have these poisoned media reptiles shot. I noticed the other day when I did the paper run that three *Daily Expresses* are taken in East End Leurbost. How comforting to know that at least three of our neighbours have a clear view of world affairs.

Another day has passed and I have learned more about the art of lone survival. Through the happy accident of dropping in on friends while they are having their meals I find little need for cooking and even less for washing dishes. I took the West End Tory for a pint and forgot my purse but he didn't mind because Harris Tweed is making that funny noise again – booming. Thus do I make small economies that will allow at least one of us to jaunt. Any sign of Calum yet?

You complain bitterly that I forgot your birthday. I keep telling you we didn't have birthdays in black-houses. Anyway, how could I possibly have suspected you were a year older when you don't look a day over 40.

By the way, I had a bad experience with the cat. While I nipped into town for a message, she dragged a whole side of sheep I was salting for your return onto the floor and the fat seems to have melted. To make matters worse, several drunks came in and slithered about spreading the grease into all four corners. I think we'll have to get rid of her.

You are no doubt wondering why I address you as 'dear'. It dates back to Calum Ruairidh Chaluim and the Rev MacIomhair. Calum's wife had also run away, so he approached the reverend for assistance with the letter. "Dè mar a thòisicheas mi, a mhinisteir?" "Feuch 'dearest," ars am ministear. "A, Dhia," arsa Calum, "nach eil sin car làidir."

I, too, thought 'dearest' was a bit strong for a public letter, and if you are puzzled about the public bit, there is a very good reason. I notice that many of our old friends have their letters published when they are long dead. This seems a very unsatisfactory arrangement because I doubt if even the posh Sundays are delivered in heaven (for which we are surely destined). For the same reason I have given Ian Stephen permission to publish some of my early love letters. It seems the so-called educated reader has an insatiable appetite for gossip and trivia and would rather read these letters than my serious poems.

PS I hope you took the children with you because I haven't seen them round the house for several days.

Y.U.T.C.C.H.
EM

1 November, 1985

MONDAY

Once again I must cross swords with The Professor. In the latest edition of the Free Church *Monthly Record* The Prof attacks Dr A J Monty White, who has written a book claiming the earth is only a few thousand years old. Although The Professor and I are at one on many issues, and no matter how much I like his style, I cannot let his criticism of Monty White go unchallenged.

Monty is not known to me personally but he is clearly a member of our own Flat Earth Society. Furthermore, being a Monty he is probably related to the Montgomerys of Ranish and therefore a cousin of mine – probably a close cousin if the earth is as young as we believe it to be. And some of us believe it to be very young indeed, even younger than Monty thinks.

It is well known – and surely I don't have to produce evidence for this as modern physicists like The Prof would demand – that in Ireland and the west of Scotland we have the best storytellers in the world with the best memories. Yet the oldest of their tales are a mere 1,500 years old. Believe me, if the earth was any older these boys would remember it. And is it not also likely that if the universe was created a slice at a time Ireland and Scotland were added at a very late date as an afterthought with the bits of bog and rock left over.

In support of his Old Earth Theory, The Professor draws on distinguished theologians like Thomas Chalmers. A powerful man, Chalmers, we do not doubt; but we have evidence that at the height of these powers he was on eight bottles of wine a day. Is it any wonder that he had little sense of time?

At one point in his crit The Professor takes a passing swipe at the Flat Earth Society. As a subscriber to this belief I take exception to The Professor's veiled suggestion that the earth is round. Has he ever tried to push a bicycle from Leurbost to Harris? If the earth was round as he claims, it would take no effort, never mind five gears.

TUESDAY

Much to my disgust, I had to take a very hypocritical stance re this flat earth argument just recently. Some city types from Glasgow had arrived to erect a steel shed for me. When they attempted to position the framework on our concrete foundation they complained that the eastern legs were somewhat short of the ground. "You poor ignorant fools," I said, "do you not appreciate that Karachi is a builder with modern ideas and likes to allow for the earth's curvature." They were bewildered by my grasp of the sciences, but I detest myself for having used false argument.

WEDNESDAY

On the MV *Suilven* the other morning (I had to swallow my pride and go looking for Maggie) I became aware, although I was engrossed in the *Monthly Record*, of the presence of a tall, serious man. I am not easily distracted from serious reading but this distinguished elderly gentleman wasn't easily ignored. His hair although sparse was the correct shade of executive grey; his clothing although carelessly casual had about it the stamp of quality, good taste and great wealth. It took me 10 minutes to recognise Iain Smith, known to my father's generation as 'Tarbh an Ach'. I always knew he would make it in the big bad world from the moment I first heard him pronounce 'Gàidhlig' with a grave accent on the 'à', as is the custom with those of us who are destined to life on the croft.

"Let me guess," I said, "you've been over to meet the SNP selection committee." "As a matter of fact," he said, "the applications were in last July and I didn't even put my name forward." I have no reason to disbelieve Iain, for I never found him to be a liar, yet I was left with the suspicion he could have told me more than he did. I resolved to observe him closely for the rest of of the voyage.

I watched him carefully as he walked through the cafeteria for a snack, and unless I detected a developing 'holy shuffle' my name is not Montgomery. This holy shuffle, as the irreverent call it, is a peculiar walk cultivated by some men who are contemplating full-time church attendance. The pace is extremely slow, with one foot, usually the right, being dragged slightly slower than the other. Often the head is slightly bent and tilted as if tuned in to a garbled radio transmission. In Mr Smith's case the development is at such an early stage he is probably not yet aware of it himself. I may, of course, be reading too much into these signs: they are possibly no more than the outward manifestation of advancing years. On the other hand, there is a vote in every painful step.

THURSDAY

I found Maggie in Inverness, but negotiations for her return were prolonged and bitter. "I'm fed up," she said, "with your presents of ladders, wheelbarrows and coils of rope. I want a decent car for myself or I stay put." What could I do? I hate washing dishes. I will have to stay out of the pubs for three years and take on a fourth job, but if that is what it takes to keep a family together it must be done.

FRIDAY

I see a letter in this week's FP from a Mr Paul Yoxon who wants to keep Skye an island. He fears a bridge would open the way for a swarm of undesirables from the south bent on rape and arson. I wonder if Paul Yoxon could be another psendonym used by Paul Cowan, editor of the *Sy Gazette*. Whether it is or not, it is reassuring to know there are people like Mr Yoxon in our midst who are willing to speak out against the dangers of immigration. Would that be the Yoxons of Glencoe or Glen Garry, Mr Yoxon?

SATURDAY

At last I have found out why Invernessians walk with their heads down. It seems incredible that these small poodles can produce so much waste unless they are on an all-bran diet. Entire streets are in imminent danger of being blocked with dog manure. Fifty per cent of the population are very poor and have their heads down looking for dogends and the other fifty have their eyes down for the ... Well, finish it yourself.

15 November, 1985

MONDAY

I am ill at ease and unable to think in the right language because tonight I have to take part in a Gaelic activity of sorts in An Lanntair. Sure, it's only for a laugh: isn't that what Gaelic is for. But still I ask myself what I'm doing in the company of these Tory pillars of the establishment: DHM, ex-Provost Ann Urquhart, Dòmhnall Lìsidh and Coinneach MacIomhair. I guess I am the token white. I'll be back in a couple of hours.

As I expected, they refused to take anything seriously. I tried to set a responsible tone, hoped even for some discourse on existentialism, but there was no chance. They had to play it for laughs. This is the old Tory trick again – keep them laughing and you won't feel their hand in your pocket. Perhaps it was just as well, because there cannot be more than five people alive today with sufficient vocabulary for a sober Gaelic discussion. And I am not one of them.

Tory or no, it must be admitted that Ann Urquhart at 84 years of age is a remarkable woman. If one were free one could quite easily still see oneself forming a romantic relationship with her.

For Stornoway boys, in BBC reverse

If there was a night like her it was not to my memory, however, from that height. When she is coming from NE by N, most often, you are allowed to bank the fire without any fear on you or those that belong to you that the house will climb up in stars. But that isn't the way she was last night because even before the cat was put out there was a bad semblance on her. She was whistling through the willows and shaking the leg-ties until you would think the roof was going to rise from the house and the chamber pot was going to fall from the dresser.

Although sleep fell on me at the end, it wasn't long that lasted because the wind rose again with a terrible blast that would put the fear of your life on you. I rose up out of my bed and went to the window to see if I could see anything but she was black dark without light or movement on the village-head. It came in on me – and it wasn't the first time – but what sort of man, male or female, could sleep through that like of storm? However, it is certain it wouldn't be a man with his livestock tethered in the ocean.

I could make out just the shape of sheep huddled in the shelter of the rushes. One thing is sure, I said to myself, it is a fortunate man who isn't as unfortunate as me. A fortunate man who knows whatever bad thing might befall his sheep he can sleep without fear the waves will smash them on the shore and leave them on the rocks without hope for the days ahead nor consolation for the days that went. Days that were not easy for him and those who weren't far away from him when he wanted them close to him.

But what is going to happen is going to happen and it is foolish to pretend that any man, male or female, is going to stop or alter those things that were promised. We were without much hope at the start of the beginning and nothing ever happened in our lives from this side that would give us cause to expect anything else. We were born as Gaels and we have no reason to expect we will not die as Gaels.

After ten minutes long had passed without sign of abatement on the wind, I took a look at the children who were sleeping in the wind-end of the house and there isn't anyone alive who could know on them how she was out. They have a while like that as we had ourselves and everyone has. But in the blink of an eye that while is gone for every man, male or female. The facsimile of their sleeping innocence is lodged in my mind's eye and it's a wonder if it won't be forever.

From here out neither day nor night will be so peaceful for one over one of them because each day and night will bring torment and worry. But fortunately, if they are spared until they reach age, we hope they will not have to put a face on the sort of agony and suffering that kept us and our ancestors in the terrible state we are in and always will be.

I took a step back through the door to see if the one that is there was aware that everything we had worked for was nearly going out of our sight, but there was a snore at her that would put the horses from the corn. What good was it me to be walking the floor and her in her hundred sleep? There was nothing for it but to lean back in the bed and put my two frozen feet on her back, but she would sleep on the daggers. She only gave one backward kick like a mare wild and fell back in her sleep. It was then I said, To the house of the female dog with it, why should I worry and put myself in a tangle? But sleep wouldn't fall with me. I climbed down the stairs and found two of the boys at the back of the door. What sort of man, male or female, could sleep through the like of this, they said. If only they knew.

FOOTNOTE Before I forget, I have this delightful little Japanese car for sale. It does 200 mile to the gallon and has several new bits. It was once owned by a holy man in Plasterfield who only drove between house and church. But the most attractive part of its history is that it was never driven by a woman. You could almost say I am giving it away.

20 DECEMBER, 1985

MONDAY

Yet another salmon theft on the west side of the island, which makes me think it is only a matter of time until someone – probably an innocent person – eats a recently-treated salmon. Occasionally, it becomes necessary to administer various medicines to sick fish, so we isolate them and delay marketing for a while. Not that it would do you much harm to eat a weakly salmon on antibiotics but, unlike pig-breeders, we care about the consumer and try to keep unnecessary medicines out of your diet.

The one I really worry about is the deadly chemical Nuvan used to kill lice. Even the instructions on the bottle worry me. Wear two pairs of gloves, stand wind-up, don't breathe, dilute to one part per million, and have oxygen standing by.

Supposing some fool was to take one of these recently-treated salmon for a friend and the friend, being a bigger fool, eats it. Observe the friend closely. Immediately he complains of stomach pains. Soon afterwards he becomes very dizzy and wants to lie down, which is just as well because by this time his legs are too weak to hold him up. At this stage the stomach pains become unbearable and the patient often produces a green-coloured froth about the mouth. There is no point in sending for a doctor then because invariably, and mercifully, death follows very quickly.

TUESDAY

Following an embarrassing incident in which a man and a boy were marooned on a salmon cage in Loch Grimshader, I've been asked by the Stornoway lifeboat crew to organise a seamanship course for fish farmers. My answer is certainly 'No'. These short trips into Loch Grimshader are an ideal exercise for the lifeboat crew, and the longer it takes Booker McConnell's "sailors" to learn to tie knots the better.

I do not believe for a moment that Calum Noo – who spent 40 years before the mast – was responsible. More likely he left the youngster to secure the boat, with predictable results. Still, they must learn.

WEDNESDAY

For some years now the Acres Boys Club has been our island's best ambassador. But what a pity they don't know what's good for them. I hear they have once again entered a competition in which early success could mean their playing football on a Sunday. Poor children. They are so young, so unaware. So easily led by the forces of darkness. The Stornoway Free Church minister wants to stop them. To stop their pocket money and their fares. What a pathetic threat. How feeble. Where is the old fire and thunder? Never mind your petty blackmail (or it is whitemail in this case?) – frighten them into obedience in the old-fashioned way.

What is Acres Boys' concept of eternity? Do they think it is perhaps only slightly longer than a period of maths? What degree of pain can they imagine? Perhaps they shudder to think of their teeth being extracted without anaesthetic, or perhaps they can imagine their nails being torn from the flesh with a pair of pliers. Or their eyes gouged from their sockets. Perhaps they can conceive of these tortures prolonged for a day or even a week, but possibly even that much is beyond them in their urgent need for immediate gratification of fleeting earthly desires.

"That much," let me warn them, is nothing. The pains of which I speak are mere midge bites and a whole lifetime is but a micro-second. Try to picture it the way it is going to be if you kick a football on Sunday. See it in your mind's eye. Try to feel the agony of a thousand demons' scalding whips as you boil and burn in that seething cauldron for time everlasting. Put your hand in the fire for one second and try to conceive of infinite duration. Do you still want to play on Sunday? See what I mean. There now, Magnus, I knew there was no need to resign.

THURSDAY

Very peculiar goings-on in the Chambers this week re that DHM business. It could easily be imagined by an outsider looking through the window that our councillors are very forgetful, or else a groat short of the shilling. I do not believe for a moment they could be induced to change their minds through threat or promise as has been suggested by some who thrive on belief in conspiracy. I am convinced this was again merely a case of old age. How can men who have 'done their good' be expected to remember on Thursday what they said on Tuesday?

While I am at it I must further deflate the gossipmongers who have been putting it about that the second man up DHM's sleeve is Boots the Chemist. There is simply no truth in this scurrilous pub talk.

FRIDAY

On my way to the Rangers Club tonight to see Hamish Imlach and Ian MacIntosh I met an ambulance tearing out of Inaclete Road. "Exactly as I thought," I said to Maggie, "and the show has barely started." As it happened, an ambulance so near the club was pure coincidence.

The gentlemen and ladies in the club turned out to be genuine ladies and gentlemen. There was no brawling, swearing, bottom-pinching or tribal chanting of the sort one normally associates with Rangers supporters. In fact, one wonders if the audience was not made up of specially-imported afficionados of Celtic folk. Whoever they were – and surprisingly they could have been more – they were very lucky. Hamish seems to have improved with age, especially his smoking song. He is, I suppose you could say, the thinking man's Billy Connolly. Funnier, too. And less desperate than Norman Maclean.

But I didn't just go along because Hamish is the best entertainer in Britain. I was there as a curious medical man. How could anyone who has been 12 stone overweight for the last 27 years still be alive on a diet of booze and fags? He is living proof, if proof were needed, that you cannot always believe everything we doctors tell you.

1986

7 FEBRUARY, 1986

MONDAY / TUESDAY

For the last few days I hardly knew myself. My physical and mental wellbeing exceeded anything I could have hoped for, even in Heaven itself. In fact I felt so good I couldn't believe it was me. The morning retching and coughing had gone. I was seriously thinking of asking the management of Lochs Football Club if I could have a trial for the coming season. At some moments I felt so good I even thought of phoning Ness.

WEDNESDAY

A magnificent winter's day. Cloudless, calm and sunny. But naturally frosty. Because of the frost we could make no headway through the ice on Loch Leurbost. Fortunately I am no hard taskmaster (no Rupert Murdoch, I). If anyone wants to go fishing in the Minch, arsa mise, I would have no objection.

Someone has kindly left a buoy on the Carannaich and there is also a new mark – the War Memorial against the Arnish module. Agus, of course, sìthean na compaist ri Seoraid Mhòr.

The catch, I must confess, was not heavy but the way the still air seemed to hold the cigarette smoke at nostril level was diabolical. Medium-sized pollack was hauled aboard and someone found the remains of a harvesting-day bottle of Trawler Rum. It was barely enough to wet the lips of the crew, yet it seemed to send them into a tobacco-rolling frenzy. They sucked, inhaled and blew until I thought they would die of happiness. And the smoke hovered over the boat as if the Good Lord was testing me. Pretty soon I asked for a smoke.

Please do not be discouraged by this apparent defeat. As a matter of fact you should draw strength from the knowledge that even the strongest of us must and will suffer temporary setbacks. It is absolutely essential at this stage that you do not buy any. Borrow by all means, but do not buy.

THURSDAY

At lunch-time in the County Hotel I came under heavy fire, not only from Sandy the barman – who has never been married and therefore does not understand stress – but also from one of my medical colleagues from South Lochs. Determined to outdo me, he had foolishly cut off the drug without prior preparation. Naturally he was suffering the usual withdrawal symptons. The protective covering of soot was wearing thin. He was coughing and spluttering into his Guinness like someone who had spent the night in Marvig with Murdani Mast. This type of withdrawal illness is very common among heavy smokers. I tried to draw this phenomenon to the non-smoker Dr Beresford's attention a long time ago but he was too young to understand. But he'll learn.

FRIDAY

Anyway, I have lapsed. The time has to be right and it wasn't right for me. I am off to London soon for a three-week course of study. You might very well ask: what does he need a course in? Does he not already know everything? Indeed, I thought I did. But if the powers-that-be judge that it is in my patients' interest that I should be familiar with their "modern methods", then so be it. I must meet strangers and strange situations and I am a nervous person. I must even, I am told, at some stage, address "them" and even, heaven forbid, lecture. I cannot do that without my prop – nicotine. So I must postpone this exercise until 28th February. There is no need for South Lochs medics or anyone else for that matter to give in just because I have.

SATURDAY

Anyway, forget for the moment all that nonsense about smoking. If you can control it at 10 a day as I do now, it is probably less harmful than mountaineering, sky-diving and eating sheep. Many months have passed since I last gave you one of my hot cousin recipes. The other night I took a notion for plain old-fashioned mince with no oriental spices or Italian accompaniments.

Into a frying pan of margarine at 187 degrees C I poured several handfuls of carrots, leeks, turnip, parsnip and onion with a sprinkling of black pepper. (Strictly no salt.) That innocent mixture's aroma seemed to me sufficiently alluring in itself, yet in deference to my carnivorous family I added one and a half pounds of lean minced steak (available only from Hector in Ivor MacAskill if you watch him). I was reasonably pleased with the preliminary tasting until she herself came along and declared it bland. (I blame Alan Frost.)

When her back was turned I emptied half a bottle of brandy into the cauldron. They all thought they had never tasted anything quite so good – not even in Leurbost school canteen. On such spontaneous moments of inspiration are the reputations of great chefs built.

SUNDAY ITSELF

On the subject of frosty Sunday mornings, several letters have been written to the local press concerning the lack of protection given to the man who must go about his business on the Sabbath. Personally, myself, between you and eye, I had my suspicions about these letter-writers. They seemed very much like trouble-making Catholics from the South bent on destroying the harmonious Presbyterian commune we had established over centuries and reinforced with integrated barbed-wire fencing.

Yes, brethren, that is what I thought. Until last Sunday morning when making my way to work down Matheson Road. On both sides of me and fore and aft cars were skidding about on ungritted surfaces. At the same time 2,000 black-clad devotees, of my own faith, slithered cautiously to church. What if through some unthinkable oversight of the Omnipotent Geometrician's one of them was to be run down? What then? Something must be done.

21 FEBRUARY, 1986

MONDAY

All my life I've harboured this terror of prison. If I'm ever caught doing something really bad, I would rather be lashed than locked up. I feel uneasy if I waken up in the morning and I cannot see 50 miles in every direction. On a good day at home I can see the mainland: on a bad day I can still see the lower half of the Harris hills. Here in Reading I can only see about 200 yards.

Much as I like trees, it is not good to have them all around you like barbed wire around a concentration camp. I have written to the local council here to bring to their attention the enormous market for fence-posts on an island we all know well.

TUESDAY

Still, 'tis amazing how quickly one gets used to prison life and the nine-to-five routine. I have a comfortable cell to myself, a sgalag to make my bed and clean the floor, and a team of cooks and waitresses to feed me. The food, it seems, is considered adequate by my English colleagues, but grossly indifferent for normal healthy people. If anyone wants to help out, food parcels should first of all be sent to this paper, where the contents will be tasted and tested. (I have many enemies.)

We have a pub on the premises, so there is no need to have any contact with the outside world. It is as if all one's responsibilities have been taken away. I can understand why some old lags prefer to stay in prison rather than face the uncertainty of freedom. I would not be surprised if I apply to stay here permanently.

WEDNESDAY

One of the lecturing jailers here has promised he will banish my fear of computers and remove their mystery for me. A decent, consicentious man, but I'm afraid he has overstimated his own ability.

I'm pleased to say I have been able to further my study and

understanding of psychology. When you lock a dozen middle-aged strangers together, they start to behave in a most peculiar and alarming fashion – especially during the first few days. The situation is further complicated when there are females in the group. Each individual male seems compelled to project his personality. Even normally-introverted men like myself talk too much and too loudly.

THURSDAY

Six or seven us of decided to visit, for a change, a traditional English pub before tea / supper / dinner. Time is short, so everyone buys his own. When I first came across this English habit 20-odd years ago I was horrified. Now, of course, I realise how eminently sensible this practice is.

There are some boys you and I know well, probably standing at this very minute in the public bar of the Caledonian Hotel, who would consider the individual-buying habit mean. But who is the meanest? The man who buys his own, or the man who has bought six whiskies and six half-pints in the Caley, then refuses to leave until all present have bought a round even if it kills them (it often does)? I once knew a fine old Highland gentleman who would never buy a round in case anyone dropped dead before their turn.

THE WEEKEND

A clean shirt, and up to London to the Regent Palace Hotel, where I am told all the country hicks meet. Strolling around Soho late at night I find very stimulating. I feel an urge to do some work on *The Novel* but manage to resist it. There seems to be an unlimited number of beautiful girls of all colours and nationalities. But you never know where they've been, so I had a bit of stuff sent down from the Western Isles to be safe. Strangely enough, I feel very secure despite all I've read about muggers. I guess we don't look worth mugging.

On Sunday we go to visit old friends from across the water who are now living out near Epsom. Now, that is a different world. All they talk about is house prices. A house is no longer a home down here: it is merely an asset. No one knows his neighbour – they only meet at the street parties they hold when the mortgage rate comes down half a per cent. An extra tin of corned beef that week, perhaps?

I go for a walk round Epsom racecourse so that I can talk knowledgeably to the West End Tory when I come home. The masochistic English at play are a fascinating lot. Cycling, running, sledging and rambling in the cold snow, they look lean and fit. Perhaps it is a good thing after all to have such a heavy mortgage you cannot afford to eat. They live a lot longer than us.

PS There is a Wicker down here with me. I am on a nice little earner as his interpreter.

14 MARCH, 1986

MONDAY

Let me make it quite clear that my decision to join Nature Conservancy was not taken lightly. After many years of tireless work for the cause, I thought it was time I started getting paid for it. Jeer and call me a do-gooder if you will, but there you have it. I am passionately committed to the survival of the peasant. Without the peasant our enjoyment of the God-given glories of these islands would be diminished if not totally destroyed.

The peasant is, and we at NCC are only too willing to admit it, a destructive animal and in some cases a downright pest. And, yes, we do concede that their numbers are increasing; but no way, and I cannot emphasise this too strongly, do we believe it is time for a cull. On this issue I and my colleagues on the Council are in complete agreement.

TUESDAY

The peasant has many natural enemies such as the seal, the corncrake and the landlord, any of which could easily wipe him out if we drop our guard for an instant.

With the exception of the landlord, there is no greater threat to the survival of the peasant than the grey seal. This dirty waterproof ferret has an insatiable appetite for salmon, which, as you all know, is the staple diet of the peasant. Extensive research by our scientists at NCC has now proved conclusively that the seal serves no useful purpose in the grand scheme of things. On the contrary, we are now in no doubt that this worm-infested carnivore exists only to pollute our foreshores and to destroy all that is sacred to the peasant.

Rumour from South Lochs has it that this ravenous beast has taken to roaming the land at night, taking sheep and hens. In view of these alarming reports, we at the Council have decided not after all to award Lord Thurso £3 million to turn the entire coast of Caithness into a seal sanctuary. To console the poor man we left him a mere half-million to do nothing as usual.

Peasants often write to ask what they should do with dead seals. Well, unfortunately they are worth very little even to pet food manufacturers, but we would like to point out that their pelts make very useful long-lasting doormats.

WEDNESDAY

The corncrake may seem to the casual observer a harmless bird and no danger to the peasant – but there, my friends, you are very far wrong. This noisy bird is one of the greatest health hazards in the Outer Hebrides.

There are few peasants who have not been kept awake by the corncrake's raucous croaking, sometimes for nights on end. I myself have spent a sleepless night hunting this bird, with near-disastrous consequences, as some of you might recall. It would hardly be an exaggeration to claim that the insomnia induced by the corncrake has knocked many years off my life expectancy.

If you are lucky enough to bag one, I think I have already given you a recipe for corncrake soup. If any of you are troubled by conscience or are uneasy about our change of policy at NCC, remember to ask yourself: which is the more important, the peasant or the corncrake?

THURSDAY

The cormorant had until recently been considered an enemy of the peasant, but I can assure you this is no longer the case. The renowned naturalist Tony Soper, himself an ex-peasant, told us on BBC2 this week that "the cormorant does not eat or damage marketable fish". This will come as a great relief to the peasants of Lochs, who were getting tired of eating them anyway.

The stag, now, is a different kettle of meat. This brute is as dangerous as a wild Spanish fighting bird. We have long ago lost count of the number of innocent peasants gored to death by rampaging stags. There is only one course of action open to anyone confronted by a stag, and that is shoot on sight. This animal cannot be considered safe until its antlers are hanging on your wall and its hindquarters safely tucked away in your deep freeze. The flesh of the stag is considered by our noble patrons to be too rich for a hungry peasant. They have politely requested that carcases of deer destroyed for whatever reason should be delivered to the landlord's castle. We at NCC are divided on this matter and leave it up to the peasant's better judgement.

FRIDAY

This brings us to the most voracious predator of them all: the landlord. Often in the past it has been touch-and-go whether an impoverished peasantry could continue to exist beside this cunning adversary. This powerful breed, easily recognised by their chinlessness and their loud mirthless guffaw, still breed in great numbers – mainly in their warm London nests.

They are at their most dangerous in August when they migrate north in huge noisy flocks. Their brief sojourn in the cold regions often proves costly for the peasant, because the landlord is obsessed with the peasant's basic food – salmon. Blood is often spilt at this time. But it is seldom the landlord's because he is well guarded by his own brood of Tonton Macoutes. He is further protected by what is laughingly called the law of the land(lord).

When they have had their fun and filled their bellies they always return to hibernate in one big cosy nest known as the House of Lords. There they slumber through the long winter months and dream of next August. One of their leaders, Lord Lazarus Biddulph, had slept until recently for 14 years. Some actually thought he might have died but were afraid to touch him. Then, lo and behold, someone mentioned the word "monofilament". The good lord leapt to his feet and delivered what they call a maiden speech.

We are reluctant to advocate the wholesale destruction of this species, for they provide moments of light relief and, what is more, theirs is the hand that feeds us.

SATURDAY

I cannot sign off this week without once again expressing my disgust with the *Stornoway Gazette*. This was their advert for *Amadeus*, the movie shown by the Film Society on Saturday night:

"Deadly rivalry … Amadeus, a film dealing with the deadly rivalry of Mazart and demon tune-smith Antonio Salieri, is being shown by the film society …"

Salieri I knew, of course, being the champion miller of his day and a son of Kris; but Mazart? Who he? Naturally I assumed Mazart was a Newmarket cowboy and that the film was some kind of modern western. Imagine my disappointment when the story turned out to be about a drunken keyboard player who dabbled in opera – with a laugh like a hyena – the whole thing the figment of some demented American's imagination. Remind me not to read the *Gazette* again.

28 MARCH, 1986

SATURDAY

The morning after the wedding. You would expect that someone who is old enough to remember the wars would have grown some sense, what? I blame my wife. For some time now I've suspected she has been trying to get rid of me, dragging me along to one social occasion after another, and all of them the sort of get-together that involves whisky.

But the liver is a wonderful organ. The largest gland in the body, I seem to remember from medical school, and nature has given us eighty percent more liver than is normally essential to keep us going. This was a very wise move on nature's part, but was eighty per cent enough?

The nervous system is another more serious concern. I believe every doctor has a duty to his patients to experiment on himself to see how much this one can take. However, this is no time for self-pity.

Jan the bride looked stunning in her new frock, and the menfolk looked very handsome in their kilts. I vaguely remember kissing Iain, the best man. I hope this was merely drink-induced confusion and not a result of my recent association with public school chaps in the South.

I have one word of warning for Jan: divers often develop heart trouble in later life. But she is not to worry. A certain seagoing gentleman from Ranish at our table last night has had several new bits sewn into his heart; his wife says she has him connected to a tractor battery under the bed and he is doing fine.

I hear of a simultaneous celebration in Portree involving young Tommy MacKenzie, a man who seemed to me every inch a bachelor. What is it with everyone this spring? Several years ago I counted 42 bachelors in our own village, of varying eligibility. Since then some have died of old age but few of them have got married. I must do an up-to-date stocktake.

SUNDAY
Day of rest.

MONDAY
As everyone in the Parish of Lochs knows well, I am always available to people in distress. My door is ever open. In the absence of confession in the Free Kirk I consider it my duty to listen to and soothe. And discretion is my byword. All subjects, no matter how personal, are classed highly

confidential. Life has few greater pleasures to offer than the satisfaction of sending someone on his way with a lighter load (especially if the load was in his wallet). Today, in the interests of the public and open government, I have to break my vow of silence and perhaps even name names.

Good plumbers are hard to find. One of them who is temporarily in Maggie's reserve army of four million recently applied for a job advertised by WIIC. They wanted an experienced, qualified plumber, and my friend felt he was the man. Thirty-five years' experience, worked on most of the council's own housing schemes with various contractors, seven children to support at the last count and an excellent plumber. Sadly, he gets a quick reply saying he isn't suitable, and this from the Personnel Department. Not even "Your application has been unsuccessful: we were looking for a younger / older man …" Just unsuitable. Fair enough, you might say, perhaps they had an application from someone with a PhD in lavatory bends.

That is not the point. What annoys so many applicants for council jobs these days is that the applications don't get past the recently-created and fast-growing Department of Rejections. Presumably someone sits and shuffles applications like a pack of cards and asks a secretary to choose one.

If and when your application reaches someone in authority with knowledge of your trade, you are asked for references and then rejected, you have no grouse. Or if you have no one will listen to you. But it is not on to be turned down by a buffer.

I feel this is what happened to my own application for Chief Executive. That is why I joined the Masons.

TUESDAY
Now I hold no grudges against Dr George, I expect a lot from him, and the first thing is to do away with the Personnel Department. I have nothing against the staff and I don't know anyone in that department. I wish them the best of luck in their next appointments, doing home help or whatever.

Come next May when I am a member, perhaps I will reveal more of my plans. I will settle first for Chairman of Manpower Services because I cannot expect to make Convener immediately – there are people to be bought first – but that shouldn't take long. Then George and I will make a powerful team, gather grey areas on a corporate basis and stuff like that. We will leave no stone unturned as we sweep out the dirty corners with a clean broom and ditch all the old clichés. I look forward to the next local parliament with some excitement.

WEDNESDAY

The wireless is a wonderful invention and a great source of education. This very day the local station provided the answer to a problem that has bothered me for years. My learned friend Kenny MacIver was talking to my eminent colleague Dr Smith, following the tragic death of a young Scottish boxer. Kenny, it was revealed, is a one-time boxing champion of Aberdeen University (1952). I didn't know this, but now that I do, much of what has been puzzling me is revealed – simply too many heavy blows to the head. I will treat him with more respect in future.

THURSDAY

Punch-drunk or not, he works hard and occasionally comes up with a good programme – like his interview with a very old lady in Coll who turned out to be the grandmother of my oldest buddy, Johnnie Walker. I suppose I'll have to pay dearly for the tape to send him, but business is business.

9 MAY, 1986

MONDAY

I have always been fascinated by the "big change". Last night I turned eagerly to the religious programme *Voyager*, which had promised us coverage of a great modern spiritual awakening in the island of Lewis. Ma-thà, what a disappointment. What a pathetic echo of the sweeping arousals of my youth. I feel I must agree with the Rev Jack MacLeod that this is definitely not the real thing. A few teenagers strumming guitars and singing what sounded to me dangerously akin to pop music does not, I repeat not, constitute a mass revival. Where was the weeping, the wailing, the swaying and fainting, not to mention the gnashing of teeth? If I am not very much mistaken, some of these youngsters were enjoying themselves. Ministers you and I knew, when ministers were ministers, would have been in there like a shot to make a hot bonfire of their guitars. It wouldn't surprise me one whit if there were some Catholics in their midst.

Although as yet the big change has eluded my own body and soul, I do not underestimate the great benefits it has brought to some boys I knew well. Boys who were so far sunk in depravity and debauchery that one could be forgiven for assuming they were beyond redemption. Boys who, when wickedness and evil were being dished out, returned again and again for further helpings. Yes, and girls too. Girls who wore lipstick, even. What does this Tom Morton of the BBC know of these things? Not much, I suspect, because he spoke in the accent of one who is a product of the city on which the light never shines. But could he not have gone, to the bother of searching for a spectacular example of a hard case turned holy? Too much trouble, I suppose, when these innocent children in the image of Cliff Richard were so easily found.

TUESDAY

Let me give you an example, though. I am sure he will not mind my using his name, because if his witness helps spur a transformation among the rest of the housing and finance departments of WIIC he will be well pleased. Brian MacLeod was, let me assure you, very far gone and yet, as he himself would admit, he would have gone further along the same road but for the fact that he had reached the end. The man was in the habit of coming to work without his trousers on. And he was certainly no stranger to bad language, strong drink, tobacco, venison and salmon. When he was younger and able I have heard it said his general demeanour and approach to young ladies could only be classed as lewd and libidinous. His long fortunate absence from the prison cells is down purely to the skill and glib tongue of expensive lawyers. In short, an infamous character.

And yet what do we have today? A new man. A changed man. Of course, I never see him myself these days. One never does see this type once they go that way. On the second or third or fourth of January this very year (he himself is not sure of the date) he woke up in the afternoon, looked at himself in the mirror and didn't like what he saw. Let us be honest, nobody would. The struggle, the inner turmoil of the following week was excruciating, but he made it. The rest of the story has passed into local folklore. The man is changed. His spiritual well-being is beyond doubt – and not only that, his physical trim speaks the story of the big change. Once an untidy 17 stone, he is now reduced to 16.9 – a walking muscular monument to months of self-denial. His friend Alex is concerned and wishes he would revert to type because he believes no one under 17 stone can carry a stag.

WEDNESDAY

Did you ever see a collection of mug shots like the one that filled an entire page of the *Sy Gazette* last week? I doubt it, unless you happened to stop outside a sheriff's office in Tombstone, Arizona in the 1960s. Would you buy second-hand promises from these aspiring councillors? I notice Mr Jerry Mugabe had the good sense to have his photograph taken on a dark night without a flash. This was a good move because the eyes give so much away. In this ward I would vote for Murdo Angus because at least he didn't shirk from exposing the mirrors to his soul. In the Goathill ward I would support Mr MacFarlane, not only because he produced the best written, most intelligent statement on the page but because of the self-satisfied proclamation of his opponent. Mr MacFarlane also had the foresight to submit a photograph I took of him in 1949.

In Benbecula they have a choice of three candidates. Mr Buchanan says he would treat the rich and the poor the same. This is a ridiculous statement. You cannot afford to treat the rich as you treat the poor – the rich would sue you. And the last thing WIIC wants is a spate of costly writs. A Mr Ray Burnett offers lucid representation in a long-winded woolly statement of the type usually associated with the loony left. Neither of the two wants to show us a photograph. Why is this? Can they be wanted somewhere? The third choice, MacArthur, mentions roads. Anyone who mentions roads is out.

The best by a long way is D H M MacIver. Have a close look at this man's face. This fellow, you can tell, has been around. Every crevice, scar and hillock on that craggy face oozes experience and a knowledge of life that should prove invaluable in the great debating chamber. Here is a man who has lived life to the full. I can imagine him saying as Lee Trevino did: "When I kick the bucket I want people to look in the casket and say, that man needed to go." Furthermore, D H M is against "the cutting down of bus services". Quite right. Donnie, so am I. If you have not already done so, go out now and vote for this man. I am confident he will be my mole and my main source of inspiration for the next four years.

THURSDAY
These are indeed times of change, some of them of a most disturbing nature. If what I read in the newspaper is true there are moves afoot (where else), probably initiated by Trotskyite subversives, to force us medical men to retire at the age of 75 – that is, in our prime. For goodness' sake, my own wife's GP is 89 and we have no intention of changing surgeries. True, he gets pulse rate and blood pressure mixed up from time to time but what does that matter. I worry occasionally, though, and I have to remind him now that my wife is 56 he can stop writing her prescriptions for the pill. "Fifty-six," he says. "Well, well, it seems only yesterday I delivered her."

Although slightly younger than him, I sometimes get confused myself. Tonight, as I sat recording the minutes of my humdrum existence, I've had one eye on the television. I could swear Tony Bennet won the world snooker championship and someone called Joe Johnson left his heart in San Francisco. Time to prescribe three spoonsful of Trawler Rum.

FRIDAY

Tonight the North Lochs Comm. Assoc. will make their first attempt to hold their AGM. Do not be afraid to attend because the present committee members are desperate to cling to office. At least I think that is what the chairman told me to say.

At a time when whispers are once again being heard of closing Leurbost secondary school we are fortunate to have Murdie Siarach as chairman of the community association and community council. Murdie was recently appointed assistant director of education and now has the clout to ensure Leurbost will not close in our time.

SATURDAY

I have had many calls from people worried about the radio-active cloud. I was amused by a lady friend from Keose who wanted to know if I would advise her to stay indoors. She had taken her pet lamb in and sent Malky out. She smokes a whole ounce of Golden Virginia every day. Until we learn more about the actual levels I would strongly urge everyone to eat only salmon and drink whisky.

16 MAY, 1986

MONDAY

A countless number of socially-aware ecologists have approached me in recent weeks urging me to "take prompt action on a matter of the utmost concern". And no wonder. I am with them all the way on this one and have agreed to become chairman of the Committee for the Prevention of Arson. Every year about this time you can watch them at it – 20,000 arsonists hacking away at our little island, burning it. How long can we allow this wanton destruction to continue? How long till we have nothing left but a rocky coastline and our main roads? How long indeed will we have roads? With a growing population we must stop them burning our native sod before it is too late.

I do not suggest that everyone should stop cutting peat, all at once, because we do realise that a significant proportion of cutters have a deep psychological need for peat. They need to look out their windows – north, south, east and west – and see house-high stacks on all sides. What comfort they derive from this hoarding we will never know. They certainly take no pleasure in dreaming of the roaring fires to come, because this class of vandal never burns peat. They merely like to look at their ever-lengthening stacks. The Parish of Ness is notorious for its miles of unburnt peat stacks. This is perhaps understandable in the cold, exposed north: they get a certain amount of shelter from the stacks. Anyway, we are not too concerned about the hoarders. If it comes to the worst, as it surely will, we can always put their peat back in the holes. The fellow we are out to stop is the man who has 10 trailer-loads of the island burnt before Christmas.

TUESDAY

Prominent among those who are determined to save what is left of the island are several of the big sheepmen. They have watched a great many of their best ewes drop dead this spring and they know the cause – mineral deficiency. Quite simply, what has happened (as we all knew it would eventually) is that the unusually high rainfall has washed essential minerals into the Minch and Atlantic. The heather, turf and peat that used to retain these minerals have been burnt by the arsonists. I see a conflict of interests developing here, but we on the committee have the backing of the powerful and wealthy NCC. Lord Thurso has donated £300,000 to our cause. I don't see how we can lose.

WEDNESDAY

Talking of Thurso and minute mineral particles, what is to be done about that lethal time-bomb with the unknown length of fuse: Dounreay. Now, I have no intention of confusing what is essentially a simple-minded readership with quantum physics and the inevitably complex language of anti-particles. (If you want to go that deep expose yourselves to the cosmic flux falling from the editorials of the *Stornoway Gazette*.) What we have in Caithness is a straightforward argument between those whose main concern in this short life is next week's paypacket and common sense.

We had the same argument in Stornoway over the NATO base, and precious few got a decent wage out of that one. The pro-nuclear camp, led by the Peter Walkers of this world, have on their side hostages who have mortgages and council house rents to pay. In that corner of Caithness their only way out of debt is Russian roulette. Some of them are quite smart – they have weighed up the odds and decided it could be a long time before the hammer falls on the loaded chamber (and what a load). Their concern for their children does not seem to extend beyond next year's Christmas stocking.

In any case, those who work at Dounreay should have little say in a public inquiry. The prevailing southerly wind would quickly carry the danger to Orkney, and if an inquiry is to have any meaning the Orcadians should be the first and only people consulted.

The French nuclear enthusiasts are often ridiculed by our nuclear establishment for their high-handed, dismissive approach to public inquiries. We are, of course, much fairer: we consult those who live upwind. If our prevailing winds were northerly, our time-bombs would almost certainly be situated on the Isle of Wight. That would amuse the French. Their leading nuclear man says: "You don't consult the frogs when you're draining a bog." You do, mate, when the chief frog is Lord Thurso.

THURSDAY

You may very well be thinking at this stage Dounreay is a long way from our problem: that is, our disappearing island. Should I not in the circumstances be urging a total conversion to peat-power? That is the way it is in the real world – full of grey areas. If I continue to encourage people to burn our island, I will walk out of the house one morning into the sea; if I support nuclear power I get blown into it.

Matters have not been helped by the unexpected return of the Barvas Navigator. He has taken to wintering in Canada, and who can blame him – no peat problem there. I was actually on the verge of sending out an SOS on his behalf (I thought he'd been eaten by cannibals) when he and Christine walked in the other night. I usually support all his crazy ideas, but his latest worries me. He wants to uplift vast stretches of peat bog from Ireland and Scotland and transport them to the deserts of the Middle East for agricultural purposes. His scheme has a lot going for it, but I will not give it my blessing until he promises to curtail his peat-lifting to Lord Thurso's bog.

In the course of a long evening I had hoped to examine the weighty spiritual conundrums with the Navigator's wife but we couldn't get a word in for him and Maggie discusing the oil crisis, investments and money matters in general. They have no more sense of eternity than the average Dounreay worker. This seems to be the problem with so many modern Protestants.

6 June, 1986

MONDAY

The salmon farming industry is going through a lean spell, so we'll all have to work together if we are going to pull through. But no matter how tough the going gets, I will not listen to any more talk about claiming salvage money. I will not hear of making capital out of my fellow man's misfortune. If Willie Bucach has to be towed to safety six times a week, then we will tow him six times a week. Should it ever be necessary, I am sure we could rely on Willie to do the same for us.

It takes a long time to master the art of small-boat manouevring in tight corners. Lining off Rockall in a 110-foot boat is not the sort of experience that is useful in the jungle called Loch Leurbost. Still, we must give the Bucach credit for toughness. Do you know of any other 69-year-old who would go walking on the bottom of six fathoms wearing wellies and oilskins and still be around the angling club to talk about it? The one who did his training in Achiltibuie is also proving to be a bit of an embarrassment.

TUESDAY

As I told you last week, I had a few bob on England for the World Cup at 16–1. I'm beginning to regret it. The least we should expect from one of the so-called great footballing nations of the world is a team of 11 reasonably fit men. What do we get? A collection of cripples swathed in bandages, held together with straps and trusses. On the other hand, this could be a sneaky Sassenach plot to lull the enemy into a false sense of security. Perhaps when the action starts they'll throw away their crutches and come out fighting fit to win me some money. But I haven't much hope.

From what I've seen so far, only the Soviet Union seems to remember the aim of the exercise is to kick the ball into the opposing team's goal. Spain are playing a devastating new formation which will no doubt catch on and quickly spread throughout Europe – a one-nine-one line up that can quickly be reformed to a 1–10–0 when danger threatens. Do not be fooled by the idiots recruited by the BBC to comment – Brazil looked as skilful and dangerous as ever and I fancy them to win the cup.

WEDNESDAY

Caught a flash of the Scots arriving late in Mexico looking a bit bleary-eyed, I thought, and surrounded by an escort of Mexican police. A recipe for disaster if ever I saw one. Will they be tempted to have a go at the polis when they've had a few? Or will the polis have a go at them when they get a bit boisterous, as Scots tend to do? The Mexican police are notorious for their unconventional nightshift routine – rape, robbery and extortion. I worry about the kilties.

THURSDAY

My own footballing career is not something I often boast about, but the souvenir room is there for anyone who cares to view it. I have no doubt I would have made the international scene but for one hulking brute of a right-back called Roddy Goosey.

At that time I was slender and extremely delicate. Roddy was seven foot and 17 stones in his size 12 boots. For two successive seasons on Goathill Park he did his best to trample me into the ground. He chipped my heels, trod on my toes and bruised my kidneys, I wouldn't have minded so much, but we played for the same team.

Some years later he nearly led to my demise in the Harris hills carrying heavy sacks through Hereward the Wake's estate, but that is another story for another day.

FRIDAY

To get away for a break from the World Cup I played golf for the second time in two years. A little practice is essential because I have been selected to represent the Western Isles in a salmon-growers' tournament somewhere near Blairgowrie in July. This is a great honour for me and I am sure the fact that I have not told anyone else on the island about the tournament had nothing to do with my selection. Anyway, I felt I was playing reasonably well until I lost my ball on the second and had to retire. Just as well, because I don't believe in practising too much in case I waste any of my good shots. And they tell me these balls cost over a pound these days.

I fear all this sports coverage is detracting from the really important event of the summer. I refer, of course, to the royal wedding. Let us hope we will soon see much more of that strapping Ferguson woman. What a fine crofter's wife she would have made. Her excessively-developed African rump seems ideally suited to the carrying of peat creels. How very useful she would be for the likes of Willie, rowing him around the loch every time his engine breaks down.

SATURDAY

A Norwegian well-boat that left Achiltibuie with salmon smolts is expected any day but I fear the worst. I am convinced those heathens in the southern isles have deliberately delayed her so we'll be embarrassed by her arrival on a Sunday. We shall see.

27 JUNE, 1986

SUMMER SPORT

OK. So, for some of us it has been a financially disastrous World Cup, but who cares. The shirt went with Brazil, and the G-string went down with England – who were not so bad and who could have done much better had the present political climate permitted them to play the black man from the beginning. (I have no doubt, and I expect confirmation from Mr Robson when I see him next week, that the arch-racialist Jimmy Hill had far too much influence on managerial tactics.)

Back to Brazil. The cause of their failure was all too familiar; exactly the same weakness that cost me to bet on them in the first instance – sentimentality. My support, our support, worldwide support for Brazil has much to do with the magicians who dazzled us in 1970. We keep clinging to the past, refusing to let great moments die. Even when death is certain we pin our last desperate hope on reincarnation. "Pele to return from a decade in some American purgatory" was the sort of headline we embraced in our wee Walter Mitty world of football. (Watching Scotland's demolition in the company of the Babylonian Iain MacKenzie was a sobering experience. "Bring on Hoddan," he kept shouting. Very sad, really.)

This sentimentality is excusable from old spectators but cannot be forgiven in management. Zico and Socrates were obviously past their best. Cold and cruel it might sound, but when one has outlived one's usefulness one should be cast aside. Footballers should be treated in much the same way as old cars that won't pass MOTs and wives who are over the tropopause.

What we are on about here is much more important than marriage and motoring. We are talking about football. See that Maradona, well! He is something special. I have studied him closely as a fan and a medical scientist. His two closest cousins in advanced evolution are the Hebridean tree and the Bragar woman.

The Hebridean tree, if and when it survives at all, must, to withstand the perpetual gales, be short and sturdy. The energy that is normally used to attain height is concentrated at the base for the development of a low centre of gravity and a substantial bottom. The same goes for the West Side woman. I have nothing but admiration for the West Side woman, by the way, and envy of their husbands, especially when I consider the spindly giraffes we produce on the sheltered East coast of the island.

Along the same lines of evolution a dedicated footballing nation has produced the first soccer superman, Maradona. Let me remind you that Rangers once or twice tried to develop small supermen like Maclean and Cooper into weight-lifters, but unfortunately destroyed agility in the process. This is only one of the physical characteristics in which Maradona is unique. He can also jump higher than Shilton-had-it-covered, and has much faster hands. He can outsprint the fastest sprinters and outstay the longest stayer. And according to my friend Jimmy Hill, he is a superb actor. Quote: "Look at Maradona, he deliberately charged that English elbow with his nose. He is now writhing about on the ground, but I can assure you because we are much nearer than the TV camera that he wasn't touched. That red stuff pouring from his nose cannot be blood because English elbows even when deliberately rammed don't draw blood. What an actor." If the laws of slander and libel did not exist I have no doubt Mr Hill would have ended with: "What a pity he is a homosexual."

Frequently, and I suppose inevitably, being one of the few now still alive who knew them all, I am asked how the present-day stars compare with "our own crowd". Ah, yes, the old days. How one yearns for them.

Gordon Smith, Stanley Mathews, Ivor Allchurch: where would they stand now? The sad truth is nowhere. They would have nothing to stand on. They would have been taken out. Referees are less to blame than modern managers who, in terror of success-seeking directors, legalised the scythe. Even that gentleman among psychopaths, Bobby Charlton, I have heard say: "A good goal, but he should never have got through. At this moment every manager in the country will be saying he should have been taken out."

Slim artists like Stanley Mathews would have been "taken out". The late, great Duncan Edwards would still have been great. My own contemporary George Best had the balance (when sober) but would be worth only £2 million against Maradona's £10 million – much the same as comparing wild unpredictable salmon with the creature bred and groomed for a purpose.

Tired and sometimes emotional after late-night football sessions I might have been, yet I still felt it my duty to stay up until 3am watching recorded highlights of Royal Ascot.

Who in Great Britain can question the therapeutic value of this grand spectacle? Where else in this strife-torn world can the common man be made to feel so close to the ruling classes? Due partly to the expertise of the BBC and the informality that is so much a part of our British way of life, one felt one could almost reach out and touch royalty.

Fergie looked every inch a princess. Royal and radiant in blue and white, bulging where bulges are appreciated, she seemed such a delightful contrast to the lanky Diana. Fergie's simple but tasteful blue outfit, a touching gesture to her Scottish ancestors, highlighted and exaggerated her most appealing and well-rounded parts. What a great pity they could do nothing about her rather fat flat face.

There is nothing much one can do at this stage except mortgage the house and lay the lot on Maradona.

19 SEPTEMBER, 1986

MONDAY
The weather this week was better than last week, but perhaps not so good as the week before. But maybe next week, DV, the weather will be better than it was this time last year, which was very bad indeed with midges as well. However, our exiles who were home for Mairead's wedding were pleased to see their old friends despite the weather which could have

been better, especially all at 24 to whom the community's sympathy is extended following the unfortunate passing away of their beloved collie aged 18. (What's going on here? – Ed.) Shush a minute. I haven't come to the best bit yet. I've been studying the parish news in the *Stornoway Gazette*, for these are tough times and a man never knows when he may have to go back to that.

Scalpay is my favourite, but South Lochs is often powerful stuff. Listen to this isolated cryptic paragraph: "Two boats anchored in the loch on Saturday night and left on Sunday morning."

That's it. No more, no less. They came and they went in the night, and if the writer knows anything else about these mysterious boats he is not going to tell us. And why should he, when he / she only gets paid 0.002p per line before tax.

I think what we have spotted here is a secret message for a person or persons unknown who, for the time being, must be considered 'the enemy'. We can be fairly certain that there is something sinister afloat on the dark side of the loch. Ships that come and go in the night always have something to hide – drugs, guns or booze are the traditional smugglers' currency. Foreign agents have been known to slip ashore in the darkest hour before the dawn. I feel it is my duty to point out to the forces of law and order that there are Irish people living on the South Side now with the infamous name of Macquire. Be very careful at all times.

TUESDAY

On the other hand, perhaps I have it all wrong. These could be two stern lines of criticism. The writer could have written what we sociologists sometimes call a deep and meaningful disclosure with a frown on his face. How dare these sailors approach the sacred soil on Saturday night, and having done so did they not realise they must stay until 0001 GMT Monday. I can almost imagine the writer's knuckles whitening on the pen as this angry sentence was carefully scribbled.

Then again, there is a possibility that these words were not so much spoken as sighed with satisfaction and relief that the boats had the decency to depart before the holy men of South Lochs got up for lunch.

I cannot remember when a short, simple sentence intrigued me so much, and I would be very disappointed to learn that this little snippet that has kept us going for 20 minutes was nothing more than a passing observation of no significance, thrown in to fill space and earn 0.002p before tax.

WEDNESDAY

Reading the News of the Maws (as Clendy calls it), I was reminded of Murdie Siarach, onetime North Lochs correspondent and critic of this column. In the early autumn of his life the mad fool has decided to embark on holy matrimony – a common enough event, even now in 1986. Yet the Siarach surprises me. Having survived 46 years of bachelorhood, and having accumulated a great deal of bread, one would have thought he'd have more sense. It is difficult enough to know at 25 if it's your body or your money they are after: at 46 when the body's done there can be no doubt.

Careful as ever with his pennies, though, Murdie is sneaking off to New Zealand to get married. We have known many who opted for the quiet dinner for six somewhere in a mainland hideout, but New Zealand seems an extraordinary length to go to avoid buying one's neighbours a few drams.

THURSDAY

I went to London the other day and I found it dirty, noisy, crowded and warm. Very warm and very crowded, especially in the Underground or 'Tube', as the natives call it. I couldn't help notice the signs were all in English. Fiercely proud of their language, these Anglo-Saxons.

Strange place, strange people; but I like the way they mind their own business. I once heard someone (probably a nationalist) say: "You could be lying dead on the street and they would walk round you." I think he was trying to be critical, but I cannot see his point. To walk round dead bodies seems to me a very sensible course of action. Only the very callous would tread on them. Some day when I have more time I'll walk down Oxford Street naked in my wellies to see if anyone will notice.

Not only will I need more time, I'll need a lot more money. At £268 return it is cheaper to go to Toronto. But who wants to go to Toronto? They already have plenty salmon there. In London, now, you have beggars. Not drunks and down-and-outs, but Third World-style professional beggars amidst enormous ever-growing wealth. I didn't offer these poor souls money because I think that is degrading: instead I invited them to Leurbost, where I run a sort of funny farm for not-so-gentlefolk in reduced circumstances.

I knew I was back from London and in my own far-from-cosy loft the moment I opened my eyes on this 262nd morning of 1986. The wind whistled low as it always does when it blows exactly from NW by North. The draught from badly-fitted bathroom windows I judged to be 6.5 degrees Celsius, and a relative humidity of 88 per cent was indicated by the viscosity of the paste glob on the topless tube. Through half-shut eyes I measured with a glance the sun's angle of elevation. The time on my Russian alarm clock registered 7.30am. All these interconnected items of information were not gauged slowly and deliberately. On the contrary, they were assimilated instantaneously and unconsciously at a speed to which man-made computers can never aspire. Immediately and effortlessly I had deduced the date must be September 18, give or take one day. Do you know what this means? It is not a special talent: I'll tell you what it means. It means I have been living on the same spot for much too long – six and a half years, to be precise. The time is long overdue for a move, not to London where you need a clean shirt every second day but to the Seychelles to feel the heat of the sun on the spinal cord – where the weather this week is much the same as last week and no worse than it was the same time last year. And no midges.

26 SEPTEMBER, 1986

MONDAY

One of the great disappointments of my week was the late arrival of an invitation from Uig community council to the presentation of the British Empire Medal to Mr Duncan Macdonald, Gisla. Ah, the Empire. How one's heart pounds at the memory – when three-quarters of the world map was painted red, and the title Lord Lieutenant meant something. Thank goodness we still have the symbolic honours and dignified ceremonies to remind us of our glorious past. Anyway, the GPO let me down again and I missed this latest celebration.

Look at the programme. 1830BST – Everyone attending presentation should assemble in the school. 1900 – The Lord Lieutenant arrives at Crowlista school. Met by John MacLeod and C J Maciver, master of ceremonies, and led to reception area when assembly will rise (unless unfit) until Lord Lieutenant signifies otherwise. 1902 – MC asks minister to give a short prayer (when the gods want to punish us, they answer our prayers). 1910 – Mr Macdonald and Lord Lieutenant approach one another. Vice Lord Lieutenant hands medal to Lord Lieutenant and then retires. Lord Lieutenant pins medal on Mr Macdonald's left breast (why always the left?) and shakes his hand. Mr Macdonald resumes his place. And so on, until 2030 when Lord Lieutenant and party take leave.

A meticulously planned evening, what? In the event the whole shebang started late, at 1932. Can you imagine the agitation? Then they forgot the hook that attaches the medal to the recipient and had to send to Carishader for it. Perhaps it's as well my invite arrived too late. I couldn't have borne the embarrassment.

TUESDAY

Once again I have suffered badly at the hands of Stornoway businessmen, and I daresay it will not be the last time. The other day I needed some plastic gloves for a rather delicate operation I had to perform. Naturally, I asked to speak to a consultant before making the purchase (it's as much as your life's worth to buy anything these days without consultation). Dr Taylor and Mr Matheson were summoned and a certain type of transparent polythene glove was recommended, but as always there was a catch – in this case Catch-25.

And this is how they make their money. I had to buy a whole carton of gloves at an extortionate price. What can you do? I bought the pack only to discover it contained 25 gloves. Who needs 25 gloves? Do these chemists really want to cater for people with an odd number of hands?

Naturally I complained, and do you know what they told me? "You'll have to buy two packs, then, and you'll have your even number. What are you moaning about?" Astonishing what shopkeepers will stoop to for the quick buck.

I hope that last paragraph is libellous, because with the novel coming out soon I want Sandy Matheson to sue me. The publicity arising from being sued by a man of substance would give sales a tremendous boost. I only wish I could tell a lie.

WEDNESDAY

Spent the morning in bed discussing with Maggie the sad matter of divorce. Although she has nothing against divorce as such, she is very much against remarriage because of the inevitable problems that would follow in the hereafter. "Can you imagine," she says, "the tedium of being harassed by several husbands throughout eternity, each of them laying claim to your body – or should I say soul?" I must admit I had not considered these consequences, but I see no reason why we couldn't all sit down on the other side to discuss these matters in a civilised fashion.

That is but one of the problems I would like Professor Macleod to preach on when he comes to the Leurbost commies this week. It is not for me to tell The Prof what to speak about, but just one thing, Donald – keep it simple. No big words, now. I don't want to hear our womenfolk coming out of the kirk saying: "A powerful man, I didn't understand a word he said." Just in case the good Prof hasn't thought of a suitable text yet, how about: "Can Catholics go to heaven?" I have several two-hour sermons already prepared on this theme in case I am asked to step in.

THURSDAY

Last night I saw a sight so strange I must doubt the evidence of my one good eye. Had it been in my drinking days I would certainly have classed the scene in the pink elephant category. Driving down from Goathill Farm behind a Peugeot saloon, I saw a calf staring at me through the rear window. In the front of the car I am fairly certain I identified Coinneach Iain and A Hogg. They appeared to be conversing normally and as far as I could make out they seemed unaware of the strange "passenger" in the back seat. The calf itself appeared quite content and was evidently enjoying the ride. I would like to hear from anyone else who might have witnessed this strange sight. Perhaps I'm going mad.

FRIDAY

Once again I must go and celebrate the wedding of a young Leurbost girl who seemed yesterday a mere child. Sooner or later it will come to us all. Your little daughter comes home and tells you she's planning to marry. But what if – and this is the horror story we all dread – she comes home with an Englishman? What then? Will your racial tolerance stand up to that one? Let us hope we are never put to the test.

10 October, 1986

The Lord of the Lagoon

DRAMATIS PERSONAE

Misty – Lord of the Lagoon

Jason – Goatherd

Absent and Present – Attendants on the Lord of the Lagoon

MacBrian – A Pirate's Ghost

Meg – A Country Wench

ACT II, SCENE I

(Act I censored on legal advice)

An oak-panelled room in the Lord of the Lagoon's Palace, wherein sits Misty himself, agitated and fuming.

Enter Jason, Absent and Present …

JASON:

Your cry for help, My Lord, aroused the town

We loosed the tether and we hurried down

What dreadful deed, what wicked calumny

Does make you frown so dark and solemnly?

MISTY:

You see before you, if you bear to look,

The shattered image of a man whose book

Lay open spotless for the world to see

That is until today, just after tea,

A woman, nay, a demon or a shrew,

Came between me and my morning brew.

ABSENT:

My liege, my Master of the Dark Lagoon

Pray tell us and do tell us soon

Who is this lass whose venom has the bite

To cause such anguish in a man of might?

Can she be human who would climb the stair
To broach you angry smoking in your lair?

MISTY *(walking about in a lather)*:

This woman, for the lack of a better name,
Lacking more in awe of me or shame,
Came north from Lochs unless I am mistaken
Before I had my morning liquor taken.
She stood there brazen and as bold as brass
And swore she'd have her husband kick my ass.

ATTENDANTS, *together*:

Naw.

MISTY:

Aye, she did, I swear it too,
Though swearing's something that I rarely do,
But when I have to I can do it well
I swore that woman on her way to hell.

JASON:

We'll swear if swear we must
But publicly our action must be just
I'm not afraid to see a woman's tear
We'll hang her husband from the nearest pier
These Maws must be reminded of our purity
My lambskin apron I will lay as surely.

MISTY:

That cheers me, friend, my brain I can now rest
(sits down)
We'll take a little medicine from the chest.

They all rise and go to the old sea chest where the malt is kept. Alas, the grog is gone. There is a note written in a ghostly hand, signed MacBrian the Pirate:

"For two score years I've paid your gross annuity
Call that wee dram MacBrian's sweet gratuity."

Grey-faced and shaken they make their way back to their seats.
MISTY:

> We must, alas, and this will lend us piety,
>
> Continue our discussion in sobriety.

PRESENT:

> If I may make so bold and to be fair
>
> (I speak, My Lord, as always through the chair)
>
> Might suit us all to let the matter rest
>
> And treat this grievous insult as a jest.

MISTY *(with quivering jowls)*:

> I beg of you to listen yet a while
>
> The woman's bad, the husband's doubly vile
>
> He casts aspersions on my own good name
>
> Furthermore to my eternal shame
>
> Ignoring my position and my fame
>
> The name he named was not my real name.

PRESENT *(who'd had a few in the Caley) giggled*:

> That's good, I like it, and I'd raise a rumpus
>
> If I could find a word to rhyme with pompous.

MISTY:

> Shut up, you fool, you miserable oaf.
>
> Sober up and try to use your loaf.
>
> We're gathered here and here we have to stay
>
> If need be for another night and day
>
> Till one of you, no matter which,
>
> Will rid me of this man and witch.
>
> I need at once a devious little plan
>
> That will forever dry his blood-soaked pen.
>
> To begin with go and book us
>
> In the notebook of Bill Lucas.

ABSENT:

> You're right, My Lord, of course you're never wrong
>
> He must be silenced and it can't be long

Or else our gossips who are blind to joke
Will spread the rumour, 'Where there's fire there's smoke'.
It goes against my principle to shoot him
But wait, I know how we can put the boot in
His masters I believe would be dismayed
To learn he practises another trade.

MISTY:

An excellent suggestion and well worded
I'll see that you are handsomely rewarded.

*A terrible commotion outside in the Corridors of Power; a crash barrier
from the Coral Reef comes flying through the door. Meg the country
wench appears in her yellow wellies.*

MEG:

Stand up, you spineless lumps of jelly,
Before I start to flay youse with my welly
Had I thought a man of bulk
So easy made to cower and sulk
My friendly warning made in fun
I would have backed up with a gun
And had I really wished to threaten
I have my own sharp deadly weapon
(sticks out her tongue)
A sword I can assure you this is
More potent than my husband's pen is.

They all run to cry in a corner …

17 OCTOBER, 1986

Dear Jackson,

Forgive me for not having written last year but I was under a terrible strain. How are things in Abu-Dhabi? Smart move that, weather forecasting where the sun always shines and the rain never falls. The only reason I write to you now is that I cannot take much more of this, and I hope you can find a job for me out there.

For seven days and seven nights it has rained here now and we are all bent double from walking against a perpetual Force 9 gusting 12. Do you sometimes dwell on how little progress we have made as scientists in influencing the weather in the last 6,000 years? (That is the age of the universe, by the way.) In the dark, far-off days when Noah built his ark, they were able without the aid of satellites to forecast 40 days ahead with startling accuracy.

What a great opportunity old Noah missed then to put things right. Why did he have to take a male and a female salmon louse on his ark? We could have managed fine without them. I think I told you last year I had become a businessman. Since the removal of the frontal lobe I feel I have adapted quite well to that world, though I still have two minor operations to undergo (local anaesthetic) before I can call myself a fully-fledged tycoon.

The first lesson we learn is never to pay any bills at all if possible. Here is an invaluable tip I was given by a publican friend. At the end of every month he puts the names of all his creditors in a hat and picks out a few lucky ones for payment. Anyone who gives him hassle doesn't even get in the hat. Unfortunately he tried the same system with his last three wives. Now he is in deep trouble. They are a vindictive lot, sacked wives.

Remember the Mod, that Gaelic festival where middle-class menopausal transvestites don tartan skirts and go native? Well, it is on in Edinburgh this week. If you ask me, it is no more than an excuse for a wild Bacchanalian orgy. Remember the Largs Mod ('66, I think), when you fell into the oily waters of the Clyde and I ended up black and blue –

another second prize following an altercation with a large American serviceman in greasy Annies. A bad lot, these Dunoonites. At least we knew how to enjoy ourselves in those days. Not like today's kids, out of their box on grass. By the way, how are you doing for grog out there? I understand your Bedouin are more liberal than the Saudis and that it is relatively easy to keep reality at bay.

Our old Gordonstoun friend, Charlie, the only half-decent man in the royal clan, is being made fun of by all the smart-asses because he talks to plants. Charlie, like you and me, is a sensitive soul, so we must support him in case his half-witted brother attempts a coup. As a matter of fact, I have asked Chuck up to North Lochs to talk to my salmon because they no longer respond to Roddy the Bosun's language. I guess, deep down, they realise they are the king of fish.

You realise you and I have reached a very dangerous age. It was brought home to me with a dreadful shock yesterday. This old woman hailed me in the main street of Stornoway. I thought at first she was selling some Salvation Army literature, but on close inspection I recognised her as one of our contemporaries (although of course you knew her better than I). She was damn near unrecognisable – nothing but wrinkles and bags where the face used to be. I felt quite ill, and of course I will not have mirrors in the house, but it does no harm to be reminded from time to time of one's mortality. For one reason or another I am no longer a cynic. The Barvas Navigator's wife and two of her friends called in the other night after a session with the mystical Professor Macleod, and I can only think this man Macleod has a powerful argument. His groupies have no fear of death, and what is more important, I suspect from their fresh, smooth skins they have managed to banish worldly care and anxiety. You will laugh, perhaps, but I have decided to apply once again to the Free Church College. Apparently my medical training is not sufficient to make me a good missionary. What does this body matter?

I see our Queen is on a tour of China. Again a decent person, the Queen, but quite thick. I have sent her some questions to ask, such as: How do you manage to feed 1,000 million people satisfactorily when there is allegedly not enough to go round? And why have our Jesuits and Presbyterians only managed to convert one hundred people in every million in the last hundred years? I don't expect her to become suddenly political, but I have hopes for her son, our friend Chuck.

Talking of medicine, our old friend and eminent colleague Dr Smith tells me foot and mouth is now rife here amongst the children, and many of them will have to be put down. This is the work of that damn IDP, and the increase in sheep numbers. The smartest move you ever made was getting out of one inexact science into another. I had two young doctors living with me last week. Three pounds an hour they get paid, after all that memorising. It is perhaps just as well they have no brains.

Still, they have all joined the Labour Party. Isn't it ironic when we are all moving to the right in old age. Remember Paul Johnson? With the fear of death begins the death of idealism. See you soon, perhaps from the pulpit.

Yours aye,
Eachann

21 NOVEMBER, 1986

Following recent talk about predestination, several readers have phoned asking me to explain in simple language what it means. My pleasure. The blunt message is that most of you have had it. You are doomed.

Normally I would pass this sort of request on to the College in Edinburgh, but since I read that The Prof refused to condemn dangerous secret societies I am no longer sure I can trust him. I take a very dim view of his soft approach to corruption and devious shenanigans involving goats and baskets of snakes. To disapprove is not enough: one must condemn and excommunicate at the risk of being seen on the Pope's side. Or is someone trying to hide something here? Is your man On The Square, as we say? We will be accused of hypocrisy, I daresay, but so what. Is the fear of hypocritical tongues what keeps us all On The Square? The fear of being caught?

But I have lost the thread with the sermon still in first gear. Predestination was the text. Most of you, I assume, will remember from your Shorter Catechism – if for no other reason than that it is easier to memorise than the longer – "He hath fore-ordained whatsoever comes to pass." But we must be careful here, brethren. "Whatsoever comes to pass" does not mean whatsoever comes to pass. No, that would be too easy. If you read further in Ephesians and Romans you will see that this fore-ordaining refers to the selection of an elite few for salvation. The lucky ones. And nowhere are we promised that the number will be other than very few.

"Whatsoever" was a bad choice of word. It might lead people to believe that every little unimportant event in the affairs of men was planned in the very beginning – like free buses to Point or even the building of a new Roman Catholic church in Stornoway. Quite clearly the latter was not predestinated, otherwise a parallel development in the form of a Catholic builders' merchant would have been fore-ordained and situated in Stornoway. That is not my logic: it is the argument of the Stornoway Free Presbyterian minister in his anti-Gaelic speech. Gaelic is predestined to die, otherwise the Free Presbyterian College would be turning out Gaelic-speaking ministers by the score. I am surrounded by ignoramuses who use terms like "predestination" and bigger words with not a notion of what they mean.

This is no doubt part of our punishment for having taught the masses to read in the first place. I used to attract a much bigger crowd to my sermons when the entire congregation was illiterate. Even our dear Editor, who is wise in many things, does not understand the subtle difference in meaning between the old, dark "predestinated" and the everyday word "predestined". This is what we are up against.

Now, where was I before the light went out? Yes. Predestination – the happy fore-ordaining, and reprobation – fore-ordaining with the black cap. Which group are you in? I am afraid there is no way of knowing. And sadly there is nothing you can do about it. There are no transfers in this game because it is all fore-ordained. Red cards were issued to the players in Team B at the kick-off. Let them play fair if they like; still there is no hope. (Excuse the footballers' jargon, but Match of the Day is still fresh in my mind.)

Another class of ignoramus you will hear frequently – usually Anglican in origin – thinks predestination was an idea dreamed up by John Calvin, the French Protestant whose real name was Jean Chauvin, from which we get the word *chauvinism* – obsessive devotion to a belief. Or was that some other Jean Chauvin? It doesn't matter to us now …

Anyway, these fools could hardly be expected to have read that other great champion of predestination, St Augustine, who lived and preached 1,000 years before Calvin. And he was, wait for it, a Bishop of Rome or Milan. Again it doesn't matter which: the important thing is, and we can be sure of this, he kicked with the left foot. What are we to make of that, then? Were the original devotees of predestination the antecedents of Ian Paisley's Papish hordes?

This theology is a tricky business. Absolutely terrifying if you think yourself in Team B. You can pray till your knees are sore but if your name is not on the list you are for it.

I think I told you this before, but I'll tell you again. About Cousin Paul and Cousin Peter. Peter was a rascal, a terrible man for the women, drinking and swearing and gambling. Used to beat his wife and children every Saturday night. Owned up to a small regiment of illegitimate children, and never paid his council house rent. But here did he not get scared after one of his binges. A smooth talker, he wormed his way into the Kirk and was a deacon in no time at all. Now he tells me he is doing fine over there and coining it in.

Poor Paul was a great man for doing good works. He studied to become a social worker in his middle years. He hoped desperately for a sign that would save his bacon, but, alas, in vain. In a panic, he finally joined the Catholics but I am afraid he left it a bit too late. Now he tells me he is poverty-stricken and living in a very downmarket corner of the hereafter. Still, his Catholic friends are praying for him in the belief that an omnipotent predestinator must surely have the power to change his mind.

I hope this complicated business is now as clear to you as it is to me.

1987

13 FEBRUARY, 1987

MONDAY

We have now passed through the difficult times and are approaching what will go down in history as the "desperate days". Every day we hear stories on the BBC about our huge collective debt – a figure with so many zeros on the end it means nothing.

The state of the nation is of little interest to most of us until they start trying to fix the blame on us as individuals. When they say the sparse population of the Highlands is £30 million in debt we can almost begin to pinpoint the bad boys, many of whom are now out of work with no hope of raising the £30 million. Even if people were suddenly to grow sense and get rid of this government, it would probably still be too late to avert hardship. I'm not quite sure how the sudden foreclosure of £30 million by building societies and banks will affect us, but what I am sure of is that it will affect us all.

TUESDAY

So what can we do? We must start in the home. There used to be three Maggies in my life – Maggie Thatcher, Maggie, and Maggie Cunningham.

Maggie Cunningham had the good sense to get married to a west-coast fisherman, so her economic problems were solved there and then – or so we thought. But the prawns became hard to find, which is why food parcels have now to be sent from Scalpay to Plockton. My own Maggie thought she was onto a good thing when I became a salmon baron, but then the Crown Estate Commissioners stepped in. The other Maggie, Thatcher, has been in all our lives whether we liked it or not, and no matter what you think of her as a Prime Minister she has some great attributes as a housewife.

Last night I saw her on TV explaining why you should never press your skirt too hard. (Although, between you and me, why anyone should want to press her skirt at all …) Anyway, what she meant was that you should never leave a crease in the hem in case fashion changed and you wanted to lengthen or shorten. "There you are, then," I said to the family. "If she has to be economical as a housewife on £265,000 a year, can you guys not put a hem on things?" You should have seen the way they looked at me.

WEDNESDAY

Economy was very much what I had in mind when I sent her to the Stornoway Fishermen's Co-op to buy an anchor and some rope yesterday. "And," arsa mise, "while you're in there buy a new shovel for the coal." Now, I know certain people about the town say I am stingy with cash, but, and well, OK, I am careful but one has to be, has one not. When I said "buy a shovel" I meant a shovel for small black peats or coal, as we all know shovels – a wee thing, that is. Do you know what she came home with? A shovel like they have in the quarry, 12 inches wide if it was a foot. Now you must remember it was not the amount of fuel she could get into the fire with one shoogle that made the difference to me, but the fear that she might strain something in the body. At the same time it must be borne in mind that a 12-inch-wide shovel through a cold winter could make the difference between a holiday in Cromore and Majorca. Just a passing thought.

THURSDAY

Talking about economy and those who were alive and are still alive yet at whom there is the memory when it was not easy to be alive, what will I do when they are not alive? One thing that is sure, when they are not alive I will not be long after them because I will not have a stocking to put on my foot that I can put in a wellington. And that is as sure for you as you are alive.

When goes away Murdag Nodaidh, Mòr Chisholm and Banntrach Sheomag, we might as well all go to the big town where there is not a need for a wellington or a stocking to go into it. For there, the women that will be there will not be like them who could knit a stocking under a creel between Loch Àirigh a' Ghille Ruaidh and Creag a' Bhodaich before the sun would go under. It is them that would not be long putting a hem on Maggie Thatcher.

FRIDAY

Now that this paper has become necessary reading for all salmon farmers, we have decided to introduce a new weekly feature listing the names of slow payers and non-payers. The first name to appear, if we start in the south, will probably be Welsh. That is all I can say for the moment. I am not in favour, like some of my colleagues in the industry, of enlisting the help of the Maryhill Mob for debt collection.

27 MARCH, 1987

Litir Mhagaidh

As the saying goes, the more you do the more you get left to do. Not that I mind doing the column this week because he is ill, and I am not surprised. After a successful fishing trip on Saturday afternoon he entered triumphantly and dumped a bag of still-live, slimy fish in the sink. I recognised the hedonistic gleam in his eye and I was glad we had already eaten because he often tries to force me and the children to eat his concoctions. I sometimes wonder that we stayed with him for so long. Anyway, he announced with great glee that he planned a wonderful new culinary creation that would not only be delicious to eat but would also offer protection against every disease known to man.

He gutted 10 fat smalags, salted and peppered the livers, placed them on a medium heat with an onion, a little water and milk for one and a quarter hours. While the livers were being reduced a pan of Kerrs Pinks was boiled and the fish fried until crisp (so the bones and all can be eaten). The spuds were then mashed, half the oily contents of pan number one stirred in and the mixture fried until a golden scab had formed on both sides. This feast takes two hours to prepare and one hour to eat noisily while being washed down with the remains of the 'soup'. It would perhaps be as well to seek medical advice before trying it, but if you want to have a go he insists you stop eating when you begin to hear a loud pounding in the eardrums. This, he says, is caused by low blood pressure in the head induced by the increased flow of blood to the bag to cope with the cargo.

For a dessert he had two large glasses of Trawler Rum which he explained was necessary to break down the fat. He declared himself satisfied and thought it was his best creation to date. But I hardly slept a wink because he spent the night on his belly like a beached whale making low rumbling noises and moaning. His bad gut today he blames on some undercooked scallops he had earlier on Saturday. I am saying nothing.

Since I became involved with this school closure business my conviction that men should have as little as possible to do with education is daily growing. This will no doubt be classed as a sexist remark, but I am now certain that all teaching should be done by women. For every one good male teacher there are twenty-one who should be discharged for incompetence. On the other hand you will seldom come across a 'bad' woman teacher. For the same reason we should have a woman director of education and a chairwoman of every education committee.

Women, you see, care about children. To the average male a child is merely a drain on whatever is left in his purse after the publican has had his cut. Do men serve any useful purpose at all, I often ask myself.

But to get back to the chairman of WIIC education comedy, Mr Donald MacLeod: I see he has latched on to the Professor's competition argument as has Donald MacKay, South Lochs. Big classes bring out the best in children, they say. Survival of the fittest. There may be some truth in this when applied to unusually-gifted pupils like the three Donalds, but we are not worried about these high-flyers who usually get by whatever school they attend. We are more concerned with average or below-average pupils whom the three Donalds would presumably throw on the scrap heap. The only competitive activity they are likely to join when they go to Stornoway is Woolworth poaching.

You may think I am a little obsessed with the big bad school, but for evidence of the psychological damage that can be caused by the Nicolson you need look no further than my own husband. Had he stayed behind in Leurbost school like other slow developers of his age, perhaps instead of the bitter and twisted individual I have to nurse today he could have been an assistant director of education like Murdoch, or like Dòmhnall Lìsidh a director of something. Perhaps I might even have been a lady of the manse, getting the flock to cut my peats.

It appears from his public statements that the chairman of education regrets the money that was spent in the southern isles and would now like to spend the entire education budget on Shawbost. Please don't get me wrong: I would like to see Shawbost get their heated swimming pool and their fur-lined gymnasium, but spare a thought for the rest of us. A chairman of sensitivity would have resigned before he closed a school. Quite clearly we will not sort out this mess until we have a woman in charge.

We didn't always lack in leadership. Not so long ago when I was young each village had a few wise men you could rely on to do the right thing and say the right things at the right time. Men who had the strength to carry more than their share of the burden. Men to whom the less fortunate could turn and could depend on in moments of crisis. James Shaw Grant would call them men of probity. Sadly, they are all gone – Niall Iain Ruaidh, Tormod Mòr and Donnchadh in Ranish. For too many senior persons now the idea of leadership is to be seen going to church, and there their responsibility ends.

These earlier stalwarts I mentioned generally gave more back to the soil than they took out, hoping to leave their patch a little better than they found it. In their place today we have educated rapists hellbent on grabbing all that can be grabbed while it lasts. They will leave to our children an island of rushes surrounded by a barren sea. You are lucky in 1987 to find a man who can be relied on to paint his windows in the Spring.

I look around me, desperately, for one real man who could be classed with the heroes of my youth, and I see only Dixie – and even he wastes time playing golf. There was one other man at No 50 but he deserted the sinking ship to teach in Oban. I am afraid, more and more, we must – like the Church of England – look to women for salvation.

3 APRIL, 1987

MONDAY

I understand a certain Tory taxi driver has taken to phoning councillors during the night asking them to get off their butts and go grit the roads. Some boy, this McKibbin.

I knew someone else years ago who made a habit of phoning his friends in the middle of the night. This other guy was a heavy boozer in those days and when he got full, usually about 3am, he became obsessed with the telephone. Convinced that all his mates would love to hear his voice, he would ring them at all hours and often he would sing a verse or two before you could put the phone down. Fortunately for us all, he took a severe dose of religion and stopped drinking.

I've never met this fellow McKibbin and for all I know he could be as sober as a deacon, but I think he may have started a new trend with his middle-of-the-night calls. I've always resented having to work during the night. If I have to be up, everyone should be up, so look out.

TUESDAY

Do you know the most irritating sound in the world today? Well, I'll tell you. "The time according to Accurist is ..." I don't know who or what Accurist is but I'll certainly never buy anything bearing the name. I often have to dial the speaking clock but I detest this Accurist thing so much I may be forced to buy an accurate Timex watch. Either that or perhaps we should all phone McKibbin's Taxis at regular intervals for time checks.

You have to admire this man's nerve. Many's the time I have felt angry enough to phone a councillor. But I would never dream of calling Sandy Matheson out of his scratcher at 3am. McKibbin also has been pestering my buddy Alec Beag. I will not have Alec Beag bullied. Anyone lays a finger on him answers to me personally.

We have a duty to try and work together on this little island if we are to survive and I am not one of these hard men who believe Tories should be ignored just because there are only nine or ten of them. As ever willing to do my bit for minority causes, I have invented a devilishly cunning little machine. We'll call it, I think, "The Personal Tory Salt Spreader".

Like most brilliant ideas, it is very simple, and more important it is exceptionally silent — ideal for Sunday mornings. A small hand cart is your first requirement. This you will, of course, fill with salt. Then you harness the cart to some poor boy on the dole. He runs in front of your taxi throwing salt for all he is worth. Hard work, I agree, but it keeps the dole figures down and lets our representatives get their rest.

WEDNESDAY

Someone once said that if six Englishmen met in the middle of the Sahara Desert they would immediately form a queue. Man, the English have nothing on us when it comes to queue-forming. The Royal Bank performance you all know about, so I'll say no more about that. Instead go along to Roddy Smith's the newsagent. There you will see the Lewisman at his most obstinate and perverse.

Poor Sandy Matheson at great personal cost and inconvenience rearranged his shop so customers could queue indoors out of the rain. By simply moving the counter from the wall to the middle of the floor he made space for the whole town if necessary to queue inside. This will be just the job, I thought, on Saturday morning when papers are late and the town ladies are desperate for the day's runners and riders.

Last Saturday was a fierce one. A howling northerly with hail showers. I couldn't believe it. Yes. You've guessed. A long line of madmen all along the street turning blue with hailstones bouncing off their skulls. I would be most grateful if anyone has any idea what makes us behave as we do.

THURSDAY

Walking the shore at low tide yesterday, I came upon several young children playing a new game. 'Lachie Dick', they call it. The game was invented by a friend of mine in Inverness and he has applied for a patent. It seems a simple sort of game, but then we are simple people. The children had gathered some winkles and were attempting to extract the live bait with a pin. Not easy, because the animal curls quickly back in its shell. Why my friend called the game Lachie Dick I have no idea.

FRIDAY

Once again she dragged me along to the Caberfeidh to see Norman Maclean. He attracts a strange mixture of an audience – teenagers, pensioners and a sprinkling of the middle-aged. A very comical fellow, Norman, but I don't hold with all this dirty talk and making fun of the Catholics and the Free Church. Why does he not have a go at the Church of Scotland occasionally? I'll tell you why. Because he had hoped some day to become a minister in that Church himself – but, as he says, he doesn't have enough previous convictions. Ha, ha: good one that, Norm, what?

Norman did a very funny wee thing about a visit to the dentist, which got a few laughs. He then told a childish joke about a visit to a Japanese brothel, and that got a lot of laughs. I am, of course, a sick person and a prude who never laughs at anything, so perhaps I am not the best person to write on these things. I see nothing wrong with mention of the word brothel in a public bar, but in mixed company … dear, oh dear.

SATURDAY

I have had some terrible dreams recently about Norwegians and consultants. As all my dreams invariably come true, I expect I shall be able to explain the Norwegian business soon.

I also hope to set up a new business venture with Moley – helicopter taxis. I am afraid that is all I can say for the moment, but you can see the first great advantage – no need for gritting on any morning, never mind Sunday. Put that in your pipe, Mr McKibbin.

1 MAY, 1987

MONDAY

When is a motion not a motion? When it is moved by Angus Graham. Don't think for a moment that what took place last week in the highest debating chamber in the Northern Hemisphere went unnoticed, Mr Chairman. Standing orders is it now, indeed? Let me make it quite clear right now that it will very soon be marching orders for the whole lot of you, you scheming devious gasbags.

But to get back to Angus Graham: where does he think he is going to get in 'there' with his honest approach? Does he not realise he has fallen among men with diseased minds? The elected 'members', as they so aptly refer to themselves, do not like anyone in their ranks to declare his or her politics. For years now the majority of Western Isles councillors have thought, if we can flatter them for a second, along Thatcher's line. Very few of them could declare this allegiance and expect to live contentedly in their respective communities, which is why they cling so desperately to the 'Independent' tag. One of the disadvantages of this alleged independence is that they cannot do any Tory braying in public.

And this is where Angus Graham has come in so very useful. Unable to attack Labour directly as a Tory gang, our Independents can now do so indirectly by attacking Angus Graham and everything he proposes. This they 'justify' in their own warped fashion by claiming their opposition to Angus's ideas is 'personal and not political'.

Many of you will be surprised that this is the level at which our great debating chamber operates. Or will you?

TUESDAY

As for last week's education committee meeting, well … Perhaps in the interests of decency and the good name of the island we should keep quiet, but already I hear questions were asked in the drinking dens of the House of Commons.

We must not lay the whole blame on Donald MacLeod, Shawbost. It was even more evident than usual that he was being led by officialdom, because he had to seek guidance for every second word.

This is nothing new. Councillors have been criticised constantly since the inception of WIIC for having to rely totally on officials for guidance. In most cases this is just as well. With the exception of the education department and housing, we seem to have a reasonable team of officials. If policy, such as it is, were to be determined by councillors, there is little doubt that Maggie would be well pleased. The public purse would be well guarded against free-spending socialists. We would have few of the services we have come to expect, low as our expectations are compared with comparable countries in the so-called civilised world. But what does that matter as long as we save money.

WEDNESDAY

After the next local election all these things will change. I look forward very much to the day when I can frustrate officialdom. I will study the legal complexities involved in the passing of a motion for the next three years. If necessary, I will always be accompanied by my own lawyer. Costly, I know, but it will be well worth it for the pleasure of being a permanent thorn in the flesh.

As a little limbering-up exercise I will work out for the benefit of cost-conscious ratepayers the damage in pound notes caused by the schools closure decision delay. Do not be surprised if it amounts to the sort of figure that would keep Achmore school going for many months. I expect it will take me until next week's issue to work it all out. Remember, I did not do a fast reading course, unlike the councillors already in situ.

Anyway, that is enough about councillors. Most of them are lacking in the meanest redeeming feature, with the singular exception of great speed and accuracy when filling in expenses claims.

THURSDAY

In the end I suppose they will have to call in a costly firm of consultants to sort out procedure at council meetings. Did I tell you my latest consultant story? This is a good one.

A Glasgow voice phoned one day and introduced itself as some class of consultant. Could it come out some day and have a look at the fish farm? What for, arsa mise. Believe me, I am tired of these guys. If it's not Ian Barley with some big noise from the Masons or somewhere, it is N D with an even bigger bwana from Rotary. I wouldn't mind so much, but, as you might guess, this type never buys anything. That is why they are rich and you and I are poor.

Anyway, to get back to our consultant: you have to admire this one's brass neck. I have been commissioned, he says, by the HIDB to do some kind of survey on salmon farming and I'm afraid I know nothing about the business. Could I perhaps come and pick your brain? How do you like that piece of cheek? Lean though the pickings may be, could I not have sold them directly to the Board at a fraction of this stranger's price? Or have we now reached the stage where the pickings from a poor crofter's brain have to go through a wholesaler?

FRIDAY

Somehow I cannot get away from politics this fine Spring – not even on the peat bank. My next-door neighbour on the moor is the West End Tory. His approach to turfing is a typical Tory's.

Turfing is, as you all know (or should know), one of the hardest jobs you'll come across in this short, sad voyage. It is the most tedious soul-destroying task this nation of masochists ever managed to invent. When faced with a bank 160 yards long you must invent little games to keep your sanity. You have to resort to diversions like: I must do the next 20 yards before that black cloud reaches the Achmore Mast.

I generally find one and a half hours going absolutely flat-out is the best way to tackle this horrible job. The first 20 minutes are torture, and it is safer to take it easy until the sweat is running freely; then you can move up a gear and shed the Damart semmit. When cutting the line, unless you have a stoker's forearms, rely on the weight of the upper body and breathe in on the upswing. If you are of the type who puts his foot on the spade, then that lesson is not for you: go to the next paragraph.

Now watch a Tory turfing. He is almost always a methodical plodder who is prepared to step slowly onto the spade as he cuts the line as if climbing stairs – gaining a measly 10 horizontal inches with each step. The difference between the Tory turfer and you and me is that he is prepared to plod along in this fashion all day. He will probably get as much turfing done in a full day as you managed in your hour and a half, and he will probably live longer. Of course, he will not do any other jobs on that day. But that does not matter to him because his is a methodical mind that is never cluttered with a dozen half-hatched plans for a single day. He is not easily bored because he has little imagination. Because we are easily bored we sometimes get classed lazy. The very notion.

26 JUNE, 1987

MONDAY

I often say to Maggie and she often says to me: "Do you regret the passing of the Empire?" "Of course, darling," I say or she says between pink gins. She knows and I know that but for women we could still be basking on the shores of Lake Malawi attended on by dusky maidens, but we won't go into that one at the minute. Too deep, Lake Malawi.

Yet we must confess we were as guilty as the next couple when it came to nipping down to the old French colonies of Mauritius and Reunion Isles for the weekend. Why these old stomping grounds should come to mind tonight I have no idea, unless it has something to do with the rumour going about that four officials and their spice are planning an official visit to Reunion.

Certain moaners you and I know well complain about waste of ratepayers' money. Please try to ignore them. I can guarantee youse all that a trip to that sun-kissed tropical paradise is not wasted. We have much in common.

On all sides of these islands they are surrounded by the Indian Ocean. Some of you will scoff, but I can assure you it is every bit as salty as the Minch. Not only that, every morning the sun rises in the East and sinks in the West, just like Shawbost. The natives are as black as Hearachs and every bit as happy. Why, then, should we not go and study them? We have much to learn, so let us have no more of this envious carping. Did you say there was a spare ticket going, Sandy?

TUESDAY

Pope John Paul and myself have had our little differences over the years. Not least of which is the choice of the name Paul. Paul, as every schoolboy knows was a Protestant, and Peter was a Catholic. You would think they would know that in the Vatican, but no. They don't encourage them to read for themselves. Anyway, we have no time this week for a theological lesson. We are too busy making money.

John Paul and I have one thing in common: we have no time for consultants. Take Dr MacPherson, for instance. The moment he decided to become a consultant we went our separate ways. Friend or foe, when the nasty costly business of consultancy arises, I will have no truck with them. MacPherson is just back from Rome. What he was doing there we can only guess. But I am glad to see your man the Pope had the good sense to take off for Poland. I suppose the Pontiff couldn't face an all-night session on cultivated mussels.

WEDNESDAY

Everyone else, including Mr MacArthur (fear a' ghuail), is at it, so I might as well add my voice to the chorus. What are you going to do about it? What are you 40 (or is it 50) Labour members going to do about the English? Forget for a moment that we are the most oversubsidised little group on the face of the Earth; let us have some blood. Where, I ask you, would we be were it not for English honest toil and their little building society accounts? In response to tabloid demand, and without my permission, the Labour Party bosses have voted for an extra layer of obstruction in Edinburgh. I would urge the hard core of Celtic fringe madmen to study the history of past centuries. The Scots are tough masters. Just be glad we are Highrish.

THURSDAY

Now, before I forget. A crowd of actors and actresses are soon to tour the Southern Isles with a play of a novel by Compton Mackenzie. Rusty of Radio Highland is responsible for the dramatic adaptation. Rusty is a clever fellow and I look forward to the entertainment. Compton Mackenzie was also very clever, but he could never understand why others were not as smart as he was. One of his greatest regrets was the advent of the Welfare State. For some strange reason he deeply resented the fact that the unemployed people of Barra could subsist on the dole. Presumably servants became too expensive. But we must not let this influence us when we go to applaud Rusty's work.

FRIDAY

All of us who intend to make a fortune someday from television writing should study a programme called *Hill Street Blues*. Despite the thick slices of sentiment deemed necessary in America, it is, next to *Soap*, the best popular programme ever produced. I wonder if it has reached Reunion Island yet? If not, there is a job for you, Malky.

SATURDAY

This obsession with the arts is spreading rapidly among peasants and horny-handed philistines. I don't know where it is going to stop. I hear Malky has been appointed Gaelic Arts Officer. Although there is no Gaelic Art as such, since I stopped doing Friday in Gaelic, this is an appointment of which I fully approve. Some critics complain that he speaks Gaelic with a Partick accent, but then so does Maggie. And who will argue that she is no artist. Malky once made a drawing of his wife Patsy and his daughter Melisssa recognised her. If nothing else, the least you should expect of an Arts Officer is that you should recognise his wife when he draws her. Of course she was younger then, so, like the work of many great artists, the picture is best viewed from a distance. (They say Patsy periodically touches it up.)

SATURDAY

Despite the huge increase in salary offered by Rupert, I refuse to write a word on Sunday. I must also warn the Brighton branch of the Clan Macdonald that this column will for the next few weeks appear in Gàidhlig. I need the practice, and also I can say what I like about him.

3 JULY, 1987

MONDAY

Perhaps some of you remember a thin medical pamphlet I produced 20 years ago called *Varicose Veins in Nurses' Legs*. Well, I've decided to resume research into this very serious problem.

Nurses, although poorly paid, spend 10 hours or more on their feet every day lifting heavy, ungrateful patients and making beds. The results are unfortunately ugly, painful varicose veins. I had hoped to produce evidence of this distressing affliction and so win a substantial pay rise for the nurses, but I had to abandon the project because of the wife. She took a dim view of me skulking around nurses' homes, camera in hand, at odd hours of the day and night.

We must be more careful this time. I have in mind to hire a few young men to do the fieldwork. When I say 'hire' I do not mean there are wages on offer, but think of the perks.

TUESDAY

Tonight I ventured into that dreadful place, the Nicolson Institute, to meet the teachers and to talk about children. A distasteful subject, but what can you do. Although they are generally not so pretty as nurses, I feel we should support teachers in their battle for better conditions. Then perhaps they will stop moaning and we will all – teachers, parents and children – be happier, wiser and wealthier. Why do we have Higher classes of 30 and over when there are unemployed teachers on the island? If this deplorable situation is not instantly remedied, we the parents have every right to sue the education department. I hope you are well insured, Mr Chairman.

I was pleased to see that most of the teachers on display were quite young. This is very encouraging, because on the whole young teachers are less dangerous than old ones. I hope we weren't tricked. It would be just like them to hide their old, mad teachers in a cupboard while parents visited. I swear I heard Gordon Urquhart's voice, and I certainly won't be going back there until the place is searched by an exorcist.

WEDNESDAY

For a number of years now I've been aware of a sneaky conspiracy of which we, the native islanders, have been victims. Someone somewhere with a lot of power has been responsible for the rounding-up of undesirables and shifting them to what they call remote islands. (Remote from where, I ask?)

This has been done so stealthily that few natives are aware of it. The plan, we suspect, is to load the islands with these misfits and then blow them up. Small matter if a few natives are lost in the process.

Many of these temperamentally unsuited persons are to be found in low-paid jobs. In better-rewarded jobs like welding or teaching natives seem to be very much in control. Perhaps this is not such a good idea, because we have the wrong natives in charge. But then, what is the alternative? You invite Englishmen and tight-fisted Scotsmen and all you get are rejects. If they would even send some Irish rebels, at least they would blend better, with their sweet Gaelic ways and attitudes.

English women. Now they are OK. Especially nurses.

THURSDAY

Leurbost school held a fund-raising hooley the other night, and pulled in £1,250. Although I resent the fact that it should be necessary to raise money in this way because 'they' prefer to spend our taxes on bombs, it was all good fun. I think almost every able-bodied woman in North Lochs turned out, and as always they were desperate to spend the Daddies' money.

When I am very old and people ask what was the happiest night of your life, I can honestly say without hesitation: it was the night I sold old Ballantyne a photograph of Mrs Thatcher for a fiver. Some say he did not have his hand up; but, with respect, I was in the best position to judge. Anyway, you should do all your ear-scratching before you come to an auction.

Brian McClair's football bought by the son and heir for £29 is one I will not forget in a hurry. Believe me, someone will pay dearly for that one – one way or another.

I think if a village raised £1,250 in one evening for the local school, we can safely assume they want to keep it open. What do you think, Donald?

FRIDAY

As I scribble this in bed with drawn blinds I stop occasionally so I can concentrate fully on feeling sorry for myself. I am in a darkened room because of the fire in my eyes and the creaking sinus passages. She has given me a packet of tablets called Sudafed and they are no damn use. Perhaps self-diagnosis is not such a good idea. If things don't improve in the afternoon I shall have to call in young Doctor Beresford. But then he is very young. One good thing to come out of being struck down in the prime of life is that I am in my second day without fags. When I get back to my place of work I am going to insist that smoking be banned altogether.

SATURDAY

I am sorry I cannot mention your play, *The Rival Monster Show*, this week again, Barbara. You didn't buy me enough whisky. Maybe you'll make up for it on the 1st of August in Portree. I find it strange that you should miss out Lewis while visiting all these lesser islands. Is it something I said?

17 JULY, 1987

MONDAY

A dull week on the croft was brightened considerably by the arrival of the Garrabost Historian. After a season locked up in Inverness he was naturally quite mad and ready for some fun. Now, his idea of fun is not always the same as mine. He wanted to get up at five in the morning to shear the old fellow's sheep. But I changed his mind on that one. If I get up at five in the morning, there are many things I would rather do than shear sheep. Anyway, my last flounder net has now been cut up for scallop spat collection, so I guess my days of hunting fish are over. I was never happy doing something illegal anyway.

Desperate for action, having been released from the classroom, he offered to mix concrete for me, or cement – anything to get dirty and break a little sweat. The trouble with trying to work with a teacher is that you must always do things his way. He shouts a lot, gets bad-tempered and then he is happy. You would think during the holidays they would try to be like other people, smile and relax: but not them.

TUESDAY

On the second day someone played a cruel, sadistic trick on us. We reached the Carannaich, three miles off Rubha Ràdhainis, only to find the Stornoway Sea Angling Club already ensconced with their feet up on our mark. I should never have shown them where it was 20 years ago, but never mind that. We tied up alongside them, seeing they had the sounder and fresh mackerel, and that was the first mistake we made. The second was accepting mackerel from them for bait. Our mackerel had clearly been treated with some evil substance the nature of which we will probably never know. In an hour or so, our 'friends' had filled a box of codling, ling and four conger eels. Our three rods had caught one small wrasse.

The Historian said "Let's go", and we did. On the way back we dropped our lines in three different shoals of mackerel and still we caught nothing. It is possible we were the victim of something more sinister than I first suspected. Perhaps the cnocan itself was involved.

Fortunately Maggie had bought some herring earlier in the day, so we fried these at midnight, pretending we had caught them. Will you ever grow up, she asked. We hope not, but I think that is where the Historian has the advantage over me. Not that my enthusiasm for play is any less, but he does not live on this island.

WEDNESDAY

I met a most interesting and unusual character today – a Stornowegian on holiday from London. The unusual and interesting bit is that he hadn't been back 'home' for 40 years except for a brief visit five years ago to bury a relative. The last time he paused for any length of time in Stornoway, someone called Muir ran the County Hotel and the town was full of kipper-houses. And, says he, what have they done with Number Three pier? I'm afraid I couldn't help him there. I am too young. He then mentioned several well-known names of men-about-town we all know well. You cannot possibly be the same age as Fingalstein and these guys, I said; they are ancient. But he was. There is nowhere on earth that ages people quicker than Lewis. Or, put it another way, there is nowhere in which people want to age quicker than they do in Lewis. There are two, perhaps three, reasons for this strange desire. If anyone can give me three reasons or more, the usual large cash prize will be his or hers. Short answers, please, to the letters page.

THURSDAY

I bought a bike today for my figure. One good thing about bike-pushing is that you have to stop and talk to people, so you get frequent rests. In a car you can speed past with a wave and a friendly smile. You could go 20 years without having to speak to friends and relatives. On a bike you are more accessible. It is difficult not to stop, even if you were fit, without being rude. It is, I suppose, a bit like pushing a baby in a pram.

Anyway, I set off in the early evening for Stornoway for the exercise. I got a lift home. If anyone can tell me where the bike is, he will be well rewarded.

FRIDAY

My friends at Lewis Offshore told me a good one the other day. A middle-aged gentleman was recently noticed moving about in the yard in what appeared at first glance to be an aimlessly strolling fashion. Later on he was seen acting suspiciously in the car park. Workers in the yard became alarmed and informed management, who blushed and said nothing at first. My own subsequent investigation revealed that the man is none other than Inspector MacArthur who was in charge of the infamous Macrae murder in Inverness. What is he doing at Lewis Offshore? Is anyone there suspected of murder most foul? If so, I feel the rapidly-ageing population of this island should be told. We must follow this one closely.

SATURDAY

One other bright spot during this dull drizzly week was Colonel Oliver North. Ollie's a cracker. If Ronald Reagan could act like Oliver North, he could have been a success in Hollywood and would never have become President. If Reagan had never become President, we would never have seen Colonel North acting. "I swear by almighty God that although everything I told you last time was a pack of lies, I'm telling the truth this time." Polls show that 52 per cent of the American nation brought up on Walt Disney believe him. Aren't they lucky they didn't grow up.

21 AUGUST, 1987

MONDAY

A man from Elgin has moved into the house next door and I fear I'll have to shoot him unless he adopts a more leisurely pace of life. As far as I can make out, someone winds him up in the morning and whatever type of clockwork he runs on, it lasts until the sun goes down.

The man is a demon with a scythe. His style reminds me of the late Ruairidh T. Bent double from the waist, to get a wider arc, he goes at it like a Dervish. What he lacks in practice he makes up for with enthusiasm. He has laid his own patch bare and has now run amok on the common grazing. It is only a matter of very short time until this corner of Leurbost is as grassless as the Ghobi Desert. What upsets me most is not that he will one day run out of control and scythe down my pine trees, but that he makes me feel guilty. I can only sit and watch him because my strimmer has lost a screw. And I'm bu … dashed if I'm going to dig out my rusty old scythe just because Maggie keeps drawing my attention to the wonderful work this man does. And, she tells me, he is partly crippled after a fall from a ladder and unable to work under full steam. There is nothing for it but to shoot him.

TUESDAY

Another person who frightens me is the good Sister Good. I have a letter from her this morning asking, among other things, for some publicity for a fundraising ceilidh on Friday 21st August in the British Legion in Stornoway. I would no more dream of disobeying a woman from South Lochs than I would of standing up to Edwina Currie.

Sister Good, as every schoolboy knows, is the power behind FIND (Food Intolerance Nutrient Deficiency). Many of my medical colleagues remain sceptical of FIND, and I must admit I too was at first a wee bit doubtful. But since I discovered that I was allergic to almost everything except lager and Murphy's I realise Anne Good is on to something. Furthermore, I see her organisation as a possible outlet for my vast stocks of Lus nan Laogh and other ancient chemical concoctions that I cannot name here. (Patents pending.)

By the way, the Master Who Doesn't Stand Upon Ceremony on Friday night is DHM Maciver. The supporting cast doesn't really matter, does it?

WEDNESDAY

Influenced by feminist friends, my wife has taken a job – some crazy notion about being independent and having money of her own. This means, I trust, that I can now claim what I earn is mine. It also means I have to do my share of the housework. There is really very little to it, believe me. It is all in the mind, as Sister Good might say. I find I have more time than ever now to watch the man next door working. From my position at the window here with the glass I can see everyone who moves in the East End.

Twice today a certain person has visited another certain party's house. What can be so important, I wonder? And who is that stranger going into Angus's caravan? A nice new car, and I can just read the number with the glasses. Pity we cannot tap into the Swansea Data Bank with the Micro. This could be an even better hobby. Your man has just come running out, jumped the fence and dashed to Billy France's. Didn't stay a minute. I wonder what the urgency was? Very worrying, this caring about neighbours. Is that Seumas, fresh out of a coronary-induced coma, chasing sheep? Frustrating, though. I could be missing something on the West window.

This is really a two-man job. At the West window I can watch Lochs, or at least I can watch 70 per cent of the pitch as I do my duty at the sink. These duties are the reason I have contributed so little to the team's efforts this season. However, if you send me an account, Coach, I'll donate 70 per cent of my gate money for all home games.

THURSDAY

What do women find to do? This is so boring. Ah, at last, a phone call. That was the *Gazette* office. Apparently their latest Editor, who had started to brighten up the paper, has been sacked. A hit-man from the South flew in, handed him his jotters and flew out again without as much as a silver handshake. "This paper," he said, "has always been grey, and grey it shall remain. Our job is to make money. Get on your bike."

Of course I must consider their offer. The job seems not too difficult – the sort of task you could manage along with the housework. Yet there is no doubt that Mr Brown is a hard man. Money as such has not been mentioned, but when he says an offer you cannot refuse, does that mean I'll be wealthy or will I waken up some morning with my prize ram's head under the bedclothes? You see my quandary!

FRIDAY

Perhaps I should have made it clear that FIND has nothing to do with the goings-on at the Callanish Stones. What dark deeds are planned around these ancient monuments we can but hazard a dreadful guess. Ancient superstition and pagan ritual have no place on our sacred soil, and I am pleased to hear Cllr Macdonald has lent his considerable weight to the opposition.

Make no mistake, for the next 13 years we can expect thousands of cabbalistic vagabonds to converge on Callanish. What these seekers-after-truth plan on this the eve of a new millenium does not bear thinking about. Human sacrifice cannot be ruled out. Listen to the sort of mystic we can expect to lead the Callanish-bound rabble. A modern American prophet: "A physically immortable human being from the realm of Shangri-la appeared in my room, in Boulder, Colorado. He wore a long robe, held a wooden staff and had long white hair. He was clearly the prophet Elijah." (No doubt made immortal by Hank Williams.)

I don't know if this business has any connection with Freemasonry or not, but I think we should have nothing to do with them. When the Earth fails to list as they expect in the year 2000 (unless the superpowers press a wrong button), we will be left with thousands of latter-day prophets looking for council houses in the Carloway ward. Cllr Macdonald is a far-seeing individual, if not actually a seer. We must be on our guard.

4 SEPTEMBER, 1987

MONDAY

Not so long ago when I was a wee boy, the Hibs were a great team. When I listened to the wireless on a Saturday afternoon I was convinced the announcer had made a mistake when he said Rangers one, Hibs nil. All evening I would listen in vain for a correction. I expected every news bulletin to begin: "Sorry, our sports results should have read Rangers one, Hibs six." The fact that the correction was never issued made me a very unhappy child, but fortunately it caused me to grow up expecting very little from life and with an abiding dislike of Rangers.

Later on, when a friend from Tyrone told me that Hibs supporters were known as green Orangemen, I understood why we lost to Rangers although we had the better team. Forty years later the best team does not have to lose against Rangers because the television camera is watching. Referees are not so easily frightened. Rangers still have the power to ban news cameramen who might show Souness in a true light, but they cannot ban sports cameras if they hope to attract sponsorship.

TUESDAY

However, now that we have seen Graeme Souness's brutal intentions, we can understand why he wanted television cameras banned. Even the most bigoted fans, who know anything at all about football, will concede that Celtic were magnificent in that first half-hour on Saturday. This is when Rangers led by the thug Souness introduced plan 'B': that is, mow them down.

In case there is some poor soul living in Ness or Unst who is not up to date with current affairs, Rangers have three basic strategies – (a) you try to buy the League in the close-season; (b) if things are not going as well as hoped for, you attack the opposition with your studs; and (c) if an opposing player scores against you during the week you buy him for Saturday, unless he kicks with the left foot. Sadly for Rangers, the Reformation was no more successful than their present team promises to be. In view of this, and that other Holy War in the Gulf, it is not surprising that I myself am, nowadays, a supporter of St Mirren.

WEDNESDAY

Although I speak as a supporter of sport it does not mean, mind you, that my participation is a thing of the past. Only the other day, or was it the day before, a young colleague called Little Hampton inveigled me onto the golf course.

Here I must register my dismay that the ferocious rough I knew in my 20s has been cut with some form of modern machinery that must obviously have been provided by the EEC. No scythe could have got rid of thon. Had the rough been as rough as it used to be, I would have lost two balls before I reached the gap on the first and would therefore have retired to the 19th and never known the level of despondency that prevailed come the Dardanelles.

I had no heroics in mind when I grasped my seven iron for my third shot on the first. All I hoped for was to get up there close. The trajectory of the ball was roughly 30° elevation and curving rapidly to the right, ending approximately 87° from the set course. This will be immediately recognised by those in the know as a 'shank'. The curse never strikes beginners or low handicappers. The debility is strictly for hackers. The word 'shank' is forbidden on a golf course, and no wonder.

The disease is thought to be contagious. Whether or not it is safe to mention the word in print I cannot say. Some golfers, I know, buy this upmarket paper because they are tired of the incessant, if not incestuous, mention of friends and relations among Stornoway's Upper-Class Golfing Dilettanti in the Greysheet.

If shanking is transferrable through print, I am sorry, Mr Whiteford, because I wouldn't wish it on a Tory.

By the fifth hole I was desperate, topping off the tee and shanking the rest. At the Short I used for the first time in my life what can only be classed "foul language". I swore on the eleventh I would never attempt this ridiculous game again. At the Dardanelles I became suicidal after 15 swipes and would have committed suicide if I could have been certain of striking my own neck. But that is only the start. My game got worse.

THURSDAY
And if there is anything worse than your first dreadful experience of shanking, it is to arrive at the so-called Clubhouse with the shutters down. Every year about this time we hear of the dire financial situation the Golf Club finds itself in. The Club has among its members many wealthy businessmen. It also has a few educated members – surely between them they should be able to work out that the problem basically is not enough drink. A barmaid is not highly paid and I am sure she would bring in enough during this uncivilised closed-hour to reduce the subs.

FRIDAY
All of which brings us to the County Hotel. I've said it before and I must say it again. If you want coffee, there are cafes in the town. Coffee takes a long time to prepare, longer even than Murphy's. Furthermore, coffee costs the publican a great deal in bartender's time. For coffee go to Horace Capaldi's and leave the bar staff to do what is expected of them – to serve those who have been shanking and met closed shutters at the Golf Club. I would have more to say on this subject but for my industrial action.

25 SEPTEMBER, 1987

MONDAY
You will naturally want to know the nature of my illness and you will no doubt want to hear the gory details of my operation. I knew when she showed me the x-ray it was going to be a tough job, a job that would take all of our combined theatre experience. The picture showed a two-

inch long stick of ivory growing from the region of my left earhole down through the gum.

I was reminded of an old bad-tempered Kafue elephant I once knew. He had an ingrowing tusk and we had to shoot him in the end. This is an alternative worth considering if you ever find yourself in my predicament, because removal of a tusk is a desperate job. On a pain-scale of one to ten it registers nine, one above childbirth and one below something so dreadful no one has ever experienced it. Not that I have personally experienced childbirth yet, but I have my wife's word for it and she has had both jobs done.

This is a job, by the way, that is better done by two ladies than one man with strong wrists. The ladies can get all four hands into your mouth at once. With one pushing, one pulling and one screaming, the task takes little over an hour. It is best done when you're awake, because then you can direct operations between screams. Up a bit, down a bit … stop, that's it.

When they let you out, then that comedian the chemist takes over. Pills to be taken four times a day after meals, he said. After meals? How are you supposed to get anything that could be classed as a meal down your bruised and bleeding gullet? Of course you cannot, so you have to eat your medication on an empty stomach – which of course makes you sick. Better by far to lock yourself away from the world with a bottle of malt. That way you still get ill, but at least it is a familiar illness.

TUESDAY

Spent a lot of time reading while I was wounded. You see a lot of rubbish in the papers but now and again you read something useful, as I did yesterday. Alas, I have forgotten what I read. Just recently I've noticed I can remember with great clarity things that happened when I was three years old but I don't know what I had for breakfast or if I had breakfast.

There would clearly be no point in starting the Autobiography now, because who could finish it? Old age can play havoc with the storage registers. They say booze can also destroy cells and the short-term memory, but among drinking men I've known I've noticed a stranger aberration. Not only do they never forget what happened yesterday, they tell you every five minutes of today. Especially if it is something of no significance whatsoever, like the fiver they lent you. Or could it be that they have forgotten what they told you five minutes ago? It is all very worrying.

WEDNESDAY

One should never tempt fate on Communion Wednesday. At exactly 508 words the electricity supply failed. Naturally, I've forgotten what the 508 words were and now we will never know. Fortunately I now remember what I read yesterday.

I had been thinking and worrying, as I often do, about North Lochs bachelors. Six years have passed since I last counted 75 of them, of varying eligibility. In that time some of the younger ones like Karachi and Lal have found a place, but the older ones, now much older, are still without wife. But not without hope, because I spotted this advert for Indonesian women.

Apparently you can now buy an Oriental wife off the shelf, much as you would buy a horse if you could afford it. I have no wish to make money out of this scheme; I regard it merely as a service for my desperate friends. A good one can be had for three grand, and hire purchase can be arranged. Not only are they wonderful servants (OK, call them slaves if you like), they don't speak your language. No one to ask where you've been when you fall through the door at midnight, or why you left your wellies on the mantlepiece. Send a stamped envelope and one hundred notes for your introduction.

THURSDAY

I saw more telly than usual during my convalescence. That wee programme about Ian Anderson of Jethro Tull was worth doing if for no other reason than to show the downtrodden peasants in the Outer Isles that Skyemen are luckier with their landlords. Can you imagine the Grimersta Mafia doing a gig for crofters in reduced circumstances? Can you imagine them period? Do they exist? How about a fund-raising concert in Harris, Ian, for fish-farmers with cash-flow problems? In return I could show you where you are going wrong with your sheep.

All I have to say about Norman's play *The Shutter Falls* I will say to him personally, except perhaps just to register my disappointment that he only showed one coffin in an hour and a half. And of course the truth hurt a bit. Who knows how many of us came into this world through a herring girl's chance encounter with a sophisticated photographer?

FRIDAY

For some time now it has been fashionable for media persons to make strange signs with their fingers when they talk to you. They raise their arms and curl their forefingers as if trying to cast rabbits'-head shadows on the wall. Often, to explain their bizarre behaviour, they say: "inverted commas". This can be entertaining but also distracting. You tend to become mesmerised with their contortions and not only forget their quotation but also the entire gist of their story.

The habit is annoying and contagious. Perhaps soon signs for all punctuation marks will evolve and there will be no need for speech. We can all sit round the table waving our hands like naval signalmen. This could be very useful for the men who mean to buy Indonesian wives.

2 OCTOBER, 1987

SUNDAY

I see many faces here tonight that are unfamiliar but not totally unknown to me. I saw them six months ago and I daresay I'll see them again six months from now. Yes, you know who I'm talking about and so do they. Men and women of all ages who think a biannual appearance in Church with a bulging envelope will absolve them of half a year's unspeakable wickedness.

Let me tell them now that this is not the Church of Rome. Salvation cannot be bought in this House. If that is your game, let me tell you now that you have lost. And, children, believe me, you have lost more than a game. Yet from one night in the company of His chosen children you could reap a harvest so rich that all the dictionaries of all the languages in the world cannot begin to describe that richness. But if you have entered here with hardened heart, if tomorrow you intend to seek the company of your old friends, be assured that you are doomed.

Ah, these so-called friends! Would not 'fiend' be a better word? You feel a bond with these friends – friends given over to the pleasures of the public house and other dens of ill-repute. This bond, my child, is not one of friendship; it is a shackle, a rope around your neck, a chain woven by the devil himself to anchor you in the pit of damnation.

Let me tell you more about these friends, my friends. They are not friends, they are your enemies and they hate you. Oh, I know, they profess to love and cherish you while there is a drop left in your half-bottle, while there is a penny left in your purse and you are top of the league. Most of all they love you while they can look at you and say, there goes someone who is worse than I. That, my child, is what gives them the most pleasure. As they sink ever lower in depravity their only comfort is you, the 'friend'. Shun them. Leave them. Leave them now and embrace those you see around you this night. For they will be real friends. They will rejoice and love you, not because they are lonely and miserable but because they delight in every new recruit who elects to join a ship that sails for ever on calm waters and never encounters a rough sea on their voyage across the Ocean of Tranquillity. No, my children, these new friends will not be fair weather friends; they will stick to you through thick and thin. Unlike your present circle of vagabonds, your new brethren will still be at your shoulder when your giro does not arrive or gets lost in the post. They will not desert your sinking ship. When your fanbelt breaks they will soothe you with cool palms and you will know the true meaning of brotherly love.

When I say brotherly love I do not mean – yes, yes, I see some of you smile – I do not mean what passes for brotherly love in the Lodge and the Golf Club where pagan ritual and sorcery is the order of every day. And I mean every day. To these boys, your alleged brethren, the only difference between Sunday and Wednesday is the spelling. And some of them are probably not aware of that little difference, blind as they are in every meaning of the word.

For that, brother, and for you because you choose to be his brother, there is only one certainty, and that is death.

As you drove here tonight, and I notice more and more of you elect to do so although you live within comfortable walking distance, you probably passed dead sheep by the wayside – an ever-present reminder of mortality. But that is only the beginning. Your present, or as I sincerely hope they now are, your past friends imagine death to be a release from their constant remorse. But they forget that death is only the beginning of an eternal torment, not only for them but for you who chose to follow them.

What awaits you all is too terrible to contemplate and I give thanks that my name has been removed from the list. I cannot guarantee you salvation, for I am not in the business of false warranty – I leave that to them – but rest assured that neither will you find it in the Sea Angling Club nor in any other club that exists to corrupt and deceive.

The punishment for ignorance is severe but is nothing compared with what lies in store for those who are not ignorant but ignore. Many of my modern trendy colleagues prefer not to remind you of that fate but let me quote a preacher from the old days:

"The torment of fire is the greatest torment to which the tyrant has ever subjected his fellow creature. Place your finger for a moment in the flame of a candle and you will feel the pain of fire. But our earthly fire was created for the benefit of man, to maintain in him the spark of life and to help him in the useful arts, whereas the fire of hell was created to punish and torture the unrepentant sinner. Our earthly fire also consumes the object which it attacks. But the sulphurous brimstone which burns in hell is a substance specially designed to burn for ever with unspeakable fury. Moreover, our earthly fire destroys at the same time as it burns, so that the more intense it is the shorter its duration: but the fire of hell has this property, that it preserves that which it burns, and, though it rages with incredible intensity, it rages forever.

"And this terrible fire will not afflict the bodies of the damned only from without, but each lost soul will be a hell unto itself, the boundless fire raging in its very vitals. The blood seethes and boils in the veins, the brains are boiling in the skull, and the heart in the breast glowing and bursting, the bowels a red-hot mass of burning pulp, the tender eyes flaming like molten balls ... Consider finally that the torment of this infernal prison is increased by the company of the damned themselves. The damned howl and scream at one another, their torture and rage intensified by the presence of being tortured and raging like themselves. All sense of humanity is forgotten. The yells of the suffering sinners fill the remote corners of the vast abyss ... They turn to their accomplices and upbraid them and curse them. But they are helpless and hopeless: they are too late now for repentance."

When you consider that that was taken from a sermon by a Catholic preacher for his flock, can you imagine how much more intense and tortuous is what could be lined up for you who should be more aware of your danger. Go home now and think on these things.

9 OCTOBER, 1987

MONDAY

October 5th 1987, SS *Suilven* ... Another crossing. Although Jim Wilkie's *Metagama* has been in my possession since last Thursday, it lay unopened until this morning. I thought it would be best read on the *Suilven*. If any ship can capture the *Metagama* atmosphere it is the *Suilven*, 55 years later. Yes, half a century later, not much has changed. True, they no longer have coal-fired boilers, but in every other respect they have managed wonderfully to preserve the deprivation of the Roaring Twenties.

Nowadays, everyone travels steerage except for the six persons who booked the cabins in 1948. The rest are crammed into two small pens like sheep or cattle. Like sheep we never complain. It is doubtful if in 1922 old Murdo Maclean would have put up with the conditions that prevail on the Stornoway-Ullapool ferry today.

Before I settled upright to read the *Metagama,* it seemed a sound idea in view of the south-west gale forecast to partake of some food. (I noticed some sensible people had brought their own sandwiches.) The cook had obviously prepared a galley-full of breakfasts before he went on holiday last month. These breakfasts, I would guess, were preserved in cooled-down fat for the duration, to be warmed when ordered and served in their own thawed fat. The sausages were undoubtedly bought in Turkey during that recent heatwave and transported transcontinental by donkey. After a certain period of decay no amount of spice can hide the guff. MacBraynes', God bless 'em, are great boys for tradition. Despite 25 years of passenger requests that the company should buy fresh bread in Stornoway, they still insist on stale buns from Inverness. Invernessian rolls are not the most palatable even when fresh: after two weeks back and fore in the sea air they are not fit for human consumption, or even for tourists. But never mind all that just now.

The voyage from Stornoway to Ullapool takes three and a half hours. The *Metagama* took only eight days from Stornoway to the St Lawrence. If the *Metagama* had been run by MacBraynes' not only would most of the passengers have starved to death, the few survivors would have been old and infirm on arrival in the New World. Three and a half hours is a fine voyage, but unfortunately it takes only about two hours to read the 'Metagama' (perhaps a lot less if you are a councillor).

This is not a criticism of young Seumas Wilkie, Well, dammit, it is. I feel a book about the *Metagama* should last you at least across the Minch once. But for all that, Seumas has done a fine job on it, and it is well worth £9.95. I liked the pictures. I always read the pictures first. If you ever study closely photographs taken of Northern Europeans who have spent 50 years toiling in the Americas, you will notice a facial similarity, particularly in their smiles. A broad, open-mouthed smile, often toothless because teeth cost money, but also slightly grim with the corners of the mouth turned down. Perhaps the harsh climate, who knows!

Now, how would I have tackled this book, I ask myself. Well, first of all, I don't fancy all that tiresome research. That could be subcontracted. And how could I fill, say, another 200 pages? The obvious answer is the voyage itself. A book entitled *Metagama* should, above all else, be about that ship's most famous voyage – eight days from Lewis to Canada. Sadly, facts are scarce; but what does that matter. Think of the stories you could invent from secret sources – and who is to say they wouldn't be true, when you consider the things that happen in the three and a half hours between Stornoway and Ullapool.

Of course we all know fine it need not be three hours. When some poor soul had a heart attack recently they managed the voyage in two and a half hours. I asked Maggie to go up on the bridge and pretend pregnancy and an imminent birth, but they wouldn't have it. "No chance," they said. "Perhaps if you were younger." So we plodded on up Loch Broom at seven knots.

I see the Russians are still here in force despite Charlie Kennedy's concern and the nearness of the Stornoway NATO base. Must have a word with Calum, see if he can either move these Russians or the NATO base.

Amazing the people you meet on the ferry ... Ewen Thompson on his way to Newcastle to look at a new boat, and he is a worried man. He doesn't speak a word of Geordie and wonders why they don't publish little phrasebooks like they do in Spain and Glasgow. Next week I'll be writing from a little island looking south on North Africa. I would take the week off but I cannot stand the thought of someone else getting my £6.50.

Perhaps I'll hitch a lift back with ET in his new boat. I still have the *Metagama's* 14 Gaelic pages to read, and that'll take me about two hours on account of the way we were taught in them thar days. Catching, the old Canadian drawl.

13 November, 1987

Dramatis Personae
King Alexander the First and Last
Douchess of Ness
Abbot of Shawbost
Archbishop of Laxay
Luis of Gaunt
Little and Large (Country Justices)
Earl Of Aig (Faithful retainer of the King)
Gress and Goathill (Two rebels)
Cardinal Park
Brutus O'Bourbon (A Southern reactionary – what else)
Sergeant at Arms / Doorkeeper to the King's Chamber
Many other unimportant characters from lower and lesser parts

Scene: The torture chamber, Alexander's Palace, Sandwick Road

THE PROLOGUE

> I come no more to make you laugh: things now,
> That bear a weighty and a serious brow,
> Sad, high and working, full of state and woe,
> Such noble scenes as draw the eye to flow,
> We now present.

THE KING:

> Now when tonight I ordered you to come
> To listen and to vote and to act dumb
> I had in mind to lecture and to teach the folly of the independent's
> breach of regulations.

DOUCH OF NESS:

> You're solid, Sandy, and you're fancy free,
> You're very nearly prettier than me,
> Perhaps if you should treat me sweetly
> My independence I would wear discreetly.

THE KING:

> I knew, dear Ness, that I could count on you
> Though in the past we've had a tiff or two
> One can assume the medical profession
> Is safe on independence and discretion.

N LOCHS:

> Hear, hear.

CARDINAL PARK:

> Sir, and this goes surely without sayin,
> I'm all for giving children room to play in
> But how much room, how much expensive space,
> Do little children need to say their grace.

O'BOURBON:

> Follow that.

SERG AT ARMS:

> Ordah, Ordah.

THE KING:

> Your part in this, friend Park, is noted well
> The distance now between us and Loch Shell
> Will shrink and shrivel like the human clay
> When tracks like magic become motorway.

EARL OF AIG:

> My lord, it seems to me a waste of time
> To have me stand just to complete a rhyme
> When all the world, indeed the whole of Point
> Knows well our politics and minds are joint.

GRESS:

> If I may raise a matter of the greatest import …

THE KING:

> You certainly may not stand up you fool
> Sit down I meant and try to loose your cool
> My men at arms who happen to be passing
> Will lift you soon as if you had been flashing.

From The Pressbox:
> Throw him out. Hang him.
> Beat …

Commotion wakens the Archbishop of Laxay.

ARCHBISHOP OF LAXAY:
> Did someone mention sheep or was it cattle
> Or was it my old brain begin to rattle
> What ever else I'll never turn my coat
> Whoever asked for it can have my vote.

THE KING:
> Now, friends, for that you have displayed,
> What will we do with all the money saved
> On English teachers, books and jotters
> And modern free-thinking rotters.

LUIS OF GAUNT:
> Can I suggest on point of order …

THE KING:
> No you may not cross my border
> When asked if you were friend or foe
> Your complex answer rang like NO.

GOATHILL:
> For years I've fought for independence …

THE KING:
> Shut up and let the Abbot send us.

THE ABBOT OF SHAWBOST:
> *(for it was indeed he)*
> My part in this dark deed deserves some praise
> I never did oppose a teacher's raise
> Yet boss and I have been compared to Hess
> For simply wishing that they numbered less.

27 NOVEMBER, 1987

MONDAY

If you ever found yourself with broken legs trapped for half an hour under a two-ton steel beam, you probably wouldn't care much which hospital took you in. Any hospital and any doctor would do. You would almost certainly not care about anything except relief from agony, so the nearer the hospital the better.

The nearer for many readers of this paper unfortunately means Stornoway. A fine hospital for the treatment of most ailments from simple childbirth to major surgery. Sadly, they have no bone man. For 25 years I have complained about this state of affairs. This is not a criticism of our only hospital. It is not the fault of hospital staff. It is the fault of our National Health so-called Service. Presumably we cannot afford to have a bone man in Stornoway.

Yet every time someone breaks a bone, one of my eminent colleagues in Stornoway Hospital has a go. After several days on the rack, the poor person being experimented upon is finally airlifted to Raigmore in Inverness to have the damage repaired. This strange form of modern torture had been going on now for as long as I can remember. Why?

Brain surgeons are smart boys (except for the odd mad one who wants to be an MP) but they are not bone men. Bone-setting is a different trade and a difficult one. Yet they all think they can have a go. For all I know, they call people in off Goathill Road when they're busy in the Hospital. "Excuse me," they say to a passing bus driver. "We have a man in here with a broken leg. Could you whip a plaster on him. I hear you're good with sheep."

"But I've never done a human."

"It doesn't matter, they're easier. There's no subsidy on them, and anyway they'll sort it out in Inverness next week if he's walking like a crab."

TUESDAY

My only concern is, of course, money. How much does all this experimenting cost the taxpayer? Loganair is already paid to ferry difficult jobs to the mainland. Why wait a week before calling them? For emergencies like a leg broken in three places with multiple cuts and bruises there is, I am told, a helicopter on stand-by.

Before we leave this very interesting topic here is a cutting from the front page of the *Stornoway Gazette*:

"An employee at Lewis Offshore's Arnish yard [how many yards have they got?] was seriously injured on Saturday when a beam toppled over him as he worked on a barge. A spokesman for the company said the accident was being investigated, and Mr Macleod's job would be open to him when he was fit to resume work."

I have no doubt that the spokesperson is being accurately quoted in the 'Grey Sheet'. But what did he mean? Assuming Mr Macleod is ever fit to resume work, are we to infer that there is some reason why his job should not be kept open? Obviously, if Mr Macleod deliberately allowed himself to be crushed under two tons of steel because he didn't like his right leg, then we must seriously examine his suitability to be re-employed – if he can walk again. After all, imagine what would happen if we take on every Tom, Dick and Coinneach who doesn't want to work weekends and then we find they take to throwing themselves under falling beams. What happens then? Before you know it they would all be at it. But thank goodness we are, above all, humane. Despite the reckless and irresponsible behaviour of our workforce, we are prepared to give them another chance. But enough.

This is the beginning of a long, long story. Those of us who are made of mere flesh and blood come out alternately in goose pimples and hot sweat as we imagine the agony. Coinneach, the victim, gained immediate entry in local folk history, keeping the head and directing operations between the occasional scream of unbearable pain. "Cut here, lift there. Pass the chain round my head." Most of us would have taken the easy route and fainted, but so much depends on those short sturdy legs.

Having survived, your man didn't demand to be taken to a recognised repairshop on the mainland. But then the stronger you are the more is expected of you, and we always expect a little too much of the strong.

God, I feel depressed tonight. In a minute I meet Rusty and Tormod a' Bhocsair to discuss our Gaelic Soap Opera. I expect to feel better after that.

WEDNESDAY

Another very important person I was supposed to meet yesterday I didn't. When I say important you'll understand exactly how important when I tell you money was involved.

There used to be a fine wee pub in Stornoway called the Club Bar. We old sailors used to gather there when Doileag was in charge. Then a few years ago they changed the name to the Neptune – a move of which we all approved. Anyway, to cut a long story short, I had to meet this important person in the Neptune. Of course he didn't wait for me, because they've changed the name again. He found the place all right, but foot he wouldn't set inside a bar named after Oliver Cromwell. This man whose ancestors suffered badly at the hands of Cromwell will not come back to the island until something is done about that dreadful name. Of course it's not the manageress's fault, it's these stupid brewers.

THURSDAY

Did you see that one about the American Judge who was blackballed because he had a drag of dagga in the Sixties? This funny world of ours gets funnier every day. The hypocrisy of those who rule us is almost beyond belief. Almost everyone of my age I know who passed through London in the late Sixties smoked a joint at one time or another. I don't think any of them became addicted although some have smoked themsleves to death on nicotine and many have become alcoholics of varying degree. But this is fine. Our rulers approve of that because they've made a lot of money out of them. But if I give the names away of these bad boys they'll never be called to the bar.

I feel terribly serious this week. I guess it must be the fault of Tormod a' Bhocsair, who has taken to preaching in his middle years. Anyway my colleagues have asked me to join them in industrial action for more money, so I'm on a three and a half day week. Many of them are threatening to join the lively new-look *Stornoway Gazette*, where the money is so much better now that cousin Kenny is in charge.

1988

15 January, 1988

Dear D. A.,

Thank you for the Christmas cards and last year's letter. Please forgive me for addressing you in the open like this, but you know what it's like nowadays. What with the price of stamps and envelopes, I don't see how the less fortunate man can keep in touch with his cousins at all. And talking of cousins, I guess you're the only proper one I have left now except for Peggy, and after 20 years working for the frightening MacInnes in the School of Scottish Buddies I cannot see her lasting much longer.

Anyway, how are things down in Durham? This university business sounds a grand lark. Is there anything I could do down there? Twenty-six years I've been working on the novel now and I'm getting tired. I'm sure I could do some research or something. Anything's better than working. By the way, what can you do with Arabic if you ever finish the course – apart perhaps from learning how to belch politely? I suppose you were already halfway there with your Edinburgh Gaelic and familiarity with sheep's heads and eyes.

Many thanks for your translation of your Arabian historian's account of their first meeting with the tall blond "Northmen". I found it fascinating and would like more of my countrymen to read it. For some strange reason many islanders like to claim Viking ancestry. You could perhaps explain this with our love of the sea, and there is no doubt that we do love it. (Our fishing boats sometimes work a four-day week now – how about that!)

That is only one reason. Perhaps we would all like to be tall and blond like you, instead of short and dark. But if we cannot be tall and blond we can at least try to claim a tall, blond ancestry – despite our Moorish features.

But, given our extreme godliness, it is very odd that some of us should be so proud of fierce forebears. My own personal theory, and please don't let this go beyond the four walls, is that we have subconsciously prepared a defence – in case we should ever find ourselves in front of Lord Mackay (na claise) on a charge of Rape, Pillage and Arson – of: "Sorry, me Lord, it's in the blood." Then finally: "OK, the Norsemen were a barbarous lot, but at least they weren't Roman Catholic." One can almost contemplate anything rather than that.

I would like to see your account of that first meeting on the Volga in 940AD published in the *Free Press*, but would we have to get permission from the University of Illinois? In any case I'm not certain that we could afford to give up advertising space. Money is all. In some respects we are no better than the *Sy Gazette*. I would ask them but some parts of your Arabic account are too "accurate". And also I'm not sure if I could extort payment on your behalf for second-hand stuff.

Not, of course, that you need the loot. Your sort never does. Once you're in on the secret of being a perpetual student, you never lack for money. I suppose innocent neighbours drop in with vegetables and other goodies because you're a poor student. They're not bad that way in Durham. At least they are not so mean as the English, but little do they know of your private income. If, however, you find yourself short of the groceries any time, give us the word and I'll send you a parcel of sheep's eyes. Perhaps we have an unfortunate picture of the typical Englishman up here – a poor soul whose idea of a feast is some lamb chop. We have a new boy here from down your way somewhere who happened to catch Carloway taking a snack the other night. Like many pioneers' stories, his description of a first glimpse of the wild was thought to be totally unreliable. His estimate of the number of chops was thought to be excessive until two people tried to lift the bin of clean bones into the dust-cart. Your Englishman is often eccentric, but this guy seems to be a competent quantity surveyor.

But there you are, despite what we learned in medical school. I saw the old fellow chasing sheep on our grandfather's croft yesterday and he looked fine. And this, remember, at nearly 80 on a diet of fat mutton and Golden Virginia. I feel that is what I should do my thesis on – Golden Virginia and the Canadian Barn Dance. You ask, as always, about old friends. Well, not a lot changes. North Lochs is still mostly bachelor. Some, like the West End Tory, will, of course, never marry because it could cost money. Others like Murdie Siarach worked out that they would need someone in old age and so made a late move. On this theme I am often approached and asked: "What is the right age?" A tricky question, I usually reply. For a woman I would say 25, and if you are a man I would say 45. At 45 a man is in his prime and beginning to mature. By the time he is 65 his wife is beginning to break down, but he doesn't care because he is nearly finished. But the man of 25 who married the woman of 25: now he has the problem of trying to trade her in at 42 for a new model.

Now you are lucky. You still have young children and a young wife. They want to go fishing with you. Wait a few years, though. Children at 14 go daft, as you should well remember. They don't want to go fishing. They don't want to know you. You are, to all intents and purposes, just a chequebook. I suppose they serve some purpose in the grand scheme, but I dinna ken what. I like a certain touch of cynicism in modern youth like the big girl's boyfriend: "Can I still come out in your old man's boat when we stop going, like?" They are smarter than we were, but I still feel sorry for him.

Take an old man's advice, though, and don't worry about anything your kids do at 14: they usually settle down about 40.

Don't think much of what they read, generally, but I stole a good book off Fiona the other night. Not sure if it was recommended by a teacher or her social worker, but either way they have gone up in my estimation. Stayed up half the night reading, and I haven't done that since *Treasure Island* in the black-house. The cause of my insomnia was *To Kill a Mockingbird*, by Harper Lee. Seems it came out in the early 60s. Must have missed it. Suppose we were fighting in the Far East or somewhere. Now I remember, you were teaching these little girls in Penang the Canadian Barn Dance. A fine book, although not on the same level as

A High Wind in Jamaica. Still, will recommend to Miss MacCuish for O-Grade, although suspect my approval is the kiss of death.

Co-dhiù, all this is very boring, but never fear, I have a great scheme for next summer: why don't we go start a revolution in some small Latin American country. If it fails we can still buy land in Paraguay for 60 dollars an acre. Some croft, what? We could have M.B. for a landlord.

Yours aye,
Eachann

26 FEBRUARY, 1988

NOTES WHILE AFLOAT

Do you know what I'm going to tell you, and this is without a word of a lie: I accompanied a colleague into his home the other day and his behaviour astonished me. "Switch off that hoover," he yelled at his wife, "and make us a cup of tea." You can hardly believe it in this day (and age) but there you are.

The poor downtrodden woman made no attempt at protest, which leads me to suspect that this sort of exploitation is the norm in many Lewis households in 1988.

I remember in '38 Fingalstein telling me of his visits to Shawbost as a young impressionable boy. Being a cultured kind of cove from Matheson Road (where even in those days women's lib was well under way), Fingalstein's country cousins were a constant source of amusement to him. He has been dining out on these early encounters for 50 years now.

Late one Saturday night he was sitting round the fire with an old crofter cousin and his family of many daughters. I forget exactly how many – six or seven. Anyway, they were all six or seven of them sitting quietly knitting. The old fellow appeared to be asleep in his rocking chair when suddenly the clock struck eleven. What followed then can only be properly understood by those who have seen Fingalstein acting the whole scene. The old boy sat bolt upright and announced: "Tha mise dol a sheubhaigeadh". At this magic word the women of the house dropped their knitting and burst into action, each to her fore-ordained task. Quick as a flash, kettle, basin, soap, water, brush, strop and razor were placed at the patriarch's disposal. Whether he nodded a thank you and actually did the shaving himself I cannot remember, and it doesn't matter. That was another time, and another place: this is now, and Stornoway, yet some men still get away with it.

Encouraged by my friend's way with his little woman, I went home and tried it on myself. "If you don't mind," says I, "I'll have my dinner on a tray in the sitting room, and when you've done that bring some coal in and …". But she didn't wait to hear me out. I think she's somewhere in Inverness now, which, if you ask me, is a bit of over-reaction. I wouldn't mind so much but for the joint account.

"How is it done?" I asked my friend. "How is what done?" says he. Your man is quite clearly unaware of his privileged position in today's woman-dominated society.

There is nothing for it but to swallow my pride and go looking for her in Inverness, which is why I write this letter to you once again from the rolling deck of my *Suilven*. A few new faces among the crew, but nothing else changes much. The bacon roll looks suspiciously like the one I rejected last October. There is fierce debate at an adjoining table about whether it really is a bread roll or some synthetic material manufactured at Long Island Insulation. A "roll" is passed around for inspection. Someone tries to tear it but fails. Another brave man tries to take a bite out of it and miraculously succeeds. But then he is an Ùigeach. After half an hour of hot discussion the consensus of opinion was that it did indeed belong to the species commonly referred to as the morning roll. The question is: which morning. Certainly not this one. Obviously the rolls are no longer bought in Inverness. They couldn't possibly age that much in 60 miles unless they've been stored in Ullapool since the seamen's strike.

The only man I could rely on, Tormod Cromarty, is on leave and Ghandi, our friendly Sgiathanach chief steward, has been transferred to the Oban run for ballast. Roddy the regular cook is again on holiday and a mutual friend assures me he is attending a cookery course in Lews Castle College, but that seems a little bit far-fetched.

All I can do in the circumstances is join that Bernera gang in the bar, where I might learn how one earns a woman's respect.

25 MARCH, 1988

MONDAY

The conversion of councillor Angus Graham, like so many island conversions, was sudden and unexpected. When he left Lewis last week for the Crofters Union meeting at Sabhal Mòr Ostaig, he was as solid a socialist as you'd meet in a day's walk. As a union delegate in his younger days he had built a reputation for honest endeavour and reliability. He never once came even close to being called a boss's man. As a councillor he is judged to be incorruptible. Yet when he could have been posing with the elite of the Labour Party in Loch Leurbost, he chose to mingle with the crofters at their annual gathering, the Alternative Skye Ball.

At every opportunity I've warned the young men of Lewis (and especially the young women) to avoid Skye if possible because the inhabitants of that last outpost of Empire are a dangerous lot. The ordinary folk are infamous for their intemperate approach to strong drink and it is well known that no virile youth is safe from the women of that mountainous island. But it wasn't the crofting women what done for Angus, but the Aristocracy. You must realise that I wasn't there myself and that all this is hearsay, so not a word outside these four walls. Exactly what happened we'll never know and we don't want to know; all I can tell you is that after our man had been shown round the ancient seat of the Clan Macdonald by Lady Clare he was heard to philosophise: "There is room on this earth for all sorts." This Lady Clare must be a powerful woman in an island of powerful women. I cannot wait to hear, at the next council meeting. Angus Graham extolling the virtues of the aristocracy.

TUESDAY

Before, during or after all this, whatever it was, was going on, our MP Calum Macdonald arrived late, but assured his friends that he had indeed found a place to stay – some B & B place, he thought: Kinloch Lodge or something like that, said he. Something like that, indeed. Kinloch Lodge is the sort of place Princess Margaret might stay when she comes to the Skye Ball, which is funny when you know that Calum is a very careful boy with his pennies – perhaps more careful even than Murdie Siarach, which is very careful indeed. Probably MP B Wilson was staying with some other Skye aristocrat like Iain Noble or Derek Cooper.

Sometimes I regret having gone for salmon when I should have concentrated on sheep, especially now that I hear Lady Clare doesn't like farmed salmon. Well, she wouldn't, would she? One shouldn't keep the King of Fish in a pen. I only say these things because they are being said.

WEDNESDAY

Meanwhile, back on the ranch, the Shadow Chancellor, John Smith (no relation to the Millionaire Cobbler), was not too proud to have a cup of tea with a common crofter. Mr Smith is definitely a type that appeals to the traditionally conservative crofter. Unbeknown to him, I have a standard set of questions with which I test potential leaders, such as how old is your grannie, and I'm pleased to say he passed that one. But then, so did Donald Dewar. When Niall Ruadh retires and the time comes to choose between the two lawyers (Gould is too smooth), I am faced with a difficult decision. Both John Smith and Donald Dewar look and dress like Free Presbyterians but at least John Smith didn't insult me. After I'd shared a black pudding with D.D. he looked out the window and announced that mine was the worst garden he'd ever seen except for one in Miavaig. These little things are not easily forgotten by a man who doesn't easily forget little things.

THURSDAY

Whatever about leaders, about Chancellors of Exchequers there is no doubt. The first qualification you look for is thrift. Here is a useful rule of thumb: "The man who looks after his own loot will not squander yours." From the present crop of Scottish Labour MPs with Highland connections, I get the impression our heritage is safe.

Back to Donald Dewar and John Smith. Both are lawyers and therefore, like crofters, more accustomed to speaking than listening. This is expected in every politician, inescapable in a Chancellor but absolutely essential in a leader.

For his final exam I took John Smith to sea in a Force Seven. My goodness, he passed with honours. He didn't flinch or duck the spray. He didn't even remove his spectacles, although perhaps this was because he didn't want to see the swell. Never mind but. I wouldn't even ask Donald Dewar to sit the test, with his higher centre of gravity and his reckless sense of humour. Don't worry, Donald: Ted Heath had a rough pair of sea-legs, no sense of humour and he sank.

Another attribute that the punters look for, especially in Scotland, is brains. I have no fear both boys would pass the 11-plus and, more important, the 51-plus because they both take care of the liver. On the other hand, in England, brains don't matter much. But accents do. This is where I think John has the edge on D.D. Although both are ferociously articulate, John retained his slow Argyll drawl while Donald had to speed up in Glasgow, because if you didn't you got knifed before the punch-line.

FRIDAY

The weekend is upon us and it's time for sport. I will say nothing about rugby because I have too much to say that has to be said because it is not being said by those who should be saying it when they're saying other things that were perhaps better not said, but if I don't say what should be said then someone else will say it because it is being said (For goodness' sake, say it. Ed.). Sorry, I've forgotten. I take it all back, Mr Roberts of

Glasgow Rangers. You can play a wee bit. Phew! What a second half. Had to get Maggie to sponge me down with a dead heron. You see, Mr Souness, younger men can have a hard game without having to resort to Chicago tactics.

22 APRIL, 1988

ANOTHER TERRIBLE JOURNEY

Never mind why, but the other day I found myself in the Lowlands of Scotland, where I saw and heard many strange things. I flew, of course – doesn't everyone these days – because although I hate flying someone else could afford the fare and you don't look a free air ticket in the mouth.

The first obstacle always on the Stornoway-Glasgow flight is the tall, dark, handsome gentleman at the BA desk. He either cannot work the computer or he pretends he cannot find my reservation. My agent tries to fool him with different names, but you cannot fool fear Chrosaboist. "Is it Eachann, H or Aimsir today?" he asks LE FIOS.

It is best to approach the pilot, who has to double as baggage handler (because times are hard on the Highland routes). Say to him: "My name is Councillor AA Macdonald." This trick never fails. All Macdonalds look alike to them, and this Cllr Macdonald (whoever he is) has a booking on every flight although he only travels every second day, and even then he is always late.

So I get to my seat by the emergency door and frighten myself with idle speculation on the age of the aircraft and the stewardess. Who is older than which, and how do they feel about being banished to the Highland Division? (Please note, I am not being sexist here: I am merely an observer of BA policy.) Like most polite passengers, I try to pay attention to her lifejacket routine, but this "girl" the other day made it most difficult. She had obviously been going through the motions for so long that she had lost interest. She wearily pulled the straps around her ample corp like an old woman harnessing herself to a creel of peat. Her instructions for action to be taken in the "unlikely event" conveyed a certain lack of conviction, as if she didn't think it was at all unlikely. She had lost the knack of smiling in the Sixties, and who can blame her. But all that can be forgiven because she was generous with the miniatures. The trouble with miniatures of Grouse is that they fire the imagination. You begin to wonder if that port prop is turning as fast as the starboard one. You ask yourself to what ridiculous extent could they carry their stringent economic strategy. Will the Captain soon be serving coffee in the terminal building and will big Joan be flying the aeroplane? I'd like to meet the joker who coined the title "Terminal Building". Give me the boat any day, for, if nothing else, they don't depress you with preparation for unlikely events.

But time is money, so we must take risks. In no time at all I was one of the crowd at Queen Street Station rushing for an Edinburgh train. There isn't a moment to be lost, so you cannot stand around gazing at departure boards like a Skyeman. Instant intelligent decisions have to be made. If there are three trains hauling at the bit, the Edinburgh one has to be the one the majority are boarding. I chased the largest flock and swung aboard the moving train like John Wayne getting on a stagecoach. Normally I would have gone for that long narrow walk looking for a smoker but I figured that by the time I got my breath back it would be too late. Anyway, Lowlanders pay little attention to "Thou shalt not" signs, so I collapsed in the nearest seat and closed my eyes.

When travelling abroad I always sport a splash of tartan and I carry a spring of heather in one ear. This encourages the natives to open up, secure in the belief that American tourists and Highlanders won't understand them. Although my grasp of foreign languages is not good, you wouldn't believe what I learned that day.

My travelling companions on the train were two middle-aged ladies from, I guessed, Sam Galbraith's constituency. At first I thought, because they were middling posh, they could have been from Edinburgh. But then one said to the other: "I was a bit naughty last week, I put on half a pound. I really went my dinger at Jim's party." A quick look in the phrasebook confirmed my suspicion. They had to be ex-Partick.

Probably two of the many elevated from the tenements to Bearsden by Skinner and Macarthur. But then I learned they were golfing ladies, so I could be wrong about Partick. Perhaps "went my dinger" is common to the entire rift valley.

When one of them lowered her voice I became quite excited and very nearly opened my eyes. I rolled my head to the starboard shoulder just in time to hear: "I haven't been to the hairdresser's for weeks; I'm scared I'll catch Aids." Now I could no longer pretend to be asleep. I stared open-mouthed, like an innocent Teuchter abroad, wondering what kind of demon barber she engaged. Did she make her appointments during what the French call "the impossible hour" or was she merely scared of being nicked on the scalp by a contaminated pair of scissors?

Whatever, it helps to pass the time and take one's mind off the gathering doubt about being on the right train. There didn't seem to be that many aboard. Could we be heading for some one-hoss town like Tyndrum or Motherwell? I thought of asking the gabby lady who hadn't had her hair done but I was afraid she would scream for a guard thinking I was making some kind of hairdressing move. Best to keep quiet in these circumstances and await the worst. The worst is the Haymarket. Hay market it might one day have been, but now it is a coal market. Why Bearsden ladies who go shopping in Princes Street don't get their councillor friends in Morningside to tidy it up I cannot understand.

What with this mad commuting, I haven't had time to tell you the reason for my wasting a good spring day in STV's primitive Leith Walk Studio. OK, I'll give you a clue: Maggie Cunningham, Kenny Maciver, Professor Ron Black and myself accepted an invitation to advertise some nightclothes on a programme called *Midsummer-night's Dream*. I must say our host, Black Angus, looked magnificent in his pyjamas. Until then I had only seen him in his sporran. (Of course later on I learned the frillies had been hired for the night by the sponsors.) Advertising makes the world go round, and it won't take Big Gus long to cotton on to the fact that hairy Highlanders like Maciver and Angus, when filmed lounging around in their shreddies, will soon attract 3am voyeurs.

I am basically a travel writer, so let me get back to my taxi on Princes Street. "Hullo, big fellow," they say, because they must say something. This Lowland greeting is very flattering. In the Highlands anyone under six feet has to live with the appendage beag; in the Valley anyone over five-seven is mòr. You wonder who suffered the most deprivation: those who stayed to subsist on kelp or those who emigrated for a diet of rivets.

My goodness, look at the time. I'll have to leave the return journey for next week.

29 APRIL, 1988

IT'S ALL COMING BACK ...

During the war one was somehow detached from the danger. One checked one's oxygen, strapped oneself in and went up to meet the Hun. One simply did what one had to do. Certainly one knew that each take-off could be one's last, but it never occurred to one to make one's Will. One was young then, of course, in the Officers' Mess, although one is old now.

This one is certainly very old and feels even older since he accepted a lift from that old wartime buddy Black Angus. "Let me drive you to the station – it's only a short hop from Leith Walk to Waverley," he said, helping me into what could have been an old Morris Oxford. He held her against the brakes long enough to check the cloud base and took off. Quite clearly a man whose mind is in the hills of Skye or back in the war shouldn't drive in a city. Your man treats all other traffic as the enemy. Every Heart of Midlothian bus is a Messerschmitt and every black taxi a Fokker. Miraculously we got to Waverley unscathed. I said goodbye and ejected the first time he slowed down in case he threatened to take me further. Thanks, Angus.

Although I fully expect to outlive them all, I made a note to make a Will as soon as I got back to civilisation. Every man of mature years should make a Will, they say. But why? Haven't they robbed me enough while I was alive? Let them squabble. I have a good mind to leave all my considerable wealth to some fictitious creature in Portree, hinting at romance and intrigue in what was in fact a dull, uneventful existence.

Anyway, there I was in the dungeon called Waverley Station, an ideal place for morbid thoughts and down-and-out Freemasons. Despite crude attempts at modernisation, Waverley smells of the last century. The impression, even during the day, is of being deep in the bowels of a very old city. Dark corners remain in which lurk Pictish winos who would slit your throat for a penny – every one a descendant of Burke or Hare.

Although ill at ease, I was sorry when I had to board the train. I was acutely conscious of an earlier, much earlier, acquaintance with Waverley in a previous incarnation. I wondered, as I sped towards Glasgow, if I'd been a man of the church bringing enlightenment to these subterranean souls. Or was it a premonition? (Mental note to read John Knox again.)

In the festival atmosphere of the Cultural Garden of Europe I felt more at home. The winos had Gaelic / Irish faces and I remembered the names of the streets and pubs. I visited the Curlers on Byres Road where Nessmen used to gather in the '50s, but the punters were all under 25 with purple hair and tartan trousers. Perhaps it's a BBC pub nowadays? In Tennents I found men of my own vintage. Someone told a new joke about Souness and Hitler but I thought it in bad taste, so I passed it to Shields for his *Herald* Diary.

At nine o'clock I thought I'd better get a bed for the night because I am old. Nae problem in Glasgow, you would think, but times have changed. The Dosshouse I often used at 2 Dowanside Road has been taken over by some kind of right-wing Kinnockian kibbutz and they wouldn't let me in. Or perhaps they were at the country lodge. Never mind, I've slept rough in many countries. But none of them as cold as Scotland, so I was forced to buy a bed on Hillhead Street in a place called Iona Guest House – chosen, naturally, because of the spiritual connotation.

My instincts, or call them divine navigators, seldom let me down, and sure enough at my bedside I found *The New Travelling Salesman's Bible in Simple English*. I won't quote from it because it clearly wasn't authorised by a king and probably wouldn't even get the Pope's blessing.

It looked to me like one of these Church of England parodies.

Early on the morning of the second day I was painfully stravaiging the mean streets when who should stop beside me and offer a lift but Anna Sturcan. "Are you looking for the Fishing '88 Exhibition?" ars ise. Well, dash it all, I was, because I wanted some cheap boxes of the type the Fishermen's Co-op have stolen from us. I wonder what kind of seventh sense these mysterious Ùigeach women possess.

In no time at all I was in what was once an ugly shipyard but is now a magnificent Exhibition Centre. Amazing what Labour councils can do. The first cove I saw was Losdaigh, explaining to the manufacturer how his (the manufacturer's) 2,000-hp machine worked and how "that would do him fine". I spotted a Shetlander or two I knew, and the Great Gatsby Mackenzie buying electronic equipment worth several million. He carries his money in a black polythene garbage bag but this fools no one. But I didn't want to embarrass him. I quickly ordered my boxes and ran to Abbotsinch.

I shouldn't have run, because you need all your strength for the type you meet at the British Airways desks. "Are you booked?" asked the short man. What happens to short men when you put them in uniform? "No, I'm not booked, I always assume the plane is half empty." "One should never assume anything," said this pompous git. Of course it was half empty, and my friend the Stewardess was in command.

We were delayed on the taxiway for 10 minutes during which the Captain called me forward and showed me some wanted notices. He held up a photo of a notorious Iranian terrorist and pointed down the alleyway to Kenny Maciver. The resemblance was startling and I would have let them take him away, but John Murray was getting hungry.

Somewhere over Skye I was delighted to hear the reassuring voice of Genghis Mackenzie. Fortunately communications in the air are not dependent on British Telecom. Can you imagine Big Fred coming to make fine adjustments to electronic hardware with a hammer and a crowbar. Let us be thankful for many things. Strangely, Dòmhnall Easy was not aboard and … but, dear me, we have run out of time again.

6 MAY, 1988

SUNDAY

Some time ago I resolved to give up preaching for the simple reason that there were already far too many people converted. Working on the assumption that the number of places on the bus is strictly limited, why risk inviting more on board? After a lifetime of good works you could find yourself without a seat. But this is a selfish attitude. Duty calls and risks have to be taken.

MONDAY

On my way to work yesterday, because I must, I was tweaking the tuning button on the car radio looking for a Gaelic sermon when I accidentally found Andy Cameron. Cameron is a decent man, for a Rangers supporter, and quite funny. For a few moments I forgot myself sufficiently to listen to him. How easily one falls into their trap. Before I could switch off in horror and disgust I heard something that shook me to the very marrow – a request from a young woman in Stornoway who had quite clearly fallen under the influence of some Barra boys.

The question we must find an answer to, and find it fast, is: to what extent have the pagan practices of the South found their way into the hearts and minds of young innocent Stornoway girls? How many more like yesterday's girl are secretly tuned into Andy Cameron when their minds should be on higher things?

We must root these people out without delay. Do not be afraid to listen at your neighbour's window for sounds of desecration, like laughter. By all means try to reason with them, but remember these are not reasonable people, so be prepared to take strong measures. Mark my words, if it's Stornoway this week it could be S Lochs next.

TUESDAY

It has been brought to my attention that many otherwise stable men are addicted to the game of snooker. This is not a game I would encourage youngsters to take up. Snooker is often played in smoke-filled dens that attract an unhealthy type, adding further to a foul and poisonous atmosphere, and bad language. Also, I regret, snooker is often a medium for the wagering of housekeeping money.

Yet it must be conceded that the sport has its attractions for men of probity, often Masons, who want to further their knowledge of geometry and trigonometry. Naturally these serious students want to watch the experts on TV and this is fine until 2359 GMT on a Saturday. Then they are snookered. What are committed youngsters to do, they often ask me? Well, now, there are several ways round this one. If your neighbour belongs to a less demanding church like the Anglican, you could suddenly remember you owe him a pound of butter. This is your entry fee. Once in his sitting-room you can watch his box with one eye while keeping a disapproving one on him.

Another ploy is to video Sunday play for viewing on Monday. Some elders take a dim view of this, although it seems no worse than reading the results in Monday's papers that were printed on the seventh day. Some wise men maintain that Sunday snooker could be watched in black and white because this offers little in the way of enjoyment and you could still pursue your study of trigonometry. But at the end of the day it is all between you and the Grand Geometrician in the Sky.

WEDNESDAY

At quarter past nine this evening, a few minutes before I was due to leave for work, we were struck by what could turn out to be a costly domestic crisis. She who hears everything said she thought she could hear a mouse somewhere. You cannot go on night-shift with a mouse loose in the house, although I know some men who would.

Ignoring all threat to personal safety, I squeezed through the hatch in the ceiling and crawled fearlessly from joist to joist. As I suspected, the "mouse" was a steady drip from a leak in the roof. Now this is no time for a plumber in N Lochs. What to do in the few minutes available? Some would no doubt have panicked and called the fire brigade (if the new director of enquiries could find the number) and others would probably have left the wee woman to cope on her own. Fortunately, there are still some of us left who can be relied upon to think quickly in an emergency. By simply placing a bucket in the right spot, having already calculated the rate at which it would fill, I was able to leave her with peace of mind. All she had to do was set the alarm every two hours to empty the bucket. With a little consideration we could all make our womenfolk's lives so much easier.

THUSDAY

I don't know how much longer I can go on. The eyesight is failing fast. (I blame these damn VDUs.) She now has to hold the paper for me across the table because my arms are getting too short to focus. I keep bumping into Robert Doig the optician, at lunchtime, but he refuses to believe there is anything wrong – more or less insinuating that I'm drunk. I know his game but. He's waiting until the price of glasses reaches 500 quid. He's not a bit like his Grandpa who gave me five hundred injections I didn't even want.

There is no need, though, to pay this extortionate price to see where you're going. In the only Sunday paper I believe, I read that cheap specs are available in New York. What you save on your glasses if you buy a few spares more than pays for the cost of the air ticket.

FRIDAY

I am astonished to receive in this morning's post an invitation from my dentist despite what I went through last year. This desperate man cannot wait until my teeth fall out naturally. He wants to yank them out and flog me an expensive set of false tusks. But I'm having none of it.

He forgets I too am a scientist. Let me give you a tip or two. There is nothing better for your teeth than this valuable compound they call plaque. Don't, on any account, let them scrape this off your teeth. It's all a con for the toothpaste industry. Plaque protects your teeth from harmful acids and rotting oxygen. Leave your plaque alone and you'll go in the box with a full set of your own chompers.

SATURDAY

It's no use. I cannot see.

20 MAY, 1988

MONDAY

This evening I was watching TV and having a few snorts with my wife to celebrate the anniversary of the relief of Mafeking when the face of William Rees-Mogg appeared on the screen. This was the first of three news items that left me exceeding wroth. The second was the final plan for the abolition of the Health Service. The third doesn't matter for the moment.

Let's take the first one first. For many years now my favourite TV programme has been *Tom and Jerry* and this fiendish censor Rees-Mogg is hellbent on having it banned. True, he hasn't said this in so many words but he has threatened to ban *The A Team*. This is not a programme I am familiar with but the children assure me it is in the same mould as Tom and Jerry, full of bloodless violence and immortal heroes who are immune to bullets. Do you sometimes feel certain you're going mad?

Why has this man Mogg been appointed, at enormous cost to the taxpayer as they say, and who appointed him? Why, none other than the chairman of the shipping company P&O, Sir Jeffrey Sterling, who is in charge of the Government's review of broadcasting. Now, you may ask yourself, what is the connection between *The A Team* and P&O? The A Team, I understand, are a bunch of anarchists who go around blowing up bad guys. The P&O chairman is the owner of many ferries that are now recognised to be dangerously unstable. Could Sir Jeffrey have got wind of an A Team plan to blow up these ferries before any more passengers are drowned? This seems the only likely explanation for the existence of Mogg the sinister censor.

TUESDAY

The collection of a Poll Tax is now thought to be impossible. They will persist for a time, of course, and some real blood may have to be spilled, but in the end they will give in. The last time they tried to impose a poll tax, if I remember right (says he dipping quickly into a child's history book), was in 1793. A few peasant heads were cracked but they quickly got the wind up when across the Channel the head of Louis XVI rolled into a basket.

The provision of cheap medical care for all, irrespective of share-holding, is something we war babies have always taken for granted. We foolishly assumed the NHS was here to stay, at least until we reached the age of hip replacement. But an older generation are not surprised that a brief period of freedom from pain for the poor is coming to an end. An oldish colleague reminds me that his first job on leaving school was the door-to-door collection of sixpences to keep the local hospital going. Now, approaching retirement, he can see himself doing the same all over again.

WEDNESDAY

Do not imagine for a moment they will not get away with the abolition of all forms of welfare. By appealing directly to greed they will succeed. Those of us, with little imagination, who haven't yet been in need of a hernia operation or had a perforated ulcer find it difficult to identify with moaning contemporaries who are always going down with something or other. If they promise us a tax rebate for being disgustingly healthy, we might just take a chance on it. The only thing that worries me is what size of tax rebate would we have to reinvest in private care if, say, we suddenly needed a kidney transplant? And what amount of insurance would cover the cost of prolonged hi-tech cancer treatment? And if they had to dip into what remained of NHS resources, would you suddenly be faced with a huge tax bill and have to sell the home as they do in America? We may have to go to war over this one. On the other hand, it is a lot cheaper to let the poor die. The poor, for statistical purposes, are all those who earn less than £20,000 a year.

THURSDAY

As I told you last week, we have good reason to be concerned with health care at this (moment in) time. Some dread disease, the origin of which I think we established was the Goat's Pen, has spread far and wide. It has certainly spread round the corner and up Church Street as far as Radio nan Eilean. I called in there the other day and found the place almost deserted. Only Jo MacDonald had escaped the plague: everyone else was off on the sick. Ciorstag Ruadh had to be called out of retirement in the Caribbean and I'm afraid she didn't look at all well. I gave her a thorough examination through the eyes of a doctor and it looks very much like a bad case of jaundice. I did what I could, which wasn't very much because she is not a member of BUPA.

FRIDAY

I honestly thought we were going to lose my old friend Daniel B. that time. A severe attack of shingles. I didn't visit or treat him personally because I didn't want to alarm him. He knows, and I know, and he knows that I know, that if the rash encircles the whole body you're a goner. However, the nurse kept me informed. One day the circle was within six inches of being complete, so I ironed my black suit. Then the next day both ends of the deadly ring had receded and we all danced a jig. We had good reason for celebration because Daniel B. is the last of the old breed – the last man on the East Coast of Lewis you can depend on, and his likes will never be here again.

SATURDAY

I stopped for a moment to watch the local fire brigade dealing with a forest fire in the Castle Grounds and wondered what madman was responsible for this near-catastrophe. This, I suppose, is the sort of caper men and boys will get up to when they have nothing else to do. Coming through Willow Glen, I met Dixie and one Robert Macrae leaving the Golf Club with what seemed undue haste. Amazing the length some folk will go to to recover a lost ball.

The simple writing of one's diary is becoming extremely difficult. In the last hour I have had 12 phone calls – two from Kenny Creed, two from Donald Taylor and eight from Jerry Luty. I have also had delivered the monthly report from the Royal Bank. Now all these people have something to worry about, but why don't they phone their own priest or minister? Now can I ever finish The Novel when I am surrounded by people who are perpetually caught up in the wheels of commerce? Thank goodness there is one close to me who can sometimes doff the cloak of reality and hang it up in the closet – a man with a true sense of eternity.

3 JUNE, 1988

MONDAY
I don't wish to fall out with all my friends in the Free Presbyterian Kirk and I hope they won't think I'm being deliberately provocative, but every man should take his wife dancing regularly. You must ensure the woman is in practice, because sooner or later she will have to take the floor at a wedding or some such occasion for making merry. Let her laze around for years and the legs go.

Look at what happened to Malky, our Gaelic Arts Officer. For 20 years he's kept Patsy locked up in that dungeon in Keose, allowing her out only once a year to lift the peats. Not only that, the rascal wouldn't admit to his meanness and obsessive jealousy: instead he put it about that Patsy had a phobia about nuclear fallout and didn't want to leave the house.

However, some mutual friends knew better and finally persuaded him to take Patsy dancing. Unfortunately they picked a rough night – the night the Cajun musicians played in Stornoway. Now, if you think a barn dance to Niall Cheòis's old box is a frisky business, it is nothing compared with the frantic contortions these Cajun boys inspire.

In no time at all poor Patsy was carried off with a severed tendon. A severed tendon is a painful and serious injury, but perhaps I had better explain to my non-eminent friends. If you've ever had to kill and skin a chicken of a Saturday afternoon, you've probably taken time, as a child, to play with the cord that controls the claw. That, then, is the tendon. So you can imagine Patsy's pain, with no connection between her bum and her toes. At the hospital we had to open up a fair stretch of her and tie a reef knot on this vital piece of fibrous rope. Take heed. Keep up the dancing and your tendons will retain their elasticity – yea, even unto middle life.

TUESDAY

The success of the Prime Minister's great evangelical mission to Scotland must not be underestimated. Some of her advisers – knowing full well that the Scots are only interested in football and religion – advised her to make a pilgrimage to Hampden Park and the General Assembly. What the amoebae that surround her didn't grasp was that Hampden was the venue for religious fervour and the Assembly the sporting arena.

She wasn't the first crank to deliver a sermon on the Mound. And if the reaction in the national press is anything to go by, she converted all the scribes. One thousand fathoms of newspaper column rested on the "high moral ground".

Even Anglican Archbishops have taken to writing about religion. Dr Habgood, the Archbishop of York, was given a large amount of space in *The Observer* to write about moral duty. I have written him a letter offering to start a fan club.

This corner of *The Observer* is usually reserved for politicians, journalists or similarly illiterate windbags. Why can we not always have this space filled by men of the cloth who, for some reason, write so much better than those who make their living at it.

WEDNESDAY

It has been brought to my notice that a couple of the Town councillors have come out of the closet and admitted the aberration of Toryism. I hope this will not be held against them in any way. When they come looking for support please try to treat them as if they were normal healthy people. Despite the present climate of resentment, these guys must not be hounded or ostracized in any way.

Angus Graham is another problem: as Chairman of Development you would expect him to attend a conference in Inverness on the most important, still developing, industry in the north-west of Scotland. Yet I hear he's been told he cannot go. It would cost the council too much money – about three hundred pounds. They can be so careful with money sometimes. I wonder if he is perhaps a Tory? Never mind, Angus, there is a better conference in Seattle later in the year. Perhaps that is sufficiently distant to interest our council. Or perhaps you can come as a guest of Orkney or Shetland, who are bright enough to know what is important. Let our boys get on with the basket-weaving and goat's cheese.

THURSDAY

For a laugh the other day I visited the Golf Club. The Clubhouse was humming with rumours of all sorts. I have no wish to poach gossip from A Whiteford and the Primitive Press, but there is one little thing. Big Fred is being sent on a course on which they hope to teach him a soft and gentle approach to the public. This seems a tough task. I have written to his employers suggesting it may be simpler and cheaper to send the entire population of these islands on a course where they may learn how to receive Fred. Say, some instruction in self-defence! It is difficult to believe Dixie is sixty-nine.

FRIDAY

Talking of characters we all know well brings me back to Sandy, our Convener. I happened to hear him on the radio the other night and, do you know, he has a way with words.

Some readers complain that I am too free with praise in this column but I cannot help it. It is not my way to carp and criticise. Let us look at it this way: we need a Convener who can think on his feet and quickly translate these thoughts into words. Bearing in mind that we are restricted in our choice to the elected councillors of the moment, can anyone see an alternative? Perhaps one, but if he couldn't get elected deputy to Dòmhnall Lìsidh, any further hope of a political career would appear to be slender.

If in the past I have not praised Sandy when I should have done, let me assure you it was purely personal. I have borne him a deep lingering grudge ever since, as School 'A' goalkeeper, he let in two soft goals in 1951.

24 JUNE, 1988

MONDAY

Every year around this time my wife makes a sacrifice to her dead ancestors. She buries, in the clay patch she calls a garden, about forty quid's worth of plants and vegetables. I don't mind this because it keeps her out of mischief, but her gesture of remembrance is clearly not appreciated by her relatives departed. No sooner has she covered my money with soil than angry souls call forth the summer monsoon. It rains then for two months. If any fern or flower escapes drowning and shows its head above ground, a south-westerly gale is summoned to decapitate it. Still, every year she goes through this futile ritual; but I don't mind, as long as it doesn't drive her to strong drink.

Yet where credit is deserved I have always paid my dues. This year she has had some success. Her cabbages survived the first few critical weeks, and she is naturally proud. Friends have been called to admire them and she has even had some photographs taken. I have been prevailed upon at great pain to build some shelter in the form of ranch fencing. Again I am happy to do this, because no expense should be spared to keep these ex-tenement dwellers contented. But just in the last few days her cabbages have sprouted a lovely purple flower. Experts from Ranish were called in and they confirmed that her cabbages were not cabbages at all; they are apparently pansies. I look forward to some interesting vegetable soups in the late summer. Never mind the taste: think of the nice colourful arrangement. Nouvelle Cuisine, I think they call it.

TUESDAY

I only mention these trivial matters to take your minds off the departure of the English team from the European Championship. A profound sadness swept through the entire western world when England were beaten, first by Ireland, then by Holland and finally by the Soviet Union. How these lesser countries managed to overcome us, who taught and civilised the rest of the world, is a total mystery not only to me but also to my good friend Jimmy Hill.

Jimmy is the fairest of commentators – without a nationalistic bone in his body – but he couldn't help pointing out that the Irish team contained very few Irish accents and the so-called Russian team was made up of Armenians, Georgians, Ukranians and, for all we know, when the ref wasn't looking, Cossacks on horseback. As for the Dutch team ... well, who could help noticing that some of them were of a very dark hue indeed, and one wonders if they could board the same bus as Zola Budd in South Africa.

Jimmy Hill quite rightly wondered if the blame for the English team's poor performance could not be laid squarely on the shoulders of John Barnes. Can one really expect someone born in Jamaica to give his all for England? Jimmy and I are asking these questions only because they have to be asked.

The gang of hooligans who went to Germany bent on pillage and arson were doing only what they should have been doing officially in National Service. And if you look at the surnames of those arrested, you'll see that many of them had an Irish or Scottish daddy and probably a Welsh ma. Sometimes I wonder if we few sports writers are the last patriots in the land.

WEDNESDAY

Talking of patriots and great sportsmen, my friend Dixie is having a hard time in the Golf Club. There is clearly a hard core of Stornowegians in the Club who will stoop as low as need be to do down the crofting golfer. And you cannot stoop much lower than to steal a man's shoes. When

Dixie returned to the Clubhouse on Saturday night after one of his net 56s his only pair of shoes had disappeared. Of course they wouldn't let him in in his spikes for his customary orange juice, and he couldn't take his spikes off because he had a vintage pair of socks on that he wears in his wellies. Bad enough, but there was worse to come. When he went to the kirk on Sunday, the elders wouldn't let him in in his spikes. "Any apparel connected with sport is forbidden," they said. Quite right, too. What shall it profit a man if he scores a few birdies yet loses his soul in the rough. The matter is in the hands of the CID.

There is more than one bad element in that Club. I have no doubt that it was Fred who bribed the Bristow Helicopter Mob to poison me on a recent visit to the club. My advice to innocent country boys is to steer clear of the place until all dubious characters have been identified and barred.

THURSDAY

I learn through the famous ornithologist Peter Cunningham, who I understand is a great admirer of the radical stance taken by this newspaper, that a Crane has been spotted on the island. I think the man who thought he saw a Crane in Uig must have been mistaken. What was probably seen was a Grey Heron grown so huge on farmed salmon that it could easily be mistaken for a Crane. Either that or some bent old Ùigeach secretly cutting peat on a Sunday.

Another possibility is the Old Celtic Crone. Although once a common sight on our shores, the Celtic Crone is seldom seen nowadays. This easily identified bird once ranged freely from the south of Spain through Donegal right up to the Butt of Lewis. The plumage is unmistakable: a black hood in summer and winter joined to a blacker cloak that reaches right down to the talons. It does not mate willingly because its disapproving croak frightens off the more timid male, which no doubt accounts for its near extinction.

FRIDAY

How to entertain my wealthier friends when they visit the island is an ever-present problem. I know they say that the man who has everything generally only wants more of the same. But men like the Barvas Navigator who enjoys eight months leave every year are extremely difficult to keep amused. Fortunately he can sometimes think of some harmless pastime for himself. Next week he wants to teach me windsurfing. He knows that I know he has an ulterior motive. When he saves me from certain death by drowning he will feast on the tale for years to come. But I am tempted to take him up on this one. What appeals to me most about the game is that, like golf, it is a complete waste of time.

But what to give him in return? I believe I have the very scheme that will not only attract the Navigator but also hundreds of wealthy tourists who will pay me vast amounts of money for the privilege of shooting my hens. When my pines grow – rapidly now, because of Maggie's fence – I will set all the village poultry free in the trees. Planeloads of Haw-Haws will descend on my croft and blast away at the hens with shotguns. I believe this is what goes on at places like Garynahine. Where are you now, Greenpeace?

1 JULY, 1988

THINGS TO DO IN BED

Some of my medical colleagues recommend a little alcohol for people like me who bear a tremendous burden of responsibility and cannot get to sleep at night. I'm afraid I must disagree with them on this one. Perhaps it works for the very old and the very young – there is nothing like a spoonful of whisky for a noisy baby – but for a man in his prime strong drink at bedtime is not a goood idea. It fires the imagination and disturbs the brain and the body.

But never mind, I have some good ideas of my own to combat insomnia. While tossing and turning in the small hours I often feel a pang of hunger. This is the very worst thing that can happen to you when trying to sleep. I used to send her down for oatcakes and cheese at these moments, but now she refuses. She says oatcake crumbs are difficult to sleep on and perhaps they are the cause of my sleeplessness.

Until my eyesight failed I used to read, and that helped. Now that I have my spectacles I thought I was on my way again, but I find they are not easy tools to handle. When you've read enough to feel drowsy you have to go through the complex routine of getting the spectacles into their case. This operation can take some time for a beginner. If you finally manage to crush your glasses into this ill-fitting "case" it shuts with a bang and you're wide awake.

I have tried all the usual ploys like walking the floor and press-ups. I've even tried counting the sheep in the field next door but it gets very cold out there at night. I cannot see how this helps any normal person.

Because of these nocturnal difficulties we have taken to playing chess in bed (what else can you do?). I also keep a box of Cadbury's Milk Tray by the bedside in case of hunger. It was a combination of these two desperate measures that very nearly led to my demise last night.

I thought if I made her sit at the foot of the bed this would help her stay awake, but it's not in her. After she foolishly lost her Queen she took the huff and moved into the spare room muttering something unintelligible about my ancestry. What can you do? I placed the chessmen by the chocolates, pulled the clothes over my head and tried to remember a speech by Geoffrey Howe. This nearly worked. I was very close to the edge when an unfortunate pang of hunger brought me back. I dropped my right arm to grope for a chocolate and sleepily swallowed a Bishop. With this wooden ecclesiastic lodged in my oesophagus I made loud and terrifying noises, but she swears she heard nothing. She can put on the Calum Searach when she likes.

There was nothing for it but to help the Bishop on his way with copious amounts of strong drink. We now have to wait and see if he has a smooth journey, but I'm not confident. I remember only too well when Bowley swallowed a plastic Robin off a Christmas cake and it spread its wings at the last moment.

One hour later, when you would have thought mortal man could take no more, what sounded like Bristow's helicopter started up in the kitchen. Apparently electricity is cheap at night, so all her noisy gadgets are programmed to start at three in the morning. But I'm no that daft. It is all part of the plot to drive me mad.

Of course I cannot go to work with a ministear-maide praying his way through my digestive tract. He might develop a splinter, or he might have had woodworm.

So I lie in bed trying to sleep. If you think it's difficult at night you should try sleeping during the day when all your enemies are up. The postman Calum Searach only blows his horn if he sees my blind drawn. I spoke to him, naturally, but being as deaf as he wants to be himself he doesn't understand. I once fired the goose gun over his head, but he pretended not to hear. His wife Maggie Ann says, "If you think you have problems, try living with him." He came home the other day while she was working in the garden and she asked him to mind the potatoes. The word "potato" registered, so he went off to water his earlies while the pan on the cooker melted. She let him have the edge of her very sharp tongue, but your man does not care; he doesn't hear.

Often about eleven in the morning we get a lull here in the East End. This is when three large men in wellies come into my kitchen to drink coffee while walking up and down shouting into the telephone as if they cannot believe it works. The general uproar is now so bad that I cannot hear Doilidh next door shouting at his dog. This is partly because Charlie on the other side has bought a grass strimmer. If I have anything at all to be grateful for it is that Atch works in Stornoway. When he retires I will certainly have to emigrate if I am still alive, which is doubtful because all this has considerably shortened my expectation of life.

I wouldn't mind if I hadn't the cleanest conscience since the Apostle Paul. I am without sin, yet I cannot sleep. Much as I hate to seek a second opinion, I fear I'll have to raid my eminent colleague Dr Beresford's cupboard to see if these younger doctors have any new painless routes to oblivion.

I wonder if anyone ever led a harder life.

9 SEPTEMBER, 1988

MONDAY

Listen, I have no time for men who try to make life difficult for their wives. If the little woman is happy to spend her day toiling in the garden, the very least the concerned husband should do is provide her with the right tools. As I sit here at the window watching her trundling her wheelbarrow back and fore, I wonder how she ever managed without it and I certainly don't grudge a penny spent on it although it was far from cheap. The same goes for the two-stroke grass strimmer and the electric mower. These are the very least in the way of modern implements the caring man should provide for his wife.

Now there are some boys you and I know well who don't mind spending the money. But having signed the cheque they feel they have done their share. They are then content to lie on the broad of their backs and listen to the sounds of industry from their beds. I am ashamed of these men and I am proud to boast I am not in that number.

When I hear her starting a machine or striking rock with spade, I sit in my swivel chair at the window where I can watch her every move. This she appreciates, and who wouldn't. No one likes playing to an empty theatre. My presence at the open window inspires her to greater effort and brings out her best moves. Occasionally I utter a word of encouragement and direction, so merrily she sings and works and her afternoons fly by. If only we could get something done about that disc in the back of her neck.

TUESDAY

I feel, at last, I can recommend that new paper *Scotland on Sunday*. Last week they sent their man William Paul to examine us. I know, we are all tired of being examined – but that is a part of the penalty we must pay for our "unique way of life". It must be unique because I have seen it written a thousand times. You may say you don't feel unique, but rest assured you are. As a part of a tiny ethnic minority you must bear with this constant examination by reporters from the first, second and third worlds.

Anyway, this William Paul from *Scotland on Sunday*. He came to the County Hotel (where else) to meet some of us who are always on duty as representatives of the far from silent majority. He listened carefully as these people always do and then to my surprise he went and wrote a fair and well balanced article in *Scotland on Sunday*. The fellow must be unique. We're unique. He's unique, Dammit, we must all be unique – so what's the point of being unique? Unless, of course, you refer to a way of life. Unique is bad enough on its own, but I don't like this condition we often find ourselves in these days. That is, almost unique, fairly unique and very unique. You wouldn't find these phrases in *Scotland on Sunday*, I'm pleased to say.

I realise some of you will hesitate to buy this paper because of a title that hints at transgression of the laws of Moses. Please don't worry. They tell me it is printed and bundled by 2300 GMT on Saturday night. It's the Monday ones that worry me.

WEDNESDAY

Winnie Ewing is often spoken of as the Greatest Living Scotsperson. I have even heard her name mentioned along with Mary Queen of Scots and John Knox, although not of course in the same breath. Imagine then my astonishment the other day when I saw this woman in the flesh. In fact she very nearly knocked me over as she stormed out of the offices of the *Stornoway Gazette* in what seemed to be a black mood. Perhaps I was mistaken because it is not easy to assess a woman's mood, even one you know well: it is harder still to gauge the mental form of a stranger in her menopausal years. Naturally I searched carefully in the columns of the Greysheet for some news of this great woman's visit, but news there was none. Possibly it was not the Greatest Living Scotsperson at all but Norman Maclean in drag. If anyone can shed light on these mysterious goings-on I will express my gratitude in the usual fashion.

THURSDAY

During the last year or so I've noticed that all the women I know of my own vintage, and some of the men, have suddenly aged. And I mean suddenly. Two years ago these people looked … Well, they looked their age. They had been growing old gracefully with a few wrinkles, whisky pouches and the odd bald patch. Now, almost overnight it seems, they are very old. Are they changeling victims of latter-day fairies, or is this something to do with Chernobyl?

With these very serious matters in mind I went along to the Nicolson Institute to see Anne Lorne Gillies and the Scottish Ensemble. I need not have worried. Anne Lorne Gillies seems to have escaped this dreadful ageing disease. And the voice is still young, although I would guess she is now well into her fifties.

Did it work, some people asked with some scepticism, this posh classical treatment of our traditional Gaelic folk songs? Yes, it did. It worked so well that when they performed the 'Caiòra' the room started swaying and I felt a touch of seasickness. I realise only we old sailors could have fully appreciated the effect, but then what do youngsters know about anything?

FRIDAY

Some of you will remember the time I had to take a certain Mr Milstead of Islay to task for making fun of the Free Presbyterians in a piece he wrote for *Punch*. I warned him but he wouldn't listen. This poor man and his family are now being hounded out of their home and off the island by the landlord.

Mr Milstead has apparently written a novel in which his landlord imagines he "sees himself". Having identified himself as a "bad character", the laird has instructed his men to throw young Milstead off Islay. There now, you see: you must never underestimate the power of the Seceeders or the Sadducees.

12 AUGUST, 1988

AN ENGLISH JOURNEY

Unless I'm wrong, which is most unlikely, it was 150 years ago my ancestor John Loudon Macadam perfected the art of road making. What have we learned since that grand old man died? Have we made any progress? Judge for yourselves: 150 years since John made his first batch of tar and gravel and the best we can come up with is the M25. But let me start at the beginning.

It was a fine day in July when we left the croft. I wanted to go to Cromore, but nothing less than Amsterdam would do for her. That is the way it is when you marry a Glasgow tenement-dweller: Cromore isnae good enough. I blame Professor Macleod, who was her confessor in Partick – a dangerous radical if ever I saw one. (Makes ecumenical noises in the fank.) Not, mind you, that I objected too much, because in Holland, I thought, they are all good Protestants like ourselves. It was the drive through England that worried me. If I knew then what I know now I would have walked.

From here to Glasgow is easy if the sun is shining and you have a sense of direction. But as you travel south there are more roads to choose from with roundabouts and stuff like that. I think we were near Ecclefechan when I noticed she had Leslie's road map upside down on her knees. And the boy in the back who hopes to get O-Level Geography next year isn't much better. By Carlisle we had several bad fall-outs and would have called at Gretna Green, if we could have found it, for a quick divorce.

Driving along the border to Newcastle, I noticed that Hadrian's Wall is in need of repair if we are to prevent further brain drainage from the north and seepage of hooliganism from the south. We stayed with friends in Durham, where we talked about house prices. We visited an old Zambian friend in Yorkshire and talked some more about the cost of housing. These people work in London and come home at weekends. I wonder if it is worth their while being alive at all. By the time we got to Essex the talk was not so much about house prices: down there they tell each other how much their houses earn each month. Everyone in England is now quite mad except Kate Mhòr and George, who are too busy on their farm to go mad. I think Kate is homesick because every night in her sleep she shouts about the hills of Coigeach. To cheer her up I tell her that since she left there is now no one at Radio Highland worth their £22,000 a year, but I'm afraid this only depressed her further.

On the ferry from Harwich to the Hook of Holland I met my first English hooligans practising for the start of the football season. Some of them looked and spoke as you would imagine hooligans should but several of them were expensively dressed and spoke posh. It is all very alarming and I wonder if they are orchestrated by a right-wing political group. Not to be outdone, a few young Scotsmen from Dundee (I would guess from their accents), in transit between an East Anglian base and West Germany, were trying to prove that no one can master the Scots at foul language.

I fell into my bunk exhausted but was soon disturbed by the Captain shouting for a doctor. Are we medical men not entitled to a holiday like anyone else? I'm sorry, but heart attack or no heart attack, I must have my rest. I ignored the call for help. Sadly, the man died and we had to return to Harwich, but that's the way it goes.

Fine big ferries they have in these other countries. Nine decks, a casino, two cinemas and a duty-free shop. Is there any possibility we could get one of these second-hand for the Minch? Or are they too comfortable?

Did you know that the average height of a Dutchman is seven feet? I guess this is nature's way of compensating for having to live in a flat, low country. Or perhaps it is something to do with having their feet in the water all the time. I wrote two thousand words on Amsterdam but I'm afraid Maggie censored the lot. Maybe she is unhappy because I wouldn't buy diamonds for her or let her come out with me at night.

Back on the farm George says: "If you're going to Goodwood, leave early. Give yourselves plenty of time for a picnic on the Sussex Downs."

I have no wish to burden you with my troubles but if I can somehow prevent the same happening to you, dear reader, well, my time is not wasted. Two hours after I made a successful entry to the M25, England's Suicide Circle, I could still more or less see my point of departure in the rearview mirror. The English are now resigned to these 20-mile traffic jams. They bring coffee and sandwiches to while away the time it takes the police to clear up the dead bodies and wreckage. For this daily ordeal they try to keep fit. They jog and don't stay up all night drinking whisky. There is something vaguely oriental about their wish for an honourable death on the motorway.

The traffic jam on a hot summer's day is not something we on the croft are well prepared for. I had on a suit to look smart at Goodwood. Not a bad suit, I thought – one she snapped up for me off the peg at James MacKenzie not so long ago for twelve pounds ten and six. It is made of the same material as cream crackers. It was nice and crisp in the morning but after two hours in the Dartford Tunnel it had gone soggy and was beginning to fray, so the members' enclosure was out. Steve Cauthen let me down badly at the end of the day. We had to spend the night in the car near Stonehenge with the rest of the hippies.

Stonehenge is not very impressive – a pale imitation of our own Callanish Stones. I suppose the Ancients started practising in the south and got it right by the time they reached Callanish.

Fortunately I found a copy of the *Gazette*, where I learn of gales and horrific thunderstorms at home, so I feel better. There is also a long letter from the Rev Angus Smith to lend me strength in a foreign field. I worry a little about not having a lightning conductor on the house. I remember that the only building in Stornoway with a lightning conductor is Martin's Memorial. I wonder if these people in the Church of Scotland suspect that Angus Smith has had it right all along. I see in the paper a photograph of my old friend the distinguished thespian Donald John MacSween, who is in training to walk round the world. He was totally bald from an early age but now appears to have lost so much weight his hair has started to meet in the middle again.

Someone drew my attention to a story in the Daily Getsworse. Apparently the Range-Rovered buckled-welly brigade who come north for the huntin' and shootin' are so desperate to prove to their friend that they've been "up in Scotland" that they carry home under their arm a copy of the WHFP. (We must assume this delicious morsel of sweet irony was served up by an innocent Express reporter.) A photograph of one of these Henrys with the paper would be worth a lot of money. Go to it, Sam. Never mind the expense.

If I had to live in the south of England I think it would have to be the West Country, if for no other reason than that it is as far away as possible from the M25.

7 OCTOBER, 1988

MONDAY

My winter is ruined. Now that it is too dark for golf I had planned to devote two evenings every week to contemplation of spiritual matters and The Novel. But some people will go to any length to delay publication of the only serious literary work to come out of these islands this century.

Anderson and MacArthur's Chief Pettifogger waylaid me one night when I was over-relaxed and persuaded me to join the Bridge Club. Now this is not the sort of bridge you and I knew in the old days when the four of us stayed up all night until one pair lost a week's wages at a penny a point. This is much more serious.

The contest takes place in a large hall set out more or less in the fashion of the Masonic Square. The compass plays a significant part in this "game". If you cannot tell where north is, forget it – because you are on a loser from the start. For maximum confusion 20 tables are scattered on the "square" in no particular order. Twenty teams, usually of two, take part. I say "usually of two", because our team, "Seumas Cleite", is different. We have a team of five and are allowed substitutes. When Chris Kelso becomes vulnerable he is taken off and rested.

How the rest of the teams came to be paired is an unfathomable mystery. The first consideration would seem to be that they must hate each other passionately, because at the end of every round a most undignified squabbling breaks out. After two minutes of this violence old Jimmy Ogilvey rings a bell, the fighting stops, all stand up smiling and thank each other politely. This hypocritical ritual probably goes back to the days of Solomon. The innermost secrets will probably be revealed to us in the fullness of time.

TUESDAY

I wouldn't like to give the impression that all bridge partnerships are based on mutual distrust. There are exceptions like Bronco and Pongo. They don't snarl at each other: Bronco prefers to yell abuse at adjacent tables. This would seem to be much more natural behaviour.

There are some pairings that are clearly undesirable and unnatural. Men team up with wives and brothers with brothers. This could easily lead to the break-up of families. But more important, partnerships based on long-lasting ties could lead to dodgy bidding. If, for instance, "M" said to "J": "There's a fierce wind blowing down Goathill Road and it has blown the leaves away", how do we know he meant: "I have a void in clubs"? Or if a Mr Taylor says to Mrs Taylor: "Terrible trouble getting ice to Harris today", does he mean: "Please lead a diamond"? You and I, Chris, as sheep among wolves, must keep the cards close to the vest.

WEDNESDAY

Sorry to keep going on about a mere game, but this obsession must be exorcised before we can go on to important things like death. Besides, I have a very sore bruise on my right shin where your man kicked me under the table last night.

Now where was I? Ah, yes, death. It would seem from the pile of pamphlets on my desk this morning that the Western Isles Health Board are determined to keep me alive and healthy whether I like it or not. Stop smoking, they say, and stop eating fat. Smoking and obesity increase blood pressure and could kill you. Every cigarette you smoke shortens your life by five and a half minutes. Is that right now? Wait till I get the calculator. Oh, dear; this statistic isn't going to persuade many to give up the drug. If you smoked 20 a day for, say, 40 years, and you suddenly see the reaper approaching when you're 70, would you rather have another three years or would you swap them for the three million happy minutes you spent smoking? It's not a tough decision. Or is it?

And then they tell me three people out of ten in these islands are overweight. How do they know I'm overweight? True, I'm two inches too short, but that doesn't mean I'm overweight; it just means I'm not tall enough, and if I stop smoking I'll be shorter still. What do they want? A nation of bad-tempered dwarfs who live till they're 73? It seems to me the biblical promise of three score and ten was carefully worked out for the 20-a-day man. I couldn't help noticing that the most violent man in the Bridge Club, Stewart, is a non-smoker.

THURSDAY

I seen a good one the other day. Yes, death again. I read in a London magazine that a writer was successfully sued for having written that someone was dead when he wasn't. I cannot understand why anyone would be annoyed to read that he was dead when he obviously was not. Surely the pleasure of having cheated the Reaper outweighed the satisfaction of a successful writ. But no. Some people will do anything for a few bucks.

We have to be very careful, because exaggerated rumours of premature death are a very common error in local papers. Take the famous Gaelic singer, Archie Grant. I cannot remember how many times I read of him as "ex", but he never sued. This piece I read has me worried now, and I can see it's going to be a nuisance. Before we ever mention a name again, in the past tense, we have to ring up and ask his missus if he really is gone. If he is, well, that's fine. Dead men cannot sue. Or can they? The evil that men do, etc ...

I told you my man quoted a good wan and I think I can "retail" it in case you missed it. From an American paper, or it could have been the *Gazette*: "Instead of being arrested, as we stated, for kicking his wife down a flight of stairs and hurling a kerosene lamp after her, the Rev James P Wellman died unmarried four years ago." That is the sort of mistake you wouldn't mind being sued for.

FRIDAY

The two men who went to Shetland to fetch back a 34' boat in the middle of the Equinox gales are still alive. I know because I checked with the Coastguard. The Ancient Mariner and Ding-a-Ling Dundee sailed into Stornoway harbour at 5 o'clock on Saturday morning. It took them 13 hours from Cape Wrath but they managed. Some say the waves were as high as the highest house; others say they were higher. It doesn't matter what the exact height was. What mattered was that the ferry didn't sail. What sort of ferry cannot compete with a 34' crab boat? Do you think they didn't want to sail until Sunday? Heaven forgive me these uncharitable thoughts.

16 DECEMBER, 1988

MONDAY

The problem with returning to an old theme is that somewhere in Ness, Skye or Harris there is an old woman with total recall who remembers which stance you took last time, no matter how long ago. On the subject of school uniforms, or for that matter any uniform, I would have been against. Yet during a brief spell in the Third World when I temporarily had some power on the equivalent of the proposed "school boards", I voted for school uniforms. This was mainly because the alternative was nakedness and the young teachers of the time couldn't be trusted to concentrate on their work while surrounded by dusky 16-year-olds with over-developed mammaries and glistening olive-skinned th ... (Enough – Ed.).

Sorry. Let's get back to the Fourth World. There is something pleasing to the eye about a regiment of identically-dressed young ladies descending daily from the Nicolson Institute and, even more agreeable, you can pretend not to recognise individuals – especially if the individuals belong to you and might want some money. Despite this obvious advantage I would still vote against, for many reasons. (The wife doesn't agree, but she is only a woman who didn't get promoted in the Guides.)

TUESDAY

One of the best reasons for not wearing uniform is that those who favour the idea are generally mentally disturbed. It may seem harmless while it applies to schoolchildren but when the aberration is carried over into adult life it often betrays inadequacies, if not outright perversion related to sadism and masochism. Another simpler reason for rejection of uniforms is that there are not enough uniforms to go round. If every little dictator in the land, and dictators are usually little, had his personal workforce in a uniform, there are not enough colours and styles to go around their fat little bodies.

Let me give you a for-instance. When our esteemed Lord Lieutenant Lord Granville visited the island recently all the Queen's men had to dress up in their uniforms for the occasion. As luck would have it, your man was delayed, which meant our old friend the PV (persecuting vassal) Colin Scott was left stravaiging up and down outside the Cabarfeidh Hotel, cap in hand, but with the rest of his uniform on. Out of the sawdust staggered an old Stornoway worthy who had seen action in three wars. He didn't hesitate. He dug some wet change out of his pocket and dropped it in the other fellow's cap. "There you are, cove, the Salvation Army's always been good to me." You see the problem.

WEDNESDAY

A couple of days ago, when I said "only a woman", I didn't of course mean only a woman. I mean she could have been a man had I been talking about the Boy Scouts. It's just the way some things read if you're not careful. Would I have the nerve to write it that way with the sort of women who breathe down my neck and criticise: Mairead againn fhìn, Maggie of the *Press & Journal*, Kate Mhòr (now of the *Inverness Courier*) and Nina of cream bun fame?

All strong women, who quite rightly insist that they should be treated as men. Yet the other night at a dinner-dance type of thing when someone – NL, I think – suggested that English idea of a kitty, in case he spent more than his neighbour, Nina was the first to renege. What is the point of having a husband, she said, if you have to pay your own way in the world? Add to that the ferocious women Buchanan, Kennedy and McCormack and you have a fine shinty team. But for gentle, soft, old-fashioned women like Muriel and Kirsty Smith, we might as well all be gay.

THURSDAY

Some time ago a Tory person came up with the idea of school boards. For several months afterwards I was regularly accosted by Frankie's Helen (I suppose since she moved to Fort William she's become a person in her own right) and asked to make it clear where I stood. Naturally I approve. I want to be on a board. It is all a matter of revenge. At every opportunity I will haul them out in front of the community and thrash the living daylights out of them. Then I would make them wear school uniforms. If their parents come to complain I'll send them to my cousin the Rev Alex Murdo for extra punishment.

I'm only sorry my old physics teacher Roddy G has retired before I could get my own back for having to follow him into the mountains on poaching expeditions when I was too young to carry a stag.

On the other hand, there will be unlimited reward for exceptional talent. There is a man called MacSween, of Irish or Hearach extraction I would guess from the name, who is worthy of the title "genius". He has the unique ability of being able to teach girls mathematics. I would nominate this man for next Pope.

FRIDAY

The extent to which women have taken command cannot be overstated. I have in front of me a long list of what fish farm workers should and should not do, and I suspect none other than Theresa Macguire is behind it. Hairnets should be worn when packing fish, it says. Our boys didn't mind that because they like to look smart on a Friday night, even Brian the Geordie miner. But they didn't take kindly to the instruction: "Nail varnish must not be used". Peter Redshaw, a bit of a dandy, took strong exception to this, and I expect a revolt on my hands. My only fear is that we are all too late to revolt now because Edwina's soldierettes are in charge everywhere.